DITCH LANE DIARIES:

ANNA'S WAY

D. F. JONES

ANNA'S WAY
Ditch Lane Diaries, vol. 2
Copyright © D.F. Jones 2015

ISBN: 978-0-9861227-2-9 paperback
ISBN: 978-0-9861227-1-2 ebook
All rights reserved.

Notes:

Cover Art by Jones Media
Editing by Alicia Street
Proofreading by Jody Wallace
Interior Design by Author E.M.S.

To my wonderful husband, my two beautiful sons,
and my lifelong friends.

Acknowledgments

I'm fortunate to have a core group of friends. They're always there for me. Most of these women are also my beta readers. I want to thank Kristi, Erin, Tammy, Ashleigh, Debby, Bettina and Denise for taking your time to read Anna's Way.

My husband, for encouraging me to follow my dreams. He is my rock. My sons, for when they ask me how my writing is going, and I go into a spiel about the storyline, and they stare at me like I've lost my bananas. Thank you to my parents, for listening while I read *Anna's Way* aloud to them. Okay, so I didn't read the steamy parts to my dad, but my mom loved it.

A big shout out to Alicia, my editor and Jody, my proofreader. After working in advertising for years, I need creative individuals to give me feedback. Both women offer constructive suggestions and comments, helping me grow as a writer. Thank you, Amanda, for designing my cover and marketing materials. You always make me look great.

And most importantly, to my readers, thank you for reading and supporting *Ruby's Choice*, book one in the Ditch Lane Diaries, and my short, "Antique Mirror," which hit number three in Romance and number six in Time Travel, under Amazon's Best Seller forty-five-minute reads, January 2016. Your support, messages, and comments are always wonderful. You share with other readers, and that makes me ecstatically happy. *Anna's Way* is for you. I trust you will love *Anna's Way* as much as I do. I love my characters in the Ditch Lane Diaries and can't wait for you to read the continuing story. *Sandy's Story* is the third book in the Ditch Lane Diaries and currently underway.

Fun Fact: Chapter Titles are songs from the late 1970's through the middle 1980's. Enjoy.

Contents

Prologue

Sympathy for the Devil

Nashville, Tennessee 1961

FROM THE TOP FLOOR OF a Third Avenue high-rise, Luc watched the busy traffic of pedestrians and vehicles on the street below. Ants, little ants. He randomly read humans' thoughts and placed a bevy of decadent sins and temptations in their minds. And today he was in a particularly bad mood since rumor had reached him that some human wards purportedly held powers of angels.

Luc had once been one of the three most powerful angels in Heaven—until he got tossed out. He had ruled the Earth and its inhabitants for the last six thousand years, fighting an angelic war over Earth's unworthy species: the humans.

Luc's meeting with a potential angel recruit and informant, Zenuael, could change his military strategy in the war. He tapped his long slender fingers on the plate glass window.

A delivery truck below turned into the driveway of the department store building across the street when a car pulled into the truck's path. The truck squealed its brakes, but Luc waved his hand, and the truck ran over the top of the Ford Falcon. The two human males occupying the car suffered internal injuries and eventually died. Two of Gabriel's angels looked up at him, and Luc laughed, giving The Creator's angels the thumbs up. Luc said, "Oh, it's the little things that make life worth living."

The rebellion had been the last time he'd seen those two angels.

Luc began to shake with anger as he went back in time and relived the moment Michael pushed him out of Heaven.

In the Beginning

LUC WALKED INTO THE ROSE Garden, a place where the angels met to hang out with their friends and looked for pairing partners. As he walked past the pale pink rose path, the female angels all turned their heads to smile, and several he had slept with in the past called out to him.

"Hi, Luc."

"Looking good, Luc."

"I love you, Luc."

He threw his hand up in salutation and chuckled as he read the thoughts of the females. Luc had the urge for a new hook up, and there she sat, Kaduntz, a gorgeous female who hadn't submitted to him yet.

Luc made his way through the male angels who were all vying to make their connections to different females. He stepped over to Kaduntz and leaned against the white column with a trellis of climbing roses in pastel pinks, yellows, and creams. The color of the climbing roses set off Kaduntz's long strawberry-blond hair and creamy, soft complexion with her warm amber eyes. Luc said, "Kaduntz, you are lovely. You're fairer than these delicate roses, and I want you. Go out with me because I want to hear you hit the high notes." He chuckled.

Kaduntz narrowed her eyes and straightened her shoulders. "Luc, just because I'm a soprano in your heavenly choir of angels doesn't give you the right to speak disrespectfully to me."

Luc leaned next to her cheek, and a sigh escaped her lips. "Oh, Kaduntz, you know I can read your thoughts, and you're in full bloom." Luc cut off the conversation and grunted. "We'll pick this up after worship. The old man is summoning me." Luc dematerialized to the palace entrance and walked into The Creator's sanctuary.

Upon entering the throne room, Luc instantly knew something

was wrong. The Creator looked pissed, and His fingers curled into a fist. Luc glanced over his right shoulder to make sure The Creator was looking at him and not someone else.

The Creator rose from His throne and shouted, "Everyone leave us, now."

The Prince along with a dozen of His warrior angels left the room. Luc held a special place in The Creator's heart, His favorite angel. They were tight. Luc made Him laugh, and he could never remember seeing The Creator get angry, much less shout.

"Luc, you disappoint me, son. Did you honestly think you could recruit the entire worship division to rebel against me and I wouldn't find out?" The walls of the sanctuary vibrated, and Michael and Gabriel appeared on either side of The Creator with their wingspans at full extension.

Luc straightened his shoulders; his chest puffed out, and his translucent wings spanned upward. "Do not talk to me in that tone, old man. I am Luc. My worship angels are ready at a moment's notice to help me take your throne."

Michael stood in front of the Almighty and shouted, "Blasphemer. You're not worthy to stand in The Creator's presence. You try to incite a rebellion within the walls of Heaven, and my army will crush you and your singing angels." Michael's sword jutted underneath the nose of Luc. "Lord, give me permission to run this traitor through."

"SILENCE." The Creator seemed to double in size and strength, but Luc didn't back down. He stood with his legs slightly apart, his hands on his hips. Luc was every bit as good as The Creator, if not better, to run Heaven and all of its subjects. He even had angels in both Michael's and Gabriel's camps ready to come under his leadership. The Creator said, "I created you, Luc. I gave you one-third of heaven's angels to worship ME, not you. And you betrayed me. I strip you of your rank and position. I'm sending you to the new planet I'm creating called Earth. You and your lot must leave immediately, or I'll have Michael's army cut you all down."

Luc became irate. "You cannot strip me of my rank and position. I will cut *you* down." Instantaneously, the throne room filled with Michael's soldiers.

The Creator went down the steps to stand in front of Luc. He turned to Michael and said, "Escort Luc and his angels out of Heaven to Earth's realm." The Creator left the room with Gabriel at his side.

Luc started throwing punches at Michael and he screamed, "No. You can't do this to me." Michael counterpunched each jab, grabbed Luc by his wings and escorted him from the palace. Luc called on his worship angels, and Michael called his army. Opening the palace doors, all of the angels in Heaven stood around, looking confused by the rumblings under their feet. Michael had two of his soldiers restrain Luc's arms while he continued to hold Luc's wings.

A third of Heaven's angels known as the worship angels' voices rang out loud and clear, "Luc. Luc. We're with you, Luc."

Michael's army surrounded the worship angels. "Today and henceforward, Lucifer's name will not be spoken within the walls of Heaven." Gabriel's angels flanked Michael's army, and they pushed Luc and his followers kicking and screaming out of Heaven.

As The Creator worked on the formation of the third planet from the sun, Luc and his army of demon angels made their home in the Earth's lower mantle, close to the liquid core known as Hell. Once Earth's formation was complete, Luc and his army were allowed to surface on the planet's continental crust.

With an air of superiority, Luc stood before his army in the Garden of Eden next to the tree of life. His waist-length, glossy, jet-black hair fell over his shoulders in waves. Luc had strikingly beautiful features, and his dark, soulful eyes looked at his followers. "I am proud, and I am strong. I am God of this planet. Earth is our home, and we will continue to grow in numbers and strength."

Kaduntz stepped away with a third of Luc's army. She yelled over the crowd, "You are the great deceiver. You alone are responsible for getting us kicked out of Heaven. The angels who stand with me now will never follow you." The earth angels disappeared from Luc's presence.

Luc shouted at the remaining angels, "If there are any left in this group who do not wish to follow me or be a part of this army—leave now. I want your complete and absolute devotion and loyalty. If you cannot give it to me, then leave now."

Luc's army began to chant his name. "Luc. Luc. Luc."

Luc bowed to his army. His translucent wings spanned out and shimmered with a rainbow of colors. "My true and faithful subjects."

Several days later

THE CREATOR ENTERED THE GARDEN of Eden and Luc materialized to sit in the tree of life. The Creator had made new beings in his likeness called humans. The old man kept trying Luc's patience. The Creator showed His new beings the layout of the garden and pointed to the tree of life.

The Creator's snowy white hair fell in one long braid down his back. He wore a long-sleeved white silk shirt over white linen trousers and stood in his bare feet. The Creator's ageless and timeless face beamed with light and love and His sapphire eyes sparkled as He gave the new beings a warm smile. The old man used to look at him with undeniable love. Luc growled, clenching his teeth. The old man said, "My dear Adam and Eve, I have given you this beautiful garden. You will never want, and you will never hunger. You will live forever. My beautiful humans, the only thing you mustn't do is take from the fruit of this tree."

Luc wondered if the old man knew he sat in the top of the tree with fruit He forbade His humans to eat. Was the old man baiting him? Or was he baiting the humans? The humans nodded in agreement with the old man. The old man vanished from the garden in a flash of incandescent light.

The human female began to explore the garden as the male slept. Luc appeared before the female. Her hand went over her mouth. Luc, the most beautiful angel in the universe, appeared to Eve as the light of love. He crooned a litany of beautiful words to the female. "The Creator has given you great beauty, Eve. He has given you this beautiful garden. Do you know why The Creator forbade you to eat the fruit of this tree?"

"No," she said timidly as she shook her head.

Luc had a way with females, and the human was no different. Eve walked over and ran her fingers through his silky ebony hair, and Luc had to control his emotions not to smack the female down for touching him. But if he could get the humans to betray the old man, it would give him leverage and a way to meet with The Creator. Luc caressed the female's face, and she closed her eyes and purred. *This female is too easy.*

The female opened her eyes and lovingly looked into Luc's. With innocence, she said, "The Creator forbade us to eat the fruit of this tree. There are many other trees filled with fruit in the garden."

Luc kissed the back of her hand and smiled. "Oh, my beloved, He just wants to test you. He wants to see if you're strong. He wants you to eat the fruit because then you'll have the same knowledge He has. You'll be like Him in every way. Eat the fruit and share with your mate. You'll see I'm right." Luc kissed her on the mouth.

The female ate the fruit, and at Luc's urging, she gave the forbidden fruit to the male. Luc neglected to tell the humans what it had just cost them. Suddenly, The Creator filled the space and screamed, "Luc."

Luc smiled and appeared before the old man and bowed. "See how easy it is to rule? The humans are mine now. Go home, old man."

The old man shook the earth. The clouds rolled across the sky, thunder boomed, and lightning struck the ground before the two humans. He shouted to the humans, "Leave this garden at once. You have disobeyed my only command. You're not worthy of this garden." He turned to Luc and Luc held his chin up in defiance. The old man said, "You have drawn your battle line, and I will draw mine. You have given away the decision of what is right or wrong so the humans may choose for themselves. They will toil until death, and you will speak as their accuser, but mark my words, you will make retribution."

"What did you expect, old man? You gave this planet to me. Did you honestly think I would allow those humans to occupy my space without being subject to me?" Luc stood with his legs apart and readied himself for another battle with Michael. He looked around, but Michael didn't appear.

The Creator shook his head slowly. With sadness, He said, "Luc, you had much potential, but your pride and arrogance have sorely disappointed me. You may still come to the heavenly meetings on the humans' behalf." The Creator disappeared.

LUC, AS THE RULER OF the Earth, controlled and manipulated time. The humans became a source of entertainment for him and his demon angels. Occasionally the earth angels led by Kaduntz thwarted his fun. Then the Prince came to Earth as a man and Luc offered him the chance to rule the Earth with him. Together, they would have been unstoppable, but alas, The Prince's people served him up to the cross.

What Luc failed to realize was that The Creator had given the humans a different choice with the Prince, who took over for Luc at the heavenly meetings on behalf of the humans. While opening the doors to humans, the Prince's sacrifice shut the doors to Heaven forever to Luc.

More determined than ever, Luc vowed to take as many of the human souls as he could from the Prince and the old man. Earth belonged to him, and he would not let it go without a fight. The humans became pawns in this game of chess over life on Earth.

Fast forward six thousand years after being cast out, and the rules of engagement changed again. Luc waited for new intelligence from a potential spy named Zenuael.

LUC SOUGHT OUT SPIES FROM heaven's guardian angels and military unit known as the AAF (Angel Armed Forces). During the mid-twentieth century, one of Luc's prospective spies scheduled a meeting to discuss new information regarding The Creator using humans as wards. Luc cultivated new spies, and Zenuael, a lieutenant in the AAF, had shown promise and interest in jumping the fence.

Luc had commandeered the top floor of a suite of offices from Tennessee bureaucrat Charlie Boatwright, who currently served jail time for poisoning his district's watering hole in exchange for money. Money, money, money—the best way to bring any human to his knees.

The interior office walls were painted a crimson red with white wainscoting. Luc had opted for the human's post-war modernist look with a George Nelson desk next to the plate glass windows, and on the left side of the room sat a Herman Miller black marshmallow sofa flanked by Noguchi glass-topped end tables.

There was a soft knock on the double doors and Luc's manservant Cole walked inside. "Sir, Zenuael has arrived. May I show him in?" Luc wished he had millions of Cole Steeles, so easy to manipulate and eager to carry out any request or demand.

Luc sat down behind the desk in a sleek black leather chair. "Yes, show him in and wait about ten minutes, then come back and tell me I have another appointment. Sometimes these angels who play both sides of the fence waste my time." Cole bowed and exited the room.

Cole Steele had sold his soul to be rich and powerful after being humiliated from the Stock Market crash in 1929. Cole had proved to be one of Luc's best recruits. He had bestowed on Cole immortality and youth until Luc decided he no longer needed him. In the meantime, Luc would give Cole the wealth and power he craved, but not until he worked decades proving his loyalty.

Zenuael entered the room with quite a presence. He stood nearly six foot three and weighed around two twenty-five, give or take ten pounds with short flaming red hair blow-dried straight, parted at the temple and smoothed over to one side. Zenuael wore a fitted black-and-brown tweed blazer with a white shirt and black pencil tie, plus black trousers paired with black leather Florsheim's. "Luc, it's been a while. I see business is great. Hans Hofmann, *nice*—goes great with the Herman Miller. So, I have information that's worth more than all of your pieces in this office including that bitch at the door. Are you ready to deal?"

Nonchalantly, Luc waved toward the sofa. "Sit down, Zen, and tell me what you have, and I'll determine the value of your information."

Zen placed his hand in his pocket and walked around the office. "Not good enough. I'm risking the Eternal Blackness just being here and I don't have time to dick around. Are you ready to deal or not?"

Pushing his chair back, Luc stood and went to sit on the edge of his desk with his arms folded across his chest. "I'll play. If memory serves, you have a weakness for young human females. I happen to have a most beautiful and exotic female that just turned eighteen, and she wants to be an actress. Oh, and did I mention she's a virgin?" Luc waved his hand toward the opposite wall, and a vision of the female walking down Sunset Boulevard in California appeared.

Luc watched as Zenuael's eyes widened and evidence protruded from Zen's trousers. Bingo.

Zenuael smiled and took a seat on the marshmallow sofa. "I want her and an oceanfront property decorated to my taste that's completely off the AAF's tracking system. The female must not age, and she must come to me freely. If I get caught, they'll make an example of me. Otherwise, I'll continue to offer you any pertinent information that comes along, for a price."

Luc threw his head back and laughed. "Why don't you just come on down and work for me and I'll give you anything earth offers."

Zenuael crossed his right leg over his left and placed the palm of his left hand on the circled cushion. "Not going to happen. I love home and, no offense, The Creator never lies. You, however, are the King of Lies."

Luc stepped over to the sofa and sat down on the other end. "Thanks for the compliment. So, not to waste any more of my time or yours, let's hear what you've got."

Cole stepped into the office and said, "Sir, you have another appointment."

Luc turned to Cole and said, "Tell them to wait." He turned back to Zenuael and raised a brow.

Zenuael said, "I overheard during a recent conference at Michael's headquarters The Creator is using select humans in the war. He's embedding into their human genome powers that have only been available to angels, the Prince, and the Spirit of Man through His DNA. I have, let's say, an intimate relationship with an angel who is a part of the human memory pool. She gave me proof." Zenuael waved his hand, and on the wall, a vision appeared of a human sitting on a braided rug in front of a fireplace talking with two little girls who looked around four or five years old.

The female exaggerated her hand motions while she talked to the younger females. "Would you like for me to tell you two a little secret? And if I do, then you both have to promise to lie down for a nap. Promise?"

The little red-haired girl grabbed the little blonde's hand and whispered something into her ear, and both girls laughed. The redhead said, "Yes, we promise."

The two little girls sat on the floor with their hands in their laps, looking at the older female. The female said, "Good because you two are wearing me out. Once upon a time, there was a woman born with special powers. The power of the angels. The woman can see the future, heal the sick, and disappear." At that, the female disappeared and then appeared in front of the little girls, who squealed with excitement, clapping their hands. The female placed her finger over her lips and said, "Shush, we mustn't tell anyone my secret. But that's not all. Soon both of you will have special powers, too. Ruby, you'll have dreams of the future." The female turned to the little blonde and squeezed her hand. "And you, my sweet Anna, will heal the sick and fight demons."

Anna's eyes went wide, and she punched Ruby in the arm. "I fight demons."

A warrior angel appeared before the human female. "You mustn't ever speak of your power or theirs again. You have no idea who could be listening. You have all the powers of the angels, and they do not yet have them. Wipe their memories of this story and put the girls to bed."

The vision on the wall disappeared.

Luc began to pace about the room and the walls in the room vibrated. "Of all the low-down, dirty tricks, to give humans the power of the angels. That makes me furious. What the hell is the old man thinking?" The black double-breasted suit Luc wore transformed into the armor of the angels, and his translucent wings jutted up toward heaven. "He is helping them again. He sees them make mistake after mistake, and He forgives them. But does He forgive *me*? Hell, no. He probably knew the whole damn time what I was going to do. He will not take what is mine. Earth is mine."

The color of Luc's eyes flashed like fire as he turned to face Zenuael. "You keep bringing me information, and I'll give you whatever the hell you want. And I want to know everything about that human and those two little females, especially the little blonde named Anna. Fight demons? Ha. It's ludicrous."

Over the next twenty-odd years, with help from Zenuael, Luc began to pursue human wards, systematically capturing, recruiting, and torturing them. Luc stripped the wards of their powers, absorbing their embedded genetic code linked to The Creator, which gave him the ability to access the outer banks of the heavenly realm, which he hadn't seen since being cast out. Luc never stayed long enough during his invasions to trip Heaven's sensors. But to be in Heaven, even for a minute, recharged his powers and gave him great strength.

Luc had taken a special interest in the human with all of the powers of the angels. Erinelle, the guardian for the human and a formidable foe, had taught the human well. The resourceful and resilient human female fought worthy battles. So Luc set his sights on the children.

Chapter 1

Undercover Angel

Everglade, Tennessee 1977

"HELP ME. PLEASE, GOD, SOMEBODY help me."

Anna glanced up from a stack of patient insurance forms she'd been tackling. She must've left the front door open after she returned from a quick tuna melt at the Drug Store Grill. Anna sprinted from behind her desk in her little office down the hall from the patient check-in counter. She slung open the door to the small waiting room cluttered with too many reception chairs and old *Life* magazines.

Frankie Shelly, Anna's piano teacher from high school, had collapsed on the floor, and her lips were turning blue. Anna reacted on instinct. Her healing power's energy tingled to life, shooting to her fingertips. About ninety-five percent of the time, her power acted like a homing device, pinpointing a person's injury or illness so she could heal them. After an hour or so, their memory of the healing incident would miraculously be wiped clean.

Anna dropped to her knees beside Frankie and prayed, "Please, God, help me heal her." She poised her hands barely an inch above Frankie's face and allowed the healing power to guide her hands downward, past Frankie's torso, to rest near her left lower abdomen. She gently pressed down with her fingertips. Anna's pulse rate pounded so loudly that her ears were ringing.

The lights in the office began to flicker, and Anna could hear the coffee table behind her scoot along the floor as her healing power hit its peak. A gust of cold wind swirled around her, and one of the old *Life* magazines hit her in the back of the head, but she remained focused. A few minutes later, the healing energy began to dissipate, leaving her extremely thirsty, with a metallic taste in her mouth. Anna noticed Frankie's color had returned to her face, and her lips were pink, not blue.

Whew. Thank you, Lord.

Frankie's eyelids fluttered open. "Anna, is that you?"

"Yes, ma'am, it's me. You passed out." Anna exhaled a sigh of relief as she rested her bum on the heels of her feet and placed her hands on her thighs.

Frankie shook her head and slowly sat up. She pressed the palm of her right hand on the chilly linoleum floor to prop her upper body. Frankie looked into Anna's eyes, and her voice quivered. She said, "I had this indescribable pain in the pit of my stomach while driving over here. I had to pull over twice to throw up. Lord, child, I thought I was dying for sure. You saved me, honey. I'm not quite sure how you did it. But electricity shot from the top of my head down to the tips of my toes. You're a gift from God. That's what you are. A miracle from God."

With a look of compassion, Anna said, "Frankie, you were passed out cold. How about I take you into one of Doc's exam rooms, and you lie down a bit while I call an ambulance? I'd call Doc, but he's on a cruise." Anna helped Frankie to her feet and linked her arm around Frankie's waist.

"Oh-oh, okay. Would you mind calling Clyde? He's still working at the water treatment plant." Clyde was Frankie's husband, and the couple shared a friendship with Anna's parents. The couple frequently came over to her parents' house to play Rook on Saturday nights.

Anna opened the door that led to the patient exam rooms and they entered the first room on the right. "I'll give Clyde a call. Hey, the hospital will probably want to run a few tests just to be sure you're okay. Are you feeling okay?"

Frankie stopped and turned to face Anna. "Whatever you did to me, I feel fine. Just a little tired." She kissed Anna on the cheek.

Anna helped Frankie onto the exam table and placed a pillow behind her head. "I'll leave the door open. I need to call the ambulance and your husband. Then I'll come right back." Frankie nodded and closed her eyes.

Anna called Everglade Hospital for an ambulance and then placed a call to the water treatment plant and talked with their receptionist. Clyde would meet the ambulance at the hospital. Anna quickly went into the break room located in the back of the office and opened the old green fridge to grab a Coke. She always got very thirsty after a healing event. She chugged it down and threw the can in the waste paper basket next to the walnut kitchen table.

A few minutes later, Anna was back in the patient room and reached out to hold Frankie's hand. "Would you like something to drink?"

Frankie gave Anna a weak smile and shook her head. "No, I'm fine. I just want to rest my eyes. Thank you for staying with me."

"You're very welcome." Anna sat down on Doc Smith's stool and braced her back against the wall. Now at the age of twenty, Anna's healing powers were growing stronger with each healing event, and she desperately wanted to understand them.

Anna's mind raced back to the time when her healing powers began. She had been fifteen when she went spelunking with her friends Ruby and Sandy to Campbell Ridge Cave, and they found a hidden room, along with ancient drawings on one of the rock walls.

THE DISCOVERY OF THE CAVE'S hidden room initially had been fun and exciting. Inside the room, one wall was dedicated to ancient drawings. Anna sat on the ground with Ruby and Sandy. Anna said, "I've got this weird feeling like we're being watched."

Tipping over a rock, Sandy found a crystal totem, and Ruby knelt down to pick it up. The girls stared wide-eyed at the totem. Ruby's voice trembled. "It looks like the totem in the drawing. I know this sounds weird, but this thing is pulsing in my hands."

The totem was around six inches tall, made out of quartz crystal, with piercing sapphire eyes. The detailed carvings made the image of the face appear real and smooth as glass to the touch. Every way Ruby turned the totem, it seemed to be watching them. She handed the totem to Sandy, who gave it to Anna, who quickly gave it back to Ruby as if they were playing hot potato.

Sandy placed her hand on Ruby's shoulder. "Put that thing back and let's get the hell out of Dodge. I've got the heebie-jeebies in here." Ruby placed the totem back in the hole. Rocks began to fall, and the ground beneath Anna's feet vibrated.

Anna glanced in the corner, and a man with long black hair stood with his arms across his massive chest, and he smiled at her. But his smile wasn't warm. It was cold, and terror shot straight to her heart. She blinked and looked again, and the man was gone. Anna screamed, "I'm out of here."

LUC MADE A POINT TO keep a check over the years on the little girl who was supposed to fight demons. He watched her and her best friends as they grew. Today, they entered Campbell Ridge Cave. Even though The Creator was winning battle after battle in the war, Luc continued to track and strip wards of their powers. He hadn't seen any real power come from the girls—yet. But as Luc entered the cave, he felt The Creator's presence. The Creator was here.

Inside the hidden room, Luc looked at the drawings on the wall. They looked to be thousands of years old. It hit Luc like a ton of bricks. The Creator had been using humans in the fight a lot longer than the twentieth century. The redhead picked up the totem and Luc instantly recognized The Creator's sapphire eyes. The totem. The Creator was using sacred places like this cave to connect with human wards. Each girl held the totem and then the redhead placed it back in the hole. The cave also led straight to the Earth's core and his home: Hell. Luc became so angry that the ground began to shake, and rocks began to fall.

The girl named Anna looked straight at him, and he smiled. Hmmm, maybe there was strength in the girl. Most humans never saw him. Another time and place he would deal with the girl. He had to meet with his generals and make a plan to start searching caves around the world. Luc wanted to smash the totem but was afraid The Creator would then realize that Luc knew His secret. Anna began to run out of the hidden room but not before Luc made her trip into a hole. He chuckled.

THE GIRLS FLED THE HIDDEN room. They ran over stones, climbed boulders, and waded through freezing, waist-deep water before reaching the mouth of the cave.

They had been sitting on a large rock, trying to catch their breath, when Anna discovered an amethyst stone in her pocket. Sandy found a hiddenite stone in her thermos, and Ruby opened her backpack and pulled out an amber-encased spider web. Then the weirdest thing happened—Anna couldn't account for the passage of time after she had held the amethyst. One minute she'd been sitting at the mouth of the cave, and the next she was back home.

The trip to the cave changed Anna's life forever. The next day, Anna had been outside, relaxing in her mom's rattan loveseat and flipping through the latest edition of Glamour *magazine, when a ruby-throated hummingbird fell onto the floor of the patio. The little hummingbird flapped around frantically, trying to fly, but it had a broken wing. Anna picked up the bird and held it gently in her hands. The healing energy surged into her fingertips, and when she opened her hands, the bird flew away. It was the first time she realized she had healing powers.*

Over the years, Anna tried many times to talk to Ruby and Sandy about what had happened in the cave. She wondered if either of them possessed powers. But every time she opened her mouth to ask them a question, it was as if an unseen force stopped her.

Anna healed injuries, illnesses, and even saved a couple of lives of people who might have died without her help. But not every injury and not every illness. Anna failed to heal her grandmother, who died of breast cancer. Her grandmother was the driving force behind Anna wanting to become a doctor. That was why she started working for Doc Smith after she graduated high school. If Anna could understand her healing power, the human anatomy, and the treatments available through modern medicine, then just maybe during her studies, she would figure out a way to marry science with the supernatural.

THE AMBULANCE'S SIRENS STOPPED ONCE they pulled into Doc's parking lot. Anna met them at the front door and led the paramedics to the patient room, and they lifted Frankie onto the gurney. Anna followed Frankie to the ambulance. "I'll check on you tomorrow."

Frankie smiled weakly and nodded. "Thank you, Anna."

The ambulance pulled out on the main road. As she turned to go inside Doc's office, she still had a funky taste in her mouth. Inside the break room, she reached into the fridge for another soda, this time, ginger ale.

Sitting at the table, Anna sipped her drink and wondered why she was given this extraordinary ability. She needed help and guidance, so she closed her eyes and said a prayer. A presence entered the room, and the hair on her arms rose. She quickly looked behind her, and no one was there. Anna called out loudly, "Who's there?"

Anna's imagination was running wild. She stood to leave and someone touched her shoulder. She screamed and ran out of the room.

Anna quickly grabbed the change of clothes she had brought to work. She was meeting Ruby and Sandy at Ditch Lane and would freaking change clothes in the car. Anna ran into the main office at the patient check-out counter to switch the phones to the answering service. She glanced up and a young man, who looked like he was in his late twenties, was staring down at her from the counter. He had gorgeous violet eyes, thick platinum-blond hair, and skin the color of caramel. He looked and smelled so good Anna nearly swooned.

He grinned and pointed to a chair. "May I talk to you for a minute?"

Anna couldn't tear her eyes away from him. He had an ethereal beauty. "Wh-who are you?"

"Please, come and sit with me in the waiting room. You just prayed for help, and I'm it." He smiled at her warmly.

One minute Anna was standing and the next she'd passed out on the floor. Anna opened her eyes, and the young man was still there, kneeling next to her. "It's okay, Annabelly. I'm here to help you. Do not be afraid." Anna's head turned up to him at the mention of her nickname. He placed his hand on the top of her hand, and she jumped from the humming electricity of their contact. He said cheerfully, "My name is Raphael."

Anna's eyes widened with alarm, and excitement coursed through her as she started to ask him a question.

Raphael helped Anna to her feet and pointed to the waiting room chairs. "Please sit down. Feel free to ask me questions, and I'll try to answer them."

Anna leaned back in her chair, dumbstruck. "Are you an angel?"

Raphael chuckled, and his smile was infectious. "You humans have to give a label to everything." He waved his hand in the air with a slight flair, sending what looked like golden glitter trailing off his fingertips. It reminded her of Tinker Bell's pixie dust. And he talked with his hands just like she did. "There are those in your world who call us angels, messengers, guardians, and on the far side of the spectrum, even aliens. Yes, I'm an angel, but more importantly"—he paused and pointed at her—"I'm *your* angel. It's my responsibility to help you develop your healing power while you learn as much as you can about man's modern medicine."

Anna shook her head in disbelief and blinked several times. Holy shit. She had prayed for help and gotten an answer pronto. "What's Heaven like?"

Raphael's face lit up with elation. "Heaven is endless, timeless, and ever-changing. Every building, every mansion, all the fields and waters are clean and sparkling with The Creator's radiance. Humans don't quite understand the depth of love The Creator has for them or His great sense of humor. He created a city based on the human concept of Heaven through your songs about mansions on hilltops and streets of gold."

Ralph crossed one leg over the other one and turned his hands palms up with his fingers extended for emphasis. "Of course, the buildings and mansions are mainly optical illusions for the new arrivals crossing over. The Creator wants to make the new arrivals' resettlement into Heaven as comfortable as possible. Once acclimated, the arrivals may create their version of Heaven, as long as the humans follow the protocols listed in the new arrival handbook."

Anna stared in shock at Raphael. *New arrival handbook?* She tried to focus on what he'd just said. She was in complete awe of this incredible being sitting next to her. "How long have you been watching over me?"

"I've been watching you since you were born into this world, and I'll be with you when you cross over to the next one."

Anna smacked her forehead with the palm of her hand. "My whole life? And do you watch everything?"

Raphael chuckled again and rolled his eyes. "I never invade your privacy unless I think you're in danger. So far, you've led a pretty good life. That's why I haven't needed to intervene until now. Anna, you've been given a great gift, but it comes with specific obligations. Do you understand?"

Anna absentmindedly scratched her cheek. "Ah, well, no, I'm just meeting you. Why me? I don't understand why I have this gift. If this gift is divine, I don't want to screw it up." Anna glanced around the office. Was this really happening to her? She was dad-blamed close to hyperventilating or possibly heading into a full-fledged nervous breakdown.

Raphael placed his hands on his knees. "I don't have all the answers, and I certainly don't want to overwhelm you right from the beginning. Let me just say that The Creator selected you because he believes you'll help those who surround you. The stone you found in the cave was merely a trigger to release the memory of the power you were given before you left Heaven. And someday you may save someone of great importance. Someone who may hold the balance between good and evil."

Anna's face fell forward into her hands. She had a guardian angel. She'd felt him many times during her life, but to see him in flesh and blood was flipping her out. Her head popped up. "I'm sorry, I'm really sorry, but I can't breathe. I have to get out of here."

Anna grabbed her purse and made for the front door. She needed some oxygen like right now. Outside, she locked the door, and when she turned around to head to her car, Ralph materialized in front of her. "Jesus, Ralph, you scared the shit out of me."

Ralph took a few steps back and threw up his hands. "Anna, I'm sorry to have distressed you. Look, if you need some time to wrap your head around everything I just told you, then I'll give you time. And I like it—you may call me Ralph."

Anna held the keys in her hand and looked into his eyes. "I feel like I'm going crazy."

A car passed by the office and honked the horn. Anna waved and turned back to say something to Ralph, and he was gone. "Freaky D. I'm losing my ever-loving mind."

A voice in the air said, "No, Annabelly. You're not losing your mind. But I wouldn't tell anyone about this encounter or you could be subject to a hospital screening." She heard a chuckle.

Anna whipped around in a circle. No one was there. She shouted, "Believe me... I won't tell a soul. Ralph?"

"Yes?"

"Just give me some time to process this information." She leaned against the door of her car and a kiss pressed to her forehead.

Anna looked up in the air, trying to find Ralph. "I do want to talk to you. I just feel overwhelmed at the moment."

"Until we meet again."

Frightened and excited, Anna vowed to find out about her powers and Ralph was just the angel to help her do it.

Chapter 2

Southern Nights

ANNA GREW UP IN THE small community of Everglade. It was a peaceful place with a slow, gentle rhythm to everyday life. She drove down the winding two-lane street lined with hundred-year-old maple trees and, in the distance, the rolling hills of the Highland Rim. Suddenly, a deer darted across the road, and Anna slammed on her brakes, screeching to a halt. The smell of burning rubber rose thick in the air. Her heart pounded as she gripped the steering wheel and slowly stepped on the gas pedal as she made her way around the sharp curve.

Good grief, what else was going to happen to her today? *Healings and angels and deer, oh my.*

Anna would think about Ralph later. Tonight, she wanted to party with her friends, not dwell on the fact that someday she might save someone who held the balance of good and evil. She yelled out, "For crying out loud, I'm only twenty." She glanced in her rearview to see if Ralph might be riding in the backseat of her car.

By the time Anna pulled down Ditch Lane and parked her car, some twenty minutes later, her pulse had returned to normal. Ditch Lane had turned into her main hangout during high school, and it was still the place where Anna enjoyed the company of her old high school friends on any given weekend.

One of the first to arrive, Anna took her time as she strolled along Ditch Lane that ended near the old washed-out bridge. On the right, an old, abandoned white plantation house with a tin roof sat off the road about five or six hundred feet with acres of farmland. The other side of the lane was wooded and full of huge cedar trees. Anna looked over the cattle grazing in the open pastures. The sun was sinking low, spreading reds, pinks, and golds across the sky, and a few white clouds drifted along the horizon.

As Anna neared the creek, she noticed Jerry starting a small bonfire. She'd been in love with him since middle school, but he didn't know it. No one did because she hadn't discussed her feelings for Jerry with anyone. Ruby always insisted she and Jerry were just friends, but Anna didn't believe it. Anna had come close to telling Ruby several times about her feelings for Jerry but was afraid Ruby would get mad at her. It would've been different if Jerry had ever shown her any interest.

Anna never had problems getting dates. She went out on dates all the time, but it was the six-foot-three, blond-haired, blue-eyed Jerry she crushed on. "Hi, Jerry, whatcha doing?"

On one knee, he blew the small flame under the sticks in the pit. Jerry stopped working on the fire, glanced up, and he grinned. "Oh, hey, Annabelly. I'm starting a fire so the smoke will send these pesky mosquitoes packing. Where's Ruby Jane and Sandy?"

"Sandy should be here soon, but Ruby's still working. She's supposed to come as soon as she gets off. Can I help?" Anna wore an orange tube top with pink horizontal stripes and blue jean cut-offs. Jerry looked straight at her boobs. *Well, at least he isn't blind.*

Jerry quickly lifted his gaze and nervously broke eye contact. "Sure, ah, go over to the creek and grab me a few of those old dried-out pieces of wood. Hey, what time does Ruby get off?"

Anna's stomach flipped. *Dadgummit.* She thought for a split second they had exchanged *the look.* It was a feeling Anna had when a guy looked into her eyes, and intuition told her he liked her. But no such luck. She gave Jerry a one-shoulder shrug. "I don't know for sure. Probably around nine thirty or so."

Anna turned around to hide the disappointment in her eyes and made her way along the dirt path to the creek. She filled her arms with as much wood as she could carry, walked back to the fire, and dropped it at Jerry's feet. Anna brushed the debris off her clothes and rubbed the palms of her hands on her back pockets.

Sandy waved at Anna as she walked toward the fire. Sandy livened any party. She had strong opinions with little filtering and constantly cracked Anna up.

Sandy could be a model for one of those New York talent agencies. She reminded Anna of Christie Brinkley, but with shimmering chestnut hair and hazel eyes that changed color with her moods. Anna never referred to Sandy's beauty because Sandy hated people who looked at her superficially. It pissed her off. Sandy worked hard and proved herself time and again with her newsworthy articles at *The Sidelines*, their college newspaper. This fall semester, Sandy would be editor in chief.

With a smirk, Sandy said, "Dude, have you lost your dang mind? It's hot as a firecracker out here. And you're building a fire?"

Jerry tossed Sandy a glance over his shoulder. "Would you rather roast or be eaten alive? The mosquitoes are as thick as thieves out here, and if the fire doesn't get rid of them, then I've got Off in my truck."

Sandy wrinkled her nose and shoved her hands into her pockets. "Yuck. I hate Off. It stinks and is so sticky. Go ahead, light us up, scarecrow." Sandy turned to Anna. "Need any help?"

"Nah, I think this is enough wood for now, don't you, Jerry?" Jerry built a pyramid out of the old sticks, and the flames began to flicker and kick up to a blaze.

"Yup, we have plenty, and hey, thanks for the help. There's beer in the cooler on my tailgate if y'all get thirsty." Jerry winked at Anna and she unconsciously wet her lips. Jerry did a double take at her mouth and stammered, "I-I see George and Lizzie pulling up and, uh, I need to talk to him. Check y'all later." Anna's shoulders slumped when Jerry left without looking back at her.

Sandy draped her arm around Anna's shoulders and butt-bumped her. "Put your tongue back in your mouth. He'll be back over here soon enough. Why don't you just go ahead and kiss him?"

"What the hell are you talking about?" Anna pushed Sandy away, walked over to Jerry's truck, and sat on the tailgate.

Sandy trailed Anna to the truck with her hands in her shorts pockets. "Honey, I have eyes, and when you're around Jerry, you look like a love-sick puppy dog."

"I do not. God, do I? Crap. I didn't realize that I was so obvious. Do you think Ruby knows?" Anna's legs dangled over the tailgate, and she began to rock them back and forth.

Sandy laughed and slapped the side of her leg. "Heck no, but she doesn't care. Ruby and Jerry are just friends. You know that. Anywho, Jerry may need a nudge, sweetie pie."

"It's so much easier to flirt with the guys I don't care about than to flirt with Jerry. I may need a little liquid courage."

"Now, that's what I'm talking about." Sandy rubbed her hands together. She opened Jerry's cooler and grabbed two beers. Sandy gave one to Anna before she leaned against the tailgate and opened one for herself.

Sandy made Anna laugh by giving her step-by-step directions on how to snag the man of her dreams. "See, honey, you walk up to Jerry real close and barely graze his arm, trail your fingers slowly over his skin while you gaze up into his eyes, all dreamy-like, bite your bottom lip, and just let nature take its course."

"Oh, you're so full of it. But I love you, sister." Anna snickered and took a sip of her beer. "Sandy, do you believe in angels?"

Sandy's brows popped, and she replied, "Of course I do. Why?"

Anna sat her beer on the tailgate. "I don't mean like the angels that we'll see when we go to Heaven. I'm talking about here on Earth. Do you believe we have guardian angels, for real?"

Sandy sat on the tailgate and drew her knees to her chest. "Yes, Anna, I believe they're real. If you believe in God, Jesus, and the Holy Ghost, then angels are part of a package deal."

Anna released a sigh. "Good, I believe that, too. Hey, Sandy, I'm glad you're my best friend and, of course, Ruby, too."

Sandy leaned over and hugged her. "Me too, jellybean."

Once the party became crowded, Anna hopped down from the tailgate, and she and Sandy made their rounds talking to several of their old friends from school who had come home from college for the summer. Rusty, one of Sandy's old beaus, was back in town and putting the moves on Sandy, big time.

Ruby's brother, George, and his wife, Lizzie, walked to the bonfire with Jerry. Jerry grabbed his cooler and placed it on the ground. He hopped into his truck and moved it down the lane to allow more room for people to gather around the bonfire before returning to the party. That was when Anna noticed Reed and Brent walking behind Jerry. She'd met Reed and Brent last semester at a frat party in Murfreesboro. *Maybe I should flirt with one of them to see if Jerry gets jealous.*

The bonfire crackled, and embers floated into the air. The fireflies lit up in the fields beside Ditch Lane and dusk became night. Anna enjoyed listening to her friends laugh and talk about the old days of high school and their new experiences with college. She glanced up at the sky to see that a full moon was on the rise. Someone cranked up their car stereo with Steve Miller Band's "Fly Like an Eagle."

George slapped Reed on the back and tossed him and Brent beers as Anna stepped a little closer to hear their conversation. George said, "Boys, so glad y'all found the place. I was afraid you'd get lost coming out here."

Reed quickly glanced at Brent before he replied to George, "We stopped by the general store and met your little sister, Ruby. Man, she's something else."

George displayed a huge grin, crossed his arms over his chest, and tilted his head to the side. "Oh, God, what did Ruby do now?"

Reed's face broke into a grin. "She just gave us directions. Ruby's pretty intuitive, isn't she? I mean, she looked straight at Brent and told him that she'd never go out with him and turned to me and said she'd meet me later."

Before George could reply to Reed, Ruby approached their group with what looked like grim determination splashed across her face. Reed locked onto Ruby's eyes and took a step toward her.

Anna elbowed Sandy in the ribs and pointed toward Ruby. Ruby ran and jumped up on Reed, locking her legs around his waist, her lips on his mouth, and her arms around his neck.

George threw his head back and laughed. "Ruby Jane, I didn't know you knew Reed."

Anna whirled around to Jerry, and a frown crossed his face. He kicked a beer can into the fire and strode away from the party toward the line of cars parked along both sides of Ditch Lane.

Anna ran after Jerry and caught his hand before he could reach his four-wheel-drive Ford truck. "Please don't leave."

Jerry's jaw clenched, and he let out a ragged breath. "Anna, I'm sorry, but I can't stand around and watch her lip-lock some dude."

Anna cupped the side of his face with the palm of her hand. He looked down to the ground and shuffled his feet, kicking up dust and rocks. Anna tilted his chin up until he met her gaze. Jerry had the most beautiful blue topaz eyes, and when he stared into her eyes, she melted like butter. "You know, sometimes love can be staring you right in the face, and you can be too blind to see it."

Jerry blinked several times and opened his mouth to say something, but stopped. He stared at her like he had never really seen her before. "W-What are you saying to me?"

Anna's adrenaline kicked in, and her heart pounded loudly. She grabbed the loops on his waistband and pulled him toward her. "Remember the night in high school when we played the Ravens? We were down by one and only seconds left in the game. You threw the basketball from mid-court and scored. We won, and the crowd roared. You picked me up and kissed me."

Jerry's hands dropped to her waist, and a lazy grin lit his face. "I'll never forget that night. I think I kissed everybody."

"But Ruby ran over and jumped on your back. You left with her. I wanted you to leave with me." Tension escalated, and the magic began to bloom in the air between them.

"Why didn't you ever tell me?" Jerry's gaze moved to her throat, down to her breasts, and back into her eyes in a matter of seconds. He wanted her, and the feeling was mutual.

Jerry's heated look seared her mind, and desire shot up her spine like a red-hot flame. Anna bit her bottom lip in anticipation. She blurted out, "I've had a crush on you since middle school, but you've always chased Ruby, and I'd never do anything in the world to hurt my best friend."

Jerry cocked his head to the side and dragged his fingers through his thick shoulder-length hair. He placed his fingers on her shoulders and began to knead her muscles. Anna had the urge to roll her head backward just as his forehead leaned down to touch hers. He said quietly, "So why are you telling me now?"

Oh, God. Jerry's fingers digging into her skin felt so good. His hand slid down her back, and he rested them close to her bum. Anna boldly looked at him through her long eyelashes and said, "Well, Ruby is a little preoccupied right now, and I thought I'd just take this window of opportunity."

Jerry laughed, and his expression turned serious. "I wanted to ask you out in high school, but I was too scared that you'd turn me down." He searched her eyes and looked at her mouth. Suddenly, he grabbed her up into his arms and kissed her with such heat and passion she seemed to float in the air. The crowd became background noise as the party melted away. Jerry kissed her under the moonlit night, and she molded against his powerfully built frame like hot wax.

Jerry briefly broke from their kiss long enough to open his truck door. He scooped her up, sat her inside, and jumped in beside her. Jerry twisted his fingers through her long blond hair and dragged her next to him. His mouth slanted slightly above hers, and right before he sealed his kiss, he rubbed his thumb gently over her bottom lip.

Dang, the boy knows how to kiss.

All of the other boys Anna had kissed paled in comparison. Jerry was farmer strong, with broad shoulders and narrow hips. Anna's temperature soared as she felt his strength under her fingertips. Why in the world would Ruby ever want to give him up? Anna knew the answer—she was in love with Jerry and Ruby wasn't.

Jerry's hands skimmed underneath her tube top and brushed briefly over her breast. He murmured, "Anna, you're so sweet."

He sucked and pulled on her bottom lip and pushed her hair off her shoulders to expose her neck. Jerry nibbled on her neck for a minute before his lips brushed back across her cheek. Jerry nuzzled against her earlobe and gently tugged it with his teeth. "Come to my house, Anna."

His sultry Southern voice was her undoing and butterflies fluttered in her abdomen. His fingers ran down her back, slipping over the curve of her behind. She said, "I want to come to your house, really I do, but I need to tell you something first."

"Hmm, okay, I'm listening." Jerry ran his tongue around the outer part of her ear and chill bumps raised on her arms.

Anna whispered, "I've never, I've never, you know…"

Jerry pushed her off him so fast it made her head spin. He moved over in the seat, gripped the steering wheel of his truck with his right hand, and leaned his left elbow on the open window ledge.

Rusty and Sandy passed by Jerry's truck, and Rusty yelled, "All right, Jerry, damn, boy. First Ruby and now Anna. Give me some of that." Sandy punched Rusty in the gut and Jerry laughed.

"Looks like you got your hands full, Bubba," Jerry said. Rusty and Sandy disappeared down the lane. Jerry's eyes were glazed over with desire when he turned around to her. "Honey, as bad as I want you, I'm not taking your cherry tonight. Damn it, Anna, you and Ruby have got to understand a man can only take so much."

Anna felt like Jerry had slapped her and replied with sarcasm, "Kiss my ass, Jerry. Since you don't want my cherry..." Anna grabbed the handle of the door and Jerry lunged over and circled her with his arms. He pulled her back against his chest and pressed his face into her hair.

With a low, raspy voice, he said, "Don't leave me, Annabelly. I'm sorry that I'm such an asshole. I just don't want you to play me."

Anna twisted around in his arms. "Jerry, I'm crazy about you."

"Crazy, huh? Well, why don't you go out with me first? And then I'll ravish you. I have an extra ticket to see REO Speedwagon at Hermitage Landing tomorrow night. Wanna be my date?" Hermitage Landing was a cool place to swim in Percy Priest Lake, lie out on the man-made beach, and listen to music at night from the stage over the water. Anna had only been once this summer.

She threw her arms around Jerry's neck and kissed him. "I didn't think you'd ever ask."

JERRY LAY SPRAWLED OUT ACROSS his bed, listening to Journey and thinking about Anna. He had gone to Ditch Lane tonight in hopes of hooking up with Ruby. Then she'd locked lips with some dude named Reed. God, he'd been fighting mad and would've kicked the guy's ass, but he seemed to be just as surprised by Ruby's actions as Jerry. What the hell had Ruby been thinking? Jerry loved Ruby but had known someday their relationship would end.

Then, a miracle happened. Anna chased him to his Ford truck, the Blue Goose. Anna Kelly, for crying out loud, had the hots for him. Jesus, kissing her had been so sweet. Anna was freaking beautiful with her long white-blond hair, eyes the color of September skies, and soft peachy skin.

When Anna's rocking body melted against him, Ruby was *his-to-ry*. Geez, he lost himself with Anna. He had dragged her into the Blue Goose and sort of felt her up. God, those milky white breasts next to her suntan lines nearly made him explode on contact. Hell, two hours later, he was still pleasantly dazed and confused.

The softness of her lips and the touch of her silky skin hit him like a tire iron to the stomach. Everything she'd told him tonight pointed to Anna being in love with him. Yes, maybe she did love him. She'd been crushing on him for years, and he'd been a total moron, completely clueless.

Ruby had blinded him for years with her fun-loving ways. Jerry and Ruby had been friends since they were rug rats. He could fight with Ruby, make out with her, and know her feelings for him would never change. He and Ruby were tight and always would be. But he wanted more—he wanted Anna.

Chapter 3

You Made Me Believe in Magic

ANNA BEGAN TO WONDER IF she had imagined the whole scene with Ralph, her guardian angel. It had been weeks since Ralph had appeared to her. Maybe he was a figment of her imagination brought on by a side effect from her healing powers. As the days and weeks passed, Anna quit looking over her shoulder for a beautiful angel named Raphael.

Summer flew by once Anna started dating Jerry. When she wasn't working, Anna would go with Jerry four-wheeling in his Blue Goose or ride horses on the back forty of his parents' farm. Ruby had fallen head over heels in love with Reed. Sandy started dating Reed's friend, Brent, among her other suitors. On the weekends, Anna and Jerry would hit the dance clubs or weekend parties with Ruby and Reed and Sandy and Brent.

A couple of weeks before the fall semester, Anna moved into a rental house on Bell Street with Ruby and Sandy. The first night they stayed in the house, Anna discovered she wasn't the only one with supernatural powers. Ruby's amber stone gave her prophetic dreams. Sandy's hiddenite stone had opened the door, giving her the ability to read minds and see visions of a person's past or future with a mere touch of her hand.

Anna stood at the stove browning hamburger meat and Italian sausage while Ruby chopped up tomatoes, onions, and peppers at the butcher block table. Sandy fired up Leon Russell's album *Will O The Wisp* on the stereo in the den.

Relief washed over Anna as Ruby talked about her dreams.

Ruby brushed the chopped veggies over into a bowl. "I met Seneca in my dreams shortly after our spelunking trip. Seneca revealed to me your healing powers, Anna, and your visions, Sandy."

Anna gasped, shaking her head. "You're shitting me. Finally. I've been healing people for five years. I tried to talk to you guys and I couldn't. The words would never come out."

"Same here. I tried many times to talk to y'all, too." Ruby walked over to the stove and dumped the bowl of the chopped vegetables into the spaghetti sauce. "In my dreams, I go into this incredible screen room where I watch these movies like vivid, full-length films of the future. Sometimes, I'm given choices to intervene on behalf of a friend or loved one, and sometimes, I'm only a witness of what is to come."

Ruby dropped the empty bowl into the kitchen sink. She sat on the kitchen countertop gripping the lip of the counter with her fingers. "Since the dreams began, I keep having this same dream, at least two or three times a year. It doesn't make a lot of sense. I'm in this very dark room, and I get the feeling that it's underground because there're no windows or doors. The walls are a dark plum or midnight blue with candle sconces on the wall, and I'm lying on a black leather couch."

Ruby slid off the counter and sat down in one of the kitchen chairs as Anna and Sandy stared at her. "Oh, okay, so in this room with me, there's a dragon with eyes of fire. I can feel the heat of its breath. But then I realize it's not me in the dream. I'm looking through someone else's eyes. Whoever it is, is frightened. I can feel the sheer terror shaking the body. I stand from the couch and look left and then right. There's no escape. I walk toward a full-length mirror. I can't see who the person is, but I feel a strong connection to them. Then I wake up."

Anna kept stirring the spaghetti sauce. "What do you remember about the dragon?"

Ruby looked at Anna and said, "The dragon is big. Its head touches the ceiling. Don't ask me how I know this, but the dragon is male. I'm scared of it. Like any minute, the thing is going to eat me or burn me alive. I wake up sweating bullets because, in my gut, I know this dragon has something to do with me. Even though I'm in someone else's body in the dream, I feel the dream connects to me. I feel like the dragon connects to us."

Sandy shook her arms out nervously like someone had walked over her grave. "Well, I wasn't going to drink tonight, but now I need one." Sandy opened the refrigerator and pulled out the ingredients to make a batch of margaritas. While mixing the ingredients, Sandy said, "Ruby, I think you need to keep a tablet by your bed, or better yet, each of us needs to start keeping a diary and write down everything we've experienced from the cave until now. Maybe we'll see a pattern between our supernatural events to give us a clue about your dream and this dragon."

After Sandy had blended the ingredients, she handed a cocktail to Ruby and Anna before she took a sip of hers. "I'll buy each of us a diary for daily entries, and I'll keep a master journal with all of our entries. Ruby, as soon as you wake up from one of your dreams, write down everything you remember. And we'll hash it out." Sandy leaned against the cabinet. "Hey, I know, let's call it the Ditch Lane Diaries. How's that for a name?"

Ruby looked from Sandy to Anna and threw her hands up. "Works for me."

Anna turned off the burner and moved the pot off the stove onto a heating pad. "Hey, here's a thought. When you're in the dream, see if you can remember anything new about the room. Is the body you're in male or female? Where's the dragon standing? Is it on the right or left? How close is it to this person?"

Ruby laughed nervously and shook her hands back and forth. "Geez Louise, I feel like I'm in an episode of *Twilight Zone* or *Scooby Doo*."

The girls laughed, but Anna was laughing out of nerves or fear, maybe both. The little kitchen seemed to get warmer, and Anna turned around to make sure she had turned the burner off.

On the far side of the kitchen, next to the back door, Ralph mysteriously appeared. He leaned against the wall and brought his forefinger to his lips. "Shh." Anna raised an eyebrow and tilted her head. Ralph said, "Ruby and Sandy can't see me and they can't hear me. Tell Ruby not to make direct eye contact with the dragon." Anna nodded in agreement.

Anna sat down at the table with Ruby. "Hey, Ruby, just to be safe, the next time you have the dream, don't make eye contact with the dragon. If you're afraid, trust your instincts. The dragon must symbolize something or someone bad, so just don't look in its eyes."

Ruby's eyes widened, and she rubbed her face with both hands. "The thought of having that dream again makes me more scared than a sinner on a Sunday."

Anna and Sandy burst out laughing. Anna said, "Ruby, you can be so funny without even trying." Headlights shone through the kitchen window. "Hey, we have company. It's either Jerry, Reed, or Brent. Any bets?"

Ruby took a sip of her margarita. "It's not Reed. He's working late tonight."

Sandy placed the pitcher of margaritas inside the freezer and then joined Anna and Ruby at the table. "Don't look at me. Brent and I had a fight, and I can't imagine him coming over to apologize. The boy never admits when he is wrong about anything."

Ruby reached over, grabbed Sandy around the neck, and gave her a noogie on the top of her head. "Y'all are like two peas in a pod. What did you fight about?"

Sandy ducked out of Ruby's grip and shoved her away. "If you must know, it was about you."

Ruby frowned with a quizzical expression. "Me? What the heck did I do?"

Sandy sighed, pulled her feet into the chair, and wrapped her arms around her knees. "It's not your fault. You're so wrapped up in Reed that you rarely notice anything else around you." Sandy rolled her eyes. "When we're hanging as a group, I catch Brent staring at you. It pisses me off."

Ruby squeezed Sandy's hand. "Honey, Brent is crazy about you. Reed says he talks about you all the time. I think maybe you're exaggerating just a teeny weeny bit?" Ruby took her forefinger and thumb to emphasize the teeny weeny bit.

Sandy interjected, "I know you're right. I might be exaggerating a tad bit, but the next time we're all together, watch him. I'm not crazy, and I'm rarely jealous. It's not like I see myself marrying him or anything. I just want his eyes on me, not you."

Ruby shook her head. "Sandy, that's the funniest thing I've heard lately, considering I've been walking in your shadow for most of my life."

A couple of seconds later they heard boots scrambling up the steps and pounding on the door. The girls laughed and said in unison, "Jerry."

JERRY STOOD AT THE KITCHEN door waiting for Anna. The door opened, and he circled her waist and drew her in for a kiss. "What's up, chick-a-roos?" He looked over and gave Sandy a smile and winked at Ruby. "Hey, sister from another mister."

Ruby chuckled and extended her forefinger toward him. "My brother from another mother."

Anna leaned against Jerry's shoulder and looked up into his eyes. "Hey, it's nice out. You want to go for a walk?"

Jerry's face split into a dimple-revealing grin. "Sure, peaches."

"Okay, let me grab a sweater."

Ever since the movie release of *Rocky*, everyone Jerry knew had started an exercise program. Anna loved to walk so they made a routine of walking most evenings around the college campus. They made a big loop around Peck Hall, down to the Admin building, and back up to Kirksey Old Main before heading back to Anna's.

Walking along the stretch known as the Grove, Anna said, "Jerry, do you miss dating Ruby?"

Jerry frowned and stopped walking. "Why would you ask me that?

Anna looked down at the ground before looking back at him. "Oh, Sandy made a comment a little while ago about Brent staring at Ruby, and I just wondered. I feel insecure sometimes about you and her. Y'all were together all four years in high school."

Jerry pointed to a park bench. "Sit, missy." Anna sat down, and he joined her, draping an arm around her shoulders. "I'll always love Ruby, but not the way you think. Ruby and I grew up together. My relationship with Ruby, most of the time, was platonic. But the night I kissed you, I knew what I had been missing all those years. I want you, Anna, not Ruby. You make me feel alive more than I've ever felt in my life. I won't lie. I'm afraid to give myself completely to you because I know as soon as you graduate you're leaving for medical school."

"Jerry, you're trying to turn the tables on me, and that's not fair. I don't have a crystal ball to look into the future. I just want you to love me as much as I love you."

Jerry took several deep breaths as he looked over campus. He pointed to an elderly couple walking in the Grove holding hands. "That's going to be us some day. I can see myself growing old with you. I'll be painting our white picket fence, and you'll be digging in the dirt in your herb garden, and we'll have summer picnics in the backyard."

"Aw, Jerry, I'm so glad you're romantic." Anna reached up as he bent down and kissed her.

Jerry held her face with both hands. "Come on, let's finish walking so we can go to Tony's Restaurant for pizza. I'm starving."

She frowned and shook her head. "Tony's? That defeats the purpose of walking."

"Nah, I'll worry about calories when I'm old." Jerry stood and held out his hand to Anna, and she placed her hand in his.

Jerry and Anna continued to walk down the sidewalk while he wondered if he would have a future with Anna. Jerry's gut got twisted up when he thought about Anna leaving for medical school. He had fallen hard for the little blonde with blue eyes. He pushed his negative thoughts away because he knew they would come back sooner or later.

Chapter 4

Angel In Your Arms

ANNA GLANCED UP AT THE big black and white clock in the Todd Library. *Dang it.* Jerry was waiting for her. She jumped up from the desk, quickly shoved her books into her bag, and bolted down the stairs of the library.

At the second floor landing, Anna tripped and fell. From down on the floor, she looked up into the eyes of the man she'd seen in the cave five years ago. He bowed to her. He was heart-stoppingly gorgeous, but something about him scared the living daylights out of her. She quickly got to her feet, slipped by him, and started down the stairs. When she looked back over her shoulder, the man was gone.

What the heck? Anna ran back to the landing and looked up the stairs; no one was there. Anna stared at the empty stairs, completely bumfuzzled. There had been a man, and she had seen him—dad-blame it. Once, maybe she'd imagined the man, but not twice.

Anna shook her head, ran down the steps and out the front door, into Jerry's waiting arms. She hugged him tightly. Jerry made a point to walk her home from school when he didn't have to work on his dad's farm.

"Geez, thanks for the awesome hug. What's up? You're late." Jerry gave her a quick kiss and threw her book bag over his shoulder.

"Oh, nothing really. Time just slipped up on me."

It was a beautiful day in October, filled with blue skies and plenty of sunshine. There was crispness to the air, and the rich greens of summer had turned to the bright yellows and deep oranges of fall.

College students filled the sidewalks going to and from classes. Students sprawled across the spacious lawns and studied under the trees in the Grove. One group of students sat around a guy who strummed an acoustic guitar while singing some folk song by The Mamas and the Papas.

Jerry caught her hand and brought it up to his lips. "Hey, Annabelly, I have to go to this thing for work on Saturday around five or so. Do you think you could come with me?"

"Hey, Jerry, what type of thing and where is it?" she teased.

"Aw, it's a harvest hoedown at Nelson Doune Farms. He throws it every year. They have tons of food, drinks, and great music. How about it, sweet cheeks?"

"A hoedown? Well, shut my mouth and call me shuggah," Anna said in an exaggerated Southern drawl. Anna had been to plenty of harvest festivals and Halloween parties, but never a hoedown. "Oh, I'm sorry. The way you said hoedown just hit me funny."

Jerry stopped in his tracks and frowned at her. "Are you finished making fun of me? I know what it sounds like, but their hoedown is fun. Mr. Nelson buys more hay from me in a summer than anyone else does in a whole year, and I live on that money. They always have a great band and plenty of dancing. Hell, last year some members of Alabama showed up and played a few songs on stage."

Anna smiled at Jerry and playfully shoved him. "Okay, okay, I'm sorry. I'm just teasing, sweets. I'd love to go with you. What time do I need to be ready?'

"I'll pick you up at four."

Anna reached up and kissed him. "I'll be ready. I really can't wait. I promise. Cross my heart and hope to die."

JERRY HAD TO LEAVE FOR work, so Anna waved at him from the front door of her house. She went through the door and yelled, "Anybody home?" No one answered. Anna dropped her book bag on the couch and stepped into the kitchen for something to drink. She rummaged in the fridge and pulled out a pitcher of sweet tea and poured a glass. Anna took a long drink and walked through the house into the den, kicked off her loafers, and sat on the couch.

Ralph appeared at her side. "Hi, Annabelly." His smile radiated kindness and emanated a feeling of love.

Anna held her breath for a few seconds. Ralph was breathtakingly beautiful wearing a pair of black corduroys with a deep purple turtleneck and black hiking boots. But it still freaked her out when he popped in without any notice. "Geez, Ralph, how about a little warning?"

Ralph draped his arm on the back of the couch cushions. "I'm not sure I can give you a warning, sorry. Now that you've had a little time to adjust to me, I thought you might have some more questions for me."

Anna tilted her head and her forehead furrowed. "I have so many questions that I'm not sure how to start. Angels look similar to humans. But you have the ability to appear and disappear, at will, from one place to another through what I assume is teleportation. But I'm not sure. And I guess I'm curious about creation in general, for humans and angels. Humans have many limitations. Do angels? And I want to know how my power works."

Ralph nodded and said, "Very good questions. The Creator made humans similarly to how He made the angels. Humans and angels have similarities, but many differences. My supernatural powers and yours are directly linked to The Creator's DNA. Human wards have been given select powers that were previously only available to the angels. The simplest way for me to explain is that it's similar to handedness. One human is left-handed while another is right. You both have similar abilities but use them differently. It's all in the DNA."

Anna twisted in her seat. Ralph didn't answer the questions, exactly. Then Anna had an aha moment. Maybe her genetic code was altered by The Creator. Maybe He gave her the ability to heal by embedding part of His genetic code into her DNA.

Ralph moved his arm off the sofa and pressed the tips of his fingers together. "Yes, that's exactly how it works. You're very intelligent." Ralph read her mind, and she added to the list of questions that kept piling up in there. He said, "Since the dawn of mankind, humans have tried to place angels on pedestals because of our supernatural powers, and some humans even revered angels as gods. Human delusions led to the downfall of many angels through time. That's why you have to be careful using your powers. Most humans wouldn't understand it, and some humans would want to turn you into a lab rat. Until you have proper training, if you need to heal someone, try to do it with as few witnesses as possible."

Anna took a deep breath and exhaled. "I was already using that train of thought. My mom almost had a coronary when I healed a deep cut she got in our kitchen. Then a little while later, she didn't remember a thing about it. Hey, was it the angels who helped the Egyptians build the pyramids? And you know how one minute you're here and the next minute you dematerialize to somewhere else? Well, I think another angel has been watching me. I thought he was a man. I first saw him at Campbell Ridge Cave, but today, I saw him in the library. Both times he stared at me, and both times he vanished in the thin air, similar to you. Ring any bells?"

Ralph tensed and faced Anna. "What did this man look like?"

Anna placed her glass of tea on a crocheted coaster on the cherry coffee table. "Well, he was tall and big. Not fat, but muscular, with long black hair, and he either had dark brown eyes, or maybe they were black. Very handsome and he smiled both times. But his smile was a little on the sinister side. Like he knew my deepest secrets or some shit."

Ralph stood quickly and straightened his shoulders. "Anna, I want to have a longer conversation about the pyramids, but I have to go. I have to report your sighting to my team."

Ralph's mood seemed to change abruptly from warm and fuzzy to rigid and cold. She looked at him anxiously. "Do you know who it is?"

"I have a hunch. I'll be back after I have gotten to the bottom of it. Anna, stay away from that man. Close your eyes. I'm going to place a veil of protection over you." Ralph placed his hands on top of Anna's head.

Anna closed her eyes and didn't move a muscle. The warm liquid heat started at the top of her head, like the cracking-an-egg-on-your-head game she, Ruby, and Sandy had played in middle school. The heat poured over her, penetrating to her bones.

"Open your eyes. You're safe, dear one. I didn't mean to frighten you. I have a team that I work with, and I want to discuss this man with them right away. Remember that I'm never far away. If you need me, just call out my name." Ralph kissed her forehead, and poof, he vanished.

Good grief. The disappearing act twice in one day set off alarm bells. Anna believed Ralph knew the man in the library. She hadn't sensed fear in Ralph; she had sensed anger.

RALPH CROSSED THROUGH THE CAMPBELL Ridge Cave portal and entered the gates of Heaven. He said, "Hi, Pete." Pete held the keys to Heaven and the master list of new arrivals.

Pete leaned against the pearly white gates that disappeared in the clouds over their heads. "Trouble with the earthlings again?"

Ralph stopped walking and shook his head. "You've been watching too much of Seneca's screen again. You have no idea what those poor souls have to live through every day while you're safely standing by the pearly gates."

Pete crossed one foot over the other. "I'm happy where I am, thank you very much. Seneca is waiting for you in the Hall of Moses, conference room zero-zero-one."

Ralph walked through the gates and yelled back over his shoulder, "Thanks, Pete."

Ralph strolled down the streets paved with gold. He could've ported to the Hall, but he loved walking through Heaven. It was pristine, no filth and no dirt. He walked through the Hall of Moses and entered the conference room where Seneca, Baldric, and Luwenia waited for him.

The walls in the Hall and conference rooms were made of crystal that resembled a sea of glass and trimmed with the purest gold to allow diffuse light to enter the room with resplendent beauty. The floors were crimson red plush carpets, and the tables and chairs were created from the oldest trees of time and space.

Seneca approached Ralph and gave him a hug. "Brother, it's been a long time. I've missed you."

Ralph kissed Seneca's cheek. "Ah, and I've missed you, brother." Ralph turned to the beautiful Luwenia, and she leaned in to kiss him on the cheek. He held her hands and said, "You grow lovelier every time I see you."

Ralph looked at Luwenia's shiny raven hair and pale complexion. He glanced down at her full lips as dark as cherries and raised his gaze to meet her shimmering aquamarine eyes with thick black lashes. She was more beautiful than all of the female angels in Heaven, and one of the most lethal, especially when it came to protecting her ward, Jerry. She said, "Raphael, you're looking good. Purple is a good color for you."

Ralph stared at her mouth, wondering what it would be like to kiss her. He dragged his fingers through his thick platinum hair. "Anna has seen Luc." He turned to Seneca. "Has Ruby seen the dragon?"

Seneca placed his hands palms down on the table. "Yes, Ruby has seen the dragon. I'm not in control of the dreams she receives. They come from The Creator. He's trying to prepare her, and the time is coming to reveal why they have the power of angels. We still have a few earth years left to allow their powers to grow."

Ralph placed his hands on his hips and stood with his feet hip-width apart. "Ruby's dream about the dragon along with Anna's revelation about seeing a man in the cave and the library may indicate that Luc has set his sights on the Campbell Ridge wards."

Baldric the Warrior had been given the responsibility to protect Sandy. He wore a coat of impenetrable armor made of gold and held a large sword in his right hand, making a figure eight with the blade. The sword had the ability to be a blade of steel or laser of light at the flick of his wrist. Baldric commanded attention as he sat down in the chair and propped his dark brown leather lace-up boots on the table. He gruffly stated, "My ward is a pain in my ass, and she constantly places herself in harm's way. That son of a bitch better stay away from my baby girl or he's going to feel a universe full of hurt unleashed on his sorry ass."

Seneca coughed several times, covering his mouth with his hand. "Baldric, may I remind you where you're sitting? Please refrain from the use of profanity. I'll have a meeting with Michael and find out if he has any intelligence on Luc's plan for Campbell Ridge."

"I'll stick close to Sandy. I swear that woman isn't afraid of anything or anybody." Baldric gave Ralph a rare smile and winked.

At once, Ralph recognized Baldric's capacity for true love. Ralph thought he would never see the day when one of them, especially the

Warrior, would find true love. But Baldric sat there at the table with the smile of a smitten man. Instead of Ralph teasing Baldric, he said, "Sandy is a worthy and true friend."

Baldric's shoulder-length hair shimmered like golden silk. His dark sea-green eyes met Ralph's. "That female has the sexual appetite of a male warrior."

Seneca and Luwenia both laughed out loud.

Luwenia placed her hand on his shoulder. "You would know, Baldric."

The tips of Seneca's fingers pressed together in prayer mode. "Now that we have the small talk out of the way, does anyone have suggestions on keeping the dragon at bay?"

Luwenia pulled out a chair and sat down, then swiveled the chair around to face the rest of the team. "If Luc is stalking Anna, then he's stalking the rest of them. Ruby sees the dragon. It's only a matter of time before Jerry and Sandy see Luc or one of his demons. We need intel, and we need to inform the AAF in case we need backup."

Seneca sat at the head of the table, and Ralph took the chair beside him across from Luwenia.

Ralph rested his forearms on the table, linking his fingers together. "I've heard through the Spirit of Man and some of the earth angels that Luc is stripping the wards' powers to help him gain access to heaven's realm. Supposedly, he uses the wards' genetic link to The Creator to breach security on the outer banks."

Ralph pushed his chair back and began to walk around the table. "The rumor has it that Luc is trying to recruit the wards first, and when that doesn't work, he strips the weaker wards' powers until they die, and the stronger wards Luc enslaves in Hell. The earth angel, Kaduntz, told me that Luc toys with and tortures the stronger wards until they either relent or die. Seneca, check with your sources and see if any of that information is accurate. Because if it is, then Luc has the Campbell Ridge wards on his radar. They need training."

Luwenia held Ralph's eyes for a long second. Time seemed to stand still as the gaze they exchanged between them released unspoken words of attraction. Luwenia finally said, "How would possessing the wards give him access to Heaven?"

Ralph swallowed hard and tried to remain focused on her question and not her gorgeous eyes. "As I said, for now, it's purely speculation and rumor. Kaduntz seems to think it has something to do with The Creator's DNA. Whether Luc is absorbing their powers through blood or the spirit, I have no clue."

Baldric slammed his fist on the table. "Give me permission to address Luc. I'll find out exactly what he's up to."

Seneca pushed back his chair and stood. "Baldric, no. This meeting is not about the long-standing feud between you and Luc. It's about the wards. Tipping him off would only give Luc time to redirect his strategies. If the rumors are valid, our wards could be taught how to ensnare him, and we will bring Luc to his knees."

Ralph, Baldric, and Luwenia all snapped their heads in Seneca's direction. Ralph said, "That makes them human guinea pigs."

Seneca took a deep breath and sighed. "This is war, Ralph, and we must use every advantage to win it. I have faith in our abilities to protect our wards."

JERRY PULLED INTO ANNA'S DRIVEWAY Saturday afternoon to pick her up for the harvest hoedown in Arrington. She wore her Levi's and a cerulean blue sweater paired with tan cowboy boots. The sweater set off her crystal blue eyes and curvaceous figure. Anna swiped on cherry blossom lip gloss and shoved it into her pocket. She pulled on a brown corduroy jacket, grabbed her purse off her bed, and ran out of the house and down the front steps to meet her man.

Jerry wore some pretty tight faded Levi's that made Anna unconsciously look straight at his well-proportioned package. He had on a white button-down, rolled up at the sleeves, which complimented his golden skin. Jerry was tan as a biscuit from driving his dad's tractor.

Anna's arms went up and around his neck, and he leaned down to kiss her. Jerry pulled back slightly and said, "I just love the way you kiss me. Are you ready to roll?"

"Yep. Let's ride." Anna walked with Jerry to the passenger side of the Blue Goose.

He placed his hands around her tiny waist and helped her up into his Ford truck. He chuckled. "Dang, Anna Faye, you're looking mighty fine in those tight-ass jeans."

The blood rushed into her cheeks. "Why, thank you, Jerry. You're looking pretty durn good yourself."

Jerry laughed loudly and walked around to his side of the truck. Anna loved Jerry's deep belly laugh. He jumped inside and gave her a smile that revealed his irresistible dimples. A rush of adrenaline shot through her. Jerry didn't know it, but tonight she was going all the way. After dating him almost six months, she'd waited long enough. Anna wanted to make love to him.

Driving down Tennessee Boulevard, Jerry fiddled with the radio dial until he found WNCM-FM, a country music station out of Nashville. Patsy Cline's "Crazy" belted out over the airways. He glanced over at Anna and caught her staring at him. "We'll never make it to this party if you keep looking at me like I'm ice cream and you're the spoon."

Anna smiled wickedly, slid over on the seat next to him, and rubbed her hand up and down his thigh. "Fine by me. You look good enough to eat."

Jerry glanced off the road for a second, and the truck went onto the shoulder. The truck sprayed gravel, and he gripped the steering wheel and pulled the truck back into his lane of traffic without hitting the passing car. "Dang, woman, I nearly ran off the road. You better watch what you say, sugar lips. Those tight jeans and your sweet sweater are making me sweat. Aw, hell, Anna, I have to show up for a little while. But when this shindig is over, I'm going to take you to my uncle's place up on Windrow Hill. I'm housesitting for them for the next couple of weeks while they're on a road trip out west in their RV. Their place overlooks Murfreesboro, and there's not a cloud in the sky. We'll stargaze."

Stargaze my ass. "Okay, I'll behave for now. I love looking at the stars." Anna giggled and looked out the truck door window embarrassed and excited by the thought of making love with Jerry for the first time.

Nelson Doune Farms was magnificent, with its rolling hills and black rail fences surrounding the perimeter of the five-hundred-acre farm. As Jerry pulled down the long pebble driveway, Anna spotted a dozen or so of the prettiest Tennessee walking horses grazing in the front lot. To the left of the driveway, there was an old brick plantation-style house sitting on a hill overlooking a small lake lit up by a string of brightly colored lights.

Jerry pulled his truck to a stop. He reached over and trailed Anna's cheek with the back of his fingers. "You make it difficult to think straight. And, well, you smell as sweet as magnolias in full bloom."

Jerry swallowed hard, and his Adam's apple bobbed in his throat. She leaned over and trailed her tongue up the column of his neck. He tasted spicy and slightly salty.

Jerry pulled her next to him and ran his fingers through her hair. His breathy kiss was hot and urgent as he pushed his tongue into her mouth. Just as she cupped his face with both hands, someone in another truck pulled up beside them and honked a horn, and they quickly broke apart.

In a low rasp, Jerry said, "Oh, God, Anna, let's get this thing over, okay? And we can pick this up where we left off." He stepped out of the truck, rushed around to her side, and opened her door. He helped her down from his truck, and her body slid down the front of his.

"I'm pretty sure I can get out of your truck by myself, but thanks." Anna inhaled Old Spice and the starch from Jerry's freshly pressed shirt.

The palm of his hands planted on her butt cheeks. "Yeah, well, then I wouldn't be able to feel your soft curves next to me." He linked his fingers with hers, and they made their way toward the party.

Anna and Jerry walked along the pebble driveway over a pedestrian bridge that led to the barn around the back of the main house. The huge barn was painted white and trimmed in black. She peeked inside the barn, and several splendid horses stood inside their stalls. The barn was spick-and-span clean and decorated for fall. On each side of the main barn doors, huge, bright yellow chrysanthemums filled large urns, and cornstalks wrapped with big orange ribbon were flanked by pumpkins of varying shapes and sizes.

Anna said, "Who'd you say this guy was? Daddy Warbucks?"

"Mr. Doune is filthy stinking rich. He sold a company in New York and retired in Tennessee. He plays at being a farmer, but his passion is horses. Nelson doesn't show his Tennessee Walkers. He breeds and sells them for pleasure."

Jerry stopped walking, and his hand cupped her chin and tilted Anna's face to meet his eyes. His piercing blue eyes shot electricity straight to her bellybutton. With a frown, he said, "I believe we may see some country music stars tonight, but don't be getting any ideas about leaving me for one of them."

"Not a chance." Anna reached up on tiptoe to give him a kiss. Jerry's expression softened. A smile lit his face, and they continued walking.

The barn party was teeming with people in country-western outfits. Anna was so glad she'd worn her Levi's and cowboy boots. A couple of men were manning two huge barbecue pits. They were roasting ribs, and the scrumptious aroma made her mouth water. There were strings of colorful lights decoratively hung from the main house to the barn. Picnic tables and hay bales were scattered around a huge dance floor backed up to a makeshift stage, and a bluegrass band was playing some kickass tunes.

A line had already formed at a gooseneck trailer laden with all sorts of food and desserts. A big burly man wearing a black cowboy hat came barreling through the crowd toward Jerry and slapped him on the back. "Hey, Mac. So glad you made it. So who's the pretty little filly you got with you?"

Anna snickered under her breath. Something about the big man reminded her of Sandy—all Yankee with a Southern twang.

Jerry smiled from ear to ear when he introduced Anna to the big man. "Mr. Doune, this is my girlfriend, Anna Kelly."

Mr. Doune flamboyantly bowed to her and kissed her hand. "Jerry's a very lucky man, Ms. Kelly. You call me Nelson, you hear? And if there is anything you need, you just holler." Mr. Nelson melted into the throngs of people.

"Are you hungry? Or there's an open bar." Jerry pointed to the bar set up under an oak tree.

Anna placed her hand on the crook of his arm. "Let's get a drink, and we'll hit the food line later after the crowd dies down."

Anna and Jerry walked toward the bar holding hands. "Aw, honey, you're in for a real treat. Zeke has this one drink where he combines sweet tea, lemonade, and Jack Daniel's. It has one hell of a kick."

The bartender wore a black cowboy hat just like Mr. Doune's and sported a huge handlebar mustache and some very hairy eyebrows. Anna started laughing and turned to look up at Jerry. "I feel like I just stepped into an episode of *Gunsmoke*, and Miss Kitty and Marshall Dillon are going to walk up any minute as we belly up to the bar."

The bartender overheard Anna and smiled. "What's your poison, missy?"

Anna gave him a cheesy grin. "Your sweet tea with a kick." She placed her hands flat on the bar as he mixed the concoction.

The bartender glanced up at her as he continued to mix the cocktail. "That's my specialty." He turned to Jerry and asked, "How's it going, kid?"

"Zeke, man, never better. I have this little honey by my side, and I'm listening to some pretty killer country tunes. What else is there?"

Zeke threw his head back and laughed, and Anna spotted a couple of gold teeth. "Boy, you got life by the balls." Zeke turned to Anna and quickly said, "Sorry, ma'am, meant no disrespect."

Anna gave Zeke a smile and picked up her cocktail. "None was taken." After she took a sip, her eyes widened, and she coughed a couple of times. "My, it's very strong, but it's really good."

Zeke turned to Jerry and winked. "Thank me later, boy."

Anna opened her mouth to say something, but Jerry interjected, "Zeke, dude, I don't need any help. I think you may want to add a little more tea and lemonade and a little less Jack."

Zeke nodded and grabbed the drink out of her hand. He poured out some of her beverage and added tea and lemonade. "Is this better, missy?"

Anna grabbed her drink and narrowed her eyes at Zeke. "You're a real bad boy, aren't ya?"

Zeke laughed so hard his shoulders shook. "Y'all go have some fun."

Anna and Jerry stepped over to one of the picnic tables and were about to sit down when, out of the blue, a tall and voluptuous brunette ran up to Jerry. She threw her arms around Jerry's neck and pressed her boobs into Jerry's chest. She completely ignored Anna.

The Amazon gave Jerry a big pouty lip. "Jerry Mac. I'm mad at you."

Jerry looked mortified, glanced down at Anna, and shrugged. "Rachel, what have I done now?" Jerry slipped out of Rachel's grasp and took a big gulp of his drink.

Rachel still didn't look at Anna and turned Jerry around to face her. "So, did you and the redhead break up?"

Jerry spit out his drink. "Rachel, Anna is my girlfriend. She and Ruby are best friends."

Rachel turned around to face Anna and checked her out from head to toe. She frowned at Jerry. "I'm only going to ask you this one time, Mac. Am I not pretty enough for you? Why haven't you ever asked me out?"

Anna flushed bright red with anger and balled her hands into fists. She might be small, but dynamite comes in small packages. Anna narrowed her eyes at Rachel and Jerry. She was getting ready to let Ms. Doune have more than a piece of her mind.

Jerry shook his head and said, "So Rachel, how many of Zeke's specials have you had?"

Rachel rolled her eyes and turned to Anna. "Hon, I don't mean to piss you off, but I've been trying to score with this hunk since I moved here."

Anna stood several inches shorter than Rachel, but she squared her shoulders, jutted out her chin, and shouted, "Get in line."

Rachel frowned. She took a step back and gave Anna a smirk. "You're pretty feisty for a pipsqueak. I'll give you fair warning. This guy, right here, is going to be *mine*." Rachel abruptly walked away and left Anna fuming.

Seconds later, Anna heard Rachel scream. Anna and Jerry ran to Rachel, who lay next to the fence row where the barnyard met the main lawn. Rachel screamed, "Snake, Snake, I've been bit by a snake."

Jerry surveyed the area quickly and caught sight of the rattlesnake slithering from the lawn into the tall field grass. Jerry jumped over the fence as Anna knelt down beside a hysterical Rachel.

Anna could feel the healing power surge into her fingertips as she wrapped her fingers around the spot where the snake had bitten Rachel. The bite was swelling fast. Anna said calmly, "Close your eyes, Rachel. Everything is going to be all right."

Anna's anger melted away. She closed her eyes and concentrated on her healing powers. She breathed in and out slowly as the power rushed into her fingers. She blocked out the background noise, the people screaming, and the footsteps crunching on the pebbles behind her. Anna held onto Rachel for a moment longer. By the time Jerry joined Anna on the ground, her powers had dissipated, and Anna released her hold on Rachel. The snakebite disappeared.

Rachel's eyes widened with alarm, and her face turned pale as a ghost. "What the hell did you do to me?"

Luckily for Anna, she had two things going in her favor. One, Rachel was drunk out of her mind, and two, she wouldn't remember a thing about the healing incident an hour from now.

Anna shrugged. "I didn't do anything. I just looked for a snake bite."

Rachel lay back in the grass with her arm thrown across her forehead.

Jerry looked at Anna and seemed confused. He'd seen the snake bite but didn't rat her out.

Mr. Doune ran up to them with someone Anna suspected was his wife, Mrs. Doune. He shouted, "What the hell happened?" The big man leaned down to his daughter, took one sniff, and shook his head. "Jesus, child, you're drunker than a skunk." Mr. Doune turned to Jerry and asked, "Did you see a snake?"

Jerry nodded and pointed to the field. "Yes, sir, I killed it. It's just a few yards from the fence in the field."

Mrs. Doune looked anxiously at Jerry first and then at Anna. "We could hear Rachel screaming all over the farm. Was she bitten?"

Anna shoved her hands into her blazer pockets. "Mrs. Doune, there's no snake bite. You may want to check for yourself to be on the safe side." Anna technically wasn't lying.

Mr. Doune placed his hand on Jerry's shoulder and squeezed. "Thank you for responding so quickly." Mr. Doune helped Rachel to her feet, and she went with her parents to the main house.

Jerry and Anna walked slowly back to the barn party. With a frown, Jerry said, "Anna, I saw the bite. I saw Rachel's ankle swollen with it. What did you do?"

Anna decided to take a chance and tell Jerry about the stones and the cave. "Several years ago, when I was fifteen, I went spelunking with Ruby and Sandy in Campbell Ridge Cave. We found a hidden room, a totem, and these mystical stones. The next day, I healed a hummingbird with a broken wing, and I've been healing folks ever since. I wish I knew how my power works. All I know is I can heal some injuries. Whatever is happening to me, I know it's a good thing. I know I'm supposed to help heal people."

Jerry didn't say anything until they sat down on one of the hay bales near the food wagon. "I've been in the cave, Anna. I found the room when I was seventeen."

Anna drew in a sharp intake of breath. Hell, she might faint. "Oh my God, do you have powers, too?" Her fingers tingled while Jerry talked about the cave.

Jerry placed his hand on her thigh before he reached into his pocket and pulled out a deep blue stone. "My stone is called lapis lazuli. It's ancient Egyptian. I've done tons of research on caves and my stone. I discovered soon after my visit to the cave that I could solve complex mathematical equations. I hated math in school, and suddenly it was a breeze. It's like that stone unlocked a key to incredible brainpower. I mean, man, did you know there are geomagnetic properties that can manipulate gravity?" Jerry paused for a second to study her reaction.

Anna grabbed his hand and squeezed. "I believe you. The miracles from Campbell Ridge are linked to The Creator. I can't believe you have a stone, too."

Jerry hugged her so tight against his chest she couldn't breathe. He allowed his hands to drop away from her. "I'm so glad I can finally talk to someone about the cave. My parents think I just woke up one day and became a genius." Jerry laughed nervously, and Anna joined him because Anna's parents had had a similar reaction when they'd witnessed one of her healing events.

"As my math skills accelerated, I began to write binary code. And now, all I want to do is write code. When I started college, I was doing some research in the library and came across the I Ching. It's this five-thousand-year-old text some folks call the Book of Changes, and it describes the binary poles of yin and yang as male and female. Many think that yin and yang is about good versus evil. But I believe it's about keeping a balance between good and evil." Jerry ran his fingers through his hair and closed his eyes briefly as if contemplating what to say next.

"The I Ching philosophy uses a broken line for yin and an unbroken line for yang. I spent hours in the library scouring over many books to help me figure out what the heck this all means. I

Ching uses those lines to develop eight trigrams, and they turn into sixty-four hexagrams. They say it's the way to the divine."

Jerry stared into Anna's eyes and swallowed hard. "I'm sorry if I'm talking too fast."

Anna brushed her hand down his jawline. "No need to apologize. I understand what you're saying about yin and yang. I'm just not sure how you use it while writing code."

Jerry kissed her knuckles and smiled with what looked like relief. "Okay, so this is the scary part—sometimes when I write code, I kinda space out. I go into the ozone somewhere. When I look down at what I've written, the code begins to change on the page. The code changes into text all by its dang self. It's like an encrypted message being decoded right in front of my eyes without me doing a dad-blamed thing. The code changes into ancient hieroglyphics, and then it's translated into English. It freaks me out."

Anna's eyes went wide with amazement, and she inched closer to him. "What does the code say?"

"The first message gave me the details of the day I went inside the cave and received my stone. The message stated that I'm to help those I love. The message ended with, "Do not be afraid for I am with you." The second time, the text revealed the New York City blackout that happened in July. In the text, it revealed the date, the time, and where the lightning bolts would strike. It described in detail what would follow. I didn't receive any specifics on what I was supposed to do with the information, and when it happened, I damn well almost died of a heart attack."

Anna shook her head in disbelief. She placed her hands palms down on the bale of hay and crossed one cowboy boot over the other. "Sweet Jesus. You'd think if the supernatural forces were going to give you information like that, they would've told you what to do with it. The first time I healed a little bird, I came close to a nervous breakdown. It's taken me years to control my emotions so I can use my power in a positive way. You need to talk to Ruby. She dreams of the future. Maybe you two were meant to work together."

Anna decided if and when she ever got the opportunity she intended on making a suggestion to Ralph that they explain things a little better for the humans. This otherworld bullshit was confusing.

Jerry met her eyes steadily. "The other information I've received is on developing new computer applications. It's amazing how my mind opens up in a code-writing session. I've shared a few of the applications with my professors, and one professor suggested that I open a software business. He said it was the way of the future. But you're the only one I've told about the New York City blackout. One message warned that there were some religious nuts out there who wouldn't fancy me sharing this information with the world. But I feel this gift is a sacred privilege even though I'm not quite sure how to use it."

Anna was a little surprised when Jerry mentioned opening a business and didn't want to overthink the complications that it might bring to their relationship when she went to med school. But at the same time, knowing Jerry had gone inside the cave and received a stone made something inside her shift like she'd found a missing piece to a puzzle. "I get it. Ralph, I mean Raphael, is my guardian angel. He told me not to tell people about my power, or they could turn me into a lab rat. The cave, the stones, and our powers are so incredible, and yeah, it's a little scary. Oh, oh, you have to start writing your episodes down in a diary. Ruby, Sandy, and I started keeping diaries. We call them the Ditch Lane Diaries. You can come to our meetings. We talk about our supernatural events, discuss our old entries, and add new ones, and Sandy catalogs them into one main journal. I'm not sure how all of this fits together, but we're getting a better picture. It's like our destiny."

Jerry slapped his hand on his knee. "I believe it is, too. Hmm, the Ditch Lane Diaries. Let me guess, Sandy came up with the name?"

Anna chuckled and nodded. "Yeah, it was Sandy's idea."

As dusk turned into evening, raucous laughter filled the conversations around them while people milled about the gooseneck trailer, loading their plates with barbecue and desserts. Several small bonfires were lit around the yard, forming a trail to the main house lawn. Jerry kissed Anna on the top of her head. "Let's get something to eat and another drink. I need it."

Chapter 5

Feels Like the First Time

JERRY LOVED HAVING ANNA UNDER his arm at the hoedown. After eating, the rest of the evening was filled with lots of dancing. The crowded dance floor flowed out into the grass. He and Anna danced the Cotton-Eyed Joe. Out of breath, Jerry pointed toward the stage. "Look, Anna, Willie and Waylon are getting ready to come on and play. I told you country music stars would be here, didn't I? Hot damn, I love Waylon Jennings."

Anna leaned against Jerry's shoulder. She glanced up and said, "Hey, who is that man standing behind them? He keeps staring at me."

Jerry spotted Cole Steele staring at Anna as if she didn't have on any clothes. It was all he could do not to go over and teach the son of a bitch a lesson on rudeness. "Cole Steele's farm connects to Mr. Doune's. The man's got more money than he's got good sense." Jerry turned Anna away from Cole, and he glared at him over his shoulder. Cole just smiled and tipped his cowboy hat.

Anna shivered and wrapped her arm around Jerry's waist. "He gives me the creeps."

"Don't worry about that asshole." Waylon walked on stage and Willie joined him. The crowd at the party went crazy when they began to play "Luckenbach, Texas." Jerry nuzzled Anna's cheek and whispered in her ear, "May I have this dance?" Anna nodded, and he led her onto the dance floor and slowly twirled her around.

Jerry and Anna went into a two-step dance with a quick, quick, slow slide motion of their feet. Other couples on the floor danced in the same direction with the same rhythm. Jerry smiled as he swirled his sweetheart around the floor again. Anna swayed her hips and hummed along with the slow tune while they danced under the stars. God, he loved her so much. He was all caught up in a happy dream. Hell, in his wildest fantasies, he had never thought Anna would be his girlfriend. Anna's eyes held his eyes, and he knew she felt the same way about him, no words needed.

As the dance ended, Jerry held onto her a little longer and squeezed her just a little tighter. In a throaty rasp, he said, "You ready to go, pretty girl?"

Anna nodded. "I am so ready to go."

AFTER THE PARTY, ANNA RODE in silence, snuggled next to Jerry in the cozy truck cab. Jerry drove them to Windrow Hill with one hand on the steering wheel, and the other arm draped around her shoulders. Anna drifted off to sleep.

Twenty minutes later, Jerry nudged her awake, and she looked out the windshield. He said, "We're almost here." He turned the truck into the narrow driveway and began spiraling upward to the top of the hill.

Anna rubbed her eyes and said groggily, "This driveway is kinda spooky."

"Wait for it... Look, you can see their house just over there." Jerry pointed to Anna's right as they crested the top of the driveway. On top of the hill sat the prettiest little white farmhouse she'd ever seen, and she could see for miles and miles over the rolling hills.

"It's beautiful. So that's Murfreesboro?" Anna pointed to a line of city lights on the horizon.

"Yup, it's the 'Boro, all right. I love it up here. My aunt and uncle are so lucky to have this place. I told them if they ever wanted to sell it to give me first dibs. I'd love to live here." He turned the ignition off. Anna hopped out and met him at the back of the truck.

Jerry pulled down his tailgate. He reached over to his cooler and dragged it over to the edge. "I have colas or beers iced down. Whatcha want?"

Jerry gave her a sweet smile, and she melted into a puddle of sappy emotion. Anna said, "Coke sounds good." Jerry opened the Coke and handed it to her.

He leaned his arm on the rail of the truck. "I have a big sleeping bag I could lay on the ground or in the back of the truck, to watch the stars come out. Your choice?"

"Do you think there are any snakes out here?" She shivered, thinking about the rattlesnake at the party.

"If you'll feel safer, I can spread the sleeping bag out in the truck bed."

"Nah, it's all right. You can spread it on the ground." Anna glanced around the property and noticed the moonlight casting long shadows across the yard.

Jerry opened his toolbox and pulled out the rolled-up sleeping bag. He shook it out and spread it on the ground. "I just washed this today so don't wrinkle your nose up at me."

It was cool that Jerry could sometimes read her mind. "Awesome."

Jerry sat down and patted the place beside him. Anna joined him on the ground, stretched her legs out, and crossed her feet at her ankles. Jerry narrated as if he worked for the planetarium. "We have a pretty spectacular view of the full moon tonight, and if you look at the two objects right there in the star configurations, they aren't stars at all, but they're planets." He pointed up to the sky. "See Venus, and over there is Jupiter. You see them first because they're the brightest in the sky."

Anna grabbed his finger and nodded, then pointed to the stars. "Yeah, I knew Venus was the first evening star to the west, and the one to the east was Jupiter. But if you look north from Venus, you'll see the North Star."

Jerry rustled the hair on the top of her head. "Very good, Anna. You get a gold star tonight." He started laughing, which made her laugh, too.

Anna lay back on the sleeping bag. She loved looking up at the stars with wonder and recited a line from one of her favorite poems: "O Stars, and Dreams, and Gentle Night; O Night and Stars return. And hide me from the hostile light, that does not warm, but burn."

Jerry rolled onto his side and propped his upper body with his elbow. "That's beautiful. Who wrote it?"

A gentle, warm breeze rustled through the fall leaves in the trees.

Acrid chimney smoke filtered through the air from a neighboring house and Anna inhaled, catching a whiff of the hay bales from the barn. "Emily Bronte," Anna said dreamily. The stars seemed so close she could almost reach out and touch them.

Jerry held her hand as they lay in silence. He rubbed his thumb gently back and forth over her skin. In the quiet still of the night, her heart began to beat faster with the promise of what would come next.

"Anna?" Jerry asked quietly, almost a whisper.

"Yes, Jerry?" Her heart beat crazy fast.

"Do you love me?"

Anna flipped onto her side and accidentally knocked her Coke over and soaked his shirt. "Oh, I'm so sorry I ruined your shirt. I can take it inside and wash it real quick."

"Don't worry about it, honey. I have a sweatshirt in the truck." Jerry stood up and took off his shirt. He shook it out and draped the shirt over the rail of his truck bed to dry. Anna couldn't take her eyes off his glorious, naked chest. She trembled with desire as she walked over to him and reached out to trace her fingers gingerly down his pectorals. She could feel him tremble, too.

Every honed muscle of Jerry's glistened in the moonlight. His beautiful physique made her mouth water. There wasn't an ounce of fat on him as her fingers trailed down to the line of hair that disappeared into his jeans.

Jerry moaned and dropped his head back slightly the moment she opened his belt buckle. He stopped her and held her wrists and searched her eyes. "Marry me?"

Anna snapped out of her daze. "Whaaat?"

Anna could feel Jerry's thigh muscles straining and quivering against hers. His eyes lingered on her face and moved down her neck as he placed his hands on the curve of her hips. She reached up as he leaned down and their lips pressed together, igniting a firestorm of passion. Anna wrapped her arms around his neck and her breasts crushed against his bare chest.

Jerry lifted her off the ground, carried her over to the sleeping bag, and gently laid her down. "Marry me, Anna."

She hesitated at first but nodded. "Um, uh. Okay, Jerry. I'll marry you."

One of his hands rested on her bum, and the other caressed the curve of her face. Jerry's tongue brushed lightly across her lips and pushed inside her mouth. Every gentle stroke of his tongue sent her reeling with pleasure. Warm tingles shot up her spine as she clung onto his biceps. She lay back on the sleeping bag and opened her arms to him.

Jerry brushed his fingers slowly over her throat, down her chest, and caressed her breast. She parted her lips, and he kissed her. Anna gripped his biceps hard and slowly slid her hands up to his shoulders and then her fingers twisted in his hair. Jerry braced himself above her with the palm of his hands pressed onto the ground on either side of her.

Jerry shifted his position slightly, so he fit snugly in the V of her jeans, and he began to move in an upward motion. The friction of him pressing against her jeans made her squirm for more. His delicious lips brushed lightly against hers, and he pushed his tongue back inside her mouth, their tongues beginning a slow and sensual dance.

Nothing in the world mattered to her right now but Jerry. The fluttering in her abdomen danced wildly. "I want to make love to you, Jerry."

Anna gently pushed him off of her and stood up. She began to undress slowly for him. Jerry watched, transfixed, as she pulled her sweater over her head and reached around her back to unfasten her bra, then let them fall to the ground. With every piece of clothing she removed, her heart pounded faster, beating a mile a minute, and the blue of his eyes seemed to glow in the dark. Finally, she stood before him completely naked.

Breathing hard and nostrils flaring, Jerry reached up and slid his fingers between her thighs and pulled her down to the ground. He began kissing her neck and came back to her mouth, running his tongue over her top and bottom lips, sucking them into his mouth. His fingers skimmed over her breasts, down her stomach and along the curve of her hips.

Jerry drew a ragged breath and whispered in her ear, "Darling, you're so out of my league." He kissed her as if to savor every sensation and every taste. He cupped her breast in his hand, gently squeezing. The roughness of his fingers against her nipples turned them into tight little beads. Jerry bent down and circled her nipple with his tongue and began to suckle her.

Anna cried out his name, and he rose up to her lips and kissed her again. He held her face with both hands. Jerry brushed his lips against her cheek and in a deep throaty voice said, "I love you."

Anna pulled away slightly and gazed up into the deep blue pools of his eyes. "I love you more."

With the moonlight behind him, he said, "Are you sure you want this?" She nodded yes.

Jerry held the side of her face with his hand and kissed her again. He murmured against her lips, "I will always love you, Anna."

JERRY COULDN'T BELIEVE ANNA WAS giving herself to him. Okay, it was a bit of a bummer when Anna had frozen at his marriage proposal. But she had said yes. The love he had for her swelled inside him and left him nearly breathless. He drank in her beauty as his hand went through her hair and cradled her head in his palm. He could feel her burning passion radiating against his skin. Anna arched her body against him, with breathy moans escaping between their kisses. Jerry knew she was ready for more, but he didn't want to rush her. He wanted this moment to last.

Jerry lifted his head, stared into her eyes, and smiled. The love that shone in her eyes told him everything he wanted to hear without Anna uttering a single word. "I'm going to try real hard to take this slow. But you're driving me crazy, and I want inside you."

Sexual heat rushed over him when she dug her fingernails into his back, and he released a moan of his own. He tried to keep himself in control, which was a contradiction because he had no control over what was happening to his body. He didn't want to hurt her, even though his carnal side wanted to take her hard and fast, but from what she'd told him in the summer, this was her first time having sex—and his.

Jerry's hand ran gently down her throat, over her shoulder, and down her arm. He entwined their fingers and brought her hand up to his lips, pressing a kiss against the back of her hand. He let go of her hand and allowed his fingers to stretch across her flat abdominals.

He traced the line down her abdomen and over her thatch of short soft blonde curls. Jerry scanned her face as his fingers ran between her thighs and slid over her soft skin, slippery with desire.

Anna's body responded so generously to his touch. It was all he could do to pace himself. He slowed down his thoughts to make this good for her. He focused only on her pleasure. He never took his eyes off her, and her eyes never wavered from him.

Anna's arousal made him crazy with want, and he bent his head between her thighs. Jerry felt her release the moment his mouth made contact with her soft skin. She twisted her fingers in his hair, and he gripped her thighs. She rocked back and forth against him, and he knew she was getting close again by her short and choppy breaths. Then Anna broke apart, throbbing and pulsating around him until he nearly lost it.

Anna looked at him with half-lidded eyes so full of desire and her lips parted. "Oh, Jerry, please, please, I want you."

Quickly, Jerry kicked off his boots and unzipped his jeans, and they dropped to the ground. He stretched over the top of her and nuzzled into her neck. "I love you, my beautiful and sweet Anna."

Jerry braced his arms on either side of her while Anna thrust her breasts against his chest. He could not stave off his ferocious hunger any longer. When she shifted her legs apart, he slid inside her silky, soft skin until he met resistance. He stopped. Anna lifted her hips off the ground, grabbed onto his hips, and pushed him past the point of no return. Anna blossomed underneath him, her legs wrapped around his hips, and she began to move in an incredible, undulating, perfect rhythm. It took all of his control to pull away, but Anna stopped him.

Anna said, "Don't, Jerry, I want you."

Wild tension began to knot in the base of his spine, building until he reached a crescendo, and he let out a yell that echoed throughout the hollow. Jerry had died and gone to heaven.

ANNA WOKE UP FREEZING TO death still naked as the day she was born, but a smile crept across her lips. Anna laid in Jerry's strong arms under the stars, and he was snoring. She giggled and tried to wrap the sleeping bag around her for some added warmth. Before Anna covered Jerry, her eyes scanned his magnificent body, ripped with muscles. Her eyes widened at Jerry's prominent arousal, and Anna couldn't help it; she couldn't stop laughing.

Jerry jumped up and turned left and right. "What? What is it?"

Anna rolled on the ground with laughter. "Jerry, are you awake?"

He stared at her in a daze as if he trying to determine if this was part of a dream. "Anna?" He shook his head and said, "It's colder than the hair on a polar bear's ass. Come on, sweet cheeks. Let's go inside."

Anna bent down and began to grab her clothes when Jerry came behind her and picked her up. "Not so fast, honey. Don't put your clothes back on." He kissed her neck, and sexual fire licked between her thighs.

"Jerry, it's freezing. I won't put them on, but let's get inside before I turn into an icicle."

"All right, honey. Take off. I'll be right behind you." Jerry grabbed his pants, opened his truck door, and pulled out a sweatshirt.

Inside the little farmhouse, Jerry draped a quilt around Anna's shoulders. He started a fire in the rock fireplace. Her teeth were chattering, so she hugged the quilt around her shoulders while she attempted to spread the sleeping bag on the floor. In no time flat, a cozy little fire blazed and Anna stretched her hands out toward the blaze to get warm.

Jerry sat down beside Anna and hugged her tight. He rubbed her arms and hands to warm her. "I can't believe we fell asleep out there. How do you feel? I could draw you a hot bath."

Anna's head fell against his shoulder. "I'm okay. I would like to go to the bathroom. Where is it?"

Jerry pointed to the hall and said, "Second door on the right."

Anna ran down the hall still bundled in the quilt, her footfalls softly padding on the hardwood floor. Inside the bathroom, she noticed blood between her legs. She looked in the little linen closet for a cloth and turned the water on hot.

After she had cleaned up, she picked up a comb lying on the counter and ran it swiftly through her hair. She didn't feel bad, just different. Anna looked in the mirror. "Ah, you're a real woman now."

Jerry stood with his muscular arms pressed against the doorjamb.

"I'll attest to that." Anna turned and the look he gave her had the air constricting in her lungs. He glanced at the cloth with blood, winced, and rushed to her side, pulling her into his arms. "Did I hurt you, honey?"

Anna tilted the angle of her head to look at him and ran her hand down his arm. "I'm fine, really. It was just my first time. That happens. But don't worry, I've been on the pill since we started dating." She grinned and touched the side of his face.

"Ah, well, I guess I should have asked you that before we did anything. I'm glad you're on the pill. But no worries, it's my first time, too. No STDs, I promise." Jerry crossed his finger over his heart.

Anna threw her arms around his neck and kissed him. "It's your first time, too? How cool is that? I love you, Jerry McDaniel."

Jerry scooped her up into his arms and made their way back to the warm fire and sleeping bag. He knelt down and laid her on the cover. "So, ahh, are you too sore to do it again?"

The buttery glow of the fire filled the room with warmth. Anna giggled and blushed. "I'm fine. I want to do it again."

Jerry stretched out beside her and traced the curve of her face with his forefinger. "I'm glad. I don't think I could keep my hands off of you if I tried."

Making love to Jerry connected her to him in more than a sexual way. Their hearts entwining, their souls mating seemed like destiny to her. She arched her back in response to his languid strokes. Jerry's skin gleamed with sweat in the firelight and scorched her with a passion she had never known. Her eyes were open this go-around because she didn't want to miss a thing. Anna held his gaze that reflected back so much love that she had to fight back her tears.

He said, "I love you, I love you so damn much." Jerry's tender touch rocked her to the core of her existence, and she knew there would never be another man who could take his place.

ANNA OPENED HER EYES AND noticed the night sky began to turn pale pink. She carefully removed Jerry's arm to run to the bathroom again. She took care of business and started to open the door when Ralph appeared in front of her. She said quietly but emphatically, "You have gotta stop doing that."

Ralph threw her a pink terrycloth housecoat hanging on the back of the bathroom door. "Sorry, I didn't mean to startle you. We can't seem to sync our schedules. Jerry will be asleep for a while." Ralph chuckled.

"I didn't think you watched." She frowned and put on the robe, tying it at the waist.

Ralph pretended to vomit. "Seriously? No way, I didn't watch, but your pheromones are off the charts, Anna. Sit." Anna pulled the lid down and sat on the toilet seat.

Anna brushed her hair away from her face and threw her palms up. "Well, I'm waiting here."

Ralph took a deep breath and exhaled. "Give me a second. I'm trying to tell you something important without overwhelming you. I believe the man in the cave and more recently in the library is Luc. Six thousand years ago, he was in charge of a third of Heaven's angels, known as the worship angels. His real name is Lucifer, although it is forbidden to say his name in Heaven. The Creator found out Luc intended to lead those angels in rebellion. Michael, at the bequest of The Creator, took his army and escorted Luc and his followers to Earth. This planet is where Luc and his demon angels made their home."

Ralph walked over to Anna and held her hands. "Once Luc found out The Creator gave certain humans like you, His wards, the power of the angels, Luc began to recruit them. He tortures the wards who do not convert, and eventually that torture leads to their death. He absorbs their supernatural power through the spirit of their soul which links him to The Creator's power. Their power is making Luc stronger." Ralph took another deep breath as he looked into Anna's eyes. "I believe Luc is targeting the Campbell Ridge wards. My team is conducting an investigation, but we believe Luc uses the wards' powers as a way to enter the heavenly realm."

Anna coughed and nearly choked on her saliva. "Whoa, hold your horses. You mean Lucifer, as in Satan, the red guy with the pitchfork?"

Ralph sat on the edge of the bathtub. "Yes, one and the same, except Luc is beautiful, probably the most beautiful angel in the universe. He looks nothing like humans imagine him."

Anna rubbed her face with both hands. "He is beautiful but gives off some seriously bad vibes."

"He does indeed give off bad vibes. He can also transform himself into human form and often appears as a sainted person or holy man. In 1232, he appeared as the Pope and reveled in torturing humans. Torturing, killing, and making humans suffer is Luc's favorite pastime. Don't look at me like that. If I may say so, you and your friends are being protected by one of the best teams from Heaven."

Anna gasped and brought her hand to her mouth. "You're talking about the Medieval Inquisition. Was he Pope Gregory IX? Do you know him?"

"Yes, yes, Pope Gregory. He is an evil, wicked angel who loves to torture humans. I'm loath to admit I knew Luc in Heaven. But hold your faith. One day The Creator is going to lock him away in a place with no doors or windows, and Luc will be alone in the Eternal Darkness forever."

Ralph knelt down before Anna and placed his hands on his thighs. "Anna, I'm telling you all of this to prepare you. You must tell me if you see Luc again or if Ruby has another dream about the dragon. I'm working to verify all the information with my superiors. The time is coming when we'll work together to win this battle Luc has against your team, and someday we'll win the war. Okay, I can tell by your eyes that you're in shock. Anna, your power is strong."

Anna was frightened and confused. She said quietly, "I sure wish you would've given me another day to bask in the glory of making love with the man of my dreams. Now I have to wrap my head around what you've said and figure out a way to tell Jerry and the others."

"No, Anna. Don't discuss our conversation with the others. At least, not until I have more concrete information about Luc's plans. I'm sorry I stole your mojo. Go back to Jerry. He's waking up. I'll talk to you soon." Ralph disappeared.

Anna walked slowly back to the front room. Jerry rolled onto his side, reaching for her, and his eyes opened. She said, "I didn't mean to wake you."

Jerry opened his arms to her, and she took refuge. "It's still early.

Let's go back to sleep for another hour or two and then I'll make pancakes," he said.

Anna pressed her face against his chest and threw her arm around his waist. "That sounds wonderful."

Anna closed her eyes. There was absolutely no way she was going back to sleep. If Luc was stalking her, then he was most likely stalking Jerry and her best friends. Anna held onto Jerry's forearm tightly. Deep down in her gut a burning grew, a desire to fight for the people she loved most in the world. The power of her healing began to tingle in her fingertips. Without her knowledge, Anna emitted a glow of light that surrounded her and Jerry, giving them both a veil of protection against Luc and his demons.

RUBY STUDIED ALL AFTERNOON FOR her Accounting II test on Monday. She was alone in the Bell Street house. Reed had to work late on campus on a new marketing program for next semester. Anna had gone to a hoedown with Jerry, and Sandy was spending the weekend with Brent in Franklin.

Ruby rubbed the tight and achy muscles in her neck. She pushed her homework aside and went into the kitchen for a couple of aspirin. She decided to lie down for a few minutes to keep her headache from getting worse. She'd finish the rest of the chapter on account receivables tomorrow.

Ruby crawled into her bed, pulled the covers up to her chin, and went fetal. A heady mixture of jasmine and vanilla filled the air as she drifted off to sleep. In her dream, Ruby made her way to the room trimmed with pure gold, its crystal walls as clear and as transparent as glass. Up ahead, crimson curtains hung from the ceiling and pooled on the floor. The curtains parted for her to enter. The glow of a thousand flickering candles illuminated her passage to the gossamer screen room. Golden, silk-cushioned seating was arranged in a semicircle around the room.

Inside the screen room, Ruby spotted Seneca and waved, and he smiled at her. He stood behind the cushions in the middle of the room with three completely breathtaking supernatural beings. The gossamer screen covered one wall of the crimson-curtained room.

On the screen, caught in a freeze frame, Ruby stood with Sandy, Anna, and Jerry, but they looked several years older. Their facial expressions seemed to be full of sadness. And standing behind them were the supernaturals in the room with her now.

Ruby turned to say something to Seneca, but he answered her telepathically, "*You know I'm your guardian angel, but you haven't met my team. This is Raphael, Anna's guardian and the lovely angel to your right is Luwenia. She's Jerry's guardian, and the big guy hanging around in the back with the sword is Baldric, Sandy's guardian. We are the guardians and protectors of the Campbell Ridge wards.*"

A brilliant light entered the room behind Ruby. She fell face-first to the floor without looking up. The light was from The Creator. The brilliant light hummed with energy radiating into the room and filled the space with such love, in the purest sense of the word. The warmth of His love wrapped around her like a blanket.

The Creator spoke to Ruby telepathically, just like Seneca. "*Ruby, I have assembled your team and the battles of life are brewing. Please remain strong and true in your friendships. You will be the glue that keeps your team together. I make way for love, and it is love that keeps your world spinning.*"

The light moved over her and out of the room. Ruby glanced up to see only Seneca remained in the room. She joined him, and they sat down on the cushioned seats. He waved his hand, gold like glitter projected toward the screen on the wall. The movie began to play. Ruby watched in utter silence. When the screen faded to white, Ruby turned to face Seneca, and he read her thoughts.

Seneca telepathically answered, "*No, I'm sorry. There are some things you cannot change. You have limits even though The Creator favors you. You're here to observe and be helpful to humans when the opportunity allows. But you're not allowed to change free will, and neither are we. There are some things even The Creator will not change because he gave humans free will. Be wary of my fallen brother, Luc. He seeks to destroy mankind. He'll use every advantage to annihilate a human soul, and he has an army of demon angels to help him. Remember, love is the greatest gift and has the most power in our universe. Love is the light, as you've seen today. Be witness, Ruby Jane Glenn.*"

Seneca drew his fingers over Ruby's face, and she awoke in her bed. The Creator had handpicked Ruby's team. Ruby had Sandy, Anna, and Jerry to help her fight the battles that were coming for them in the future.

There was a light knock on her bedroom door. Reed opened it and stepped over to her bed. Ruby smiled up at him and silently gave thanks to The Creator for Reed. He was her rock.

Ruby threw her cover off and scooted over in the bed. "Come and get in with me. I need you to hold me."

Reed took off his jeans and shirt and crawled into bed beside her. He pushed his arm under her head to cuddle up next to her. "Honey, you're trembling. Wanna talk about it?"

Ruby drummed her fingers on his pecs and pressed a kiss on his chest. She angled her face to meet his gaze. "I had a dream tonight."

Reed tensed. She had told him all about her dreams. Heck, he'd been in one of her dreams, and she smiled at that sweet memory.

Reed stroked her back and asked, "Does someone die?"

"Nope, not today." Ruby's face nuzzled against the curve of his neck. She stretched her arm across his chest and fell into a deep sleep.

Chapter 6

Don't Bring Me Down

Spring 1979

OVER THE NEXT TWO YEARS, Anna and Jerry were virtually inseparable. If Jerry wasn't with Anna at the Bell Street house, she was with him at his parents' farm. They spent every free minute together, at school, going to parties, celebrating holidays, including Ruby's wedding. After their wedding, Ruby and Reed would often visit at the Bell Street house. When Ruby moved out of the Bell Street house, Jerry unofficially moved in.

Anna's senior year at MTSU clipped by at a frantic pace, and she began the laborious process of applying to medical schools. At first, all of the schools she applied to were in-state, but after the fall semester had ended, Anna began to apply to every med school in the southeast region. She needed a scholarship and had to expand her possibilities for getting one. Anna and Jerry had discussed her goal of going to medical school, but she neglected to tell him she applied to out-of-state universities.

One evening, Anna came home after having dinner with Jerry and her parents. She and Jerry stepped inside the Bell Street house. Ruby and Reed were sprawled out on the couch watching *M*A*S*H*, and Sandy was in the kitchen making brownies.

Anna slipped off her shoes. "Hey, Ruby and Reed. I didn't know you two were coming over tonight. Something smells great."

Sandy stuck her head in the den and said, "You're smelling my mama's brownie recipe, and they'll be ready in ten minutes." Sandy ducked back into the kitchen.

Ruby placed her hands on the back of the couch, and Reed placed his chin on Ruby's shoulder. "We came over to watch *M*A*S*H* and Sandy cooked supper. Hey, you have some mail, Annabelly." Ruby winked. Ruby and Sandy both knew she had applied to several out-of-state colleges.

Anna glanced at the large envelope from the University of Florida. Her hands trembled when she stepped over to the mail basket on the side table next to the wall closest to the hallway.

Anna looked anxiously at Jerry, Ruby, and Sandy. She ripped opened the envelope and began to read the letter. "Oh my God. I don't believe it. I just don't believe it. They're offering me a Presidential Scholarship. It's a full ride." Anna's parents were prepared to take out a loan against their home to pay for her medical school, but Anna didn't want them to do that.

Anna, Sandy, and Ruby screamed at the same time. They were jumping up and down when Anna caught Jerry's frown. She stopped and said, "Jerry, I didn't say anything to you because I didn't think I had a chance in hell of getting it. I still can't believe it." Jerry remained quiet and crossed his arms over his chest. Anna noticed his jaw tick. Quietly, Ruby, Reed, and Sandy made a hasty exit into the kitchen.

"Are you mad at me?" Anna couldn't believe Jerry would be angry. This scholarship was her chance to be a real doctor.

With a frown, he said, "You should've talked to me about it, Anna. We're supposed to get married, remember? Damn it to hell. I want you to live your dream and all, but you didn't even discuss the possibility of going to Florida." Jerry's hands were shaking as she reached out for him, and he backed away from her. "Don't, Anna. I can't have you touch me right now."

With palms up, she said, "Jerry, I'm sorry. I didn't want to worry you. I didn't think I had a chance of getting a full ride."

Jerry's face turned red, and his nostrils flared as he stepped in closer to her. He yelled, "That's a crock of shit, and you know it. You didn't tell me because you didn't want me to try to talk you out of it. You know I've been in negotiations with BCS to sell them several of my software programs. You *knew* my business plans. I just placed a deposit for office space, and you didn't have the damn decency to tell me you could be moving? I'm opening my new Tech World in June. You made a life-changing decision without even asking my opinion. So what are you going to do?" He placed his hands on his hips and glared at her.

Okay, so maybe that had been the real reason Anna hadn't told Jerry. She didn't want to be talked out of it. But Jerry just yelled at her. He had never done that before. An awkward silence lengthened between them. She was at a crossroads: stay with Jerry in Tennessee or go to medical school in Florida.

Like Alice in Wonderland, she slipped down the rabbit hole, and then she got angry. "I should've told you, and yeah, I guess I didn't want you to talk me out of applying. But how can you even ask me what I'm going to do? You know how hard I've been working the last four years to get into medical school. Of course, I'm taking it. I don't want my parents to mortgage their house when I can go for free. You're acting like a real dick right now. Do you think your freaking business is any more important than me becoming a doctor?" Jerry hadn't even congratulated her.

"Well, I may be a dick, but I'm not stupid, and right now, you're a real bitch." Jerry turned toward the door, and Anna grabbed his hand. He jerked away. They stared at each other for what seemed like an eternity, but in reality, it was only seconds. He said, "I guess we just want different things. I thought you wanted a life with me. I thought you would go to school in Tennessee, and I'd start my business, and we'd get married. But now I see that I was wrong."

Anna poked her forefinger into his chest. "I love you. I do want to marry you. But I want to be a doctor, too. If I can go to school for free, then I'm going to do it, and if you can't wait for me, then don't."

Jerry stormed out of the house and slammed the door in her face.

JERRY'S BODY SHOOK WITH ANGER as he raced down the steps of Anna's front porch. He strode to his truck and opened the door, sliding behind the wheel, and peeled out of her driveway. Jerry wanted to kick his own ass. He'd known the day was coming when Anna would leave for medical school. He'd thought at the worst she'd end up in Knoxville, a four-hour drive, not eight to Gainesville. What hurt him the worst was that Anna never indicated one damn time she was applying to out-of-state schools. It was obvious Ruby and Sandy knew all about it.

Driving past campus, Jerry turned onto East Main Street and drove to Faces. Faces was a local disco and bar that drew college students and yuppies. Monday night in the 'Boro (as the locals called it) was Deadsville, but Faces seemed to have a decent crowd by the number of cars in the parking lot. At least, he wouldn't look like such a loser getting drunk by himself at the bar. He stepped out of the truck, shoved his hands into his pockets, and walked inside.

A huge chandelier hung inside the foyer. The club sported stylishly multi-colored lights and two huge, mirrored disco balls, but no one was on the dance floor. Tonight, the club had its recess lighting set to dim, and white candles sat in glass hurricanes on the tables. The club's manager played Harry Chapin's "Taxi" on the stereo. A quick glance around the room showed a smattering of people at different tables, but Jerry didn't take the time to see if he knew anyone. At the back of the bar, Jerry slid onto one of the high-back cherry bar stools with thick black padded seats.

The bartender, Rod, took a bar towel and wiped down the counter in front of Jerry, then placed a coaster on the dark walnut bar. "Hey, Jerry. What's up, man? You look like hell."

Jerry raised his head and growled. He said, "No shit, Sherlock. Sorry, bad night. Give me a shot of Crown and a Heine."

"You and Anna have a fight or something?" Rod pulled a beer from the cooler and poured Jerry a double.

Jerry grunted and said, "Or something."

"On me, bro. Let me know if you need to talk." Rod moved to the other side of the bar as if whatever Jerry had might be contagious.

Jerry knocked out the shot without blinking and chased it with his beer. Heat from the whiskey hit his full stomach. He looked at the green bottle and turned it slowly around in his hands before setting it on the bar. Jerry felt lost.

Someone placed a hand on his shoulder, and Jerry looked up into Rachel Doune's eyes. She was a knockout in a tight-fitting, light gray tailored suit, and she wore a low-cut, black see-through blouse with a black lace bra. Jerry was a boob man and Rachel's boobs demanded his attention.

"Getting your eyes full, Mac?" Rachel chuckled and slid onto the barstool beside him, resting her forearm on the bar. Rachel swiveled around in her chair and propped her black pumps on his chair's foot rail.

Jerry slowly moved his gaze up her throat and looked into her eyes. With a scowl, he said, "I'm not in the mood for your smart ass remarks, Rachel. Why are you so dressed up?"

Rachel threw her hands up in surrender mode. "I'm sorry. Dad and I donated a couple of fillies to the MTSU Equestrian Society, and I just wrapped up dinner and drinks with the Department Head of Agriculture. He left with a sizeable donation and seemed pretty damn happy. I was heading out the door when I noticed you sitting over here by your lonesome. Where's the little woman?"

Jerry tensed and waved to Rod, who walked over to him. "Another shot and a Heine and whatever she wants."

Rachel smiled at Rod, and he straightened his spine and grinned. Rachel said, "Cape Cod, Rod, and please use the Absolut, not the rotgut." Rachel batted her eyelashes. Rod's nostrils flared, and he looked like a dog in heat.

Jerry wanted to warn Rod he was flirting with disaster. Rachel was a man-eater. Rod placed the drinks on the bar, leaned in toward Rachel, and said, "You want to hook up later?" Rod was handsome for a dude, Jerry guessed, but not even close to Rachel's league.

Rachel placed her hand over Rod's and smiled. "Aw, aren't you sweet." She turned away from Rod to face Jerry. She said, "Tell me what happened, Jerry. I'm a very good listener." Rod threw the bar towel in the sink, frowned at Jerry, and went back to the other side of the bar.

Jerry laughed and took a long pull from his beer. "I think you hurt Hot Rod's feelings."

Rachel glanced over her shoulder and looked back at Jerry. "So not going there. Come on, Mac. I see that you're well on your way to getting drunk, and I have no plans. Plus, I'm staying at our house on Main Street."

Jerry wasn't taking Rachel's bait of subtly mentioning her house on Main Street. Rachel had been trying to get her hooks into him since she'd moved to Tennessee. He held his beer in his hand. "I'm celebrating tonight. Anna has received a full-ride scholarship to medical school. Yay." He twirled his forefinger in a circle and took another long pull. Oh, what the hell. He chugged the rest of his beer and set the empty bottle on the bar. "She's going to the University of Florida." Jerry dragged his fingers through his hair, and his shoulders slumped. Rachel was quick to place her arms around him. He couldn't help it. He hugged Rachel back.

Rachel rubbed Jerry's back softly. "I'm sorry, Jerry. I know how much you love her." Her arms dropped away, and she slid back onto the bar stool. "I take it you didn't know she had applied, and that's why you're so upset?"

Jerry scratched his head and turned to Rachel. Without much thought, he began to ramble on about his relationship with Anna. From the beginning until tonight, and Rachel listened and never interrupted or offered advice, which he appreciated. When he finished talking, he felt better but was shitfaced. "I think Anna believes we're going to keep up a long-distance relationship. But I can't do that, Rachel. I mean I could, but eventually, I would resent her. I know in my heart our relationship is over, and it hurts like hell."

A tear trickled down his cheek, and Rachel took his face in her hands. "Jerry, I wish I could tell you that it's going to be all right. That everything happens for a reason, and you'll find your happily ever after. But I don't believe that bullshit." Rachel's hands dropped to her slender thighs, and she leaned back in the stool. "You're going to hurt for a long time. But you're strong, Jerry, I've seen it in you, and you'll survive. Dad said your business opens in June. Well, that should be your focus. That's where you need to place all of your energy. Computers are the way of the future. You're going to be rich, my friend. And while money can't fix a broken heart, it can sure as hell give you plenty of toys to occupy your time. Anna is going to live her dream. You live yours."

Jerry reached into his back pocket and pulled out his wallet, but Rachel stopped him. She said, "I've already paid the bill. My treat."

Jerry stood and began to weave back and forth. He held on to the back of the chair for support. Slightly slurring his words, he said, "Rachel, you're all right. You try to be this uptight rich bitch, but you're not. You're solid. Thanks for the drinks, but I gotta go." He turned to walk out of the bar and stumbled. Rachel ducked her head under his arm and linked her arm around his waist.

She said, "Jerry, you can't drive. You can stay with me, and I'll bring you back in the morning."

Jerry pointed his forefinger at her. "No hanky panky, Rachel."

She laughed and said, "No hanky panky."

THE NEXT MORNING, LUC WALKED from the antebellum courthouse in the middle of town square down the historic East Main Street with stately Victorian and Italianate façade homes dating before the United States of America's Civil War. That war between the states was one Luc had sunk his teeth into pitting brother against brother. Over a million lives lost, and families split apart forever. He smiled at the memory.

Luc walked down the tree-lined sidewalk with its old oaks and maple trees to Rachel's driveway. A bucket truck pulled in front of Rachel's Queen Anne house and stopped on the side of the street. A man got out and put on goggles and hard hat. The worker pulled a monster chainsaw from the toolbox on the side of the truck. Luc chuckled. "Now, that piece of equipment could do some serious damage." The man stepped into the bucket and ascended to the trees close to the electrical wires. The traffic was steady, and Luc decided to play with the human. The man fired up the chainsaw and began cutting down tree limbs.

Luc glanced to the left as a beat-up Oldsmobile approached the truck. The older lady who was driving turned on her car's blinker to go around, but Luc waved his hand and made the Oldsmobile plow into the back of the bucket truck. Luc heard an agonizing scream and materialized at the top of the maple tree. The man in the bucket truck dropped the chainsaw and cut off his arm, and blood sprayed in a steady stream. The lady in the Oldsmobile began screaming as blood ran from the bucket onto her car and passing drivers stopped to help. By the time another human male lowered the truck's bucket, the worker had bled out.

With an evil grin, Luc said, "Another banner day at the office and that human is one of mine." The soul departed from the physical body of the human male while two of his death demons engulfed it. He waved. "Bye-bye."

By the time Rachel pulled into the driveway, an ambulance and police cars were on the scene. Rachel pulled her car into the garage, and less than a minute later she walked up the front steps.

Rachel frowned and gave him a weird look. "Who are you? And what happened out there?"

Luc rocked in Rachel's front porch swing. He'd watched Rachel and Jerry come into the house last night from the bar. He knew Rachel wanted more from Jerry than a casual relationship. If Luc could offer her Jerry on a silver platter, the Campbell Ridge wards would be weakened. It would be easier for him to absorb their powers if their team split apart.

Luc waved his hand toward the truck still sitting on the street in front of her house. "Someone just died. And I'm your new best friend. Please join me on the swing and I'll spin you a tale." Luc smiled seductively at her. Rachel seemed mesmerized and willingly sat down and listened to his proposal.

"Well, Rachel, do we have a deal?" Luc looked inside Rachel's soul. Baelezael, a Demon of Jealousy, had already made a home in her soul years ago. Baelezael smiled back at Luc as Rachel fell quickly into Luc's trance. "Come forth, Baelezael." The demon angel departed from the soul of Rachel.

Baelezael stretched his neck and spanned his black wings. His black eyes resembled what the humans called alien eyes. He had greasy, inky, shoulder-length hair, and the tint of his skin was a coppery orange with Rachel's blood plasma. "Ahh, Master, it feels good to stretch."

Luc smiled and squeezed the top of Baelezael's right shoulder. "You have done well with this soul, my son. Keep up the good work, and when this soul becomes mine, you will be promoted to divisional leader of the Southeast region of the United States. I have plans for this female. See to it you carry out my demands or don't report back."

Baelezael bowed before Luc and said, "It will be as you wish, sire." Baelezael entered Rachel's soul again, and she awoke from the trance.

Rachel nodded. "We have a deal."

RACHEL LOOKED DOWN AT HER watch. It was nearly four o'clock in the afternoon. She had no recollection of coming home from dropping off Jerry. That had been hours ago. Rachel didn't remember walking up the steps or sitting on the porch swing. She shook her head. Surely the blanking out episodes wasn't starting up again.

She went inside the house and up to her bedroom. She grabbed the pillow Jerry had used last night and inhaled. It still smelled of him. She was crazy about Jerry, and Anna was moving to Florida. Something inside her soul told her to be Jerry's friend, and that would lead them to a deeper relationship. Yes, Jerry McDaniel would be hers someday.

FORTY-EIGHT HOURS PASSED WITH no word from Jerry. Anna left several messages, and he never returned her calls, so she decided to drive out to Everglade. Thunderclouds rolled in from the west and lightning struck in the distance. Spring in Tennessee could be beautiful one minute and tornadic the next. Anna flipped the car radio on to check the forecast. Heavy rains were on the way to Murfreesboro as she drove down Salem Highway toward Jerry's house.

Jerry had every reason to be mad at her, but she had to take the only full scholarship offered. Anna had to try to make him understand how important going to the University of Florida was to her.

If BCS bought his software package, Jerry's business would be taking off in the right direction. She wouldn't hold him back in his ambition to succeed. Surely he would do the same for her. A couple of years ago, Jerry had turned his parents' detached garage into an apartment and computer lab. He would be moving to Murfreesboro after graduation and was set to open his new business, Tech World, during the first week of June.

Anna pulled into Jerry's driveway and noticed his truck parked next to the fencerow of old cedar trees. She glanced into the rearview mirror and rummaged through her oversized purse until she found pink lip gloss. She applied it to her lips, checked her teeth, and quickly ran a brush through her hair.

Anna stepped out of her car and walked along the sidewalk to his door. Jerry's cat ran out of the shrubbery and threaded its body in between Anna's legs. She reached down and scratched behind his ear. "T.C., what are you doing outside?" The cat purred. Anna knocked on the door. There was no answer. She tried the knob. It was unlocked, so she walked inside.

Jerry was asleep on the couch. She looked down at all of the empty beer bottles strewn about the floor. *Uh-oh, this doesn't look good at all.* He still looked gorgeous in a disheveled sort of way, his thick blond hair tussled and his luscious lips slightly open. Anna eased down on the couch and curled up beside him. She placed her head on his chest and threw an arm around his waist. She took a deep breath and waited.

Jerry stirred restlessly and opened his eyes. He glanced down at her. He seemed so distant and withdrawn but didn't move or push her away. He said gruffly, "What are you doing here?"

Anna's mouth went dry, and she choked out, "I-I've been trying to call you, and you never called me back. You missed school today, too. I-I wanted to see you."

"Anna, what's the use? You're leaving. It's over. It's all over. Don't you get it?"

Anna didn't know what she could do or say to make it any better. "Jerry, I love you. Please love me back."

Jerry tensed. His whole demeanor resonated with sorrow. He dragged his hand across the stubble of his beard and pushed Anna off him. Jerry stepped over to the window, placed his hands on either side of the window frame, and looked out at Versailles Knob. Anna ducked underneath his arm. She pressed her face against his chest and wrapped her arms around his waist. He didn't hug her back, which made tears spring into her eyes. Anna angled her head against his chest to peer outside the window.

Gusts of wind blew the budding flowers and trees back and forth like they were dancing to the howl in the air. Anna heard the thud of his heartbeat against her ear. A brilliant flash of lightning struck across the sky, followed by a loud boom of thunder. Anna whispered, "I can't stand you being mad at me. I love you so much."

Jerry wrapped his arms around her. "I love you, too. But do you have any idea how I feel? You're breaking me up into a million pieces. Hell, it's worse than Humpty Dumpty." A small smile curved his lips.

Anna drew in a deep breath, and her pulse leaped with a little hope. She hated the awkwardness between them. "Yes, I know exactly how you feel. I'm leaving you to go to medical school. But Jerry, it's the only scholarship I've been offered. I don't want my parents to mortgage their home when I can go to school for free. I get that I'll not be seeing you for months at a time. And there's a chance we won't make it. It's ripping my heart out, too. Come with me, Jerry. But please, please, don't shut me out and don't turn me away."

Jerry trailed a finger over her cheek. "If you would've only asked me before you applied to the University of Florida, I would've made different plans. I would've followed you to the ends of the damn earth. You didn't give a shit what I thought. You didn't even talk to me about it, Anna. You just mailed off the application and accepted the scholarship without considering my feelings or what it would do to us. Anna, you knew I was making plans with my business. It's too late now. I'm not going to stand in your way, but you can't stand in mine, either."

Anna ran her hand down his biceps and caught his hand in hers. "You're right. I should've trusted you. But I was scared. Hell, I'm scared to death of losing you. But I also know in my heart that I'm making the right decision about school. I want you to succeed more than anything, and I'm not going to stand in your way. Can't we try a long-distance relationship?"

THE NIGHT JERRY HAD HIS big fight with Anna, he woke up the next morning in bed with Rachel. He sprang from Rachel's bed like a scalded dog. Thankfully, they both still had on clothes. Rachel had reassured him nothing happened and took him back to his truck. He had never cheated in his life. Even now, he guiltily looked down at Anna. The realization hit him in the chest that Anna was leaving. He shouldn't feel guilty about anything.

The scent of Anna's perfume filled the air when she snuck into his place and laid her sweet little body next to him. Evidently, being pissed was a huge turn-on. Part of him wanted to flip her over on her back, and the other part wanted to kick her out the damn door.

The stress of Anna moving away, along with him opening a brand spanking new business, had lit a very short fuse to his temper. Jerry loved Anna, but she'd hurt him. He wanted Anna to succeed beyond her wildest dreams, but not discussing her school options with him had driven him crazy mad. She'd cut him to the core by excluding him from her decision-making process. Anna could've told him before he locked into a twelve-month lease on the office space for Tech World, and he had just placed another lease on a condo he thought they'd both live in—married.

Anna waited until the last damn minute to ask him to move to Florida. Well, right now was a day late and a dollar short. But, God help him, he still wanted her as he held her in his arms and kissed her. It didn't change his feelings. He loved Anna, but their relationship was over. He knew it and was pretty sure she did, too. And it didn't matter she was leaving him for school. Nothing mattered except she would be gone. The heart doesn't grow fonder with separation. Separation just makes the heart grow harder.

Jerry looked into Anna's deep blue eyes. She had the face of an angel. He took a deep breath. "Anna, we can try to make a long-distance relationship work, but you're going away for a long time. And we have little time left together before you leave. I guess I can follow my mom's motto and just take it one day at a time."

Jerry scooped her up in his arms and carried her to bed. "I need you to make love to me."

Anna nodded and pressed her face into the curve of his neck. She murmured against his skin. "I love you, Jerry."

Time slowed, and his anger lessened as he caressed her soft skin and ran his fingers over her lovely face. The rhythm of their love was perfect. He couldn't take his eyes off her, and the love she returned sent him over the edge into oblivion.

Later, as they lay in each other's arms, he stroked her hair, her face and entwined their fingers together. Who was he kidding? He would never get over her. Anna's moving away was going to crush him. There would never be another Anna in his life. That knowledge gave him great sadness, but life goes on and so would he.

Jerry thought about all the laughter and the love they'd shared over the last two years. It had been a gift, really, a reprieve from reality. He would stay with her until she moved. Then he couldn't see her again. It would be too painful, a reminder of what they had once shared.

Chapter 7

We Are Family

A U-HAUL TRUCK SAT IN the Bell Street house driveway. Anna, with Sandy's and Ruby's help, had packed most of her belongings, and they were clearing out the rest of the house. Sandy had packed her things a few days ago. Sandy had landed an entry-level position as a field reporter for the Channel 3 News in Nashville, and she started after graduation.

Sandy came inside the back door and wiped sweat from her brow with the back of her hand. She sat down on one of the boxes and propped her elbows on her knees. "That's about it, kiddo. All you have to do now is drive that U-Haul next Monday to the Sunshine State. I know you're excited about the cute little apartment your daddy found."

Anna took a brief break to drink a Dr. Pepper. "Promise me you'll come and visit. We'll drive over to St. Augustine for some fun in the sun."

Sandy jumped down, draped her arm around Anna's shoulders, and gave her a hip bump. "You know it, sister. Fun in the sun, cold brewskies, and hot guys with suntans."

Anna wrapped newspaper around a glass and tucked it in the box. "Oh, Sandy, I'm going to miss everyone so much." Anna choked back her tears.

"Well, we're going to miss you more." Sandy hugged her. "Listen to me, you're daring to live your dream. You have a great gift from The Creator, the ability to heal. You're doing the right thing." Sandy grabbed a piece of newspaper, wrapped another glass, and stuck it in a box.

With sadness, Anna said, "You think so?"

"I know so. Wow. This house is empty. It's like the night we brought Ruby here on her twentieth birthday, remember?" Sandy walked around the empty den and looked out the window toward campus.

Anna sighed and wrapped the last glass with newspaper and stuck it in the box. "It feels like yesterday when we moved in, and now it's over. Ruby's married, you're moving to Nashville, and I'm on my way to Florida. Life goes by too damn fast."

Ruby had left about thirty minutes earlier to meet Reed after work. Anna reminisced about Ruby and Reed's wedding. It had been a wonderful evening close to Christmas, and three inches of snow had fallen. Everglade Farms had been decorated for Christmas, a virtual winter wonderland. Anna had stared at Jerry during most of the ceremony. His smiling eyes had returned her knowing look that someday it would be them saying their vows. It was such a happy memory. Ruby and Reed were meant to be together.

Anna loved Jerry very much, but she wasn't so sure their relationship would survive her moving to Florida. She'd made a colossal mistake by not telling Jerry the moment she applied to the University of Florida. If she had just talked to him months ago before his plans, before hers, then he could be moving with her. God, she was an idiot.

Anna was a complete bundle of nerves as she taped up the last box. Tears glistened in her eyes. "I'm doing the right thing leaving, aren't I?"

"Come on, honey. Stop second-guessing. You were born to be a doctor, and I'm going to be the next Barbara Walters." Sandy grabbed the rubber band around her wrist and pulled her hair up into a ponytail. She grabbed a box and headed out the back door.

Anna sat on the floor and looked around the empty house. It was hard to believe, but this time next week, she would be living in Florida.

ANNA AND HER FRIENDS HAD met at the back entrance of Murphy Center one hour before the MTSU graduation ceremonies began. Anna,

Jerry, Ruby, and Sandy were in their caps and gowns, and Reed had his Minolta 35mm capturing every moment. Their families had already left to find seats.

Ruby hugged Sandy, Anna, and then Jerry. "I'm finally graduating with the best friends in the whole wide world." Tears began to stream down Ruby's face, and Anna reached up to brush them away.

"It's going to be okay. We're all going to be okay." Anna tried to convince herself as much as she tried to convince Ruby.

Sandy bellowed, "Come on, y'all. Stop your caterwauling. This is the best time of our lives. We've made it through college, and we're beginning our next chapter. It rocks!"

Anna caught Jerry's hand and smiled. He had agreed to drive her to Florida and help her move into her new apartment. Jerry had forgiven her, but the awkwardness remained between them.

Reed adjusted the lens on his camera. "Come on, one more shot, and I'm going to grab someone to take a group shot of all of us."

Reed snapped a few more shots and asked another graduate to take a photo of all five of them together. Anna knew the moment the camera flashed it would be a memory that would never fade away.

Reed dipped Ruby backward and kissed her. "I'm so proud of you, wifey. George and I will be the ones whistling the loudest when you guys walk across the stage. Then y'all need to get your asses out to our house where the real party will get started."

Jerry leaned down and kissed Anna. "I'm proud of you, too."

Anna clutched at Jerry's arm and accidentally knocked his cap out of his hand. "Sorry 'bout that." She bent over and picked it up. "I'm proud of you, Jerry. You're going to accomplish great things with your new company. And before you know it, I'll be back here opening up a practice, and you'll be a millionaire selling those software programs of yours."

The pomp and circumstance music started, so they separated and took their respective places in the processional line.

By two o'clock, everyone had met back at Ruby and Reed's house. Reed had spared no expense to celebrate his wife's graduation from college. He had hired a local event company that set up a dance floor and hired caterers, along with a bartender and a DJ.

Anna and Sandy helped Ruby with the last-minute details. Ruby went over the checklist with the caterers. Sandy made sure the bartender had plenty of glasses and ice, and Anna gave the DJ their playlist for the party.

It was hot for early May, with loads of sunshine and bright blue skies. The DJ cranked up Earth, Wind and Fire's "That's The Way of the World" and music filled the air. Two dozen patio tables, chairs, and umbrellas were scattered across the backyard, and strings of Japanese lanterns hung from the maple trees to help illuminate the area through the evening.

Jerry walked over to Anna at the DJ table. Something about him today reminded her of a posh Robert Redford with a John Wayne swagger. It was going to be so hard not to see him every day. Jerry picked up a vinyl record and flipped it over to check out the title.

The DJ started playing The Manhattans, and Jerry grabbed her hand. "Hey, let's boogie."

"Sure." Anna twirled around and shook her tush. "Let's do it."

On the dance floor, Jerry pulled Anna next to him and nuzzled his face in her hair. "You smell like oranges, and I love oranges." He nibbled on her ear, and she giggled.

Anna grabbed the loops on his waistband and shook her head. "Stop, you're making me have chill bumps. And for the record, I know I screwed up. I should've asked you to come with me a long time ago. I wish you were moving to Florida with me."

Jerry's brows drew together, and his facial expression softened. "I can't, Anna. I just hired two new techs and a new assistant. Besides, you need to focus on school. I'll visit, and you'll come home for the holidays. If the Lord's willing and the creek don't rise, we'll be married when you become a doctor."

The DJ played a song by Aretha Franklin, and Anna swayed back and forth in his arms to the music. She leaned her head on his shoulder. Anna loved hearing him say they'd be married when she became a doctor, but she had a feeling things between them would never be the same again.

Jerry cupped her chin and said, "Hey, this is supposed to be a party, not a funeral. No more talking about Florida."

She nodded okay. "You're too good to me."

He chuckled and twirled her around. "So true, so true."

Anna nearly crashed into Sandy and Brent. Brent had graduated in 1977 with Reed. He'd been in California on business but flew back in time to celebrate their graduation. Brent and Sandy had dated for a while and remained friends after their breakup. Sandy was famous for staying in contact with all of her old beaus.

"What's up, Brent? Long time no see, brother. How've you been?" Jerry danced with his elbows bent, hands in fists and rocked his shoulders back and forth to the beat.

Brent wore a pair of RayBans and strutted his dance moves. "The West Coast is where it's at, brother. I just landed a new account out there. Hey, man, you need to go with me sometimes. Can you dig it?" Brent grinned at them.

Jerry said, "Since I'm going to be on my own, I may have to take you up on the offer." Anna elbowed Jerry in his ribs.

"Ouch, what was that for?" Jerry winced and started laughing.

"You know what that was for, and California couldn't handle you," Anna said sarcastically.

Ruby came over and grabbed Anna's hand. "Can you help me in the kitchen?"

Something was up. Anna followed Ruby inside the kitchen through the house and into the master bedroom, and Ruby shut the door.

Nervous now, Anna said, "What the hell is going on?"

Ruby looked downright mean and placed her hands on her hips. "I just overheard Reed talking to Brent before y'all hit the dance floor. The night you and Jerry had your big fight, he got drunk and spent the night with Rachel."

Anna felt like she'd been sucker punched in the gut. She couldn't breathe and started to cry.

Ruby sat beside her. The door opened, and Sandy walked in. Ruby said, "Shut the door."

Sandy said, "What's wrong, Anna?" Ruby frowned and shook her head.

Anna brushed the tears away from her eyes. "Did he sleep with her? Tell me, did Jerry sleep with Rachel?"

Sandy's eyes widened, and her mouth dropped open. "Double dog damn. Anna, man, I'm so sorry." Sandy looked at Ruby and said, "What the hell is wrong with you? Couldn't you wait until after the party?"

Ruby fumed and shouted, "No, dad-blame it. I couldn't wait. Anna has raked herself over hot coals about leaving Jerry. If he did sleep with Rachel, Anna needs to know."

Sandy put her hands on her hips. "Well, Ms. Busybody, don't you think maybe it would've been wiser to tell her after the party ended?" Ruby flipped Sandy the middle finger.

Anna went over to the dresser and grabbed a tissue from the box. "Stop it, you two. Stop it! I mean it." Anna walked out the door and went to find Jerry. He stood at the bar with Reed and Brent. She stormed over to him. "Jerry, a moment, please." She frowned at Reed and Brent, grabbed Jerry's hand, and dragged him to the side of the house.

Jerry said, "What's the matter?"

She was breathing hard, and her fingertips tingled with energy. "Did you sleep with Rachel?"

Jerry took a few steps back and paled. He stammered, "Ah, well, technically, I spent the night with her, but if you're implying I had sex with her, you have it all wrong." His face turned red, and his voice quivered with anger. "It was the night you dropped the bomb about Florida. I kind of got wasted and couldn't drive. Rachel was at Faces and staying in town, so I crashed at her place instead of killing myself driving home."

Anna paced back and forth without saying anything for a couple of minutes. She stopped and looked into his eyes. "Jerry, you know that woman is in love with you. Why do you think she wanted you to crash at her place? And if you were trashed, how do you know you didn't sleep with her?"

Jerry placed his right hand on his hip. "Damn it, Anna Kelly. Do you honestly think I would cheat on you? And if you do, then you don't know me, and maybe you never did."

Tears threatened to spill again, and he leaned down and caressed her face. "Annabelly, I'm in love with you. I would never cheat on you, ever. I'm sorry I didn't tell you, but there was nothing to tell."

She glanced up and blinked a few times. "Promise?"

Jerry tilted his head to the side. "Pinky promise." He held his little finger out for her to take it. She did.

She threw her arms around his neck. "I love you, Jerry. I hate this—I hate this feeling of separation between us."

He pulled her into his arms, hugging her. "Me, too. Come on. I have a bone to pick with Ruby."

"No, Jerry. I don't want to ruin the rest of the party,"

Jerry brought her hand to his lips and pressed a kiss on it. "Okay, but she is going to get an ass chewing when it's over."

Through the rest of the afternoon, Anna laughed and reminisced with her friends about their college glory days. The older adults began to leave as night fell. Reed informed the hired help they could leave. Finally, the only ones left at the party were Anna's oldest and dearest friends. They sat at one of the tables, munching on chips and eating barbecue.

Reed extended his hands out. "Look, I want you all to spend the night. No drinking and driving."

Collective sighs and "oh, dads" came from Brent, Sandy, Anna, and Jerry.

With a look of concern, Ruby said, "He's serious, y'all. We've been partying all day."

Brent turned around sheepishly and looked back at the group. "Well, I'll stay if you guys try some of this ganja I brought back from the West Coast."

Sandy went over, jumped on Brent's lap, and draped an arm around his shoulders. "Ooooh, Brent, you've turned into a bad, bad boy."

Reed waved his hands and shook his head vehemently. "No way, man, I'm not smoking that shit."

Ruby brushed the hair from Reed's forehead, leaned in, and planted a kiss. "Oh, come on, Reed, live a little. It's not like we'll turn into stoners with one hit." Everyone roared with laughter.

Reed played Crosby, Stills, Nash, and Young's "Teach Your Children" on the stereo and placed a speaker in one of the windows. The Japanese lanterns sparkled in the backyard and candles flickered on the tables. Thirty minutes later, they were laughing their butts off over the dumbest stuff.

Jerry fired off one-liners left and right that had them doubled over with laughter. "You know if you crossed a bear and a shark, it could shit anywhere?" Jerry tried to catch his breath from laughing.

"Okay, okay. The last one, I promise. What's a day without sunshine?" He grabbed onto Anna's hips when she tried to stand up, and he said, "It's a day without you."

Anna shook her head, giggled and kissed him. "Aw, Jerry, you're stoned, but God, I love you." The tension from earlier in the afternoon had dissipated, and it was fun to be together with everyone again, at least for one more night.

God knows when we will all be together again.

Chapter 8

Makin' It

JERRY DROVE ANNA TO FLORIDA in the U-Haul with her VW Bug in tow. A wall of silence went up between them when they crossed over the Florida state line. The trip took ten hours, with stops, to pull into her new apartment complex. Anna should've been ecstatic, but a deep sense of dread came over her.

Anna and Jerry unloaded her mattress first and struggled with it on the stairs. Jerry said, "Hold up. Let's switch places. I'll push, and you can pull." They swapped places in the stairwell and finally got it through the door. Once they had the mattress inside her bedroom, they collapsed on top and crashed for the night.

The next morning, Jerry nudged her awake. "Come on, sleepyhead. Get up. We have work to do."

It took nearly all day to unload the truck with her furniture and boxes. One of her neighbors, a young med student named Wes, offered Jerry a hand with the furniture while Anna unpacked the boxes.

Wes was from Texas and starting his first year in med school. He was tall and gangly with glasses and dark red hair. Jerry bonded quickly with him and made a point to ask Wes several times to watch over Anna.

The following day, Anna and Jerry drove over to St. Augustine's beach to catch some rays and swim in the surf. Late in the afternoon, they walked along the beach.

Jerry stopped walking and turned to her. "Anna, I've been thinking. I want you to hear me out before you interrupt."

Instinctively, her stomach did a few flips at the seriousness of his tone. Anna nodded okay while her worst fear came to fruition.

Jerry said, "I'm flying home tomorrow, and I think it's best for us to make a clean break. I'm not angry with you. I've been thinking about it for weeks." He placed his palm on the curve of her face and moved his thumb gently back and forth across her cheek. "I wanted to make sure you were safely moved into your apartment before I said anything. It's just going to be too hard on both of us to only see each other two or three days every six months or so. It'll hurt too much. And you don't need the added stress of worrying about me or what I'm doing. I'll always love you, I will. But I have to let you go. Do you understand?"

Anna staggered back and plopped her rear down in the sand. She dropped her face forward into her hands and began to cry. Jerry dropped down beside her and wrapped his arms around his knees, digging his feet into the sand. Anna shook her head back and forth, but Jerry remained silent. She wiped her tears away with the back of her hand. "Jerry, I don't want to break up."

He sighed deeply and tilted his head toward her. "I know you don't. I know you like having me in Tennessee waiting for you. It must feel like some insurance policy, but I just can't do it. Anna, I'm not saying we can never be together again. I just think it's best for us to work on our careers for now." He placed his hands palms down on the sand and leaned back.

Anna leaned against Jerry's shoulder and cried until she could cry no more. "I know it's the best for you. But it's not for me. I can't stand the thought of you being with someone else."

"No worries about me dating for a long time, sweetheart. You're kind of a hard act to follow if you know what I mean."

Anna pushed him back into the sand and straddled him. "Jerry, I want you to know there will never be another man for me. You can be sure of it. I came here to study. I don't want to spend my life with anyone but you." She leaned over and kissed him, and he enveloped her in his arms.

ANNA WATCHED JERRY'S FLIGHT TAKE off the tarmac with a buzz of noises in the background of the airport terminal. She turned to leave and passed by people standing in line at the check-in counter to board the next flight. Adrift in a sea of unchartered waters, she passed the lounge filled with laughter and soft music. Anna stepped through the sliding glass doors, made her way to her Bug, and drove back to the apartment.

Anna changed into her gym shorts, T-shirt, and running shoes and went for a long run. She pushed herself to the limit. Her muscles screamed by the time she unlocked the door to her apartment. She threw her keys in the glass bowl on the table next to the door. Exhausted and depressed, she fell asleep on the couch.

ANNA'S BIOCHEMISTRY CLASS WASN'T OVERLY large. She'd waited a lifetime to sit in her first class at medical school and found a seat near the back of the classroom. Anna noticed only two other women in a class full of men. Her professor came in and began to go over the class objectives for the semester. Anna took meticulous notes and tried very hard to keep up. At the end of class, she ran to her apartment, threw herself on the bed, and screamed in frustration. *What in the world am I doing five hundred and forty-six miles away from the man I love?*

She picked up the phone and dialed Ruby's home number on the off chance she was home from work. Ruby still worked for Everglade General Store but was working on a deal with Mr. Burns to buy the store.

"Hello, Jackson's residence." Ruby sounded so much like her mother, Lee.

Anna sat up on the bed and tried to quit crying. Her voice cracked. "It's Anna."

Ruby said, "Honey, what's wrong?"

Anna walked outside to the small balcony with the phone and sat down in the chair next to the wrought iron bistro table. She began to vent her frustrations. "Oh, Ruby, I shouldn't be here. I hate it. I miss Jerry. I've been to one freaking class, and I'm in way over my head. How in the world did I ever think I could be a doctor? I want to come home." Anna was near hysterics.

Ruby stayed quiet until Anna finished her rant and she began her pep talk. "Anna Kelly, I love you like a sister, and you're not upset about the class. You're the smartest person I know. You're experiencing separation anxiety because you miss Jerry, your family, and us. Once you get settled, you'll ace this class and all the others. Your biggest problem is you miss Jerry. And well, honey, there's not a lot I can do to help you, except to say he's as miserable as you are. Right now, darling, you have to try not to dwell on him. Focus all your energy on school. And when you're not doing homework, you need to work out and meet some new friends. Are you still there?"

Anna calmed down, listening to Ruby's voice. "Of course, you're right, and I did meet one of my neighbors. Maybe he'll want to study together. Thank you, Ruby. I feel stronger when I talk to you. Watch out for Jerry. I love you."

Ruby smacked her lips in what sounded like a kiss. "I will, and I love you, dumpling."

Anna hung up and stood to look out over the balcony. She had a view of a lovely pond with gorgeous plant life. Anna chuckled to herself. Her dad had rented the apartment on the second floor on the outside chance an alligator might meander into the complex. She hadn't caught a glimpse of a gator yet.

Anna grabbed her books, shoved them into her backpack, and strapped it on her back. She hopped on her bicycle and rode over to the library to study. Anna slammed the book shut after about thirty minutes and looked up to find Ralph staring down at her.

He smiled and pointed to a chair. "May I sit down?"

Anna nodded and crossed her forearms, resting them on the table. "Long time no see. What's up?"

The library was full of students, and all of them were oblivious to this beautiful being who radiated such love. Ralph radiated a soft glow of light around the frame of his body. "Now, Ms. Anna Faye, it's time to start your training. I know you're distracted by leaving your home, but in a few weeks, you're going to be so busy the loss will lessen. You're on the right course. When you faced a tough decision, you took a path rarely taken. Grab your book bags. I'll meet you at your apartment." Ralph dematerialized.

Anna straightened her spine and left the library feeling stronger.

She unlocked her bicycle and began to pedal faster and faster as the balmy breeze hit her face. Anna's guardian angel said she'd made the right decision.

At the crosswalk, Anna stood on the concrete with the bike between her legs and shouted, "I can do this. I will become a doctor."

A man in a sports coat and jeans stood at the crosswalk with her. He turned around and said, "You can do anything if you're willing to work hard enough for it."

Anna smiled at the man. "It's my first day of medical school. Thank you." She pedaled to the Tom Thumb market and bought a six pack of baby Millers. She threw them into her bag and rode her bike to the apartment. Inside, she found Raphael lying on her couch with his hands behind his head.

Anna threw her keys in the glass bowl on the table and walked through her little den into an even smaller kitchen. "Hey, I bought beer. Do you want one?"

Raphael smiled again, his teeth dazzling white. "I only consume organic nutrition from my home. I've never consumed human food or drinks, ever. Similar to what humans refer to as being vegan. However, I do love the colors and the smells of your foods and the ingenious ways humans prepare it. Thank you for offering."

Anna placed the beers in the fridge and wasted no time opening up one for herself and drank it pretty damn fast. "Ralph, how does the healing energy work? I want to know why I can't heal all injuries or illnesses."

Ralph motioned for her to sit down with him on the couch. "I briefly discussed with you about how the healing energy is a direct link to The Creator. He uses your electrons and neutrons through an embedded genetic code to link chemically up to His energy. There are some aspects of the energy I don't understand. I wasn't meant to. You're unable to heal some humans because their destinies are sealed. Those souls are on a different path. All human bodies have an expiration date. Try to remember that angels aren't allowed to interfere with human free will."

Anna sat cross-legged and took another sip of beer. "Okay, so you've mentioned the free will part. Will you teach me everything you know?"

Ralph turned and sat cross-legged to face her. "I had to allow you to grow and mature as a human. But I would love to teach you. I have great faith that you're ready now. The Creator has great faith in you, and He has great faith in all humans. And yes, before you ask, all humans are important. Some humans lose their way, and demons consume many. There are humans who simply ignore their gifts. Their rational intellect tells them not to believe in the supernatural. But the answers have always been there for any human who seeks the divine. Knock and the door will open. Seek and you shall find."

Anna raised her hand and said, "Give me five." Ralph met her hand with a smack. She smiled. "So where do we go from here? What do I need to do to help?"

Ralph touched the side of her face with his hand, and warm tingles shot across her cheek. "You and your friends have such a genuine eagerness and willingness to help."

Over the next few years, Ralph began to teach her about her powers, and Anna's entire perspective began to change on life. Anna had been chosen by the divine, and she delved into her medical studies like a madwoman. Ralph worked with her daily and taught her how to conceal her power and control the elements around her, so she could heal people without anyone or anything detecting her.

Anna hadn't exaggerated to Jerry about her school workload. She barely had enough time to breathe, much less sleep and brush her teeth. Anna only saw Jerry a handful of times throughout medical school. At first, Anna talked to Jerry once a week, but as time passed, the intervals between their phone calls grew longer and the messages she left for him went unanswered. Until the day came when they had just quit talking. Life moved on.

Anna settled into a maddening, fast-paced routine and took full loads every semester as well as going to summer school and intersession. She spent long hours studying and memorizing material for every course. The doctors at the university hospital took notice of her work ethic when she started her clinical rotations. Anna's schedule was very intense, but she'd been relentless in her efforts. She never complained and worked shifts no one else wanted. She covered for people who couldn't make their shifts. Anna's sole purpose in life was to heal, and her drive landed her a residency at the Hall of Saints Hospital in Pensacola.

Murfreesboro, Tennessee 1984

THE FIRST YEAR AFTER ANNA left took an emotional toll on Jerry. He had to remind himself to wake up, put his feet on the floor, and breathe. The days turned into weeks and the weeks turned into months. Ruby and Reed had been his lifeline. Jerry practically lived with them during the first year known as "life without Anna."

The Ditch Lane Diaries monthly meetings had switched to conference calls and, more often than not, Anna was absent. Ruby and Anna had up-close-and-personal relationships with their guardian angels. Jerry knew his angel's name and felt her presence from time to time, but no visuals. Whenever Jerry received an encrypted message, he would discuss it with Ruby. The supernatural events that had been so important in his past now seemed to make an appearance only in his professional life.

On the weekends, Jerry still helped his dad on the farm, and he became friends with Nelson Doune. Nelson became a valuable mentor to Jerry's business. Nelson had been the one who suggested using Rachel to host employee events and dinner parties. She was a big hit with the Tech World employees. Jerry and Rachel's friendship evolved into a professional relationship, albeit one with flirtations.

Jerry threw himself into building Tech World. He hired two exceptional programming students who had turned into full-time hires. By the second year of business, Jerry's sales had doubled, and his success kept growing year after year. Eventually, he acquired enough capital to buy a commercial lot and hired a contractor to build him a commercial building to meet his specific needs, including climate control environment for his servers. Jerry hired Reed as his marketing consultant, and Tech World was projected to be in seven figures by year-end. Jerry had a staff of fifty employees, and he worked hard every day to make sure those employees kept their jobs and stayed happy. Happy employees yielded profits in a big way for Tech World.

Jerry walked through the double doors of his new building. His receptionist, Sarah, waved. He smiled and revealed a basket of pastries in his hand. "Good morning, Sarah. Would you like a pastry? Freshly made from Everglade General Store."

Sarah turned several shades of red and said, "Mr. McDaniel, they smell wonderful, but I'm trying to lose weight for summer. Thank you."

Jerry frowned and shook his head. "Sarah, you're beautiful just the way you are. You don't need to lose weight. But I guess that means more for me. Is everyone in this morning?"

Sarah straightened her shoulders and nodded. "Yes, sir. Everyone is here."

"Great! At nine o'clock, make an announcement for all employees to meet in the warehouse. I have some news." He winked and walked down the hall corridor. Several employees shouted greetings, and Jerry waved or said hello. He hit the button on the elevator to the second floor. When he stepped out, his assistant, Kaye, waited for him.

"Good morning, Mr. McDaniel. You have a full calendar today. Hmm. Uh. Ms. Doune is in your office. She doesn't take no for an answer."

Jerry chuckled and offered a pastry to Kaye, who took a chocolate-covered donut. "Ms. Doune never takes no for an answer. We have a meeting in the warehouse at nine. If you need to change my schedule, please give me about twenty minutes to tell the employees the good news." He whistled as he walked through his office door. Rachel stood looking at his Chris Chambliss signed jersey his dad bought him for his birthday last year.

Rachel wore a tailored black suit with a white blouse, and her hair was pulled back tight at the nape of her neck and secured with a black clip. She turned and smiled. "You're late."

He kissed her on the cheek. "I'm celebrating this morning, and I have pastries from Ruby. Want one?"

"You bet your ass I do. I want her cinnamon buns. So what are you celebrating? And why am I here so early? You know I hate early meetings." She took a bite out of the cinnamon bun, and he went around and sat at his desk.

Jerry grabbed one of the donuts with confectioners sugar and placed it on a napkin. "I closed the deal with Weston-Hall Enterprises. Seven-figure contract."

Rachel ran around the desk and hugged his neck. "Jerry, I'm so proud of you. When did you find out?"

He patted her hand. "Last night. I received a phone call around eight. And you're here to help me throw a party for the employees. I couldn't do this without their help or yours. I'm giving every employee a hundred-dollar bonus in their check this Friday. I want you to line up caterers, music, and an open bar. The works. I'm flying high, my friend." He took a bite of his donut and washed it down with coffee, two creams, two sugars. Sarah came over the loud speaker system. He grinned and said, "Come on, let's tell them together." He grabbed Rachel's hand, and they walked to the elevator and went to the bottom floor.

Jerry noticed that his employees looked apprehensive. He quickly hopped onto of one the spools of wire and whistled. Everyone stared at him. He shouted, "I have awesome news. We closed on the deal with Weston-Hall last night, and we're going to celebrate this Friday. We're going to throw a party, and each of you will receive an extra hundred bucks in your paycheck this week." The employees yelled and whistled with excitement. "Now, y'all get back to work." Jerry laughed, and several employees came over to shake his hand and thank him. He looked up at Rachel and smiled. Today was a good day.

New Year's Eve

JERRY RODE IN THE BACK seat of the limo he'd hired for the evening, heading to the Nelson Doune Farms annual New Year's Eve Bash. He intended to celebrate tonight because Tech World had had another record year. *Not half bad for a farm boy from Everglade, Tennessee.* He stepped out of the limo in a custom-fit Armani Tux, diamond cufflinks, and a pair of black Salvatore plain toe oxfords. Jerry's hair was shorter now and feathered off his face.

People entered the main house in evening gowns and tuxedos. Inside the house, black and gold balloons, streamers, and glittering décor filled the rooms. Music blared from the ballroom on the second floor. Jerry grabbed a flute of champagne offered by a passing waiter.

Jerry zeroed in on two hotties in the library when he glanced up, and Rachel appeared on the staircase. Holy hell. Rachel wore a sleeveless black evening dress with a plunging neckline that seemed to go to her navel, but a wide velvet belt prevented his view. The belt cinched at the waist and accented her voluptuous curves. Rachel waved and descended the stairs. He offered her his hand, and she took it.

Jerry kissed the back of her hand. "Ms. Doune, you're looking quite beautiful tonight."

Rachel reached over and kissed his cheek. "Right back at you, Mac. You clean up well for a farm boy. Every woman here is staring at you."

Jerry placed her hand in the crook of his arm and walked them to the bar in the library. "And every man is staring at you."

Rachel laughed out loud. "Then let's make them all jealous as hell."

The evening passed with more cocktails than Jerry could count. At midnight, Jerry and Rachel were on the floor dancing to Al Green's "How to Mend a Broken Heart." He pulled her close, his hand resting on the curve of her ass. The music stopped, and Nelson took the microphone and started counting down, "10-9-8..." But Jerry didn't hear anything. He locked on Rachel's eyes, his gaze dropped to her mouth, and she licked her top lip as everyone screamed, "Happy New Year." Jerry grabbed her by the nape of her neck and crushed her with a kiss.

Rachel grabbed his hand and said, "Come with me." Jerry followed her and raced to the east wing of the house. The next morning, Jerry woke up in Rachel's arms and his life began again.

Chapter 9

Separate Lives

Pensacola, Florida 1985

ANNA RENTED A BRICK GUEST house from a former patient she'd treated when she first came to her residency at Hall of Saints Hospital. Cary Stewart was a well-off man in his seventies with no kids of his own. She'd saved Cary's life. He'd had a massive heart attack in the ER, and with the miracles of modern medicine along with her healing powers, Cary had recovered astoundingly fast.

Anna stopped by frequently to check on Cary during his stay at the hospital. They would get into long conversations about Tennessee. His grandmother had lived on a farm in Bethesda. She enjoyed Cary's sense of humor.

On the day of his release, Cary made her an offer she couldn't refuse. "Look, I learned from one of the nurses you're looking for a place to rent. My place has a guest house I normally rent out to tourists. I'm happy to offer it to you. It has two bedrooms with a daybed up in the loft. We have a swimming pool, and the ocean is only a stone's throw away. How about it?"

Anna sat down in a chair next to the hospital bed. "Sounds expensive. How much?"

Cary tapped his finger next to his temple. "You pay the utilities, and we'll call it even. You did save my life." He reached over, grabbed his pen and pad off the side table, scribbled, and handed the note to Anna. "Here's the address. Come and check it out."

Anna took the note and read the address. It was close to the hospital. "Cary, I don't know what to say except thank you. I'll come and check on you tomorrow, and then I'll check your guest house out."

Anna accepted Cary's offer but insisted on paying him a fair amount of rent. The tropical oceanfront property had a pool and private access to the beach. Carey and his housekeeper, Maria, became her friends during her two years of residency in Pensacola.

AFTER ANNA'S SHIFT AT HALL of Saints, she went for a long walk on the beach. It had been a particularly hard day for her. She'd lost a patient. Her mind retraced each step of the case, and she couldn't find anything she would have done differently. Anna had even tried to use her healing powers, but she lost her patient anyway. She thought about the fifty-year-old woman, still in the prime of life. The patient had been admitted to the hospital with stomach pains, no fever, no chills, only stomach pain. By the time Anna had been made aware of the case, it was too late. There had been a tear in the abdominal wall. An abdominal aortic aneurysm. The worst part had been going out to the family. Her husband and two sons were in the waiting room.

Anna went over to the Densen family. "Would you please come with me?" The look of terror struck across the husband's face, but the two teenage boys were unaware of the life-altering event she had to tell them. Inside the family consultation room, Anna looked at the husband and the two boys. "Mrs. Densen suffered a tear in her abdominal wall. It's what we call an abdominal aortic aneurysm. I tried to repair the damage, but too much time had lapsed."

The oldest boy, who looked to be sixteen or seventeen, said, "May I see Mom?"

Anna held the boy's hand and looked at the father. "Yes, you can, but I'm sorry to say your mom has passed away." The husband broke down in tears, and the sons stared at her in shock.

The older boy said, "No, my mom is okay. She's taking me to my baseball tournament this weekend. Mom said she just ate something bad."

Anna placed her hand on his shoulder. "I am sorry. You may come with me now, and I'll take you to her room." The husband was inconsolable as he and the boys followed her to the room. Inside the room, all three broke down and cried and Anna had cried with them. She said, "Please take as long as you need. I will be at the nurses station."

Now, Anna walked on the beach with her heart broken. She didn't understand why she could heal some patients and not others. As the sun began to set, Anna made her way to Cary's boardwalk, past the grounds, to her house. Inside the kitchen, she sat at the table numb for the family who had suffered the loss of a beloved spouse and mother.

The telephone rang three times before she heard it and the machine picked it up. Ruby was on the line. Anna went over and grabbed the phone from its docking station. "Hey, Ruby, I'm here. Just a little slow today. What's up?" A chill came over her, and the hair on her arms rose. Ruby let out a big sigh. Anna said, "What's wrong? Tell me. I can see you twirling the ends of your hair right now."

Ruby laughed. "Girl, you know me too well. I've been struggling with this phone call. I had a dream years ago right after we moved into the house on Bell Street. I knew you and Jerry were going to break up. I knew he was going to start dating Rachel. I should've told you, but I was told to observe and not to interfere. But when I found out a month ago Jerry was getting married, I knew I had to tell you, but I put it off until now."

Anna interrupted Ruby and said, "What? Married? You knew we would break up and didn't tell me? You knew he and Rachel would start dating? Why, Ruby? Why would you keep that from me?"

Ruby blurted out, "I did try to keep you two together without breaking my oath to Seneca. I talked to the two of you. I'm not allowed to interfere with free will. You made your decision, and he made his. I have an awful feeling in my gut this is all wrong. In my dream, I didn't see Jerry walking down the aisle with Rachel. There's still time to change the future."

Anna sucked in her breath as big tears began to well in her eyes. "When?" She closed her eyes. *Not Jerry, please God.*

Ruby's voice faltered. "I—I should've told you sooner. I'm sorry. In June, the week before you move home."

Anna grabbed a tissue from the box of Kleenex on the polished cherry end table next to the couch. She walked into the living area and sat on the couch. "You should've told me," Anna said hatefully.

Ruby snapped back at her, "That's not fair, and you know it. We talked about the pros and cons of you moving to Florida. Jerry broke up with you before you went to your first class at medical school. You had choices. You made the decision to stay. Did you think you could go away for six years and things around here would stay the same? Jerry was devastated when you moved to Florida. He practically moved in with Reed and me."

It upset Anna that Ruby was taking up for Jerry. "I did what I thought was best for him and me. Medical school was friggin' hard. It wouldn't have been fair to either of us. Hell, Ruby, I just lost a patient today. And now this?"

Ruby's voice softened. "Oh, honey, I'm sorry about your patient. I'm sorry about my poor timing. You don't have to explain. I understand, and you have my undying support. Honestly, I didn't think Jerry and Rachel would last. But to Rachel's credit, she does seem to be crazy about him. But I know in my heart that Jerry still loves you. I just know it. I had hoped he would call you and tell you. I had to tell you so you would have time to stop it before Jerry ruins his life and Rachel's."

Anna shouted, "Me? How in the hell am I supposed to stop it? For years, I've tried to see Jerry whenever I came home. I wrote him letters that went unanswered. I left him messages that he never returned. He's moved on, Ruby. I can't believe it. I just can't believe he's getting married. I guess I thought when I moved home somehow we would end up together, but this isn't the movies, and we're all grown up and living separate lives." Anna sucked in two quick breaths and covered her mouth to hide how hard she was crying. She picked up the remote and threw it across the room, just barely missing the mirror on the wall.

"I don't mean to take out my anger on you. I'm glad you finally told me. I love you, but I can't talk right now. I'll call you later." Anna hung up before Ruby could reply. She ran to her bed, grabbed her pillow and began to sob. In the back of Anna's mind, she always thought she and Jerry would get back together. Anna had been a complete and utter fool. She'd been consumed with becoming a doctor. If she was honest with herself, during the grueling years of medical school, she'd completely pushed Jerry to the furthest corners of her mind.

Anna had become a successful physician. Hell, she had offers coming in from all over the Southeast region of the United States. She achieved success, and now Jerry was getting married. It wasn't his fault. It was hers, but damn it, that news just split her heart wide open with pain.

On a whim, Anna picked up the phone and dialed Jerry's new number. Ruby gave her his new number a couple of months ago when he moved into his new house. Why hadn't she called him then?

The phone rang twice, and he answered. "Hello, this is Mac." Anna frowned. Ugh. Rachel's dad called him Mac.

"Jerry, are you getting married?" There was dead silence on the line. Anna could hear him breathing. "Jerry, are you still there?"

"Yes, Anna," Jerry replied quietly.

"Yes, you're getting married?" Anna wrapped her arms around the pillow and hugged it tightly.

Jerry let out an exasperated sigh. "Yes, Anna, I'm getting married."

Anna's tears rolled off her face like Niagara Falls. "Do you love Rachel? Do you love her like you used to love me?" She leaned back against her headboard, closed her eyes, and tried to breathe in and out of her mouth slowly. Again, a silence that seemed to last for-friggin'-ever.

Jerry replied rather angrily, "Why in hell are you calling me now? Why? We haven't dated for six years. I haven't talked to you in, what, three years, and *now* you call me?"

Anna's stomach twisted in knots as memories of Jerry flooded back to her. Those feelings triggered an avalanche of pain rolling down a hill of sorrow. "I tried calling you. I wrote you letters, but you never called back, you never wrote back. You didn't answer my question, Jerry Douglas McDaniel. Do you love her? Have you stopped loving me? I have no hold on you. I get it. You told me once I belonged to you. You told me never to forget it. Well, I'm still in love with you. I went to school and held you in my heart for six long years. Well, I'm tired of being alone. I need someone to hold me and

love me, too. So you be happy, Jerry, and maybe someday I will."
Anna's breathing was choppy and shallow from crying.

Jerry's voice was ragged and his breathing heavy. "I never got any letters or phone calls. I thought you'd moved on. Anna, you love medicine a lot more than you love me. Rachel loves me. And I may not love her as I loved you, but it's real, it's solid, and it's dependable."

Separated by four hundred miles, the air between them charged, as though sparks shot between the phone lines. "I don't understand. I don't understand why you didn't get my letters. Why didn't you get my messages on your answering machine? Don't you think that's odd? And you know exactly why I pursued medicine. It's the same reason you write code. It's why you've been so successful selling your software. It's because we're the chosen. Could you stop developing software or writing binary code?"

His voice softened. "No."

Anna cradled the phone in her collarbone as tears echoed in the pitch of her voice. "Jerry, I don't want you to marry her, but if you love Rachel, then I wish you a lifetime of happiness. But for the love of God, if you don't love her, then please don't do it. Jerry, please don't marry her." Anna curled her fingers around the receiver so tightly they were going numb.

Jerry replied, "I have to go Anna. I'm sorry, I just have to go." He hung up on her. He effing hung up on her!

Anna threw the phone down, fell back on her bed, and launched into a crying jag that would go on the rest of the night and way into the morning.

IN HIS KITCHEN, JERRY STOOD frozen in total shock from Anna's call. He closed his eyes and imagined his hand against the curve of her face, feeling the soft warmth against his skin. God help him, he still loved Anna. Over the years, he had learned to live without her. Then Anna called and all that time didn't matter anymore. Had Anna written and called? What happened to the letters? The messages? It was odd.

Jerry stared outside to the deck on his back porch and wondered. His betrothed, Rachel, sat at their patio table addressing their wedding invitations. Did Rachel delete Anna's messages and throw away Anna's letters? Surely not. Rachel loved him, damn it.

Rachel was good to him. Jerry had even gotten used to the idea of marrying her. Rachel would turn thirty soon and wanted kids, so she'd proposed to Jerry. He'd been honest with Rachel. She knew how he felt about Anna. It wouldn't have been fair to marry her without her knowing the truth. But Rachel kept pushing him and pushing him, so he finally agreed to marry her. He and Rachel had similar interests, and well, she was a wildcat in bed.

Jerry wanted a family and Rachel was willing to give him one. In real life, you learned to make concessions. He cared for Rachel and loved her in his way. He would be good to her. But he would never love Rachel like he loved Anna. Now, out of the blue, Anna called and begged him not to marry Rachel. He wanted to punch something hard.

Jerry walked through the kitchen door, stepped onto the patio, and kissed the top of Rachel's head. She smiled up at him, and guilt racked his soul. "Hey, I have to drive out to the farm, and then I'm going to have a beer or two with Reed, okay?"

Rachel stood up, threw her arms around his neck and kissed him. "Sure, hon. Have fun and call me if you drink too much. I'll come and pick you up."

Jerry left the house and punched the gas pedal of his truck as soon as he hit Salem Highway. He hit the dashboard several times with his hand. "Damn her. Damn Anna." He cranked up his cassette tape deck with tunes from Zeppelin. How could talking to Anna for a few minutes put him in such a tailspin? Jerry had asked Anna to marry him—twice.

Memories flooded back to him that had been locked away a long time ago: *I will marry you, Jerry. I'll be back home opening my practice before you know it, and you'll be a millionaire from selling those software programs of yours.*

"Son of a bitch. Why did life have to be so damn complicated?" Jerry drove to his parents' house. Jessie and Bill were on their houseboat at Centerhill Lake. Jerry strode through the sliding glass doors, went straight to his dad's liquor cabinet, poured a shot of Crown Royal, and tossed it back without blinking. And then he poured another one.

Jerry picked up the phone and dialed Anna's number. The phone rang twice and went straight to Anna's answering machine. His voice was full of angst. "Anna, I just don't get it. I never got any phone calls or letters. What did you expect I'd do? Wait forever? Now, out of the blue, you decide, oh hey, I'll call Jerry, and he'll just stop what he's doing after six years and come running back to me. Well, life doesn't work that way, baby."

Jerry started to hang up when Anna answered. He could hear her sniffle in the background, and suddenly he felt like a total jerk. His stomach did a funny flip. The years melted away, and Anna was back in his arms.

Anna's breaths were uneven from crying. "I'm sorry, Jerry. It's all my fault. I should've married you when I had the chance. I was selfish. I thought I was doing what was best for both of us." She paused, and Jerry heard her blow her nose. She said, "I want you to be happy, and if Rachel makes you happy, I'm glad for you. But remember, I'll always love you."

Anna stabbed his heart with a knife and twisted it. Jerry kicked the trash can across the kitchen floor and paced back and forth. What should he say? What should he do? Jerry replied, "I'll always love you, Anna. Always."

Jerry heard Anna crying again, and before he could say anything else, she said, "Goodbye, Jerry." Then she hung up.

JERRY DROVE STRAIGHT TO RUBY and Reed's and hopped out of his truck. He strode around to the back of the house. Ruby lounged on her outside chaise, sipping on sweet tea and reading a book. She glanced up and smiled at him, and her smile faded. Jerry scowled at her and pulled a lawn chair up next to her. "Why, Ruby? Why did you have to tell Anna I was getting married?" He ran his fingers through his hair in frustration.

Ruby sat up, straightened her shoulders, and narrowed her eyes at him. "I love you, Jerry. God knows I do. But I love Anna, too, and she deserves to know the truth before she moves back home and finds you married to Rachel. Anna will be moving back here in less than a month to start her practice. I know Reed told you. And besides, I knew you were too chicken to make the call yourself." Ruby crossed her arms defiantly.

Jerry glared at Ruby, but the wind went out of his sails. He slumped against the back of the chair. "Yeah, I'm a big fat chicken, and she's my Achilles heel. Anna called me crying, which, by the way, ripped me to shreds."

Ruby reached over and placed her hand on his thigh. "You want some tea?" She leaned in across the chair, brushed the hair from his forehead, and kissed him there.

"Come on, Ruby Jane, I need something stronger than tea, for crying out loud." Jerry closed his eyes, and Ruby disappeared inside the house and returned with a cold beer for him.

Ruby sat next to Jerry with her hands on her knees and gave him a pleading look. "Please don't marry Rachel. You don't love her. You'll only end up hurting Rachel and yourself in the long run. Rachel deserves better, and so do you."

Jerry jumped up and waved his arms all about and shouted at Ruby, "Why shouldn't I marry Rachel? She loves me, damn it."

Reed turned the corner of the house after getting home from work, walked in front of Jerry, and placed a hand on his shoulder. "Whoa, brother, stop yelling at my woman like that, or I'll be taking you to the woodshed."

Exasperated, Jerry said, "I'm sorry, but your woman called Anna and told her I was getting married." Jerry plopped down hard on the chair and turned up his beer.

Reed leaned over and kissed Ruby soundly on her lips and ran his fingers gingerly down her cheek. "How are you feeling, doll?"

Ruby stood and circled her arms around Reed's neck, looking into his eyes with adoration. "Honey, I'm fine. I'm just pregnant and the mornings are the worst. I'm sorry if I worried you." She turned and gave Jerry a big grin.

Jerry's eyes widened, and he faced Ruby, returning a big grin of his own. "Pregnant? Y'all are going to have a wee little one?" He ran over and pulled Ruby into his arms and gave her a big hug and kiss. "Oh, Ruby, I'm so happy for you." He turned and hugged Reed and shouted, "I'm going to be an uncle." Jerry and Ruby weren't blood, but they were tighter than most brothers and sisters. His eyes watered with happiness for his best friends.

Jerry quickly stepped inside the house and grabbed a beer for Reed out of the fridge. He walked back through the French doors and tossed the beer to Reed. "Here's to Ruby's health and a healthy baby."

Jerry sat down and looked around Ruby's backyard. Soon, Ruby and Reed would have a child playing back here. He smiled as he pictured a swing with a slide in the back corner of the yard under the old oak tree.

Jerry was envious of the kind of love Ruby and Reed shared. Reed kissed Ruby, and Jerry coughed conspicuously, and they quit kissing. "Ruby said I needed to call off the wedding. What do you think?"

Reed shook his head and smiled at his wife. "Honey, I know you love Jerry and Anna. But this is Jerry's life, and he has to make his own bad decisions."

Jerry quickly drank the rest of his beer and placed the empty bottle on the patio table. "Well, on that note, I think it's time for me to leave. Ruby, tell Anna if you talk to her I'm sorry."

Chapter 10

On the Dark Side

ANNA HAD BEEN WORKING IN the emergency room for almost eighteen hours, and her energy was beginning to wane. It was times like these when she was so bone tired she questioned becoming a doctor at all. During those weakened moments, her thoughts raced wildly about Jerry's impending marriage. Her feelings were running the gambit between jealousy, hatred, and sorrow.

Amy, the head nurse in the ER, walked over and tapped Anna on the shoulder, which brought Anna back to reality. "Dr. Kelly, there's an elderly patient in bay five who's raising hell. Help!" Amy turned swiftly, and Anna followed her to the patient bay.

Anna grabbed the patient's chart and quickly glanced over her stats. As she walked with Amy to the rowdy patient, Anna said, "Mrs. Appleton in twenty-two needs an EKG, Mr. Williams in fifteen is on the schedule for a CT, and Ms. Underwood in nine is ready for release. But make sure you place in her release instructions that she has to follow up with her doctor in two weeks."

The rowdy patient's name was Gertrude Travis, age eighty-five. Anna stepped over to the edge of the patient's bed and asked pleasantly, "Now, what seems to be the problem, young lady?"

Ms. Travis bolted upright out of the hospital bed, swung around, and landed a solid punch to Anna's right eye with the strength of a much younger woman. The patient ripped the IV out of her arm and lunged for Anna's throat.

The crazed look in the woman's eyes scared the shit out of Anna. Anna staggered backward and nearly crashed into the workstation behind her. Two techs, Randy and Gator, along with Debby, another nurse, rushed over to help restrain the patient. Anna took a second to gather herself and calmly said, "Give her a five-milligram injection of haloperidol. If that doesn't help to calm her down, then add fifty milligrams of diphenhydramine and follow with two milligrams of an oral benztropine. We need complete labs on her. Once you have Ms. Travis sedated, send someone to get me in the bunker. I have to place some ice on my eye and rest for a few minutes."

Nurse Amy made additional notes on the chart before handing the script to Debby, who swiftly turned and ran to fill the order. Amy said, "Dr. Kelly, why don't you go home? Dr. Forrester is here, and Dr. Chandler just came on shift." Amy waited for her reply.

The mention of Jack Forrester made Anna nervous. The devastatingly handsome head resident was a constant reminder of what she didn't have in her life anymore—a man. Jack was an excellent doctor, and she respected his work ethic. But Jack had groupies—residents, med students, and staff who worshiped him.

Anna squared her shoulders and took a deep breath. "Amy, I know you're concerned about me, and I'll head home as soon as you get me Ms. Travis's blood work results." Anna patted Amy on the shoulder and made her way to the bunker.

Anna headed down the busy hospital corridor. She'd been visibly shaken by the patient's attack. She turned left at the admin offices and walked into the doctors' bunker at the end of the hall. The bunker was a place for doctors and residents to grab some quick shut-eye or a bite to eat.

The bunker had a common room with a small kitchen, a round black table with matching chairs, and a worn brown leather couch. The television mounted high in the far left corner of the room played the local news. Anna grabbed the remote off the square oak coffee table with too many *Travel* magazines and *Sports Illustrated*. She hit the mute button on the remote.

A door to the right led to a small bedroom with two bunk beds. The hospital had the linens changed every shift, so Anna grabbed a pack of ice out of the freezer, wrapped it in a clean towel, and headed for the bunk bed.

It would be nice if she could use her powers to heal herself, but she found out early on that it wasn't possible. Years ago, Anna had tumbled down the stairs at high school and busted her knee. She'd placed her hands over the wound, but she had no tingling in her fingertips. Anna painfully made it home, and her mom drove her to the ER for stitches.

Anna flipped on the nightlight next to the bunk beds, turned off the overhead lights, and collapsed on the bottom bunk. She placed the ice pack over her eye and winced. *Damn, that hurts.* She should clock out but was too exhausted to ride her bike home. Fifteen minutes was all Anna needed to recharge and then she'd check on her patient and leave for the day. Anna couldn't get Jerry off of her mind. Part of her wanted to fly home to Tennessee and beg him not to marry the Amazon. She drifted off to sleep.

ANNA WOKE ABRUPTLY IN THE bunker and glanced at the clock. She had only been asleep for twenty minutes and dreamed of walking in the Grove with Jerry. Her rational mind told her to leave Jerry in the past. But Anna's dream reminded her of the love they once shared. The last time she'd been with Jerry, she told him there would never be another man for her, and six years later, those words still rang true.

Anna dragged herself off the bunk bed and walked into the bathroom to splash cold water on her face. She grabbed a clean hand towel and gingerly dried around her eye. She inspected her very swollen and badly bruised eye in the mirror. "Jesus, that old woman packs a powerful punch." In the mirror reflection, Jack Forrester stood behind her.

"Anna, turn around and let me take a look." She'd seen Jack's grim expression enough to know he wasn't in the mood to argue, so she turned around to face him.

"I'm okay, Dr. Forrester. It looks worse than it feels," Anna lied through her teeth. It hurt like hell, and she could barely see. She placed her hands on her hips as Jack examined her injury.

"We need to run a CT and check to see if you sustained a concussion and if you have any retina or cornea damage. I'll touch base with Dr. Chandler, and after your tests, I'll give you a ride home.

I know you rode your bike today." It was more of a command than a request. Jack turned and walked out of the bunker.

Anna frowned. She rode her bike every day. "Wait a minute, Dr. Forrester. It's going to be one hell of a shiner, but I'm okay. And I'll ride my bike home because I'm pretty sure it won't fit in your sports car." Her words came out with more bite than she intended.

Jack turned and narrowed his eyes at her. "I don't like being argued with, Dr. Kelly. You're under my care and supervision when you're a resident at this hospital. Your eye is swollen. It's protocol." Jack stopped abruptly and added, "Do you want me to lose my job?"

"Well, no, sir, I don't."

"Good, I'm glad you agree." He turned and walked to the ER.

An hour later, Anna's test results showed no damage to her eye or a concussion. She did have a terrible migraine. Anna walked to the ER nurses station, and she threw her hands up to the staff, including Dr. Forrester. "I'm fine. I have a migraine, but that's it. I've clocked out, and I'll see you guys tomorrow."

Jack handed a chart to Dr. Chandler and walked over to Anna. "Not so fast, Dr. Kelly. You don't need to ride your bike in the heat." He turned to a tech named Michael, but everyone called him Gator. "Hey, Gator, do you still drive a truck to work?"

Gator looked up and nodded. "Yes, sir, Dr. Forrester."

Jack placed his hand on Gator's shoulder. "You won't mind dropping off Dr. Kelly's bike at her home later?"

"No, sir, Dr. Forrester." Gator looked anxiously from Jack to Anna.

Anna reached into her drawer and pulled out her bag. "Jack, that's not his responsibility. I'm riding my bike home. How would Gator know where I live, for goodness' sake?" She turned on a dime and made for the exit doors when Jack caught up with her.

"Jack? Really? Around these parts, people call me Dr. Forrester. If you're crazy enough to ride your bike home, then you give me no alternative but to follow you in my car." Jack swiftly walked past her toward the physician parking lot.

At the bike rack, Anna grabbed the key out of her scrub pocket and unlocked the chain around her bike. Seconds later, Anna pumped her bike pedals gaining speed until she approached the intersection.

Anna had reached Bayou Boulevard when Jack pulled up beside her in his sports car and revved his engine. She nearly wrecked. Anna stopped and stood on the ground with the bike resting between her legs. She scowled at Jack as he rolled down his window and smiled. She shouted, "Are you intentionally trying to scare the crap out of me? I nearly wrecked. Go away." Anna motioned for him to leave. She stood up on the bike pedals and began to pump faster. Minutes later she turned into her driveway.

Anna parked her bike in the main garage and walked around the side of the house. She became light-headed walking up the steps to her front door and fell backward, landing in Jack's arms. She blacked out.

Anna didn't know how long she'd been passed out, but Jack must have taken it upon himself to snatch her keys and carry her inside the house. When she came to, she was lying on her comfy chintz couch with a cold cloth on her forehead.

Jack took her pulse and looked freaking smug. "I told you not to ride your bike home." Anna looked up into his rather gorgeous gray eyes. No man should ever be born with such thick black lashes when she had to wear mascara. Jack was movie star beautiful, but he wasn't cocky. On the contrary, he seemed shy at times.

Nauseated and dizzy, Anna closed her eyes. In hindsight, letting herself get dehydrated from riding in the Florida heat, after being assaulted by a patient, was probably a very stupid thing to do. But she would never admit it to Jack. He nudged her gently, and she opened her eyes slowly. "What, Jack?"

He handed her a glass of water. God, she hated that he'd read her mind. Jack pulled her into a sitting position and placed his arm around her shoulder to keep her steady. Anna drank half a glass. When Jack pinned her with a look, she drank the rest of the water. "Thank you, Jack. I'm sorry, I should've listened to you. But I hate it when you're right."

"Ha. I don't believe it. An apology. Once more, please," he said and leaned his ear to her mouth.

Anna whispered, "I'm sorry."

Jack withdrew his arm and stood. "Good. I want you to drink one more glass of water. Does your head hurt? And tell me the truth." He looked down at her with his hands placed on his narrow hips. She nodded yes. He went into the kitchen for another glass of water. "Drink, all of it. I'm going to get my bag, and I'll be right back."

Anna started to open her mouth in protest, but Jack shook his head back and forth. She refrained from what she wanted to say to him. *Like, enough already, please get out of my house*. But she would have conked out on the hard concrete sidewalk if Jack hadn't followed her home.

Anna's head felt like it was in a vise and little white dots were swimming in her vision from a major migraine. She drank the rest of the water when Jack came back inside the front door.

He sat down next to her, opened his medical bag, and pulled out a syringe. Anna threw her hands up and said, "No, Jack, if you give me pain meds, I can't work."

Jack filled the syringe and pushed the plunger into the barrel to release the air. "Anna, this is a mild sedative for your migraine. I hate to tell you, but you're not working until next Tuesday. Doctor's orders. Which arm?" She took a deep breath and offered her right arm.

As the needle pierced her skin, the meds began to burn going into her veins. Seconds later, her head wasn't hurting at all. She felt completely relaxed. Her tongue became thick as she looked at Jack and gave him the thumbs up. "I'm feeling no pain now. Thanks."

Jack laughed and suddenly seemed younger and not so stiff. Anna giggled and started laughing loudly at her drug-induced thoughts.

Jack tilted his head to the side and placed his hands on his thighs. "What's so funny Anna?" Anna pointed to him and laughed some more.

Jack flashed her a most charming grin, showing nearly perfect teeth. One of his front teeth just barely lapped over the other one. He said, "Me? I normally don't get *that* kind of response, but I'll take it, considering it's coming from you. Come on. Let's get you into bed."

Anna snorted; she just couldn't help herself. It was the drugs talking. "You've never tried to get me into bed before, Jack. What's up? Are you pitying the poor, overworked resident?"

Jack helped her to her feet. She placed her arm around his waist, and he wrapped his arm around hers. "Anna, since you're on drugs and will likely not remember a thing about this conversation, I'll just say you don't need my pity. You're perfect."

"What did you say, Dr. Yummy?" And the long hours of her work day combined with the pain meds made Anna melt into slumber.

OUTSIDE ANNA'S BEDROOM WINDOW CERULEAN warblers were singing to each other from one of the old oleander trees. In the stillness of early morning, she lay in bed listening to their sweet song. For once in a long time, her mind was at peace. She didn't need to tick off a to-do list. *Oh, shit. Did I call Dr. Forrester, Dr. Yummy? Oh, for heaven's sakes, kill me now.*

Anna stretched and yawned, then swung her legs over the bed. Still groggy from the drug Jack had given her and sat for a couple of minutes before she stood up. Anna opened her bedroom door, shuffled her feet slowly into the kitchen, and poured a glass of milk. She was hungry but still too queasy to eat. Her eye was swollen shut.

She stepped into her living room and gasped. Dr. Freaking Yummy slept on her couch in his boxer shorts and T-shirt. *Holy cow.* Anna eased down into the oversized loveseat next to him. Jack was really hot. *Oh, this deserves a phone call to Ruby and Sandy.*

Dang. The man must work out every day of the week. Jack's T-shirt draped over well-defined pecs. He didn't have the body of a body builder but was beautifully sculpted, nonetheless.

Jack must have sensed Anna's presence and opened his eyes. He sat up and stretched his neck to the left, then the right. "You look terrible. How do you feel?"

Anna took a drink of milk and tried to look at him over the rim of her glass. With a smile, she said, "Geez, thanks for the compliment. I feel better, but it's hard to see."

Jack glanced around the room, walked over to the light switch on the wall and flipped on the overhead light. He scoured through his bag and pulled out his penlight. He lifted her chin and leaned down close to her face, and she suddenly became nervous. Anna wondered, for the first time, what it would be like to kiss Jack. She hadn't thought about kissing anyone in a long time.

Anna tried to push Jack's hand away, but he grabbed her wrist. "Why do you love to infuriate me so? I swear I say black, and you say white. Anna, you were hurt yesterday. It's the hospital's responsibility to make sure you're okay. I need you to follow the light for me." He looked in both her eyes and turned off the penlight. "Do you think you can take a shower by yourself?"

"Of course. Were you thinking of helping me?" Anna teased him, and he started to rebut when he realized she was joking. Anna just bet most of the staff didn't receive personalized attention from the chief resident.

Jack crossed his arms over his chest. "Finally, I hear laughter in your voice after nearly two years. You do have a sense of humor. Who knew? If you show me where you stash your coffee can, I'm going to make a pot of coffee while you take a shower." Jack seemed to wait for her to argue with him, but she only nodded in the affirmative and walked into her kitchen. She opened the cabinet and placed the can of Folgers on the countertop.

Anna turned to face Jack and placed her hand on his arm. "I like my coffee really strong. Thanks, Jack, for staying with me."

"I think I can handle it. Now skedaddle," he said and swatted her behind. Jack flirted with her.

"Hands to yourself, please." She smacked his hand playfully and backed away from him. She left the kitchen and made her way to the master bathroom with a smile on her face.

Anna yearned for the warmth of a man's love. Having Jack inside her house in his boxers and making coffee made her miss the warmth of Jerry's big, loving arms. She'd been alone for too long.

Anna stepped inside her bathroom and leaned against the door for a second before she reached over and turned on the shower. She wheeled around to check her eye in the mirror, and Ralph appeared beside her bathroom sink. "Holy shit, Ralph, you nearly made me have a heart attack. Why can't you whistle or something to give me a heads up?"

Over the years, Anna had gotten some weird looks talking to Ralph in public. Since he was invisible to all but her, people looked at her like she was crazy. Maybe she was a little crazy. Ralph had become her closest companion since she'd moved away from Tennessee. Most of the time, she was too exhausted to socialize, so days and sometimes even months passed without her doing anything outside of the hospital. She suddenly felt old in her twenty-eight-year-old body. Life was passing by her.

Ralph brought his slender forefinger up to his lips. "Shush. I'm sorry I wasn't there to help you yesterday. I was in a closed-door meeting, and I had no connection to the Earth in the operations room. An earth angel contacted me this morning and told me two demons possessed the old lady who knocked you out yesterday. I'm not sure from which division, but I'm searching now. Unfortunately, Ms. Travis died."

"What?" Anna said, incredulous.

Ralph gave her a smirk. "Shush. Do you want Dr. Freaking Yummy to think you've gone mad?" Ralph resembled humans in many ways, but his otherworldly beauty set him apart. She constantly stared at him in awe. He said, "Have you seen Luc?"

Anna held onto the lip of the bathroom counter. "No, why? Do you think he carried out the attack?"

"No, but he may have sanctioned it. I'm not sure, but I think the demons were trying to possess your power. They could've succeeded, but Gator and Randy reacted swiftly to restrain the possessed woman. I like big old Gator. He has a genuine and loving soul."

Ralph motioned for her to sit on the toilet seat. "When did Ruby last dream about the dragon?"

"Ralph, you're making me nervous. I missed the last couple of meetings. To the best of my knowledge, it was last December. You think Luc is coming for me, don't you?"

He said, "I think Luc has been watching you and your friends for a long time. I have a meeting with our team soon. I'm sorry I can't heal your eye, or the good doctor would probably have a stroke. If you want, I'll do it later."

Anna opened her mouth to interrupt, but Ralph stopped her. "I'll explain in depth when you're alone. No worries, Annabelly. You're safe for the moment."

"Geez, Ralph, somehow I think you're blowing smoke up my ass, but if you say I'm safe, then I trust you." Anna reached over to check the water's temperature and turned to say something, but Ralph was gone. It drove her insane how one minute he was there and the next minute—poof.

AFTER ANNA HAD DRESSED IN black leggings and an oversized blue jean shirt, she walked barefoot into the kitchen.

Jack sat his coffee cup in the sink and brushed a lock of his ebony hair away from his forehead. "Anna, I guess it's time for me to leave. I'll check on you tomorrow."

Anna leaned against the kitchen cabinet and looked into Jack's eyes. "Ah, thanks again for taking care of me, Jack." He grabbed her hand. Anna's eyes widened, and he abruptly let her hand go.

Jack reached inside his dark gray suit, pulled out a silver business card holder, and handed her his card. "Call me if you need me. My home number is on the back."

Anna nodded okay. Jack walked out the front door without looking back. A tiny spark had ignited between them, and it made her excited and nervous. Jack was her boss, and as the old saying went, you don't shit where you eat.

Anna decided to put Dr. Yummy and his boxers out of her mind. She had free time. She still had one good eye, so she intended to veg out on her comfy couch for a movie marathon. She opened her video cabinet and selected some of her favorite old movies.

Anna went into the kitchen for another cup of coffee. She'd barely popped the VHS tape of *The Philadelphia Story* into the player when her phone started ringing. Anna reached over to the table next to the couch and picked up the phone. "Hello."

Ruby's voice trembled. "Are you okay? I had a dream you couldn't see. Some evil old woman was trying to hurt you."

Anna wiggled her toes before stretching her legs out, and she sank into the soft cushions of her couch. "Calm down, mother hen. I'm fine. I did get coldcocked by a patient who was possessed by demons. Hey, when was the last time you dreamed of the dragon? Ralph seems to think Luc is targeting our team. I'm sorry I missed the last two meetings. But I'm almost through with my residency, and I'll be coming home soon. I'll have more time." Anna sipped her coffee.

With a sharp intake of breath, Ruby said, "Geez Louise, I had a dream about the dragon two nights ago. Then last night, I dreamed about the woman who attacked you. Were you scared?"

"I was scared during the attack, but not anymore. Good grief, how are we supposed to protect ourselves from something we can't see? I think Ralph needs to teach me how to spot a demon. I get some bizarre people in the ER, for real. Surely, they're not all possessed. Now that is a scary thought." Anna shivered at the possibility.

"Are you in much pain?"

Anna grabbed the remote for her VCR and pushed the pause button. "Nah, not really. But hey, I'm on sick leave for four whole days. Can you believe it? I haven't had free time since before med school. Can you fly down? Please, please, please," Anna begged. Ruby would come if she could get away from the store.

Anna could just picture the wheels beginning to turn in her best friend's mind. Ruby had bought the Everglade General Store from Mr. Burns and had three full-time employees, plus a manager. She had added a café and covered outdoor patio where the local musicians jammed on the weekends.

Ruby said, "Hmm, I guess I could see if Rose could cover me for a few days. Want me to call Sandy?"

"Oh, Ruby, that would be *totally* awesome." Anna giggled. Ever since the movie *Valley Girl* had hit the theaters, med students and nurses were constantly saying "totally" and "for sure."

Ruby took another deep breath. "Look, I'll talk with Sandy and check the available flights and call you later with the details. Hopefully, Sandy will be able to get off early from the TV station. Did she tell you she's up for an AP award for one of her investigative reports?"

Anna propped her elbow on the arm of the couch. "No, she didn't. That's awesome. Do you need me to pick you up from the airport?"

"Nah, I'll rent a car when we get to the airport."

Anna hesitated, then said, "Ruby, have you talked to Jerry? Did he tell you I called him?"

Ruby sighed. "Yes, I talked to him. I know I should've kept my big mouth shut, but I just hate to see him make a mistake. He still loves you."

Anna held her breath for a second, and she said, "He has a funny way of showing it. I'll see you tomorrow. Love you." Anna hung up. Did Jerry still love her? Could he marry someone else? She had to quit thinking about him and pressed play on the VCR.

Chapter 11

Sunglasses at Night

ANNA TOSSED AND TURNED FOR most of the night due to bad dreams about Jerry and Rachel. The first rays of sunlight burst through her bedroom window. She sensed Ralph before he sat on her bed and shook her foot gently. Anna threw her pillow at him. "Leave me alone, Ralph."

Ralph began to tickle the bottom of her foot, and she shoved him off the bed. He said, "Anna Faye Kelly, I've watched you from a baby to adulthood, and I've never seen you wallow around feeling sorry for yourself. Get up." He shook her again, and she bolted up and tried to open her eyes, but they were too swollen.

Ralph gasped. "Saints preserve us. Lie back down. I'm going to make it all better, and then you're getting in the shower while I cook crepes for breakfast."

Anna giggled at the mention of crepes. Ralph didn't eat human food, but he loved to show off his culinary skills and the art of great food presentation. Crepes sounded delicious, and since she was depressed, her body craved sugar.

"Crepes with strawberries and cream cheese?" she asked with her hands in prayer mode.

"Yes, with strawberries and cream cheese and my secret sauce. Now lie back down." Anna lay back, and Ralph placed his hands over her eyes. The same energy Anna used to heal others was now being used to heal her.

Less than a minute later, Ralph removed his hands, and Anna blinked a couple of times. She didn't feel any pain, and thank heaven, she could see. Anna threw her comforter off, ran into the bathroom, and looked into the mirror. It blew her away how the healing energy worked. Anna had no signs of her injury or any swelling from crying during the night. She stepped back into her bedroom to thank him, but Ralph had already left to cook. She could hear him banging pots and pans in the kitchen. Her guardian angel rocked. Anna did a little dance because she had three more days off, and her best friends were coming into town this afternoon.

Anna's master bedroom and bathroom were nearly as big as the whole guest house. The bedroom had a mahogany pineapple four-poster bed, two end tables, an armoire, and a dresser with a full-length mirror. The interior walls were painted a soothing sage green, and the trim was painted white. The adjoining bathroom had clear glass shower doors and a Jacuzzi tub in the corner. She had two oval sinks with white cabinets, and the mirror had beveled edges that went all the way to the ceiling. Anna loved her bedroom oasis and often came home from work and went straight to the shower. Afterward, she would crawl into her big, beautiful bed to read before falling asleep.

Jerry's impending marriage popped back into her mind. He'd gotten awfully upset with her for someone who was about to be married. He shouldn't even care what she thought. It gave her the tiniest bit of hope he might rethink his decision before it was too late. At least, he knew she still loved him whether he married Rachel or not. Anna was glad Ruby and Sandy were flying in later today so she could talk to them about Jerry.

Anna pulled on a pair of white cotton shorts and a pink polo shirt and walked out of her bedroom. She stopped in the foyer long enough to quickly sort the junk mail from the actual bills in the mail basket. Anna left the bills in the basket and made her way into the kitchen, opened the pantry door, and threw the junk mail in the trash. Suddenly ravenous, she inhaled the sweet aroma of crepes with strawberry sauce.

"Ralph, you've outdone yourself. The food smells divine, and the arrangement is beautiful." Ralph had arranged a beautiful tropical bouquet mixed with large and medium heliconia and big red ginger with pieces of deep green foliage and placed them in a glass vase in the center of her kitchen table.

Ralph was busy folding the crepes, and he said, "Grab yourself a cup of coffee and I'll make you a plate." Anna poured a cup and sat down. She held the coffee cup in both hands and peered out through the sliding glass doors to the swimming pool. The water shimmered from the brilliant sunlight. It was going to be another gorgeous day in paradise. Anna glanced over at the main house and didn't see any movement from Cary.

Cary normally piddled around the yard in the morning. She loved Cary's old Floridian plantation home with its swaying palm trees and huge, moss-draped oak trees and gorgeous pink oleanders. The luscious landscape around his oceanfront property offered the illusion of seclusion while being in the midst of a subdivision.

Ralph set a plate of strawberry cream crepes in front of her. "Bon appétit."

"Ralph, you cook like a French chef." Anna took a bite and moaned with delight. "God, this is wonderful. I wished you'd taste it. It's superb."

Ralph sat down at the table. "It pleases me very much you enjoy my cooking. You look much better now that you've showered and no longer have those horrendously swollen eyes. Anna, your eyes are the color of the ocean on a bright, sunny day."

Anna cut into her crepe. "Aw, Ralph, you're sweet. You must have some pretty bad news if you're buttering me up with crepes and compliments."

Ralph leaned back against the chair and placed his hands on his thighs. "After your attack, I had a meeting with Seneca, Baldric, and Luwenia, the guardians of Campbell Ridge." Ralph had explained to Anna early in their relationship that every human had a guardian, although most humans never acknowledged them. The guardians assigned to Anna and her friends were part of an elite force of angels sent to protect the Wards of the World.

Anna took a big bite of crepes while she continued listening to Ralph.

He said, "You've heard Ruby talk about Seneca. He's the leader of our team and has great wisdom. Baldric is Sandy's guardian, and the lovely Luwenia is Jerry's. We placed new shields of protection over each of you. We frequently change the shields' coordinates with a pattern of numbers based on the golden ratio overlaid with our energy fields. For now, you're safe. Your detection by Luc's bootlickers is nearly impossible."

"That is so over my head. Wait a minute. You just said the *lovely* Luwenia? Ralph, you sound like you're in love. Oh, is a bootlicker the same thing as a brown-noser?" Anna asked before taking another bite of her crepes and licking the sauce from the corner of her mouth.

Ralph flushed and stammered, "L-Luwenia? She's beautiful, but I'm not in love with her. I've never been in love with anyone." Anna smiled to herself. Ralph was in love, but he didn't realize it yet. *Hmmm, that brings up some more interesting questions.*

Ralph leaned over the table and nervously began to fiddle with his flower arrangement. "Bootlickers and brown-nosers both kiss ass. The bootlickers I'm referring to are demon angels, and they do whatever Luc commands them to do. See, when wards use their power, it releases a light invisible to the human eye, and that light beam radiates toward Heaven. It's how demons detect and track wards. I did receive confirmation from the AAF that Luc is actively recruiting wards. If a ward refuses to work with Luc, he strips their power until they pass away into Heaven. There's also a rumor Luc is enslaving the stronger wards."

Anna coughed and nearly choked on her crepe. She took a sip of coffee and said, "What are we going to do?"

Ralph went over to the stove, grabbed the crepe dish, and offered another one to Anna, then left the plate on the table. "We're going to fight, Anna. That's what we're going to do. Luc uses human weakness. You need to get a handle on your jealousy regarding Rachel."

Anna snapped. "Wonderful. Just freaking great. That's why those freaking demons attacked me. I had worked a long shift, and at the end of the day I couldn't shake the feelings of hatred and jealousy against Rachel, and I felt sorry for myself. So I guess I opened myself up to them."

Ralph knelt down before Anna and turned her to face him. He held her hands and said, "The Demons of Jealousy are from one of Luc's most powerful divisions. Be careful, because those nasty beasts will dig their claws in deep. Let it go. Let it all go. It's when you allow those emotions to consume every waking moment that the demons take hold. Once inside your soul, they're extremely reluctant to leave.

Even those humans who classify as The Order of the Ever After have to fight demons. No human is immune. Oh, well, except during the time when the Prince of Peace walked the Earth as a human."

Anna frowned and broke away from Ralph's grasp. She walked over to the fridge and took out the OJ. She glanced over her shoulder before pouring herself a small glass of juice. "Prince of Peace. You mean Jesus?

Ralph rose from the table and walked over to the sink to wash dishes. "There are some humans who refer to the Prince as Jesus. There's been a war going on between Heaven and Hell since the birth of mankind, and it'll continue until the bitter end. Most humans turn a blind eye to it. It's like watching one of Jerry's high school basketball games. We're the home team. Every time a human offers a kind word, a lending hand, a generous heart, our team adds points to the board for the home team."

Anna joined him at the sink and took a dish towel out of the drawer to dry while Ralph washed. He said, "The home team is playing a cunning and ruthless competitor who likes to lie, cheat, and steal. He takes cheap shots, and his players are deceit, revenge, greed, jealousy, hatred, vanity—the list is endless. When their team gets the ball and makes a basket, it racks up points by taking pieces of a human soul little by little, day by day, chipping away until nothing's left but a mere shell of what the human used to be."

Anna stopped and stared at Ralph. He was right. Something inside her knew those aspects of life that destroyed a soul were part of a much larger and darker picture. Ralph had given her insight, and she intended to be more careful. But she was only human, after all.

Anna opened the cabinet above her head and neatly stacked away her dishes. "I always try to do what is right and you know it. But it's going to take me a while to get over the fact that the man I thought I would spend my life with is marrying someone else. And don't look at me like that. I know it's been a long time since we've been together, but I never got over Jerry. I still love him." Anna scraped the remains of the food down the garbage disposal and flipped the switch while the water ran into the drain. "Ralph, do angels have relationships in Heaven?"

Ralph shoulder-bumped her and said, "There are some things the human brain is not equipped to understand. Our relationships are different from yours. There are no tears in Heaven, no chances of a broken heart. Maybe being witness to great love is why I love coming to Earth. And maybe true love is why some angels choose to stay. I hate seeing you suffer, but to love someone so much it still hurts years later, just thinking about them, is a gift. Besides, Jerry isn't married yet. So what are you waiting for?"

Anna leaned against the kitchen cabinet. "It doesn't feel like a gift. And what am I supposed to do, drop everything and go to Tennessee? Should I throw myself at Jerry's feet and beg him not to marry Rachel?"

With compassion, he said, "If I ever have the chance at true love in my life, like you've had, I'd do anything to keep it. You humans can have such thick skulls. Dates back to your primitive beginnings. You never grow out of it."

Ralph took off the yellow plastic gloves and replaced them back under the sink. "You have to clean your house for your guests and then go for a walk on the beach. It's beautiful today." Ralph was right. She had guests coming to visit, and Jerry wasn't married yet. Maybe Anna still had a chance to get him back. She walked into the den and whirled around to say something to Ralph, but he'd disappeared again.

ANNA GLANCED AT THE CLOCK on her bedside table. Ruby and Sandy were due to arrive any minute. She felt like a teenager again waiting on her best friends. Anna had worked like a dog all day cleaning her house, and it sparkled. She couldn't remember the last time her house was this clean.

Anna had vacuumed her silk drapes and dusted her plantation shutters. The cherry coffee table and end tables gleamed from the furniture polish. Anna could even see her reflection in the black granite counter tops and appliances. She left the vertical blinds opened to the sliding door. It offered a splendid view of the pool and main house. Last, Anna arranged the overstuffed cushions on the chintz sofa.

ANNA WORE A STRAPLESS, CORAL tea-length sundress and paired it with a white sweater. She grabbed her pearls out of her jewelry box and clasped them around her neck. The pearls had been a gift from Jerry the last Christmas they had spent together.

Anna made an eight o'clock reservation at the new Temps Restaurant and Beach Club. The five-star restaurant had opened on Valentine's Day. Temps offered excellent Floridian cuisine, and their bar had spectacular views of the ocean with direct access to the beach. Anna had only been once with Amy and Gator. They had gone for drinks one Friday after work.

The doorbell rang, and Anna flew out of her bedroom to open the front door. All three girls screamed and hugged each other tightly. Anna showed Ruby and Sandy inside her house, and they went through the short foyer to the living area. Anna said, "Ruby, I've placed you in the downstairs guest room, and Sandy, you're in the loft. The loft has a wonderful little deck with views of the ocean."

Ruby grabbed Anna's hands and stretched out her arms. "Anna, you look wonderful. I thought you were hurt?"

Sandy grabbed Anna's chin and turned her left, then right. "Ralph does good work."

Anna sat down on the arm of the couch. "Yes, he does. You guys go ahead and leave your suitcases in your rooms. I have reservations at the swankiest joint in town, and if we leave right now, we'll have time for cocktails before dinner."

Sandy looked down at her work clothes. "You have to give me fifteen minutes to change clothes and freshen up."

Ruby removed the strap of her purse off her shoulder and set the purse on the end table. "Me, too. Swanky? I've never known you to be an uptown girl. But what the hey, we only live once. Where's your phone? I have to call Reed, so he doesn't have a fit. I'm *so* married."

Anna playfully shoved Ruby and giggled. "You've been so married since the day you locked lips with Reed." Ruby crossed her eyes at Anna and stuck out her tongue. Anna pointed to the kitchen. "There's a cordless on the counter just inside the kitchen door on the right, or you can use the one in my room for privacy."

Ruby snorted. "Privacy around you two? Get real." Ruby stepped over to the kitchen, grabbed the phone out of the dock, and dialed. "Reed, honey, I'm here... Yes, sweetie, I'm fine. We're heading out for dinner and drinks, and I'm sure we'll be late getting back... No. I'm not drinking. For heaven's sake. And I love you, too. I'll phone you tomorrow. And hey, don't get too trashed with Jerry tonight." Ruby hung up and turned to find both Anna and Sandy laughing at her.

Sandy leaned against the couch and slipped off her Valentino pumps. She held them by the straps with one hand while rubbing the arch of her foot with the other. "Why's Reed so adamant about you not drinking? It's not like you've ever been a big drinker. What gives?"

Ruby's face split into a big grin. "I'm pregnant."

Anna and Sandy both screamed. Sandy dropped her shoes, ran to Ruby, and hugged her.

Anna placed her hand on Ruby's belly. "You do have a special glow going on. How far along are you?"

Ruby placed her hand over Anna's. "I'm seven weeks or so, and I've just started having morning sickness. I sure hope you have saltines. If not, we need to stop at the store before we come back home tonight. I brought my herbal tea."

Anna took a step back and said, "I have plenty of crackers. A baby, a sweet baby. I can't wait. Who's your OB?"

Sandy rolled her eyes. "I'm starving. We can talk all about our baby over dinner. Besides, we're going to spoil Ruby's kid rotten."

Anna looked at Sandy and smiled. Boy, she had missed her friends. "Okay, y'all, go on and leave your suitcases in your rooms. I'll go and pull my car out of the garage. Oh, I have to wear sunglasses tonight just in case I run into someone from work. They won't understand how quickly I've recovered. The last one out locks the door."

Anna left through the sliding glass doors in the kitchen while Ruby and Sandy crooned Corey Hart's, "Sunglasses at Night." Anna shook her head and laughed at her friends. She walked around the pool to the main garage. She had bought a new VW Quantum and rarely drove it unless she was going to the grocery store or it was pouring down rain. Anna backed out of the garage and pulled around to the side of the guest house where Ruby and Sandy were waiting. They had changed into sundresses, too. She said, "Y'all look gorgeous. Now get in and put on your seatbelts."

Sandy opened the back door, and Ruby opened the front

passenger door, and they jumped inside. Sandy said, "Lady with the baby gets shotgun, and as usual, I get stuck in the back."

Anna turned around and said, "Thanks, Sandy." She pulled out of the driveway and headed the short distance to the restaurant. Along the way, they chatted about the flight from Nashville.

Sandy leaned in and placed her hands on the back of the front passenger seat. "You're never going to believe who we saw on the flight."

Anna glanced in her rearview at Sandy. "Who?"

Ruby let out a sigh and turned to Anna. "Brent and he's still hot."

Sandy placed her forearm on the armrest. "Damn right. He looks good and still not married. I gave him my number. Maybe we could have a quickie reunion if you know what I mean." Sandy wiggled her eyebrows up and down. "But then again, Brent has always had the secret hots for Ruby. You should've seen him being gaga over our girl until Ruby told him she was pregnant, and he turned white as a ghost."

Ruby twisted around in the seat to look at Sandy. "You have an overactive imagination."

Sandy laughed and said, "It's what wins me awards, baby."

"So, what's Brent doing down here?" Anna clicked on her left blinker and pulled into the restaurant's valet parking.

Sandy reached down for her clutch purse. "He's bidding a job in Destin. I told him we're staying with you. Is your number listed?"

Anna pulled her car to a stop, handed her keys to the valet, and turned to the girls. "Yeah, my phone's listed. If he calls, I'd love to see Brent. Hey, we're a little early. I'll put our name in with the hostess, and we'll go around back for cocktails. The sun's setting and the view is killer."

Anna, Sandy, and Ruby followed the lush tropical path to the back of the restaurant until they were in the bar area. The club had a Jimmy Buffet sound-a-like band playing music. Anna said, "I never get tired of Jimmy Buffet, white sand beaches, and the Florida sunsets. Oh, I see a table." The girls followed Anna to a table, and a waiter came over to get their drink order.

Ruby ordered water, and Anna ordered for her and Sandy. "Two Sex on the Beaches, please." Anna glanced at Sandy. "Have you ever had that?"

Sandy laughed so hard she had to hold onto her sides. "Not the drink, but I've had sex on the beach." Anna rolled her eyes and shook her head and laughed. It was good to know some things never changed.

The girls easily fell into their old routines. There was something pretty spectacular about having best friends. Even though miles, and sometimes months, separated them, when they got together it felt as if they'd just seen each other yesterday.

At dinner, Anna ordered the chef's feast for them. The seafood came on one huge platter, and they shared it between the three of them. Scallops, shrimp, and oysters baked, fried, and broiled. Anna placed her hand over Ruby's and said, "Don't eat the oysters, just to be on the safe side. You'll thank me in the morning."

Ruby placed her hand over her mouth and closed her eyes. A minute later, she said, "No worries, the thought of oysters makes me sick. Fried shrimp is all I want and bread. Lots of bread and butter."

Sandy popped a fried scallop in her mouth and moaned. "God, girl, this food is choice. I haven't tasted seafood this good since I went to Aruba last year with Paul. And don't ask. He was some dude I interviewed last year. He's in the music industry in Nashville, and it was a fling. So, Ruby, please enlighten us on how you and Reed stay so much in love? I mean, for the rest of us, it's hard. The moment you think you've found Mr. Right, it doesn't take long to figure out his flaws. Either you burn or get burned."

Ruby tore off a piece of bread from a basket on the table and began to slather it with butter. "Oh, Sandy, I hate you jumping from one guy to the next. Doesn't it get old?"

Sandy tensed slightly and added with a touch of sarcasm, "Well, we don't all get to marry a Reed, do we?"

Ruby's eyes brightened, and she smiled, revealing her beautiful pearly whites. "Don't get testy, my dear bestie. I didn't mean to hurt your feelings. I just worry about you." Ruby's face lit up as she began to talk about Reed. "I don't know how we do it. All I know is I love Reed more now than I did when we first started dating. Y'all will always be my best friends, but Reed, he's my soul mate."

Anna took a sip of her cocktail and smiled. "And now Reed is going to be a daddy. I'm so happy for you both."

Ruby looked down briefly while she pushed her salad around

with her fork, and she looked up at Anna. "He is sweet and kind. It's not like we don't fight. We do. But it's over stupid stuff like putting the toilet seat down or leaving toothpaste in the sink."

Anna sighed with a tinge of jealousy. "So how is Jerry? And what happened after he called me?" A smattering of conversations swirled around them in hushed tones from different tables. A whoosh of air passed her as the wait staff ran back and forth from the kitchen.

Ruby's amber eyes flickered in the candlelight. With a quirk of her brow, she said, "I told him not to marry Rachel."

Anna spat out her bread. The lady at the table next to them turned her nose up and placed her back to Anna. Anna rolled her eyes at the old woman and turned back to her buddies. "What did Jerry say?"

Ruby added some lemon to her water. "Well, he yelled at me. Jerry was letting me have it when Reed came home from work, and Reed chewed his ears off." Ruby laughed and reached over to squeeze Anna's hand. "Honey, Jerry's still in love with you, and from where I'm sitting, you're still in love with him. Don't let him marry Rachel."

Anna sat stiffly in her chair and waved to the waiter, who came right over. She handed the waiter her credit card. "We're ready to check out, please." When the waiter walked away, Anna turned back to Ruby and tried hard to keep her emotions under control. "Ruby, I called Jerry and begged him not to marry Rachel. I told him if he still loved me at all, not to do it. Jerry told me he was sorry. Sorry. So what the hell am I supposed to do?"

Anna looked at her two best friends. "I want your opinion on something that's been bugging me since I talked to Jerry. I tried calling him over the years, and when he never replied, I wrote him a few times. The last time I reached out I wrote him a long letter telling him how much I missed him and I still loved him. Jerry said he never received any of my messages or my letters. I want to know how long Rachel has been with him and whether you think she deleted my messages and trashed my letters."

Sandy drank the rest of her cocktail and set the empty glass on the table. "I wouldn't put it past her. Rachel started hanging around Jerry right after you moved to Florida. She was pretty slick about it and played the friend card first. Her father set it up with Jerry for

Rachel to start hosting these dinner parties and stuff for Jerry's business. Annabelly, you need to have a face-to-face with Jerry. If you two are still in love with each other, the sparks will fly, and he'll take his blinders off. Rachel has gotten her claws dug in deep, and believe me when I say that she gets what she wants."

Ruby munched on the last piece of bread, pressed the cloth napkin to her lips, and laid it down next to her plate. "Sandy's right. Rachel was pretty slick how she handled Jerry. But Jerry didn't start dating her exclusively until New Year's. That's when Reed told me he, well...when he...slept with her for the first time. Jerry doesn't talk to me about his love life, but he does talk to Reed."

Anna signed the dinner tab. "Well, I didn't expect him to remain celibate. I have this feeling Rachel sabotaged me. Of course, how would I prove it? I'll need more than a miracle to have a face-to-face with Jerry before I finish my residency. I still have a couple more weeks left. Even if I could get out of my residency before then, isn't Rachel living with Jerry? Come on, let's go back to the bar. The jams should be cranking by now, and I want to dance."

The girls went back to the bar, and Anna pointed to the beach access. "There's a table over there next to the little pathway that leads to the beach." They walked over and sat down.

Sandy placed her purse on the table, and her eyes widened. "Hotties at three o'clock, and I do mean H.O.T."

Anna looked up and said, "Double damn." She slumped down in her seat and put her sunglasses back on. "Crap, it's Jack. Of all the times for me to run into him. I'm on sick leave, dad durn it, and I'm out clubbing."

Ruby strained her neck to get a look at Jack. "Geez Louise, Anna. That's Dr. Yummy? Why haven't you closed the deal with him?"

Before Anna could reply, Jack and another handsome man stepped over to their table. Jack said, "Anna? Hey, I thought that was you. How are you feeling? And who're your pretty friends?"

Anna straightened her spine and said, "These are my two best friends, Ruby and Sandy. Girls, this is Jack, my *boss*."

Sandy reached out and shook his hand. "Hi, Jack. Why don't you and your friend pull up a chair?" He gave Sandy a million-dollar smile.

Jack pulled a chair next to Anna and reached over to shake

Ruby's hand. "It's so nice to meet you both. Friends of Anna's from Tennessee?" Anna moved her chair over to make room for Jack's. He pulled off his jacket and draped it on the back of the chair, then leaned in and introduced his friend. "Anna, this is our newest board member, Dr. Frank Howard. Frank is breaking new ground with his research on Alzheimer's."

Frank reached over and shook her hand. "Dr. Kelly, your team speaks highly of your work." Frank turned to stare at Sandy with an another-one-bites-the-dust look splashed across his face. "Are your friends visiting for long?"

"No, they're here for just the weekend," Anna replied.

Anna listened silently as her friends chatted away with Jack and Frank, and the drinks just kept coming. Jack placed his arm on the back of Anna's chair. He leaned in next to her ear and said, "Dance with me, Anna?" She took a deep breath and her knee started bouncing up and down. The band played "One More Night" by Phil Collins. Sandy kicked Anna's leg, and Anna kicked her back.

"Okay, Jack, let's dance." Anna rose from her chair. Ruby and Sandy were smiling at her like two Cheshire cats with a bowl of cream.

Jack led her onto the dance floor and pulled her up close to him. It had been a long time since she'd been in the arms of a man, even if it was Jack. God, he smelled good, too. Anna had the irresistible urge to run her tongue along the cord of his neck.

Jack nuzzled his cheek next to hers and muttered, "Anna, you smell like a little slice of heaven."

Anna tilted her head to the side and looked up into his eyes with a laugh. "It's the shrimp scampi."

Jack joined in her mirth and with a low drawl said, "Maybe...but you sure as hell smell good enough to eat."

At work, she and Jack talked over cases fairly easily, but right now she couldn't think of a single thing to say. Her body had taken over her brain, remembering him in boxers, but it didn't change the fact Jack was still her boss.

Jack kissed her so fast she didn't have time to react. The dance floor seemed to blur, and the thumping beats of the music filled her ears. Instinctively, Anna hauled off to smack Jack across the face, but he caught her hand.

Anna became weak in the knees and didn't think she could walk back to the table. "What in the blue blazes do you think you're doing?"

"Anna, it's just a kiss." Jack lifted her sunglasses and froze. His mouth dropped open, and it hit her a second too late that there was no evidence left from her eye injury.

Jack stumbled over his words and said in apparent disbelief, "H-How, how? W-What did you do? I-I don't understand."

Anna took a step back from him and threw her palms up. "It's a miracle, Jack. I woke up and went to the mirror, and my eye was completely healed." It wasn't a lie. She just left out the part about Ralph. Jack shook his head back and forth. His kiss was forgotten in the face of a miracle.

Anna went back to their table, and Jack followed her in silence. Anna looked at Ruby and Sandy and gave them a shrug. She placed her sunglasses back in her purse. Jack couldn't take his eyes off Anna, but his look had nothing to do with desire. He kept looking at her like she belonged under a microscope in a petri dish.

Sandy sipped on a dirty martini and said, "Well, you two certainly looked cozy out there." Jack nodded but kept staring at Anna. Sandy was trying to play matchmaker, and it just wasn't going to work.

Jack turned to Frank. After a long pause, he said, "I told you how hard that patient hit Anna a couple of days ago. Well, look—she doesn't have a shred of evidence left from the injury. Her eye was completely swollen shut yesterday. It should still be swollen, and she should have a bruise. Any ideas?"

Anna, Ruby, and Sandy each did their best to keep a straight face. They all knew it was a miracle. Ruby said, "You mean to tell me you've never seen or heard of medical miracles?"

Frank stood and put on his glasses. He went around the table and brought a penlight out of his coat jacket. "Anna, please follow the light for me. I just want to see for myself." Anna blushed, but she followed the penlight. He clicked the light off and placed the pen back in his coat.

Anna jutted her chin and defiantly said, "Unexplained medical miracles go unsolved every day. I just happen to be one of them. I didn't come back to the hospital today because of exactly what you two are doing to me now. I'm not a specimen, and I'm trying to enjoy my time with my girlfriends. You're embarrassing me, Jack."

Frank turned to Sandy and offered her his hand. "Would you like to dance?"

Sandy stood and placed her hand in his. "Frank, I would love to dance." Sandy and Frank stepped away from the table.

Ruby grabbed her purse and stood. "Sorry to leave you, Annabelly, but I have to go pee. Pitfalls of pregnancy."

Anna chuckled under her breath, and her gaze returned to Jack. The look he gave her made her hold her breath for a long second. She'd been so focused on becoming a doctor and establishing her reputation in her residency that dating had never entered her lifestyle equation. Jack was seriously handsome and a wonderful doctor. She was leaving in two weeks, so why was she placing the quietus on any interaction with him?

Jack stared at her like she was crème brûlée, and it made her nervous. She didn't need any more complications in her life. "Jack, stop looking at me like I'm one of your groupies at the hospital. You have no effect on me." Anna glanced up to make sure lightning didn't strike.

Jack gave her a slow and sexy smile. He brushed his lips next to her ear and whispered, "I beg to differ, Anna. Your eyes are dilated, and your pulse rate is off the charts."

Anna pushed the chair away from the table and left Jack sitting by himself. *Off the charts, indeed.* Night had fallen, and the beach club glowed from the tiki torches and candle globes on the tables. She muscled her way through the crowded dance floor to Sandy. "Jack's getting on my last nerve, so I'm walking down to the water."

Frank pointed to Jack, who stood behind her and had heard every word.

Sandy chuckled and said, "You tell 'em, sister. We're not going anywhere. You go for a walk on the beach. With this moonlight, you might get lucky." Jack and Frank both laughed at Sandy's comment.

Anna stomped away without looking back. Why was she so angry? Was it Jack? Or was she angry at herself? Maybe a part of her wanted to get back at Jerry, or maybe she wanted to live life again and was too afraid. As her feet hit the sand, Anna slipped off her sandals and ran barefoot to the shoreline. Once she reached it, she stopped and let the slow ocean waves roll over her feet. The moonlight was so bright that Anna could see a couple making out near the boardwalk.

Jack ran up beside her, and she noticed he had stopped long enough to take off his Italian loafers and roll up the bottom of his pants.

He shouted over the waves, "What did I do, Anna? How do I get on your nerves? Is it because I want you? Or is it because you want me?"

Anna turned around and yelled back, "I don't know. I think it's because I've been alone for too long and you scare the hell out of me."

Jack scooped his arm around her waist and held her head with the palm of his hand. He kissed her senseless as she clung onto his biceps. She circled her arms around his neck. Then Jack abruptly let her go, and she lost her balance and landed in the sand on her rump. She looked up at him with her head tilted and he helped her to stand.

Jack gingerly ran his hand along her arm and then backed away. "Anna, I don't want to scare you. Hell, it scares me, too. I've never felt like I do when I'm near you. I know I'm your boss, but in another two weeks, you'll no longer work for me."

Jack's eyes seemed to glow in the moonlight, and his chest heaved up and down as if he was having a hard time breathing. He ran his fingers through his hair. "Anna, I want you, and when you make up your mind, you know how to find me." Jack left her and walked back to the club.

Motionless, Anna stared out at the ocean. The moonlit night, the sand, and the ocean were aesthetically the stuff that made romantic fantasies. She didn't think it was the fact she wanted Jack necessarily; she just wanted *someone* to love her. Someone to hold her. And Jack was hot and sexy as hell.

Chapter 12

Cherish

THE NEXT MORNING ANNA WOKE up to Ruby being sick in her guest bathroom. Anna threw off the covers and ran to her. "Honey, sweetie, is there anything I can do?"

Ruby waved Anna away, and in a weak and shaky voice, she said, "No, I wish. This baby makes me throw up every morning. I'll be okay soon." Ruby threw up again while Anna opened the linen closet and pulled out a washcloth. She filled the cloth with cold water and wrung out the excess before placing the cool cloth on the back of Ruby's neck.

Sandy groggily entered the guest bathroom, and in a gravelly voice, she said, "I feel sick, too, but it's from too much alcohol. My head's killing me. Aspirin, please?"

Anna glanced up, noticed Sandy had on Frank's shirt, and cringed. "Is Frank upstairs?"

Sandy bobbed her head up and down. "Sorry, I couldn't help myself. Aspirin?"

Anna placed her hand on the door. "Ruby, I'll be right back." Anna turned to Sandy and butt-bumped her. "Come on, slut. I have some aspirin in the kitchen." Sandy playfully pushed Anna.

Light footfalls fell across the tile floor as Sandy followed her into the kitchen. "Just because I have a healthy sexual appetite doesn't qualify me as a slut. If I were a man, I would be a stud."

Anna laughed out loud. Inside the kitchen, Anna reached over the hood fan and opened the cabinet to grab a bottle of aspirin. "You're a studdess."

Sandy opened the fridge, pulled out a Coke, and popped the top.

Anna handed her two aspirin. Sandy said, "Thanks. I like Frank. He's super sweet."

Anna exhaled a deep sigh and leaned against the kitchen counter. "Thank God I'm not going to be here for much longer. For goodness' sake, Sandy, he's on my board. And you need to be drinking water, not Coke. Does Frank like you?"

Sandy placed her hand on her hip and cocked her head to the side. "Really? The man only asked me to marry him a dozen times last night. No, I'm serious. Frank wanted me to fly to Vegas last night and get married."

Ruby slowly entered the kitchen and eased down in a chair. "Anna, would you please make me some herbal tea, and I need a few crackers."

Having Ruby and Sandy in her kitchen reminded Anna of when they'd all lived together in college. "Sure thing, sweetie. You only have a few more weeks left and your morning sickness should be over. Are you taking prenatal vitamins? You look as though you've lost weight since Christmas." Anna handed Ruby a box of saltines. Sandy walked over and snatched a couple of crackers out of the package and handed the box back to Ruby. Sandy jumped up on the kitchen counter and nibbled on a cracker.

Ruby groaned and slumped down in the chair. "Ugh. A few more weeks? Oh, God, what in the hell was I thinking? Why in the world would a woman want more than one child?"

Anna chuckled and put the teapot on the stove to heat. "I promise, once the baby is born, you and Reed will want another one. I've heard mothers forget all about the sickness and the pain of childbirth once they hold their precious little bundle of joy."

Sandy hopped down from the counter and stepped over to Ruby. She brushed the side of Ruby's face with her fingers and made a sad face. "Poor baby. No kidding, Ruby, I hate seeing you sick. I don't think I ever want to get pregnant if I have to throw up like you did this morning. I thought you were going to pass a lung." She leaned down and gave Ruby a quick kiss on her cheek.

Anna and Ruby chuckled at Sandy's comment, when Frank walked up to Sandy, shirtless, pulling her to his chest. Ruby ogled him, and Anna's mouth dropped open. Who knew that Frank was a sex god under all of that Mr. Good Doctor apparel?

Sandy circled her arms around his waist and reached up to kiss him. "You want some coffee, Frank?" Frank kissed her with passion, dipping her backward.

Anna turned around and poured hot water into Ruby's tea cup, then looked at Ruby and pointed to the door. Ruby grabbed the crackers. Anna and Ruby stepped outside through the sliding glass doors. They walked over to the patio table next to the pool and sat down.

Twenty minutes later, Sandy joined them wearing her bikini and sunglasses. "Frank's gone. He's sweet and a great lay, but dadgummit, he still wants to marry me." Sandy always ran in the opposite direction anytime one of her suitors even suggested the "M" word.

Ruby took a sip of tea and nibbled on crackers. "Sandy, Sandy, what are we going to do with you? Do you think you'll ever settle down?"

Sandy pulled her shades down over the bridge of her nose. "Cherish me, Ruby. I would have to find the equivalent of me to settle down, and men like that are in short supply."

The ocean breeze lifted the saltines off the table, and Ruby grabbed them. "What do you want to do today? We've got one good day left, and it's all yours." Before Anna could reply, Ruby farted so loud it sounded like a shotgun going off. Sandy snorted, and Anna started laughing so hard she nearly peed her pants. Ruby waved her hand behind her butt and held her nose. "I'm sorry, guys. My body and brain are no longer synced or in control."

Sandy and Anna howled with laughter and tears rolled down their faces. Sandy said, "First puke, now poot. No thanks, I'm never getting pregnant. Geez Louise, Ruby Jane."

Ruby stood, placed her hand on her hip, and slightly pointed her foot outward as if she were posing for *Vogue*. She said, "Didn't y'all know that puking, burping, and pooting is all the rage in *Parents Daily*? Let's go to the beach. How 'bout it?"

Anna stood and smacked Ruby on the rear. "Only if you sit downwind."

LESS THAN AN HOUR LATER, they had two beach umbrellas and four chairs on the beach with a cooler full of beer and water. The sand glistened in the brilliant sunlight and umbrellas dotted up and down the beach. The summer season hadn't quite hit yet. There were a few families with young children happily making sand castles and playing in the water as the ocean waves ebbed and flowed and crashed onto shore.

The balmy breeze coming off the ocean filled Anna with a mixture of happiness and sadness. She was happy about moving back to Tennessee, but part of her would always belong on the beach. Even on Anna's worst days, when she lost a patient, she could walk on the beach and regain some peace. She would miss Florida very much.

Anna stripped out of her shorts and T-shirt, down to her bikini, and shucked her flip-flops under her beach chair. "You don't have a baby bump yet? I hope I look as good as you do when I get pregnant. Have you thought of any names? Do you want a girl or a boy?"

Ruby reached down and lovingly ran her hand from one side of her stomach to the other and kicked off her sandals. "Reed and I don't care if it's a girl or boy. We just want this baby to be healthy and happy. We've decided to hold off on names until I finish with my first trimester. Y'all remember my dream about miscarrying, and I just don't want to take any chances." Ruby unrolled her beach towel, spread it over the beach chair, and sat down.

Anna adjusted her sunhat and tilted her head to face Ruby. "You and the baby are going to be just fine."

Sandy spread her beach blanket on the white sand and began to apply suntan oil with a splash of sunscreen. "Well, if it's a girl, name her after me."

Anna kicked sand on Sandy's foot, then reached over and opened the cooler, grabbing a bottle of water. "Ruby doesn't have to answer that, and it's not fair to put her on the spot."

Sandy wrinkled her nose and leaned back on the blanket, propped on her elbows. "Geez, Mom, I was only kidding." Sandy closed her eyes and tilted her face toward the sun.

Tears sprang to Ruby's eyes and her voice quivered. "What if I'm not a good mother? What if I scar the kid for life?" She leaned forward and placed her hands on her knees. "I love Reed so much it hurts. I was so in love with creating a part of Reed and me that I completely forgot I have to be a mom. And it dawned on me. I'll be a mom forever, not just until the kid turns eighteen. Being a mom lasts for life. What if the child hates me?"

The temperatures began to soar as the sun rose to its noonday position in the sky. Anna looked at Ruby's panic-stricken face. Ruby had always been the leader of the three girls. Ruby was always the one Anna counted on for stellar advice on life. Now Ruby looked like she just got caught stealing Granddaddy Campbell's whiskey back in high school, completely terrified.

Nearly every Friday after school, Anna and Sandy went to Ruby's house for a weekend of fun. Ruby's mom would have pizza or spaghetti waiting for them with tea cakes. Anna could still remember how Ruby's house always smelled of something sweet baking in the oven. They played kick the can in the backyard, and Sandy would flirt with George, Ruby's older brother. The three of them would stay up late, make prank calls, and watch movies like *Breakfast at Tiffany's* or *An Affair to Remember*.

Anna squeezed Ruby's hand. "Whoa, big girl. Just hold on a cotton pickin' minute. You and Reed are going to be wonderful parents. You're kind and loving, and so is Reed. The apple doesn't fall far from the tree. Your child will love you. It's those damn bootlickers trying to place doubt and fear in you. You stop it, right now, and I mean it."

Ruby drew her brows together and said, "What are bootlickers?"

Anna chuckled and leaned back into her chair. "Ralph calls demons bootlickers. They play on your fears and anything else that can weaken the soul. Don't let them get away with it. You're much stronger than that."

Sandy sat up and drew her knees close to her chest. "Demons. Grrr. Don't you just hate them?" Sandy glanced up in the sky and shook her fist. "You're never going to beat me. Do you hear?"

Ruby grabbed her beach bag, rummaged inside for her lip balm, and brushed it across her lips. "You're right. I know all of this, but I'm only human, and I do have fears. I'm sorry."

Anna applied sunscreen and handed off the lotion to Ruby. "Fear by itself isn't what draws them. It's the obsession of fear, all-consuming fear of a particular thing you can't control. You acknowledge a fear, and then you let it go. I have no doubt your kiddo will be crazy about you. Let your fears go." Ruby nodded and took a deep breath and exhaled.

Sandy dragged her fingers through her long chestnut hair and twisted it up off her neck before she secured it with a hair clip. "I brought the big diary with me. We probably need to make new entries. And for the record, it's just not fair for you two to have real interaction with your guardian angels." Sandy sniffed. "Ha. He's here. I smell him."

Squinting, Anna put on her sunglasses. "Who do you smell?"

Sandy turned to face Anna and Ruby and said, "My guardian."

Anna's face broke into a grin. "Well, that's a first." Ruby burst out laughing.

Sandy threw her palms up and shrugged. "Well, I do. He smells like cocoa and vanilla, and the smell gets stronger when he's in heat. And God knows, y'all know how much I love chocolate." Anna burst out laughing and slapped her hand on her knee.

Ruby choked on her water and started coughing. "What the heck?"

Sandy crawled over to the ice chest, grabbed a beer, and placed it inside a cozy. Sitting on the beach blanket, she said, "This is my theory. My guardian angel has a crush on me." She chuckled and shook her head. "I mean, come on, what else could it be? He's just afraid he won't be able to control himself." Sandy waved a hand over her body, and with a sideways smile, she added, "How could he resist? Sometimes I feel him watch me when I'm falling asleep, and sometimes I can feel him when he lies down next to me. I dreamed one night he kissed my forehead."

All of a sudden the beach umbrella flew out of the sand. The three girls scampered after it and caught the thing before it crashed into one of the sand dunes. Once they had the umbrella securely placed back deep down into the sand, Sandy said, "I betcha a hundred dollars that he's the one who blew the umbrella out of the sand."

Ruby took another gulp of water and brushed some sand out of her chair. "I didn't think angels had sexual feelings. I think Seneca is asexual. I know he loves me, but it's like he loves a tree or something. Anna, what about Ralph?"

Anna pulled a beer out of the cooler and popped the top, and

Sandy threw her a cozy. "Ralph and I are close, but it's like he's my brother. But I do think angels experience the feeling of desire. I think angels are more like us than we realize. Yesterday, Ralph and I were talking about true love. He said if he had a chance at true love, he would do just about anything to keep it. He also mentioned Jerry's guardian in a loving way. I think Ralph may be in love with her, but he just doesn't realize it."

Sandy sat her beer down next to her thigh and grabbed the radio out of her beach bag. She fiddled with the knobs until she picked up some music. "Wise man, that Ralph. Why wouldn't angels be able to fall in love? True love is the real driving force in the universe, baby."

Anna turned quickly to Sandy. "Oh-oh, Sandy, I know the name of your guardian."

Sandy bolted around to face Anna and spilled her beer on the beach blanket in the process. "What? Really? What's his name?"

Anna clapped her hands with excitement. "Oh, this is good. Ralph had a meeting with our guardians, Seneca, Baldric, and Luwenia. Baldric the Warrior is what Ralph called him. He's your guardian. I kind of feel sorry for him, though. Sandy, you'd try the patience of a saint."

"Well, that's a friend for you. Tell me the damn truth even when I don't want to hear it." Sandy eyes widened with alarm. "Oh my God. When I was a little girl, before I moved to Tennessee, I had an imaginary friend named Baldric. That *cannot* be a coincidence. You hear me, Baldric? I know your name, baby. So anytime you get good and ready to show yourself, I'm ready."

Sandy stood, walked to the edge of the shore, and waded knee-deep into the ocean before she dove head first into the waves. Sandy broke the surface of the water, swimming on her back and kicking her legs hard. Anna and Ruby looked at each other before jumping up and racing into the water. Anna could hear the laughter of her friends when she dove head first into the chilly ocean.

SINCE THE ATTACK ON ANNA, Baldric had been stuck to Sandy like glue. Sandy had a knack for getting herself into difficult situations. He remembered the first time he saw her, twenty-eight years ago. Sandy had been a beautiful baby and pretty, precious toddler. When she'd been a little girl, he'd watched her jump rope and get into fights with boys on the school playground. She had bloodied more than her share of noses, even back then. She'd been fearless.

Sandy's father, Hugh, had wanted a son. Baldric watched Sandy beg for attention from her father. Sandy excelled in everything she did and gave more than 110 percent effort. Most of the time, her dad just simply ignored her. Her mom, Sally, loved her but always put Sandy's father first. Sandy had grown up without really feeling parental love.

As an only child, Sandy played alone for most of her young life. So Baldric became her imaginary friend. One day he bent the rules and appeared in her bedroom while she played with her dolls. "Hello, Sandy, my name is Baldric. Would you like to play hide and seek?"

Sandy had jumped up from the floor and thrown herself into his arms. "Yes. Yes. Let's play." He knew he wasn't supposed to reveal himself so early, but Sandy had been very lonely, and he just couldn't help himself.

One night changed the way how Sandy viewed true love. Hugh had invited his boss, Ben, over for dinner at their house. At nine years old, Sandy was already blossoming into a beautiful young lady. Ben paid close attention to Sandy all night.

Ben even got down on the floor and played Scrabble with her. Sandy had been ecstatically happy. When it was time for her to go to bed, Ben said, "Sandy, would you like for me to tell you a bedtime story? I know dozens."

Sandy jumped up and down with delight. "Yes, Mr. Ben, please."

Hugh stood up from his chair and replied, "Absolutely not, young lady. Now go upstairs, brush your teeth, and go to bed."

Dejected, Sandy slowly made her way upstairs, brushed her teeth, and went to bed. As Sandy drifted off to sleep, her bedroom door opened, and Ben snuck inside and sat on the edge of her bed. Baldric watched in horror and grew enraged. He materialized downstairs to her father, bypassed her father's guardian, and placed thoughts in her father's head of what Ben wanted to do to his daughter upstairs. Then Baldric ported back into Sandy's room.

Baldric watched as Ben shook Sandy awake and her eyes

widened with the excitement of an innocent. "Sandy, darling, wake up. I'm here to tell you that story I promised."

Ben smiled, and Sandy jumped up and down on the bed saying, "Yes, yes, yes." Ben picked Sandy up, and she wrapped her arms around his neck. Ben sat Sandy on his lap and began to stroke her hair and back as he told her the story of Sleeping Beauty. Sandy's innocent eyes shone with excitement and relished in every detail of the story. Ben ran his hand under her nightgown, up and down Sandy's bare leg.

Sandy frowned and tried to get off of Ben's lap, but he held her tightly. Ben said, "Don't be afraid. Prince Charming did the same thing to Sleeping Beauty."

Hugh burst into her bedroom and nearly beat Ben to death. Sandy stood in horror while tears streamed down her little face. She decided Prince Charming didn't exist and made up her mind to never fall in love.

The next day, Sandy's family packed up everything that belonged to them and moved to Tennessee, where Sandy's aunt lived. Sandy met Ruby on the first day, and they became fast friends. Sandy had fallen in love, and it was with the whole Glenn family. Sandy stayed with the Glenns more than she stayed at home. In Sandy's mind, the Glenns were her family.

With every passing year, Sandy grew into a beautiful, smart woman. He had fallen in love with her and vowed to keep her from harm, even if it meant breaking the rules of Heaven.

When Sandy started high school, she became curious about sex. He knew most guardians didn't watch their humans in sexual situations, but he couldn't help it. Baldric was afraid for Sandy and never wanted her to be abused again. Baldric read Sandy's mind with every sexual encounter, and with each one, a part of her became that scared little nine-year-old girl who only wanted someone to love her. Unconsciously, Sandy still looked for a human Prince Charming, and there were none who filled Sandy's desire of the heart.

Today, Baldric followed Sandy to the beach. Her sense of humor made him laugh all the time. The topic of conversation had turned, and Sandy started talking about him. It was the first time Baldric realized Sandy could feel his presence. She had felt him lay beside her and watch her sleep, and she'd felt him kiss her forehead. And to

Baldric's great shame and horror, Sandy could smell him when he was in heat. Guilt washed over him. *Jehoshaphat.* He'd watched her having sex and imagined she was making love to him. That was a huge rule breaker. But he'd been in love with Sandy for so long and couldn't help himself. *Saints preserve me.*

Baldric had to do something, anything to stop Sandy from talking about him. He had grabbed the umbrella pole and tossed it up high in the air. The girls ran after the umbrella and put it back down in the sand. Then Anna dropped the bomb and told Sandy his name. Sandy remembered him, and now it was time to get reacquainted. *God have mercy on my soul.*

AFTER DINNER, ANNA MIXED UP a batch of Maria's margaritas. Maria worked for Cary and had the best recipes in town for food and beverages. Anna made a virgin drink for Ruby and not-so-virgin ones for her and Sandy. A full moon lit the sky and everywhere the fragrant smell of hydrangeas, old garden roses, and ocean breezes drifted in the air. They sat around the wrought iron patio table next to the pool, laughing and reminiscing of old days.

Sandy went inside and brought out her Ditch Lane Diary. She read over the last few entries and added the information about the attack on Anna at the hospital. Sandy placed her finger on the side of her nose and her thumb under her chin. "I'm working on a new story and need you to give me your two cents' worth."

Ruby chuckled and propped her feet up on the chair next to Sandy and wiggled her toes against Sandy's thigh. "Nah, but I'll give you a Yankee dime's worth." Sandy playfully pinched Ruby's little piggy.

Anna held her drink with both hands. "Wait, before you get started, do I need to make another batch of margaritas?" Ruby and Sandy shook their heads no. The frogs sang out in the night, and the stars overhead twinkled across the inky black sky. "Okay, Sandy, let it rip."

Sandy gave Anna an exaggerated bow. "Here goes. I had to do a fluff piece on the new convention center coming to Nashville. I met with Cole Steele of Steele Enterprises. He's the one who brokered the deal." Sandy could've modeled for a sculpture of Athena Parthenos. She became light and fire when she talked about her work. "The day I met him, my cameraman and I got caught in a thunderstorm. I was completely soaking wet when we arrived at his office. But I just thought we would shoot him and do cutaways of me later after I changed clothes."

Anna gasped and threw her hand over her mouth. "I saw Cole years ago when I went to a hoedown at Nelson Doune Farms. Cole was there, and I caught him staring at me. Something about him gave me the creeps."

Ruby rubbed her lower back and stood up. "Don't mind me. I just get aches sometimes. It's weird, but I can feel this baby grow. Please, do go on."

Sandy smiled at Ruby and said, "You want to go inside, pumpkin? You could stretch out and kick your feet up on the couch."

"Best idea I've heard all night. Okay, Anna?" Ruby replied.

Anna stood and grabbed her glass. "Sure, grab your drinks, and I'll turn off the outside lights." Anna walked into the main garage that held the lighting for the patio and pool. She switched off the floodlights but left the pool lights on and went back into her house.

Ruby stretched out on the couch, placed a pillow behind her head, and propped another pillow under her knees.

Anna took the quilt off the rack in the corner of the room and spread it over Ruby. "Comfy, cozy?"

Ruby tucked the quilt under her chin and rolled onto her side. "Perfect, Mom. Go on, Sandy. But if I fall asleep, I'm not rude. It's just the baby makes me tired, and I can fall asleep at the drop of a hat."

Sandy leaned down and kissed Ruby on the forehead. "I'll fill you in on what you miss when we're flying home tomorrow." Sandy got comfy on the loveseat, and Anna kicked out in the recliner. Sandy said, "Anywho, I walked into Cole Steele's office soaking wet. Anna, you've seen him. He's ruggedly handsome, but there's something downright scary about him. He was pleasant enough and answered all my questions. The whole time I was interviewing him, he looked at me, and it wasn't in a flirty way, but I had a sense he wanted to hurt me." Sandy took a sip of her drink. "When I shook his hand, I didn't get a reading—no visions and no past thoughts. It was weird. That never happens. I get tingles when I feel my power kicking in. I can read people by barely brushing next to them. I ping off the wall with energy. I had the power. I felt the energy, but he blocked my reading some way."

Anna waved her hand back and forth. "Ooooh, oh, I got a seriously bad vibe from him. He looked at me that way, too. He's bad news, Sandy. Stay away from him."

Sandy leaned her head against the back of the loveseat. "I can't, Anna. I have an instinct with my stories. He is a big story. While Eddie and I were editing the piece for the ten o'clock news, I get this phone call from my friend, Brenda, who works at NPD's dispatch. She asked if I could meet her for a drink. She had some scoop. Well, I met her and found out the scoop was about Cole."

Anna sat cross-legged, unwrapped a Hershey's Kisses from her bowl of candy and popped it into her mouth and threw one to Sandy. Anna pointed to Ruby and said, "Sawing logs."

Sandy chuckled and unwrapped her piece of chocolate. "Can you believe she's going to have a baby? Makes me feel my clock ticking."

Anna unwrapped another piece of candy. "Oh, hush up, we have plenty of time before our eggs shrivel up. Do go on. You've got me on the edge of my seat. What happened with Brenda?"

Sandy flipped her hair behind her shoulders. "Brenda meets me at the Gold Rush, you know that bar on Elliston Place, and we go to the back of the bar. Before our drinks arrive, she tells me she overheard a conversation between the chief, as in police, and this guy from city council. Of course, I ask her who the man was from the council and Brenda drew a blank or was afraid to tell me. So I held her hand and saw the man's face."

Sandy propped her upper body on her elbow and placed the palm of her hand on the side of her face. "The councilman went to see the chief in fear of his life. Cole Steele sent a thug to strong-arm him about passing the resolution for the new convention center, but that's not what piqued my interest. The chief reassured the council member he would take care of it, and as soon as the guy left, guess who the chief called?

Anna leaned in and said, "Cole Steele."

Sandy nodded. "Uh-huh. One and the same. I've started a secret folder on Mr. Steele. I want to do an exposé on him. There's something rotten about Cole, and after everything we talked about today, I think maybe he's one of Luc's bootlickers or maybe Cole is Luc, if he can take human form."

Anna felt a panic attack coming on. She hadn't had one since her first year in med school. "Sandy, drop the story. Please, leave it alone. You don't want to mess around with Luc. He hates us."

Sandy sat up and placed her hands on her thighs. "The hell I will. We're wards for a reason, and I think this guy may be the reason I have this power in the first place. I'm going to run Cole Steele out of town on a rail. Hell, I might even tar and feather the bastard."

Rattled, Anna slowly breathed in and breathed out. "Sandy, I hope you're teasing, my Huckleberry friend. You have to make me a promise. If you feel like you're getting in over your head or you get frightened, you'll call us. Remember, we're a team, and we're stronger together."

Sandy was likely dancing with the devil, and it terrified Anna. Sandy yawned and stretched. "I will, I promise, but I'm not backing down until I know everything there is to know about Cole Steele and what he's doing in my town."

BY THE TIME RUBY AND Sandy left for the airport, Anna had begun to make her plans to move back to Tennessee. Her friends needed her home. The love for her two best friends had been the real constant in her life. Their love never let her down and to date had never broken her heart.

Ruby was pregnant, and Sandy was getting in way over her head with Cole Steele. She felt it in her gut. And Anna didn't know how, but she was going to get Jerry back before he made the disastrous mistake of marrying wretched Rachel.

ON THE WAY BACK FROM Heaven, Ralph dropped by the in-between to speak to Michael, the Commander in Chief of the Angel Armed Forces. Ralph needed to make a full report about the bootlickers' attack on Anna.

Ralph needed to find out how many other attacks had happened to other wards recently. He also wanted to fish any information from the Secretary of Defense, Naphetina. The army must react with swift and immediate action if there were any escalations or changes in Luc's strategy. The wards would have to receive combat training if the threats were becoming a reality.

Michael's headquarters was military regulation. He had a sentry of angels placed at every exterior wall, and inside the walls, warrior angels were armed to the teeth at every door. Angels didn't use conventional weapons. They fought with weapons, like Baldric's sword, devised by The Creator, Himself. The bows and arrows, daggers, and swords could travel through space and time with any warrior angel. Plus, each warrior angel had the ability to use the light of love. Any of these weapons could annihilate any demon, including Luc, to the Eternal Blackness. The Eternal Blackness was a place where unruly beings were separated from The Creator, and for some, the sentence was for all eternity with no hope of parole.

Michael's headquarters was a massive white structure, and it housed all of the maps and coordinates of the universe. Every divisional leader in the AAF met with Michael on a weekly basis to offset any new devious trick or strategy Luc threw their way. The divisional leaders and Michael shared any relevant findings to the angel's core teams on a need-to-know basis, and those teams would pass down any pertinent information to the Freemasons of the world.

Ralph passed through the halls until he reached Naphetina's office. He stuck his head inside her door. "Naphetina, you're looking well."

All angels were created beautiful, but Naphetina didn't possess the beauty of Luwenia. However, Naphetina had cunning wits and exceptional strategic military skills. That was why Michael had made her his second in command. "Ralph, to what do I owe the pleasure of seeing you today? Please sit down."

Ralph sat in one of the white wingback chairs in front of her desk. "My ward, Anna Kelly, was attacked by the Divisions of Jealousy and Sorrow. She's a healer. I have information from the earth angels that Luc has been recruiting wards, and with the weaker wards, he is sucking their power until they pass. The stronger ones become prisoners. I need information. I need a plan of action."

Naphetina pulled her glass screen magically from thin air and swiped her fingers across the screen several times before stopping. She looked over at Ralph and leaned her forearms on her desk. "This was an unsanctioned attack without Luc's knowledge."

Ralph frowned and stood straight. He placed his hands on her desk and leaned forward. "And you believe him? What about my other allegations?" Ralph knew he was seriously treading in dangerous waters, but Naphetina needed to know the truth, even if he got slapped with an infraction.

Naphetina's citrine eyes flashed at him. "Please, watch your tone with me, Raphael. I didn't say I believed him. I said it was unsanctioned. Luc's speaking with Michael in his office now about Anna's attack. As far as the other allegations, it's marked classified. Don't stare at me. I don't know, either."

Ralph's eyes bulged with anger, and he said, "What? You don't know? Are you kidding me? You know what this means? Luc's going after the Campbell Ridge wards. They need training for combat at once."

Naphetina rubbed under her chin with her fingers. "You'll need to discuss civilian combat training with Michael. I'm not sure another attack is imminent in this decade, but I'm not ruling it out. A report came in recently about a ward being killed mysteriously in Australia. Of course, Luc denies any knowledge of the attack, too. Ralph, the humans aren't the only ones suffering monumental losses in this war. Our warrior angels fill the treatment center daily with the injuries inflicted by the demon angels of earth. And there will be more human casualties, and that includes the wards."

Ralph frantically paced back and forth, and his military boots pounded hard on the white and gray marble floor, creating an echo that rang out in the halls. "I have to talk with Michael and get back to Earth. Did you know there's a rumor going around among the earth angels that Luc is trying to breach the outer banks of the heavenly realm?"

Naphetina's eyes turned from citrine to blood red, and she gripped the edge of her desk. "No, I've not heard. He would have tripped the sensors. My team would've been alerted to the breach. I have to go. Good day, Ralph." She dismissed him.

Ralph intended to train Anna with or without Michael's

permission. She needed to know who and what was coming for her and her friends. Ralph arrived at Michael's door and reached up to knock. The door opened, and Luc walked out into the hallway.

Luc scanned Ralph from head to toe and smiled. He grabbed the top of Ralph's left shoulder and squeezed hard, and Ralph shrugged out of Luc's grasp. "Well, hello, nephew. I hear you're having some trouble with your ward, ah—what's her name? Oh, yeah, Anna."

Ralph straightened his shoulders, his face level with Luc's, and replied, "You have been stalking my ward. Stay away from her or there will be consequences. Do you hear me? And please do not refer to me as your nephew. You're no longer part of our family. You're a disgrace, and I'm not afraid of you."

Luc smiled wickedly. His eyes looked as cold as the marble stone under his feet. He leaned in next to Ralph's ear and whispered, "You should be." Luc vanished.

At five foot ten, weighing around two hundred twenty-five pounds, Michael was the best warrior in all of the known universes. He stood at the door in golden armor with a dark crimson sash across his breastplate. Luc was afraid of Michael.

Michael also loved Ralph. "Don't let that twerp bully you. Luc's number is coming up." Michael gave Ralph a big bear hug. "You make me proud, son. Come in and let's talk."

Chapter 13

Yah Mo B There

ON THE DAY ANNA RETURNED to work after the attack, she rode her bike to the hospital. She thought about all of the people she had saved and those she had not. Life and death went hand-in-hand. Sometimes death was quick and painless, and at other times, death came agonizingly slowly and painfully. For each person, the experience was uniquely different.

When death was imminent for one of Anna's patients, she could feel the Angel of Death lurking in the shadows and knew no amount of medicine would keep him away. The only thing Anna knew for certain, without a shadow of a doubt, was that there was life after death.

Even without Ralph in her life, Anna would've believed in an afterlife. She had experienced the whoosh from the Spirit of Man descending over her many times in her life, giving her peace when she needed it most.

As soon as Anna clocked in for her shift, she was given an update on the current patients in the ER and proceeded to make her rounds. In the emergency room, lives could be lost or saved on any given day. In life-threatening situations, Ralph had taught Anna how to combine her healing energy with her medical skills without alerting staff or affecting her environment. She no longer made tiny tornadoes or knocked out the power grid. Ralph had trained her well. She had developed nerves of steel when lives and seconds counted.

Anna's morning swiftly turned into late afternoon before she finally took a break and headed to the bunker. She walked inside to find Jack eating a late lunch at the kitchen table.

Jack's eyes met hers, and a sweet, dizzy feeling fell over her. "I want to apologize for Friday night," he said. "I was out of line." He took another bite of his salad.

Anna swallowed hard. Jack regretted kissing her. "It's okay. No need for apologies. I'm a big girl." Anna went to the fridge and pulled out her lunch bag.

Jack pushed his chair away from the table and placed his leftovers in the trash can. "All of the residents are expected to put in an appearance at the American Heart Ball this Saturday night. It's formal." He looked into her eyes for a moment too long, and the silence was deafening. Jack slipped his white coat on and walked out the door.

Through most of her lunch, her mind bounced from Jack to Jerry. The two Js. She still loved Jerry, but Jack had made her feel something again.

ANNA THREW AWAY HER TRASH and placed her empty container back into her lunch box. She looked up when the bunker door opened, and the man she'd seen in the cave and the library walked inside wearing a pair of jeans and a Hawaiian shirt with sandals. Anna gasped. She looked into his cold, dark eyes, and her blood thundered through her veins.

The immortal Luc had immense beauty with perfectly proportioned features. Glossy black hair fell over his shoulders, and a menacing smile revealed perfect teeth. Luc radiated an all-consuming darkness, and evil seemed to pour out of every molecule, like sap running from a sugar tree. Luc took a step toward Anna and she tried to back away but couldn't. She stood immobile. He shut and locked the door with his mind. Anna glanced up at the clock, and it read 3:05 p.m.

Luc spoke with a silken tongue, smooth as glass and sweet as chess pie. "Most humans don't possess the intellect to see me. But you saw me in the cave and the library. I'm impressed, Dr. Kelly."

Anna's stomach flipped, but she stilled her nerves with a silent prayer. With calm assurance, she said, "I'm not afraid of you."

Luc laughed loudly and rubbed his hands together in excitement.

"That's what Raphael said to me only a moment ago. Oh, but wait, you call him Ralph. Very cute." Luc stepped closer and placed his hands in prayer mode. "You can't lie to me. I read your thoughts, even your prayers. It's truly delightful to rule by fear. You're wasting your healing talents with The Creator. You could go places with me, even run a hospital of your choosing. Have a wing dedicated to your name."

In an instant, Ralph materialized in front of Anna. His shimmering, translucent wings spanned the width of the room, shielding her. "Back off, Satan. You devious, bottomless pit of putrescent rubbish."

Luc wore an insane smile and shook his head back and forth. "Tsk, tsk, tsk. Raphael, Raphael, you cannot defeat me. You need to stick with healing. You have no stomach for violence. It's not in your nature. You're going to get this very talented human killed and yourself maimed for life. Give her to me, and I tell you what—I'll leave her friends alone. I'll even allow Ruby's baby to live."

Anna stood on her tiptoes and tried to stick her head around Ralph's wings. That burning feeling crept inside her gut, and the urge to protect her friends and even Ralph overcame her. An intense glow outlined the frame of her body, and she shouted, "You stay away from Ruby and her baby."

Three more angels appeared next to Ralph. Anna assumed the angels were Seneca, Luwenia, and Baldric, based on the descriptions Ralph had previously given her.

The Guardians of Campbell Ridge held weapons in their hands. Ralph held two daggers in each hand. Baldric whipped out a sword that hissed through the air and created an electrical charge in the room. It glowed with incredible, pulsating light. Baldric bent his knees in readiness for an attack. Seneca and Luwenia spanned their wings to overlay Ralph's wings, making a wall of protection around Anna. Luwenia's bow and arrow aimed at Luc's chest, and small blue spheres that emitted an extraordinary amount of energy hovered in the air less than an inch above Seneca's hands.

Luc snapped his fingers, and immediately behind him, the room filled with demons. The demons' bodies resembled humans, but their heads were reptilian. Their mouths opened, revealing sharp, pointy teeth and oozing what appeared to be saliva. The bunker became a living thing. The walls seemed to pulse, and she knew they would cave any second. The two sides prepared for battle.

Her battle—Luc wanted her. Crap on a cracker.

With an air of aloofness, Luc waved his hand about the room, spreading the stench of death. Luc casually walked closer to Ralph and gave Anna a piercing look, and it felt like hands were roaming over her body. "Anna, you do amaze me. The Creator has given you some incredible gifts for such a small human."

Luc turned to Raphael and said, "Do you want this to go down right now in a place already filled with human suffering? I will destroy this place. I will level it to the ground, and every human here will die." Luc's laid-back attire swiftly changed into what appeared to be a steel meshed breastplate, and a rainbow of colors filled the room when his wings spanned out and broke the ceiling's surface.

Ralph's voice resonated with the strength of a warrior and was music to Anna's ears. "I will fight for Anna. I will do what is necessary to ensure her safety."

Suddenly, the room filled with incandescent light. They were no longer in the bunker but in a tropical place with lush forest. Anna glanced up to see raging waters gushing over a towering waterfall. Another angel appeared behind Luc, and he grabbed Luc by the wings.

All hell broke loose.

Anna stood in the flat valley in the midst of a supernatural battle in what she could only describe as a glass bubble. To her right, Baldric battled two demons, ducking and weaving while swinging his blade with incredible speed. When his sword made contact with a demon, it disintegrated into ash.

In rapid succession, Luwenia released flaming arrows to plunge deep into a demon's chest, which had the same effect as Baldric's sword. Seneca threw the blue spheres of light, which exploded at the moment of impact against the demons. One by one the demons disappeared.

Ralph body-slammed the demon heading straight for Anna. He grabbed the demon by the head and headbutted the demon into ash. Ralph flipped around before the next demon could grab his wings. He threw consecutive punches to the demon's gut and an uppercut to the demon's jaw.

Anna screamed, "Watch out, Ralph. Nooo." But he didn't hear her and the demon stabbed Ralph with a dagger to the kidney. Ralph's knees hit the ground.

Luwenia shot an arrow, hitting the demon between his eyes. Luwenia picked up Ralph and placed her hand over his injury. In less than a minute, Ralph was back on the balls of his feet fighting the last demon. Ralph swiftly reached in his side belt, withdrew another dagger, and slashed the demon across the jugular. The demon's ash floated in the air, disappearing before it hit the ground.

Anna turned to the fight between the short and stocky angel and Luc. Luc shouted, "I've waited an eternity to fight you, Michael." Luc escaped from Michael's wing hold. He drove his fists into Michael's face, knocking his head back. Michael recovered fast and, with a swift kick of his right foot, Luc hit the ground.

The sound of thunder echoed throughout the valley, and screaming winds blew the trees and plants violently back and forth. Ralph screamed, "Baldric and Luwenia, guard Anna."

Ralph threw himself in the middle of the battle between Luc and Michael. Michael shouted, "Stay back, son, I have this bastard." The second Michael looked at Ralph, Luc punched Michael in the gut, and he doubled over, gasping for air. Ralph flew in the air and slammed Luc into a huge evergreen tree, giving Michael time to regroup. Ralph wrapped his arm around Luc's neck in a chokehold.

At the same time, Luc brought up his left foot and crashed it down on the top of Ralph's left foot while Luc elbowed him hard in the ribs, allowing himself enough time to escape from Ralph.

Luc flew into the air with his wings spanned at full extension. He shouted, "This is only the beginning, my brothers." He disappeared in the howling wind.

ANNA WOKE UP ON THE couch in the bunker. She glanced up at the clock on the wall, and it still read 3:05 p.m. *Holy Smokes.* Anna looked around the room, and Ralph was nowhere in sight. She intended to get the full scoop on the battle that went down today. Time had stood still during the battle between Heaven's angels and

Hell's demons. She shook her head in disbelief. Nothing in the room seemed amiss.

Anna had to get back to work and would discuss the apocalypse with Ralph later. *Yeah, that's what I'll do. Focus on work, focus on work, that's what I'll do.* She repeated her mantra all the way back into the ER.

TODAY HAD RELEASED A SHIT storm of trouble for Anna with her coming face-to-face with the leader of the dark world. She was ready for a bottle of merlot and a long hot soak in the Jacuzzi. Anna wiggled the key in her front door and pushed it open to find Ralph had created an obstacle course in her living room.

Anna threw her backpack down on the floor and sagged against the couch. "Whatcha doing, Ralph?"

Ralph wore a pair of navy blue sweats and a white, long-sleeved T-shirt with a pair of cross-trainers. He stood on a small ladder, nailing up blankets on the wall on the other side of the room. Ralph stepped down from the ladder and, with a look of pure determination, he said, "You have to start training. After the battle today, you must be prepared in case Luc decides to make another impromptu visit with you again."

Anna could see lines etched around Ralph's gorgeous violet eyes. In the whole time she had known Ralph, he'd always been so upbeat. Now he seemed tense and a little on the edgy side. "Today was not your fault."

Ralph walked over to her and pulled her up into his arms. He hugged her and then took a step back. "I should've known he was coming for you. Luc could've taken you. He could've killed you. Anna, I know I'm not supposed to form emotional attachments to my human, but you're like the daughter I never had, and I failed you today." Ralph's head fell forward, and his shoulders slumped.

Anna tilted his chin up, and his eyes met her gaze. She said, "You saved me today. You have never failed me. If I could choose from all of the angels in Heaven to be my guardian, I would pick you every single time. I love you. You're my rock, Ralph."

Ralph dropped to his knees and with his head bowed, he said, "You're too magnanimous, Anna."

Anna knelt down beside him and placed her hands on either side of his face. She smiled broadly, and he smiled back. "Ralph, we make a good team. Remember, The Creator doesn't make mistakes. But right now, I'm pooped. I'm going to grab a glass of wine and soak in the Jacuzzi for about thirty minutes. I'll tell you what... You let me relax, and then you can train me on how to be a warrior ward." She snickered and said, "Oh, I like that—warrior ward. I'll have to tell Sandy to write it down in the diary."

Ralph stood first and helped Anna to her feet. Ralph's smile warmed her, and the stress seemed to disappear from his face. He said, "Anna, wait on discussing this event until the other guardians have talked to their wards. Go and relax. I made lasagna with French bread and a tossed salad. Fighting makes me restless and cooking releases tension. I'll get you a glass of wine and bring it to you."

"No, my brave protector, take a load off. Do whatever you do to relax, and I'll be back to eat dinner later. By the way, dinner smells heavenly." Anna went into her bedroom, shutting the door behind her.

ANNA LIT LAVENDER AND VANILLA aromatherapy candles around the tub and dimmed the light switch. She laid her Walkman with Wham's *Make it Big* tape ready to play and placed her glass of merlot on the marble ledge of the tub. Anna stepped inside her Jacuzzi and immersed herself. A few seconds later, she broke the water surface. "Ahh, now that's what I'm talking about." She took a sip of wine and placed her headset on her ears and pushed play. Anna used her toe to push on the jets, and the soothing pulsating streams of water began to knead her tired and aching muscles. She released a moan of delight and leaned her neck against a rolled up towel.

As the music played, Anna began to unwind, pushing the thoughts of today's battle away, and she allowed her mind to get into the slow grooves of George Michael singing "Careless Whisper." She glanced up at the ceiling before closing her eyes.

At twenty-eight years old, Anna had an incredible desire to have sex. Maybe it was the fact she could have died today. She needed to make love every once in a blue moon and cringed at the thought of how long it had been since she'd done it. So she fantasized about Jerry making love to her.

But thinking about Jerry making love to her only created a deep longing for him, and the empty place inside her heart seemed to grow larger. Anna reached for her wine and drained the rest of the glass. The jets made her legs feel like jelly, and she took a washcloth out of the basket and lathered it up with Savon de Marseille soap.

Anna quickly dried off, applied body lotion, and combed her hair. She pulled on a pair of black leggings and an oversized sweatshirt, then grabbed a pair of socks and her running shoes. Anna's bare feet slapped on the tile floors as she strolled into her new workout area.

Ralph sat on a stool in front of her bar. "You're positively glowing."

Anna's cheeks flushed pink, and she dropped the shoes next to the couch. "A bath with wine and jets can work miracles, and I had a few fantasies about Jerry, too."

Ralph burst out laughing. "Well, that answers for the glow. Come on, let's get you fed and later we'll work out."

The food was delicious, and the carbs gave her a renewed energy. Anna followed Ralph back into the workout area. She slipped on her running shoes and said, "Ralph, what happened today? It was weird when we went into the forest, and I was suddenly in this glass globe. It scared me to death watching you fight. I guess you were right. Luc is after us or, at least after me?"

"Michael threw us into an alternate realm to protect the humans in the hospital. We had to take you with us. Other demons could've shown up. The protective globe shielded you against the supernatural energy and weapons dispensed in the battle. Luc will make another attempt at you, and you have to be ready when he does."

Anna stood with her hands on her hips. "So where do we start?"

Ralph walked behind her and wrapped his arms around her midsection. He placed his hand on her diaphragm. "First, I want you to concentrate on breathing. In through your mouth and then exhale out. Feel the steady rhythm. Breathing exercises help to keep you centered. I've placed three objects on the kitchen table."

He moved her back about five feet from the center of the table. "I placed a pillow, a five-pound bag of sugar, and a twenty-pound bag of potatoes on the table. I'm going to teach you how to use the energy you displayed today in the bunker. I want you to move those objects off the table with your mind. I laid a painter's drop cloth down on the floor to catch debris, so don't wrinkle your nose."

Anna frowned and turned to face him. "Uh, my healing shoots to my fingertips, but that energy today came from my gut. When Luc mentioned hurting Ruby and her baby, I experienced this intense burning right in the middle of my abdomen." Anna placed her hand over her belly button.

He smiled and said, "That is exactly where your life force begins. Anger is a good thing if you use it in the right way and it doesn't develop into hatred. Are you ready?"

"Ready as I'll ever be," Anna said. She shook out her arms, loosened up her neck, and did a few leg stretches.

Ralph took a step away from her and said, "Now raise your arms, but not higher than your shoulders, and point your fingers level toward the pillow." Anna did as he requested. "Good, now I want you to think about Luc. Think about how he made you feel and next, think of your life's energy force."

Anna pointed to the pillow and concentrated on the burning growing inside her stomach, and she thought about Luc. The energy shot to her fingertips. "Okay, the energy is at my fingertips, so what do I do now?" She lightly bounced back and forth on the balls of her feet and thought of Muhammad Ali. She was going to fly like a bird and sting like a bee. No, that wasn't right. She was going to float like a butterfly and sting like a bee.

Ralph leaned in next to her ear and said, "The pillow is Luc's chest. You want to push him against the wall. NOW."

Ralph yelled at her, and the energy shot from her fingertips across the room and the pillow exploded into a massive amount of down feathers floating in the air. "I exploded the dad-blamed thing."

"Excellent." Ralph walked over to the table and positioned the sugar in the center of it. "You have an extraordinary gift. I didn't know if this would work. You blew the thing apart. Which means, once we get your power under control, you'll be able to blow demons apart."

Anna straightened her shoulders and readied herself for the five-pound bag of sugar. She felt like Annie Oakley in *Annie Get Your Gun*. She had the movie and might pop it in later if she didn't fall asleep first. "I'm ready to try to aim at the sugar. Why don't I just try to push it off the table without you yelling at me? You nearly made me pee my pants."

Ralph leaned against the other wall with his arms crossed over his chest. "And the student teaches the instructor. I love it. Go for it, Annie Oakley."

Anna relaxed and allowed her mind to concentrate on the energy that hummed steadily in her fingertips. The energy shot from the tips of her fingers and blew the bag of sugar off the table, slamming it against the wall. Thankfully, the bag didn't burst apart.

Anna made a gesture with her fingers like they were imaginary pistols. She blew on the tips of her pointers and placed her energy guns back into her invisible holsters. "Wow, Ralph. Why haven't you taught me this before?"

Ralph stepped over to her and placed his hand on her shoulder. "Let's sit on the couch for a minute." They sat down, and Anna sat cross-legged to face him. He said, "It's against the rules for angels to teach humans this kind of power. Some humans would use it in the wrong way. Without permission, I risk getting fired from my position, but the risk is worth it after what happened in the bunker today."

A wave of panic rose into her throat at the thought of losing Ralph. Anna reached over to hold his hands. "Ralph, I don't want to lose you, and I don't want you to get into trouble."

"I discussed your training with my dad today before he went home." Ralph gently touched the side of her face before placing his hands on his thighs.

Anna leaned into her comfy couch pillows and stretched her legs out, so her feet rested in Ralph's lap. "Your dad? I thought The Creator made angels?"

He massaged her foot in a slow stroking motion, pushing his thumbs into her arch. "As I've said before, angels and humans are similar. My biological father is Michael. He's in charge of the Angels Armed Forces over Heaven and the Universe. He is the one who saved the day. And before you ask, I wasn't conceived out of love or lust, but out of necessity. My biological mother, Ahneeta, is in the New Soul Departure Division. They both love me in their way. There are some angels who fall in love in Heaven. Angels who fall in love are paired in a commitment ceremony. But most angels are paired out of necessity to create more angels as the populations of the universe increase and as the demon angels increase their numbers."

Anna sank further into the couch on the verge of sleep. "Ralph, I want you to fall in love. I think you care for Luwenia more than you realize. She saved you today. The way she reacted and the way she looked at you made me think she loves you, too." Anna made a motion with her forefinger and thumb. "Maybe you love her just a little more than you're letting on."

Ralph placed his hands on her calf and squeezed her muscle. "Maybe, but I don't think Luwenia sees me as a romantic interest. The kidney shot would have put me in our treatment center, but Luwenia healed me. Any member of my team would have responded the same way."

Anna grinned, and before she nodded off to sleep, she yawned and said, "You have to make a move, Ralph. She may be afraid of the same thing. You need to flirt with her once or twice and see if she responds."

Ralph rubbed her shin and said, "Maybe I will."

Chapter 14

All She Wants to Do Is Dance

ANNA HAD BEEN SCHEDULED TO work the night shift this week. She took the opportunity to shop during the day for a new dress for the ball. After finding the perfect dress, she made a quick trek to the dreaded grocery store. Anna hated fighting people in the grocery store aisles and check-out lines. Anna chuckled a few times thinking about her newfound powers. She'd never abuse her powers but giggled as she imagined pushing the people who blocked the aisles out of her way.

After putting up the groceries, Anna wolfed down leftover lasagna and drank a glass of milk. She needed to remind Ralph to start cooking lighter meals, or she'd gain two hundred pounds. She stacked her dishes into the dishwasher and turned it on.

On the way out of the kitchen, she found a note. It was from Ralph.

I'm so proud of you. Last night, I didn't have time to work on the power of love. Remember, love is the greatest power within you. The love of light when properly used will work miracles beyond what your mind can comprehend.

May love light the way, daughter of my heart,
Ralph

AFTER ANNA HAD CLOCKED IN for the night shift, she noticed Jack sitting on a stool in the nurses station talking with his groupies—two female residents and one male resident. They were so far up Jack's ass Anna was surprised he could even sit down. Why she cared brought up questions she didn't want to face, much less answer. Jack walked over and handed her the patient cases for the night without so much as a how do you do or a kiss my ass.

On the night shift, Anna was the one in charge. No two patients were ever the same. For the rest of the week, Anna worked with patients who experienced varying respiratory conditions, chest pain, broken bones, and abdominal pains.

The hours were long and hard, but also rewarding. The staff respected Anna, and it felt good to know they could count on her, depend on her. And whether Jack wanted to admit it or not, he knew she was a good doctor.

Anna's shift was ending and the day shift was clocking in. She looked up to see Frank walking down the hall with the Chief of Staff, Charles S. Vanburen, M.D. Frank smiled and threw up his hand to wave to her, and she waved back. Anna spotted Jack stepping out of the elevator. Anna nonchalantly moved to the end of the nurses station to hear their conversation while she continued filling out the remaining forms for the day.

"Jack, have you met our newest board member, Frank Howard?" Dr. Vanburen asked.

Jack grinned and held out his hand. "Frank, good to see you again. Yes, I took Frank out last Friday night."

Frank shook Jack's hand. "I had a great time going to Temps. I met Dr. Kelly and some of her friends. Chaz, Dr. Kelly is a real gem."

Dr. Vanburen clamped his hand down on Jack's shoulder. "Dr. Forrester, I always hear good things about Dr. Kelly. She's doing an outstanding job in the ER. Her residency is ending soon, and I want to keep her. I know you'll make that happen for me, won't you, Jack?"

Anna turned slightly to watch Jack's reaction. Jack tensed but replied quickly, "We're proud of Dr. Kelly. She's one of our best and brightest. I'll do my best to keep her at Hall of Saints." Anna wondered if Jack meant it.

A few minutes later, Frank walked over to Anna at her workstation. "Hey, if you're about ready to wrap up, I thought we could grab some breakfast."

Anna smiled at Frank and quickly looked at Jack, who looked like he was on the verge of a coronary watching her with Frank. She said,

"I just finished my last report, and I'm starving. Let me grab my bag."

THE DAY OF THE BALL filled Anna with both excitement and anticipation. She had the day off and booked appointments to pamper herself with a massage, followed by her hair stylist for a few highlights. Anna typically wore her hair in a French twist at the hospital, but tonight she was letting her hair down. Her stylist used a skinny curling iron to make long cascading curls down the middle of her back and cut bangs to frame her face superbly. After her hair appointment, Anna proceeded to have a manicure and pedicure. And for the *pièce de résistance*, she had her makeup professionally done.

Anna bought a beautiful backless evening gown at Tina's Wedding and Formals on Wednesday. The silver dress had a wide, rounded neckline that fastened at the back with a deep oval cutout and small shimmering sequins. The skin-hugging dress accented Anna's curves, and she paired it with silver sandals that had three-inch heels. Last, she added simple diamond earrings. Anna took one last glance at her reflection in the mirror and made her way to the garage.

Cary met her and dangled his keys to his black Jaguar. He kissed her cheek and said, "If I were twenty years younger, I would sweep you away, my dear. You're stunning."

Anna's cheeks reddened. "Cary, the Jag? Are you sure?"

He placed the keys in her hand. "Absolutely. More than sure. Have fun."

Oh, she felt like Cinder-freakin'-rella. "You're too good to me. Thank you, Cary."

It was dark by the time Anna pulled into the valet parking, and the young male attendant was falling over himself to help her out of the car. Anna grinned and tossed the young man the keys, and he whistled, either at her or the Jag, maybe both. She straightened her shoulders and walked inside the country club.

Patrons of the hospital and its faculty filled the ballroom. Anna made small talk with a couple of the residents and turned to go and say hello to the chief and his wife when Jack intercepted her. Anna looked straight into his smoky gray eyes, and her mouth went dry. Jack wore a black shawl collar tuxedo and a batwing bow tie with a white shirt. If she was playing Cinderella, then Jack filled the bill as Prince Charming.

In a low throaty voice, Jack said, "Anna, you're truly ravishing tonight."

Anna trembled under his intense stare, but she managed to say, "Thank you."

"Do you have a date?" Jack asked, looking over her shoulder for an escort, and slid his hand inside his coat pocket.

Anna looked down and glanced quickly to the left as the big band began to play "At Last." The female singer had a voice that would make Etta James proud. She said, "No, I'm solo tonight."

Anna's spine tightened as Jack reached out his hand and said, "Then may I have this dance?"

Anna found herself nodding as Jack guided her onto the dance floor. He placed one hand low on the small of her back, and the other held her hand. Anna placed her other hand on his shoulder and concentrated hard on dancing the waltz.

Jack gave her a look that made her pulse race. "Anna?"

Anna breathed in his spicy lavender scent. "Yes, Jack?"

"I want to kiss you again. I want to make love to you, Anna."

A slow smile curved his lips and stabbed her with an intense longing. Gazing into his eyes, Anna allowed herself to be swept away in the moment.

Cinderella danced the waltz, and she was having fun for a change. Anna floated on air as she swayed with the rise and fall of the waltz. Jack, an excellent dancer, moved with grace as he circled her around the ballroom dance floor. And he wanted her.

Everyone in the room stared at them, but Anna ignored them. In her mind, all the people simply faded away, and she and Jack were the only ones left dancing in the room. A feeling of passion washed over her like the turbulent waves of the ocean.

Jack desired her, but her heart still belonged to someone else. She said quietly, "Jack, you know I'm moving back to Tennessee. Whatever might be happening here won't last."

Jack pressed her tightly against the length of him and whispered, "You haven't even given me a chance."

The music ended. Anna let go of Jack's hand and walked away from him. She turned down the long corridor of the club and ran into the women's restroom. Anna went over to the mirrored vanity. She'd been so tempted by Jack. After years of missing the warmth of a man's love, Anna shook with need. Jack could satisfy her physical need, but her emotional tie had always been with Jerry. At one time, he filled the need of her heart, but now Jerry had a fiancée.

Anna entered the ballroom and walked over to talk to Dr. Vanburen and his wife, Lisa. "Good evening, Dr. Vanburen. Lisa, I love your dress. It's a wonderful ball. Thank you for inviting me."

With a smile, Lisa said, "Anna, you're simply too gorgeous for words. You're quite the belle of the ball tonight. There's not a gentlemen or lady here who has taken their eyes off of you. Did you come with Jack?"

"No, I'm alone. Jack just asked me to dance," Anna replied.

Dr. Vanburen said, "I want you to have a great time tonight."

"I intend to do my best." Anna grabbed a flute of champagne from a waiter when he offered his tray to them. She took a long drink and left the chief and his wife to the bevy of people vying for their attention.

Anna waved at Dr. Jones, another resident in the ER. He stood near the bar, and she walked toward him. Wes had been her neighbor in Gainesville. "Hi, Wes. You're looking very dapper."

He pushed his glasses back into place after checking her out. "Anna, you have curves? What's up with Wolfman Jack?" he said with a chuckle.

"Oh, Jack just asked me to dance." Anna had no more gotten the words out of her mouth than someone walked up behind her. She turned to find Jack staring into her eyes. Wes excused himself, leaving Anna to fend for herself.

"Why did Wes leave? I know some of the staff call me Wolfman Jack. No biggie," Jack said jokingly.

Anna shifted uneasily on her feet. "I'm not sure why Wes left. Hey, I see some ladies looking over here, and they seem to be very unhappy. Why would you waste your time with me when you could be scoring somewhere else?"

Jack's expression turned serious. "Because I don't want to talk to anyone else."

Anna's inner goddess did a couple of cartwheels. "I don't know how to respond to you. You're my boss."

Jack placed his hand on her bare back, and a soft breath escaped her lips. He said, "Not for long. And if I don't tell you now I how I feel, I may never get another chance."

A tall, leggy blonde came over and kissed Jack on the cheek. "Jack, your parents said you would be here tonight. I would love to catch up."

Before Jack could reply to the blonde, Anna said, "Jack, I'll talk to you later. I see Dr. Chandler, and I want to say hello." Anna turned to leave, and Jack grabbed her hand.

"Anna, don't leave." Anna's hand dropped away from his grasp.

She said, "I'll be around, and you know where I work." Anna walked away, leaving Jack with Blondie. Anna was moving soon, and her heart couldn't take another disappointment. She didn't turn back to see Jack with the gorgeous blonde.

Just like Cinderella in the fairy tale, Anna decided to flee the ball before she turned into a pumpkin. She made a hasty exit before she did something stupid like run back to Jack.

Anna pulled out of the club parking lot and drove down the highway. The stars shimmered across the velvety sky. It was a beautiful night for riding along the beach highway. Tonight had been fun. Anna loved dancing and glowed with happiness.

Anna pulled Cary's Jag into the main garage and placed the key on the wall. She locked the door to the garage behind her and took her time walking toward the front door of her house. The warm ocean breeze blew her hair off her shoulders. The lights from the pool shimmered, and the palm trees slowly swayed.

Suddenly, Jack appeared out of nowhere and pulled her into his arms. He kissed her with uncontrollable passion. Anna's body responded to his touch, to the feel of his hard body pressed close to hers. Jack's lips were gentle yet demanding, his tongue exploring hers. His hands seemed to be everywhere.

JACK EXCUSED HIMSELF FROM CAROLINE Wilkins, a family friend, and he ran after Anna into the parking lot. Out of desperation, he jumped into his car and flew to Anna's home. Something inside him told him if he didn't pursue her tonight he wouldn't have another chance.

After he had parked in Anna's driveway, Jack stepped out of the car and followed the sidewalk to the main garage. He froze. Anna walked beside the pool with the ocean breeze blowing her hair off her shoulders. *A goddess, a five-foot-four goddess.* Anna had more strength and courage in her little pinky than most people did in their entire body.

Jack burned for Anna, craved her like an addict did his favorite drug, and she was his drug of choice. He ran to her and pulled her into his arms, crushing her with a kiss, and the passion between them exploded in the warm night air.

Anna pulled away slightly, her lids heavy with desire. She stared into his eyes and said breathlessly, "Would you like to come inside, Jack?"

Jack kissed her hand and held it. "After you, beautiful."

Inside her house, Anna threw her purse and keys on the table next to the door and her phone rang. She answered it. "Hello?" The color drained from Anna's face. "I'm so sorry, Ruby. I loved him so much. He was like my grandfather, too. Yes, I'll get a flight tomorrow... Yes, honey, I'll stay with you. I love you, sister." Anna placed the phone back into the dock on the table and looked at Jack with a sad smile. "I have to go to Tennessee. Ruby's grandfather passed away. He was like family to me." A tear threatened to spill down her cheek. "Granddaddy Campbell was the patriarch of Everglade Farms and mentor to so many. It's an end of an era."

Anna slipped off her shoes and walked barefoot into the kitchen. She pulled a phone book out of a drawer and called the airlines to make flight arrangements. Anna hung up the phone and reached for Jack's hand. "I'm sorry. I like you very much, but I have to pack, and if you stay, I'm afraid I won't get anything done. When I get back, we can go to dinner, okay?"

Jack felt like a silly teenager. "Okay, if it's what you want." Call it instincts, but Jack had the feeling he'd lost Anna before he ever had the chance to make her his.

Anna grinned, lifted a brow, and released his hand. "Yeah? Good, Jack. It's a start in the right direction."

Jack shoved his hands into his pockets and took a step away from her. "I'll change your schedule at work. Please call me when you arrive in Tennessee and let me know you're okay." He kissed her briefly on the cheek and walked out the front door.

Chapter 15

Crazy for You

ANNA FLEW INTO THE NASHVILLE airport and picked up her rental car at Hertz. She drove straight to Ruby's house. Anna had called her parents before she left Florida. She explained she would be staying with Ruby while she was in town and would see them later at the funeral home.

Four cars and a truck were in Ruby's driveway, so Anna parked in the grass. She stepped out of her rental, took a deep breath, and exhaled. She loved the Tennessee air. She went around to the back of the rental car and grabbed her suitcase out of the trunk.

Anna walked along the sidewalk with her heels clicking on the concrete. At the front door, she knocked with no answer and pushed the doorbell with her finger. Anna was about to let herself in when Jerry opened the door. She looked up into the deep blue pools of his eyes and sucked in a breath. Her butterflies danced wildly in her chest.

Dang. Jerry had turned into one hell of a good-looking man. Anna nervously glanced down at her bag. Jerry reached down to pick up her luggage and barely grazed her arm, and she jumped from the electricity of their contact.

Sparks flew in the air between them as he stared down into her eyes and a slow smile curved his lips. "Hi, Anna. I'll put this in their guest room. Everybody is out back on the patio." Jerry turned and took the stairs two by two with her suitcase.

Anna had been holding her breath and began to breathe again. The instant she looked into his eyes, she knew she still loved Jerry and neither time nor space had lessened her feelings.

170

Anna gathered her wits and stepped through the French doors onto the patio. An overcast sky cast dark shadows on the people sitting around the table. It took a second for her eyes to focus on Reed, Ruby, Sandy, and Rachel. Anna's spine tightened when she met Rachel's eyes. Anna ran over to Ruby and hugged her. "Ruby, I'm sorry. I loved Granddaddy so much. I can't believe he's gone."

Ruby's eyes and nose were red from crying. She sniffled and said, "He loved you so much. He didn't suffer, thank God. Mama found him in bed and said he just looked like he was sleeping. He went peacefully in the night. Sit by me." Anna sat down beside Ruby on the chaise.

Sipping on a glass of tea, Reed sat in between Sandy and Rachel. He said, "I'm glad you were able to get a flight on such short notice. Do you need to freshen up? We aren't heading to the funeral home for another hour. You have time."

Anna held Ruby's hand and smiled at Reed. "Yes, I think I will freshen up and change clothes. Are we riding together?" The thought of riding with Jerry and Rachel made her queasy.

Ruby gave her a squeeze. "Reed and I are going to leave a little early to be with Mom. Sandy's going to drive you, and Jerry and Rachel are coming later."

Anna glanced over at Rachel. "Hello, Rachel. I trust you're well?"

Rachel sat with her fingers linked and her forearms on the wrought iron table. Her eyes widened, and she smiled a little too brightly for the circumstance of their gathering. "I'm great." Rachel's expression turned solemn, and she shook her head. "It's just very sad about Granddaddy."

Anna's blood began to boil. Rachel didn't know Granddaddy, not like Anna knew him and loved him. But Anna knew it was only the green-eyed monster of jealousy raising its ugly head. She tried to reign in her emotions. "Yes, it's very sad. If you all will excuse me, I think I'll take a shower. I'll see you later at the funeral home. Sandy, come upstairs when you're ready to go." Anna kissed Ruby, Reed, and then Sandy. Anna turned to walk inside and crashed smack dab into Jerry's chest in the doorway.

Jerry held her wrists, and it felt like lightning rods on a summer afternoon. Anna gazed up into his eyes, and the way he looked at her made the air back up in her lungs. Anna thought Jerry felt the jolt, too. Anna stammered, "I'm—I'm sorry. I didn't see you there."

Jerry chuckled, still holding onto her wrists, and suddenly he realized what he was doing. He let her go quickly and shoved his hands into his pockets. "Oh, you're fine, Annabelly." Jerry's simple reply and the brief recognition she saw in his eyes, seconds really, let Anna know Jerry still cared for her. There was no way to explain it. Trying to explain their love would be like trying to explain how Mozart wrote symphonies.

Anna stepped inside the house and ran up the stairs. Her body shook with desire and nervousness when she closed the bedroom door. The look Jerry had given her left her burning and quivering with passion. She still had a chance, albeit a small one.

Anna plopped down on the bed, fell back, and draped her arm across her eyes. Jerry was engaged and downstairs with his fiancée. Anna opened her eyes and found Ralph staring at her.

Ralph jumped up and down on the bed, like a kid, making the bedsprings squeak. "Well, Annabelly, taking destiny into your hands? Seize the day, my daughter. But a small warning—remember, choices, free will, and all that jazz?"

"Wow, really, Ralph? No other words of wisdom from your millennia of experience?" Anna jumped off the bed, opened her suitcase, and began taking her things out.

Ralph placed his hands on Anna's shoulders and turned her to face him. "Don't shoot the messenger. There's no way around it now. Someone will be hurt. It'll be either you and Jerry who suffer or Rachel. Ultimately, it's your decision. Anna, your way will pave the future course of three lives. That kind of decision, I've only witnessed and seen the consequences. I've never been privy to experience the kind of love you share with Jerry. But I think you would live a life of regret without trying to get Jerry back. For what it's worth, I believe he's your soul mate. And Jerry and Rachel aren't married yet."

A lonely tear escaped down her cheek, and she brushed it away with the back of her hand. "There's only one way, Ralph. I did enjoy the attention I received from Jack, but there has only been one man for me, and it's Jerry. If he'll have me back, I'll suffer any consequences. I love him, and you saw it downstairs—he still cares for me, too."

Anna walked over to the window, opened the curtains, and peered down at the patio. Jerry must have sensed her and looked up. Their eyes held steady for a long minute, but it was clear their love was still alive, and Anna was going to fight for it.

"COME ON, ANNA. WE'RE GOING to be late," Sandy screamed up the stairs.

"What time is it?" Anna grabbed her little black purse, pulled out her red lipstick, and applied it to her lips with precision. She wore a sleeveless crepe black dress that cinched at the waist and hit right at her ankles with a wide black leather belt and black slingback pumps. Anna fastened the pearl necklace Jerry had bought her in college as Sandy burst into the room.

"Half past a monkey's ass. Geez Louise, woman." Sandy recognized the necklace and fanned her fingers out. "Wowzer. You look fabulous. Going bear hunting tonight?"

"As a matter of fact, I'm going Jerry Beary hunting tonight. I needed my good luck charm." Anna smiled and said, "Let's ride, Clyde."

Anna and Sandy went downstairs, out the front door, and into Sandy's silver Corvette with T-tops. Sandy reached over and squeezed Anna's hand. "You better be careful. Rachel will be watching you like a dang hawk."

Anna rolled her eyes while she fastened her seatbelt. "I'm not afraid of Rachel. All I need is ten minutes alone with Jerry to see if he still loves me. If he does, then Rachel can go back home to Daddy Warbucks."

Twenty minutes later, Sandy pulled into the Smith Funeral Home parking lot. Sandy rode around the parking lot twice before finding an empty spot around back. Anna and Sandy walked through the back entrance, opened the door to the kitchen area, and peeked inside.

Anna said, "Church women cook the best." They walked inside and looked over the spread of food scattered on several tables.

Sandy scanned the desserts and pinched off a piece of brownie. "Girl, you know that's the dad-blamed truth. Death brings them in by the droves." Anna smacked her on the arm, and Sandy lifted one shoulder, saying, "What? It's the truth."

Anna and Sandy left the kitchen and walked into the sanctuary after signing the guest register. Anna hugged George and Lizzie. "I'm sorry about Grandaddy. He's going to be missed by everyone."

George kissed her cheek and then Sandy's. "You two look like you're up to no good, and Sandy, you have chocolate in the corner of your mouth. Y'all hit the kitchen first?"

Lizzie elbowed him. "Shush. You did, too, and you know it," she said, and George chuckled.

Anna said, "Your poor mama is going to be exhausted, bless her heart. The receiving line is out the front door and down the sidewalk. Is Ruby in line, too? She doesn't need to overdo it while she's still in the first trimester." Anna quickly noticed the pain flicker across Lizzie's face. George and Lizzie had been trying to have a baby for years. Anna grabbed Lizzie's hand and squeezed. Lizzie smiled weakly.

Sandy touched Anna's arm. "We need to find Ruby and pay our respects. George and Liz, we'll talk to you before we leave."

Anna and Sandy made their way through the crowd of people and made small talk as they inched their way to the front of the line. Anna and Sandy ran into their parents, who were sitting together in one of the pews.

Lee and Harry, Ruby's parents, stood next to the casket, and Ruby sat in a chair beside her mother. Anna gave them each a kiss. "I love you all so much. I'm here if you need me for anything."

Lee held Anna's hand. "Anna, we've missed your smiling face around here. Ruby says you're moving home soon?" Lee had no more said the words when Jerry and Rachel walked up behind them.

Anna said, "Yes, ma'am, less than a month now, I'll be living right back here for good. Now, don't y'all over do it. I'm sure the guests will understand if you need to take a break." Lee kissed her cheek and Anna noticed Rachel's face turned bright red.

Anna and Sandy sat on the front pew of the sanctuary and began to talk with some of their old friends from high school. Granddaddy Campbell had brought in people from all over Middle Tennessee and beyond tonight. Anna wouldn't be a bit surprised if Granddaddy's spirit hovered around, listening to all the wonderful stories people were telling about him. He was one of the kindest people Anna had ever known, and she had never heard him say a bad word about anyone.

Anna grimaced, knowing she couldn't say the same thing about herself. Rachel chatted away with Ruby and Reed. Anna noticed Jerry leave through the side door of the sanctuary toward the kitchen. She leaned over to Sandy and said, "I'm going bear hunting."

Sandy chuckled and said, "Good luck."

Instead of drawing attention to herself, Anna decided to go out the front door. Once she was safely out of Rachel's vision, Anna ran toward the kitchen. She opened the door, and Jerry stood near the desserts eating a piece of chocolate pie. She stepped up to him and placed her hand on his arm. "That stuff will make you fat."

Jerry licked a piece from the corner of his mouth and chuckled. "True, but what fun would life be without a little sugar?"

God, Anna hadn't realized how much she missed him and nearly reached up to kiss him, but stopped herself. "You've been a good friend to Ruby and Reed. You were good to me, too." She choked back tears, and her heart filled with such intense emotion that his expression softened.

"Anna, I'm sorry. I should've called and told you I was getting married. I was chicken, to be honest. Besides, you hate me anyway."

"So not true. Jerry, I—I..." Anna was about to beg him not to marry Rachel when she strolled into the kitchen like a queen.

"Jerry, hon, I've been looking for you everywhere. I should've known you'd be in here stuffing your face." Rachel turned slightly to Anna and smirked. "I just can't feed the boy enough. It's like he has a hollow leg or something. Come on, hon, we need to be out there for Ruby and Reed." Rachel tossed another glance at Anna and said, "You know what I mean." Jerry shrugged and allowed Rachel to usher him out the door. *Like a dang lap dog.*

Anna shook her head and mimicked Rachel's voice, "I know what you mean, *and hon*, you mean to keep him as far away from me as possible."

Someone coughed, and Anna turned to find Brent standing in the doorway, smiling at her. Brent did get better looking every year. She wished she had the hots for Brent, but she only felt friendship.

"Excuse me, Anna, if you want to continue talking to yourself, I'll leave you to it." Brent laughed and pretended to walk out the door.

Anna ran over to Brent and threw her arms around him. "Brent, how the hell are ya? I'm sorry. I was trying to talk to Jerry, and his fiancée snatched him away. Why hasn't some lucky woman snatched you up?"

Brent stretched Anna's arms out to get a good look at her. "Watch it, precious, sounds like you might be a little bit jealous. As for me, there's only one woman I'll ever love, and she's married." Brent stepped away and placed his hand on his hip.

Anna's hand went over her mouth in surprise. Sandy always talked about Brent having the hots for Ruby. "No, I don't believe it. Are you talking about Ruby?"

Brent walked over to the brownies and grabbed one. "No comment."

Anna grabbed a brownie, too, and turned to look at him again. "Brent, Sandy said you always had a thing for Ruby, but I didn't believe her. Did Ruby ever know?"

Brent took a bite of brownie and poured a glass of sweet tea. He swallowed and said, "No, and don't you be telling her something like that, either. She's pregnant. Besides, I love Reed and Ruby. What good would it do now? Maybe someday I'll find Ms. Right."

"Aren't we a pair? If you want to know the dad-blamed truth, I'm jealous as hell. What did Scarlett say? I'm just pea green with envy." They both laughed.

Anna shoved the brownie into her mouth and her cheeks puffed out. Brent draped his arm around Anna and said, "Anytime you feel like making Jerry jealous, I'm all in." Brent hugged her.

AS THE FINAL VISITORS LEFT the sanctuary, Ruby, Sandy, and Anna sat on the front pew staring at the casket. Ruby said, "Do you think he's in Heaven?"

With a raised brow, Anna said, "Granddaddy was a saint. If he's not in Heaven, then I don't know who would be. Yes, I believe he's in Heaven."

Sandy stood and twisted left and right as if to get a kink out of her back. "Let's go to the kitchen and start wrapping up the food. We need to take it to your mom's for the wake tomorrow."

Anna squeezed Ruby's hand. "You and Reed go home. Sandy and I will take care of the food and take it to your mama's house."

Ruby stood with Anna. "I'll walk with y'all to the kitchen. I'm pretty sure Reed's in there making a plate now. Poor man's been starving to death. I've been so sick with the baby the last thing I've wanted to do is cook."

Sandy grunted and rolled her eyes. "Reed's a grown man, and if memory serves, he knows how to cook. You've just pampered him to death for the last eight years."

The girls chatted away as they walked down the hall toward the kitchen. They were giggling about Rachel catching Anna with Jerry.

Harry stood next to the kitchen door. A sad smile lifted the corners of his mouth and tears glistened in his eyes. "Girls, it's good for an old man's soul to see y'all together and laughing again. Brings back so many memories." The girls ran over and placed their arms around him. Harry started crying and that made the three of them cry. He took a step back and reached up to wipe the tears from his eyes with his forefinger and thumb. "I'll be okay. I'm just becoming a big ole softy."

Ruby reached up on tiptoe and kissed her dad on the cheek. "It's just the way I like you."

Anna followed Ruby and Sandy inside the kitchen, but Rachel had already wrapped and packed all of the food and was on her way to Everglade Farms with Jerry. Reed held onto the only plate left.

Reed snarled and turned his back to them. He glanced over his shoulder and growled. "Sorry, but I'm starving, and I'm not sharing." He turned back around and filled the room with warm laughter. "Just kidding, want some?" And offered his plate to them, but the girls refused.

Anna fumed with anger, and she gripped the lip of the kitchen counter. "Well, I'm so freaking glad *Rachel* took care of everything. She's just made herself indispensable around here. First Jerry, and now my best friend and her family."

Ruby placed her arm around Anna's shoulders. "Rachel will never replace you, not in a million, zillion years. I'm exhausted, and I'm craving Tony's cheeseburgers."

Sandy and Anna said at the same time, "Yuck."

Ruby shrugged. "Sorry, but this pregnant woman needs to eat, and the baby wants Tony's."

FOR THE LAST THIRTY MINUTES, Jerry had been staring down at his blank legal pad. Talking with Anna on the phone hadn't come close to preparing him to talk with her face-to-face. Just seeing Anna in the flesh had thrown him for a loop. He pulled out the bottom drawer of his desk and lifted a box of paper. He grabbed an old photo of him and Anna at Ruby's wedding. He stared into Anna's eyes, and a sharp pain hit him in the middle of his chest. What the hell had he had he been thinking when he'd agreed to marry Rachel? He was a damn fool.

A soft knock at his home office door and Rachel stuck her head inside. "May I come in?"

Jerry placed the photo quickly back in the bottom drawer and waved her inside. "You need something?"

Wearing a long pale pink nightgown with a matching robe, Rachel walked behind his desk and kissed him on the head. "No, silly. I don't need anything. I was just checking on you. You were quiet tonight, and you've been in your office for the last two hours. Are you coming to bed?"

Jerry glanced up at her. "Oh, I'll be along in a little while. I'm just playing catch up. Don't wait up. You go ahead and go to sleep."

Rachel hugged him and pressed her face next to his. "Don't stay up all night. We have to leave early in the morning."

"Oh, I won't."

Rachel walked to the door, paused, and turned back to him. "I love you."

Jerry didn't smile, but he glanced down at the drawer and said quietly, "I know." He could sense Rachel knew what this was about, but she wasn't saying anything. Jerry had never told Rachel he loved her, and after seeing Anna tonight, he could barely look Rachel in the eyes. She left the room and closed the door.

Jerry couldn't keep this façade up and knew he should've called off the wedding long before Rachel addressed the invitations. He was a damn idiot. Part of him wanted to think he could marry Rachel, but he just couldn't go through with it. Whether he ever ended up with Anna again or not, he knew he couldn't marry Rachel. After the funeral tomorrow, Jerry would tell Rachel, and then he would tell her dad. He wasn't looking forward to either one of those conversations.

Jerry began to scribble notes regarding the new project he had signed on to do for The Baer Company. He wrote for twenty minutes before he stopped again and looked down to read back what he'd written and froze. The words on the page began to change into ancient hieroglyphics and rearranged in an orderly manner into English. It had been over a year since the last message.

An intermediary has been chosen to save her soul. Blood must be spilled to preserve the balance between good and evil. The sun will darken, and the earth will shake when the chosen must set her free or lose both of their souls. And so goes an end of an age.

Jerry read the message over and over again. Who was the chosen one? Whose soul needed saving? *Shit on toast.* He thought of Ruby and the baby, Anna, and Sandy.

The Campbell Ridge wards needed a meeting, fast, but it would have to wait until Ruby buried her grandfather. He would give Ruby time to grieve, and then they would meet and discuss his message.

The wall clock quietly chimed two o'clock in the morning. Jerry stood from behind the desk and walked over to the maroon leather couch to lay down. He reached behind him, pulled his mother's old quilt off the back of the couch, and covered up. Jerry couldn't sleep with Rachel again. He wouldn't sleep tonight period, but he needed rest even though his brain wouldn't shut the hell up.

THE NEXT DAY WENT BY in a blur for Anna. The funeral started at ten and, in no time, she and Sandy were leaving the cemetery for Everglade Farms. Anna said, "I've not had one chance to be alone with Jerry, and I fly out tomorrow. I think my window is closing."

Sandy drove down the curvy backroads of Everglade and whipped around the slower traffic. "Anna, I have a plan. Rachel loves to smoke cigarettes. I'll take her outside after she's had a few cocktails and you can corner Jerry. I think I can stave off the woman for about fifteen minutes so you can work your charms."

Sandy pulled into Ruby's parents' driveway, drove around to the back of the house, pulled down the tractor lane toward the barn, and parked. "The whole community must be here. Good grief. Did you get a look at the cars?" Sandy turned off the ignition and chuckled. "Let's go and kick some Rachel Doune ass." Anna didn't have a clue if Sandy's plan would work, but she had to try something.

Jerry was the first person Anna saw when she walked into the Glenn's house. He leaned against the stairwell with his arms crossed over his chest wearing a navy blue suit and black shirt. Jerry's eyes locked with Anna's. The molecules in the air charged with electricity, kicking up a furor of fire flooding Anna with the warmth of his love.

Jerry's face lit with a smile, and it felt like seeing the sun for the first time in years. Her pulse raced, and her fingertips tingled with power. Anna swiftly looked around the room and didn't see any sign of Rachel.

Anna made a beeline to Jerry. "I need to talk to you, alone. I have no idea how because Rachel pops up everywhere. Will you please talk to me in private?"

Jerry leaned close to her ear and whispered, "When and where?"

Anna sighed with relief. That was all she needed to hear. "Sandy intends to feed Rachel cocktails and suggest she go outside to smoke. We might have a few minutes then, okay?" Jerry's eyes turned a shade darker. He undressed her with his eyes, and she trembled, leaving her knees feeling weak. She grabbed onto his hand and held it tight. "I feel the same way about you."

Anna noticed Rachel walking out of the kitchen. She quickly turned to Brent, who was talking to George and Lizzie. Anna placed her arm around Brent's waist.

Brent smiled down at Anna and circled his arm around her waist. He whispered, "Are we playing a game?" Anna nodded.

Out of the corner of her eye, she noticed Jerry tensed and his jaw muscles clenched. She looked down, and Jerry's right hand balled up into a fist. *Hot dog. Jerry's jealous.*

As the afternoon wore on, the neighbors and church folk began to leave until the only people left were the Glenn family and a few family friends, including Brent, Sandy, Jerry, Rachel, and Anna.

Sandy plied Rachel with cocktails all afternoon. Sandy winked and nodded to Anna when she led Rachel outside to the backyard. It was showtime. Anna whirled around the room and spotted Jerry near the front door watching her. Anna nodded, and he walked up the stairs. Anna glanced across the backyard once more and made a mad dash up the stairs. She made the top step and started down the hallway when Jerry opened Ruby's old bedroom door and pulled her inside.

Anna threw her arms around his neck, and he circled her waist. Searching his eyes, she said, "I don't need a man to complete me. I need love to complete me, and it's the love I have for you that makes me whole. I've made a ton of mistakes, but there's one thing I know for sure. You, Jerry Douglas McDaniel, are the love of my life."

Jerry held her face with both hands. "All it took was one look into your eyes, and I knew I was still crazy for you, all of you, and I can't go another minute without making you mine."

Anna's eyes widened with surprise. "What are you saying?"

Jerry brushed a strand of hair behind her ear and caressed her cheek with the palm of his hand. "I didn't sleep last night. All I could do was think about you, about us. I don't have any proof, but I think Rachel may have deleted your messages and thrown away your letters. I didn't think you loved me anymore, Anna. I can't marry Rachel. God forgive me. I don't mean to hurt Rachel, but I don't love her. I love you. I always have."

Jerry leaned in only inches from her face. The warmth of his sweet breath and the spicy scent of his cologne made it hard for her to breathe. His loving eyes searched hers, saying everything and nothing. Anna's adrenaline kicked in high gear. The clarity she had at this moment was razor sharp.

An emotional force unleashed between them as Jerry's warm lips made contact with hers, and they slammed against the wall. His lips were gentle and rough, alternating between kissing and sucking her top and bottom lips. His tongue licked the corners of her mouth, and he gently traced the outline of her lips before he plunged inside. His knee pushed between her thighs, and her heart skipped a beat.

Jerry scooped her up in his arms, carried her over to Ruby's bed, and lay her down. He traced his fingers along her jawline, down her neck to the swell of her breasts. Jerry pulled back slightly, looking at her as if she were a lost treasure he had just found. He covered her with a blanket of kisses and gently ran his hand over her breast and squeezed, and she stopped him.

"Jerry, we can't do this, not here in the Glenn's house. As bad as I want to make love to you right now, I can't. I love and respect them."

Jerry brushed his fingers over her cheek. "Anna, I'm sorry. The long and short of it is, I damn well near died when you left. But now I feel like my heart is going to explode with happiness. I don't want to let you go." Anna choked back her tears and reached up to run her fingers through his thick hair.

Jerry kissed her again. "I'm sorry, Anna. I should've never agreed to marry Rachel. It wasn't fair to her or you. Will you forgive me? I know you may think I'm nuts, but let's run away. I want you to run away with me. I've always wanted to marry you. Always. Will you run away with me?"

Anna kissed him hard and hugged him with all of her strength. "In a Tennessee heartbeat, I will. I'm staying at Ruby's. What time will you come for me?"

He rolled onto his side, propped on his elbow. "I'm not sure yet. It could be late. Will you wait for me? I promise I'll be there. I have to tell Rachel, and it's going to get real ugly."

Anna couldn't take her eyes off of his face. "Yes, I'll wait for you. I'll be ready. If you like, I could go with you to talk to Rachel."

Jerry pulled her on top of him and ran his hand down the curve of her spine. "Bad idea. She's jealous about everything, especially you. It's my mess, and I'll clean it up. I have to go. Rachel will be looking for me, and I don't want to create a scene here. I love you, Annabelly." They sat on the side of the bed. He hugged her again. "Is this real? Are you really here with me?"

She gently touched the side of his face. "I'm here."

Jerry walked to the door. He cracked it open and paused before he strode back over, pulled her up into his arms, and kissed her one last time. "Damn, I missed you." Then he left, leaving her standing next to the bed. Her heart hammered faster than a horse running the Kentucky Derby.

Anna pressed her fingers to her lips. She couldn't believe it. Jerry was coming for her tonight. Anna stepped over to Ruby's vanity, picked up a hairbrush, and began to brush her hair. She opened a tube of coral lipstick and applied it to her lips.

Anna went over to the door and peeked outside. She didn't see anyone, so she quickly walked down the hall and into the bathroom.

Anna's skin flushed pink. It wouldn't take a rocket scientist to figure out what she had been doing. Anna began to breathe in and out slowly to settle her racing pulse. She looked around the drawers in the cabinets until she found Lee's makeup case. Anna tried to make herself presentable before she went back downstairs.

Anna had waited for ten minutes before she descended the stairs. On the bottom step, Sandy grabbed her hand and dragged her outside. Anna followed Sandy around the back of the house. Sandy stopped and turned to face her.

Sandy threw her hands in the air in apparent frustration. "Have you lost your mind? I see you certainly did a lot of talking. I'd know that look a mile away. I have some whiskey in the glove box of my car if you need to take a shot. Jesus, Anna, you said talk to Jerry, not have sex with him. I'm pretty sure Rachel's drunk and that may be the only thing that saves your hide this afternoon."

Anna rolled her eyes. "Don't have a cow. I didn't have sex with Jerry. We just kind of made out." With a wide grin, she said, "But we're running away together tonight. He's coming for me at Ruby's." Anna opened the door to Sandy's car, reached inside the glove box, and twisted the top off of a small bottle of Crown Royal. She took a sip from the whiskey bottle and handed it to Sandy.

Sandy took a sip of whiskey. "What the hell does that mean?"

Anna squared her shoulders. "That means if Jerry doesn't change his mind, and he comes for me tonight, we're running away together. Dad-blame it, Sandy. I wasn't kidding around. My heart has always belonged to him, and you know it. I'm marrying Jerry if he still wants me, too."

Sandy leaned her back against the car. "Holy shit, I mean h-o-l-y shit."

Anna started walking back toward the house, and Sandy followed a few steps behind. They entered the house by the back kitchen door. Anna glanced into the den where Rachel had her arm around Jerry's waist. It was all Anna could do not to go over there and rip Rachel's arm off him. Anna began to breathe hard and started toward the den when Sandy grabbed her hand.

Sandy whispered, "Do not go in there. Let it go, Anna."

Ruby walked into the kitchen, leaned over to Anna, and whispered in her ear, "Looks like you've got your way, Annabelly." She kissed Anna's cheek and placed her right hand on her right hip. "Reed just told me y'all were running away tonight. I just knew Jerry still loved you. I'm so glad you came home. You've saved Rachel and Jerry from a lifetime of sadness. He would've never been happy, and Rachel would've been miserable."

Anna said excitedly, "I still can't believe it." She was afraid to say much, in case things didn't work out.

Chapter 16

Love Is a Battlefield

JERRY AND RACHEL DROVE BACK to his house in strained silence. He'd built the house with the help of some of his subcontractor friends. The three-bedroom brick house was the last house on the right in a subdivision located next to a large farm. Jerry had planted trees and landscaping in the front yard, but the backyard still had an old tractor lane with established trees from the family who'd previously owned the farm.

Jerry parked his truck beside Rachel's red Mercedes. He walked into the kitchen and grabbed a beer out of the refrigerator. Rachel locked the door and draped the shoulder strap of her purse on the back of one of the kitchen chairs.

Jerry ran his fingers through his hair. "I need to talk to you."

Rachel stretched and yawned. "Hon, I'm exhausted. Can't this wait until tomorrow?"

Jerry turned and faced Rachel and pointed to the chair. She sat down and looked up at him. "Rachel, I'm not going to mince words here. I'm just going to tell you flat out."

Rachel narrowed her eyes at him and placed her left forearm on the kitchen table. "What are you saying, Jerry? Tell me flat out about what? That you banged Anna upstairs this afternoon? Do I look like an idiot? I could smell that bitch on you from a mile away. Now can I go to bed?" Rachel stood, but Jerry placed his hand on her shoulder to stop her from storming off.

Jerry looked into Rachel's eyes and calmly said, "I can't marry you. I don't want to marry you."

Rachel punched Jerry hard in the stomach, and then she gave him a roundhouse to his left eye. Jerry grabbed both her hands firmly to stop any further assault.

Rachel trembled, and her eyes bulged with anger. She shouted, "You cocksucker. Do you expect me to be a laughing stock among our family and friends? I thought you just needed to get her out of your system."

Jerry narrowed his eyes at her. "If I let you go, are you going to hit me again?"

Rachel took some deep breaths in and out and shrugged out of his grip. "I'm not going to hit you."

Jerry stepped away from Rachel and leaned against the kitchen cabinet. "Rachel, I will never have Anna out of my system, and I've told you how much I love her. You've always known, and I've never lied to you about my feelings for her."

Rachel ran over to him and reared back to smack him again, but Jerry grabbed her wrist. "Jerry, you lied to me. You said you could be happy with me. You said we would have kids. You said you would marry me." She stepped back to the table and placed her hands palms down to support herself, then stood there breathing hard.

Jerry closed his eyes briefly and said, "Yes, I did. I said all of those things. I'm sorry, Rachel, I am. I wanted to believe I could go through with it. And God knows you worried the shit out of me until I said yes. But I was honest and told you I was in love with Anna before we ever agreed to get married. You know I care for you, but you also know I've never loved you. You deserve more than I can give you, and so do I. I know you think you love me. But I'm just something your daddy couldn't buy." Jerry shoved his hands into his pockets. "I'll take full responsibility, and I'll tell your parents."

Rachel grabbed the glass flower vase off the table and threw it at Jerry. It smashed against the cabinets, missing Jerry's head by inches and spraying fragments of glass across the room.

Jerry quickly ducked and shouted, "You crazy bitch. Have you lost your damn mind?

Rachel's eyes were bloodshot and red. "Hell, yes, I'm the crazy bitch that is going to be your worse fucking nightmare. You will not call my family or my friends. I swear as I stand here, Jerry Mac, if you don't marry me, you'll come home from work one day and find your precious little Anna has met with some accident. Maybe a little battery acid to the face would do the trick." She glared at him in a fit of fury.

Jerry strode across the room and slammed Rachel against the wall. His nostrils flared, and his tempered soared at the thought of Rachel hurting Anna. "I swear to all that is holy, if you touch one hair on Anna's head, I'll kill you."

Rachel blinked and began to struggle to get out of his hands, and she kneed him in the groin. He stumbled backward. With hatred, he said, "I've never struck a woman in my life. But if you touch me again, I will. If you go near Anna, I swear, woman, I'll kill you with my bare hands. Do you understand me, Rachel? Do you hear what I'm saying?"

Rachel stepped over to him and spat in his face, and he wiped it off with the back of his hand. She shouted, "Do you think I care if you kill me? I don't. If I can't have you, then she can't, either."

Jerry grabbed his truck keys off the counter and started toward the door. Rachel ran and grabbed his arm. "Don't do this, Jerry. Don't leave me." He jerked away and looked down at her with sadness. What had he seen in her? He'd never even known Rachel, not really.

Rachel let him go, straightened her shoulders, and jutted out her chin. "If you walk out the door, I'll call my daddy. He knows some pretty unsavory people from back east. They're really good at cutting off fingers and making people disappear. It'll be kind of hard for Anna to practice medicine without fingers."

Jerry looked at Rachel and saw nothing but pure evil. A quiet calm came over him, and he knew he was in the presence of his guardian. He said in a low and even tone, "I'm leaving. You have one week to get your things out of my house." And he walked out the door, got into his truck, and drove straight to Nelson Doune Farms.

RACHEL WATCHED IN DISMAY AS Jerry pulled out of their driveway. Had it only been two days ago that Jerry had held her in his arms and made love to her? Then her life turned completely upside down with the passing of Joseph Campbell.

Rachel's stomach muscles had clenched with panic yesterday

when Anna had bumped into Jerry at Ruby's house. The look the two had exchanged had Rachel all twisted up inside. She had tried to act like everything was normal. Jerry had been most attentive to her through the funeral—until this afternoon, that is.

Rachel and Jerry had gone to the wake at Everglade Farms after the burial. Rachel had pitched in and helped Lee and Ruby in the kitchen. The more the afternoon wore on, the more cocktails Rachel drank. She had wanted to smoke a cigarette and Sandy asked her to go outside for some air. Rachel hadn't thought anything odd about Sandy's request until she walked back into the house and found Jerry and Anna gone.

Rachel had shot Sandy a knowing look. Sandy had played her. That bitch was going to get hers, too. Rachel had stood in the Glenn's den barely comprehending the conversations carrying on around her. That was when she'd noticed Jerry descend the stairs. He'd strolled over to the bar and poured a shot of whiskey. He tossed it back without blinking. Then he'd joined her. Jerry had talked and laughed with Brent and Reed, but Rachel smelled the whore on him.

Rachel had shaken with anger on their ride home. Jerry had driven in silence. She'd followed him inside to the kitchen where a sense of foreboding engulfed her. Like she had a weight placed around her neck. Jerry had broken their engagement. Rachel had addressed and stamped their wedding invitations, and they were in the outgoing mailbox at Jerry's office. The church had been booked, along with the country club for the reception.

Now that Jerry was gone for good, Rachel slowly made her way into the living area and picked up a photo of her and Jerry skiing in Colorado last winter. She placed the photo back on the mantel and turned around to look at her well-ordered and stylishly-decorated home. No, not her home. Jerry told her she had one week to move out. Damn it all to hell. After all the time they had shared, he gave her one week to move out. Rachel flew into a rage. She placed her hands on the mantel and swept their photos off with such force they smashed into the wall before crashing to the floor.

"Watch it, human. You nearly hit me." Luc leaned against the wall with one foot over the other. He walked over to the mantel and reached down for one of the photos. "Fun times, huh?"

Rachel looked at the man standing by the fireplace. "You. You're the one who did this? You're the one who was on the porch?" She went to hit Luc, and he threw her against the wall with his mind. Rachel fell to the ground and blood trickled from her lip.

"Be careful, human. I gave you the boy. You couldn't keep him. Now he's gone back to Anna, and their team is solidified again. You worthless piece of shit."

Rachel's eyes went wide with terror. She didn't move from the floor, but her body rose off the ground, and she was thrown again into the couch. Rachel screamed, "I think you just broke my arm, asshole."

Luc laughed. "Really? And I wasn't even trying. Now, why don't you tell me what you're going to do to prevent Jerry from marrying Anna? Because if you don't, the demons inside you now will seem like silly schoolgirls on a picnic when I get inside you."

Panicked, Rachel closed her legs and Luc roared with laughter. He said, "I'm not going to fuck you, idiot. I'm going to fill you with so many demons that you'll go completely insane, and you won't be passing into the great white hall, but you'll reside in the red room of death."

Minutes or hours passed. Rachel couldn't remember trashing the house. She looked around at the destruction. Her arm hurt, and her lip was split. *How in the hell did I do that?*

She picked up the phone and called her father.

Hazel, her parent's maid, answered the phone. "Nelson Doune Farms."

Rachel's voice quivered as she said, "Hazel, I need to talk with Dad."

"Ms. Rachel, he's in the study with Mr. McDaniel."

Rachel gritted her teeth. Jerry had gone straight to her dad. She let out a heavy sigh and said, "Thanks, Hazel. I'm sorry if I woke you."

"Ms. Rachel, are you okay?"

Rachel shook her head. "No, Hazel, I'm not." She hung up, glanced around at the aftermath of her destruction, and dialed zero. "Operator, would you give me the phone number and address for Anna Kelly in Pensacola, Florida, please?" Rachel jotted down the information on the notepad next to the phone. She called and booked a flight to Florida.

Rachel grabbed her overnight bag and threw in some clothes and toiletries. She flew out the back door and jumped into her car. On Interstate 24, Rachel smashed the gas pedal to the floor, drove to the Nashville airport, and boarded the plane in first class.

JERRY PULLED UP TO THE security gate and found Zeke asleep. He rolled down his window. Jerry whistled, and Zeke shot out of his chair like a silver bullet. Zeke looked at his watch. "Kind of late for a visit, isn't it, boy? Is Mr. Doune expecting you?"

Jerry shook his head and leaned his forearm on the edge of the car door. "No, it's urgent. I have to talk to him now."

Zeke walked over to Jerry's truck and his eyes widened. He whistled. "Rachel slugged you? Man, that's going to leave one hell of a shiner. I guess you're lucky she didn't kill you. But I'm not surprised. Rachel's a wild one. I'll phone, go on ahead."

"Thanks, Zeke." Jerry pulled up the long driveway and parked in the circular drive in front of the main house. He walked up the steps to a huge veranda with its white columns and huge planters overflowing plants and vines. Jerry pressed the doorbell, and the door opened. It was Hazel, the Doune's maid.

Hazel fastened her robe around her tightly. "Mr. Doune will be down in a minute. He said to put you in his study. Would you like a drink, Mr. McDaniel?"

Jerry smiled at Hazel with kindness. "No, Hazel." She ushered him into the study and left. The room was full of Nelson's taxidermy trophies from all over the world. The floors were covered with genuine Persian silk and wool handmade rugs. He walked around the back of Nelson's elaborately-carved eighteenth century American desk. It was a bonnet-topped mahogany secretary, carved with a block-and-shell. Behind the desk, Jerry looked out at the Doune estate through eight-foot windows.

Jerry couldn't shake from his mind all of the horrible things Rachel said to him. It was all he thought about on his drive to Arrington to speak with Rachel's father. He couldn't take any chances with Anna. Rachel had threatened Anna with serious bodily harm.

Nelson walked into his study with a heavy brocade robe tied over his paisley silk pajamas. He didn't say anything at first but walked straight to his liquor table, reached for his bottle of Hennessy, and poured a drink for himself and one for Jerry. Jerry picked up the glass and took a gulp.

In front of the fireplace, Nelson went over and sat down in a leather chair and crossed his leg over his knee. "Please sit down, Jerry. I assume this must be pretty damn important to get me out of bed."

Jerry sat down in the matching leather chair next to Nelson. "Sir, I wouldn't be here if it wasn't. I broke off my engagement with Rachel tonight."

Nelson's eyes widened as he looked at Jerry's black eye and frowned. He took a long pull from his drink and set the glass down on the marble-top walnut side table. Nelson took a deep breath. "Would this have anything to do with Ms. Kelly coming back to town?"

Jerry held the tulip snifter in his hand and nodded. "Yes, sir, it does. I'm sorry. I never intended to hurt Rachel or your family. But I can't marry her knowing I'm in love with someone else. I should've called off our engagement before now. I should've never agreed to marry her. But your daughter is the most persistent person I've ever known and doesn't take the answer no well."

Nelson chuckled and said, "She, unfortunately, takes after me, son. I do think of you as my son, and I looked forward to having you in my family. But if you don't love Rachel, in the long run, you both would live miserably. I take it by your black eye Rachel didn't take the news well."

Jerry glanced down to the rug for a second before looking back at Mr. Doune. "No, sir. That would be an understatement. Rachel threatened Anna with battery acid and said you had friends in New York who would cut off Anna's fingers and make her disappear."

Nelson winced at Jerry's words, then pinched the bridge of his nose with his forefinger and thumb. He leaned back in his chair and looked at Jerry. "Rachel should've never threatened Anna. I'm sorry. As for me and my contacts, you have no reason to fear. I would never hurt you or Anna. My daughter, however, is another story. There's no telling what she'll do." Nelson stepped over to the fireplace, placed his hand on the mantel, and turned back to face Jerry. "Rachel has experienced control issues in the past. Her erratic behavior was one of the reasons we left New York. She accidentally killed her best friend."

Jerry fell back against the chair and gulped the rest of his drink. "Dear God, what happened?"

Nelson shook his head in sadness. "Her friend, Vanessa, came to me with concerns over Rachel. Rachel had made some sexual advances toward Vanessa that she wouldn't reciprocate. I suggested that she place some distance between herself and Rachel until things blew over."

Nelson poured another drink and sat back down across from Jerry. "Vanessa told Rachel her parents were sending her away to a boarding school in England. Rachel lost her temper and pushed Vanessa. She fell from the top stairs of our balcony. The poor girl broke her neck and died instantly." He took a long pull from his drink. "It was an ugly scandal, and I had to pad a lot of wallets to keep Rachel out of jail. I moved here in hopes of building a new life for Rachel and us."

Jerry ran both hands through his hair. "Jesus, Nelson. You knew Rachel fixated on me from the beginning. You didn't stop her or warn me. You need to lock her up and throw away the damn key because I swear I'll kill her if she hurts Anna."

Nelson shot Jerry a menacing look. "Do not threaten me, boy. As crazy as she may be, Rachel is still my daughter, and I'll protect her. You should've never agreed to marry her. I'll try to talk to her tomorrow, but if I were you, I would get Anna out of town as fast as you can. I'll see if I can find Rachel a new play toy in the meantime."

Jerry stared at Nelson in shock. "You—you used me as her play toy. You used me. Can't you see Rachel needs to be in a hospital?"

Nelson drank the rest of his cognac and sat the empty glass on the table. "Yes, I'm afraid you speak the truth. I'm not proud of what I've done. I know she should be in a facility somewhere. You won't understand until you have kids of your own. She's my baby girl." He turned to Jerry and said, "It's time for you to leave, Jerry. Where's Rachel now? I need to bring her home."

Jerry stood to leave. "She's at my house. After our fight, I told her she had one week to get her things out."

"Jesus, Jerry, she'll burn the place to the ground. I've got to go. Let yourself out." Nelson walked swiftly from the room.

Jerry picked up the phone and called Reed. The phone rang twice before Reed answered. Jerry relayed the events of the evening. "Reed, tell Anna to be ready in twenty minutes. We're flying out of here tonight."

ANNA KEPT LOOKING AT THE clock as she nervously paced the floor. It was nearing midnight and still no sign of Jerry. Maybe he had changed his mind. Ruby and Reed had gone to bed around ten. The telephone rang, and Anna froze. She waited in the living area for Reed or Ruby to come out of their bedroom.

Reed and Ruby walked out together, and Anna could tell by the look on their faces that whatever had happened, the news wasn't good. Anna propped herself against the sofa to keep from falling to the ground. "For the love of God, what's happened?"

Reed had his arm around Ruby, and she leaned against him with tears in her eyes. He said, "Get your things quickly. Jerry broke his engagement and Rachel has threatened you. He believes Rachel will try to carry out her threats. You and Jerry are flying out tonight."

Anna's eyes watered, and she looked over to Ruby, who was visibly frightened. She turned and took the stairs two at a time. She began throwing her things into her suitcase. Ralph's words played like a broken record. *Someone will get hurt.* Anna had her bags packed and was downstairs in nine minutes. Jerry came in the front door, and Anna threw herself into his arms.

Jerry held her tight and placed kisses all over her face. "Anna, if anything happens to you, I—I..."

She stopped him and placed her fingers over his mouth. "Don't. It's over, and we're together." She turned and went to Ruby and hugged her tightly. "Ruby, I love you with all my heart." Anna glanced up to Reed and said, "Take care of my sister."

Ruby squeezed her hand. "Go. Call me when you get to Florida. Let us know you're safe. I'll call Sandy. Do you want me to call your parents?"

Jerry walked up beside her and caught her hand in his. She

looked up at him. "No, I don't want to worry them. I'll call them in the morning."

Jerry let go of Anna's hand and hugged Ruby and Reed. "I'll leave my truck at the Holiday Inn. I don't want to leave it here and cause problems for y'all." He turned to Reed and said, "I have an extra set of keys at my office. I'll call Kaye in the morning and let her know you're coming Monday to pick them up. Take the truck and put it in my dad's barn. Reed, one more thing, would you take one of the deputies and check on my house. Nelson thinks Rachel might try to burn it to the ground. Call your real estate buddy and tell him I want to place it on the market. I don't care what he can get for it. I just want to get rid of it."

Reed clasped Jerry's shoulder. "Be safe, man. I'll take care of things here."

Jerry draped his arm around Anna. "Let's go, Annabelly."

Anna waved as they walked out the front door. Outside, she looked up at Jerry. "Do you think it's safe to go to my house in Florida? Cary has a security system."

"Anna, I don't care where we go as long as it's far away from here."

ANNA AND JERRY STEPPED UP to the ticket counter at the Nashville airport and inquired on flights to Pensacola or any destination close to the area. Jerry leaned his forearm on the counter and smiled warmly at the ticket agent. He said, "See, we're eloping tonight." Jerry kissed the top of Anna's head, and she smiled up at him.

The female ticket agent swooned and began to type. "You're in luck, Mr. McDaniel. They're just boarding 1205 to Pensacola now. If you hurry, you can make it. Would you like coach or first class?"

Jerry handed her his credit card. "First class."

RACHEL'S EYES WIDENED IN UTTER shock when Jerry and Anna boarded her flight. She sat two rows behind them and slumped down in her seat. As soon as she noticed them fasten their seatbelts, Rachel slipped out of her seat and dashed into coach. She went up to a flight attendant. "I'd like to request a favor. My old boyfriend and his new squeeze just boarded this flight. I don't want to sit behind them. Is it okay for me to sit back here in one of the empty seats?" Rachel pressed a hundred-dollar bill in the flight attendants' hand.

The attendant nodded and smiled. "You leave everything to me." A tear ran down Rachel's cheek, and the flight attendant patted her shoulder and walked away from her station toward first class.

Rachel sat down in the back, next to a window, but kept her eye on first class. It was still dark outside when the plane took off. An hour and a half later, the flight landed, and the attendant came back and told her Jerry and Anna had exited the plane. Rachel stayed back until all of the passengers left and then made her way to a coffee shop in the terminal. She wanted to give Jerry and Anna plenty of time to leave the airport.

After Rachel had finished her second cup of coffee, she went to Hertz and rented a black Audi sedan. She walked out of the terminal, and the warm Florida breeze hit her face. Rachel found the rental and made her way to the hotel on the beach. She rented an oceanfront suite, threw her bag on the bed, and looked inside the desk drawer for a phone book. The sun was coming up as she opened the sliding glass door and peered out at the slow ocean waves rolling onto the white sand beach.

Rachel sat down in one of the plastic chairs on the little balcony. She thumbed through the yellow pages until she found a local gun shop, and she ripped the page from the book. They opened at eight.

Rachel opened her purse and pulled out a vial of cocaine. She lifted a bump to each nostril and sniffed. Jerry had been clueless about her love for the white pony. She had worked for years cultivating the relationship with the farm boy turned computer geek. Jerry wasn't only gorgeous but sweet and kind.

At first, Jerry playing hard to get had been part of a game to Rachel. A contest of wills. Rachel had become his friend and hung out with him so much over the years that he'd given her keys first to his condo and then to his house. That was how she found out Anna had attempted to reconcile with him, and luckily Rachel had intercepted several phone messages and letters. She had deleted the messages and thrown away Anna's letters, all except for the last one. Anna's last letter begged Jerry to come back to her, and that letter gave Rachel fuel for her fire.

Rachel had finally won, and they were supposed to get married until that bitch flew home on her broomstick. Rachel took another bump. She had no intention of going to sleep, not until Anna Kelly had a bullet in her brain.

Chapter 17

Lay Your Hands on Me

ANNA COULDN'T BELIEVE EVERYTHING THAT had happened in the last couple of days. A smile curved her lips. *Good things do come to those who wait.* She pushed all thoughts of Rachel out of her mind.

Jerry had come for her just like he promised, and they had escaped to her home in Florida. Anna believed in fate and destiny. She laid her head on Jerry's chest, felt the thump of his heartbeat, and watched his chest move up and down while he slept.

Rays of sunlight shot through her bedroom window. She was too excited to sleep. Her fingers played with the hairs on Jerry's chest, and he stirred. Anna whispered, "Jerry, are you awake?"

"Uh-huh." He rolled over, wrapped his arms around her, and pressed his face into her neck. "Aren't you sleepy?"

Anna rolled back over to face him and brushed the hair from his forehead. "No, not at all. I still can't believe you're here with me—in my bed. I'm too excited to sleep. Lie back for a minute. I'm going to heal your black eye." Jerry closed his eyes, and the tips of her fingers tingled as she placed them over his eye. A minute later, she said, "Open your eyes. Your black eye is gone."

Jerry's beautiful blue eyes opened and looked into hers with such love. He leaned in and kissed her softly on her lips. She ran her tongue over his lips and into his mouth.

Jerry broke from her kiss and glanced at the clock on her nightstand. "It's nine o'clock, marry me?"

Anna giggled and kissed him again. "Really? Are you sure?"

Jerry's hand ran down to her bum, and he squeezed. "I've always wanted to marry you. I just got sidetracked for the last six years. You think it's too soon?"

"Hell, naw. I'm ready, Jerry. I'm never letting you go again. Would it be okay if we walked over to Cary's first? I want you to meet him and Maria. They've been wonderful to me while I've lived here. And I would love to get married on his front lawn with the ocean as a backdrop. Cary's place is like something out of *Better Homes and Gardens* or maybe *Southern Living*." She sat up, crossed her legs, and fiddled with the edges of her pillowcase.

Jerry squeezed her hand. "Don't be nervous, Anna. I would marry you on the moon if you asked me right now." He sat up and leaned against the headboard. "But I only have the clothes on your chair. Is that all right with you?"

Anna grinned. "Not to worry. Just down the street is Paul Parsons Men's shop. He has everything from jeans to tuxedoes. We'll stop by and pick you up a pair of off-white pants and a white button-down after we get our license. I have a long, creamy white dress I bought last year for a fundraising event for the hospital. You'll love it."

Jerry pulled her up into an embrace. "I'd love you in your birthday suit."

"It won't be anything fancy, but I would like to tell our grandchildren one day about my wedding day."

Anna leaned against his shoulder, and he kissed the top of her head. "Lots and lots of grandchildren."

She happily replied, "Lots and lots."

He said, "Let's take a shower. Then we'll go to Cary's and *then* we'll go to the county clerk to get a license."

She playfully jumped off the bed and teased, "Oh, no, no showers together until you say I do."

Jerry jumped off the bed, buck naked, and gave chase. Anna ran into the bathroom, and he scooped her up from behind. "Are you kidding me? I'm not waiting another damn minute to see you in the buff, woman."

As his head bent down to kiss her, he smelled good. A trace of sweat and masculine musk filled the air she breathed. Jerry brushed her hair off one of her shoulders and kissed her neck. He took a deep breath and let out a moan that sent shivers up her spine.

Anna reached out and placed the palm of her hand on the curve of his face. A shock of his blond hair fell forward, and she twisted her fingers in his silky, soft hair. She murmured, "Oh, I've missed you."

Jerry trailed his fingers down her cheek and across her bottom lip. He leaned in and pulled and tugged on her bottom lip, sucking it into his mouth. An intense sensation hit her hard. She pulsed and throbbed with need from his kiss.

She whispered, "I love you." His eyes darkened, and his lids were hooded and heavy with desire. The chemistry between the two of them rose higher and flowed like a raging river.

Anna pulled him to her mouth, and years of pent up passion exploded. She kissed him savagely, drawing him to her, cupping his face with her hands. Her tongue licked the edges of his lips, and she began nibbling his lower lip and gliding softly over the top before delving her tongue into his warm mouth. Tasting and twisting, balancing between playful and passionate. One of Jerry's hands kneaded her bum while the other worked its way up her torso.

"Sweet heaven, that's what you are to me. Sweet heaven." He kissed her again and again.

The anticipation of having him inside her made her squirm under his touch, and she pleaded, "I need you to touch me."

JERRY LAID HER DOWN ON the bed, and the love he had for Anna hit him square in his chest. Anna pulled her T-shirt gown over her head and threw it on the floor. She was perfect to him in every way. The streaks of sunlight cast a honey glow on her sweet, fragrant hair. The curve of her beautiful face and soft peachy skin as she lay on the bed was a vision to behold. Jerry marveled at her beauty from her firm breasts to her flat stomach right down to the thatch of soft, blonde curls of her sex. He adored her.

With a hoarse voice, he said, "You're as pretty as a picture lying there with your dreamy eyes staring up at me. God, Anna, my damn heart feels like it's going to jump right out of my chest." He held her delicate hand, reached down, and licked and sucked the sensitive flesh between her fingers.

Anna closed her eyes and released a breathy moan. "Oh, God,

Jerry, what are you doing to me?" She opened her eyes and wet her lips.

Jerry glanced up and smiled. "I just want to give you pleasure, my sweet Anna."

Her smile lines around her brilliant blue eyes creased with laughter, and her pouty pink lips parted. She said, "I've dreamed of you here, just like this, with me." Anna pinched his arm.

"Ouch, I'm here, I promise." He chuckled and rubbed his arm. Jerry leaned down and kissed her slowly and deeply, and he circled his arms around her. He ran one hand down her back to cup her butt cheek. He was having a hard time breathing. It had been six long years since he had seen her lovely body. It had been six long years since he had made love to her. He laughed out loud.

Anna's face leaned in less than an inch from his. "What's so funny?"

Jerry brushed a strand of hair away from her face. "I'm laughing because I feel like a kid staring at the front counter candy, and you're the candy."

Anna brushed her soft lips across his. "I know what you mean. I can't keep my hands off of you. I want to kiss you, to hold you, to touch you and to feel you inside me." She kissed him softly on each cheek, and he closed his eyes to the wonderful sensations of her touch on his skin. She kissed each eyelid and the tip of his nose before pushing her tongue inside his mouth.

Jerry quickly flipped her onto her back and propped himself on his side. Then he bent down and latched onto one of her nipples, sucking and pulling until she released a throaty sigh. His hand ran gently along the curve of her calf and caressed the soft skin at the back of her knees. Anna's fingers traced from his shoulder blade down his back with her nails digging into his skin.

Jerry moved from one breast to the other, pressing kisses south to her navel. He ran his fingers across the plane of her flat abdominals, downward over her short soft curls, and over into her glistening sex. Anna quivered and jerked when he stuck his tongue in her belly button. He murmured against her skin, "Ticklish?"

"Very ticklish."

Jerry glanced up into her sweet, lovely face and saw the raw, sexual hunger in her eyes. "Oh, honey, I need you, and I need you now."

Jerry swiftly shifted and began trailing kisses up her inner thighs. He loved the feeling of his lips next to her soft, slippery folds. Anna opened for him like the petals of a morning flower basking in the sun. The silky taste of her made him moan in pleasure as she arched and lifted her hips against him. He gently pressed deeper and teasingly pulled away. He began French kissing her until her body responded with total satisfaction, reflected in the color of her heated skin that flushed pink. Instead of releasing her, he lingered there, loving her for a moment longer until her love slowly ebbed.

"Ahh—oh, Jerry, I need you now. Please..." She begged and gripped his biceps.

Jerry rose above her and placed his hands palm down on either side of her. Anna relaxed her legs, and he slid between them. "Anna, oh, you're so ready, aren't you, love?"

Anna moaned and arched again. "Yes, for crying out loud, Jerry. Quit tormenting me. I need you, damn it."

Jerry nearly lost it from the first touch of her warm silken skin wrapped around him like a tight, hot glove. The scent of her sweet arousal coiled and fisted in his lower spine. Jerry's blood pounded through his veins, and he throbbed inside her as he tried to make the moment last.

Anna was so hot that his body shook and trembled with desire for her. He strained with an urgent need to release to the point of sweet pain. He was crazy with the want of her as he slowly stroked her and she released her little, throaty sighs. His heart nearly burst with love as he screamed out her name. The love he felt for her was why poets wrote love poems. Jerry's last thought before he melted into oblivion: *Anna.*

ANNA AND JERRY STROLLED PAST the pool through the lush gardens of Cary's estate. They held hands, rocking them back and forth, as they walked up the steps of the back porch to the double doors. Anna pressed the doorbell and turned to smile at Jerry. She had been humming an old Doris Day tune her mom used to sing to her when she was a little girl. She caught the smell of the ocean breeze and let out a deep sigh. Everything about this moment was perfect.

Jerry leaned over to her and whispered, "You've been living in paradise."

Anna butt-bumped him. "Nope, I just started living in paradise today."

RUBY CALLED, AND ANNA'S PHONE went straight to her answering machine. She sniffled and brushed the tears away from her face. "Anna, it's Ruby. Please call me. Rachel's in Pensacola. I've had a dream. Rachel's in your house with a gun. Please, please call me as soon as you get this message. Be careful."

Reed wrapped his arms around Ruby. Her head fell against his shoulder, and she cried. He said, "There, there, baby, please don't cry, princess. It's tearing me apart, and you've done all you can do. Think about the baby. You're still in your first trimester. Please, honey."

Ruby tried to steady her breathing and looked up into his eyes. "I'm so tired, Reed, so very tired of these dreams. I don't know if they're a curse or a blessing."

RACHEL PARKED DOWN THE STREET at the public beach and walked to Anna's house. She had watched Jerry and Anna have sex through the bedroom window like a Peeping Tom, but Rachel had no shame. She had no pride left. Hate was the only thing left inside her. Rachel slipped into Anna's house through the sliding glass doors next to the swimming pool when Jerry and Anna left for the big house next door.

The telephone rang, and the answering machine picked up the call. Rachel listened to Ruby's message. Then she pressed the delete button. She went through Anna's rooms, picking up things at random and smashing them to the floor. Rachel picked up a photo of Anna, Jerry, Ruby, Reed, and Sandy. It must have been their graduation from MTSU. They were in their caps and gowns. Rachel opened the frame, lifted the photo, and ripped it into tiny pieces.

Rachel stepped into the master bedroom, and the scent of sex made bile rise in her throat. She fled from the room, ran into the guest bathroom and threw up. Rachel turned on the cold water, cupped her hands under the faucet and pressed her face down into the water, anger and hatred boiling inside her, festering and rotting her soul.

Anna's front doorbell rang, and Rachel ignored it. She stepped into the kitchen and rifled through Anna's fridge. There was a knock on the sliding doors and Rachel lifted her head. *Jesus, what a hunk.* A good-looking man stared back at her and smiled.

Rachel opened the door. "Yes?"

Jack took a step back and said, "Hi, I'm looking for Anna."

Rachel laughed bitterly, and she said, "Aren't we all? Who are you?"

Jack shoved his left hand into his pant pocket and shifted from one foot to the other. "I'm Jack. I work with Anna at the hospital. I was just checking to see if she was back from Tennessee." Jack wore a pair of off-white linen trousers and a black, short-sleeved silk shirt untucked. She looked him over from his head to his sandals. Another time, another place, and she'd be jumping his bones.

Rachel opened the door wider and waved him inside. "Come in. We'll wait together." Rachel noticed a full pot of coffee and cups on the kitchen counter. She turned to Jack and said, "Want a cup of coffee?" Jack smiled, and his Hollywood good looks blinded her.

Jack walked into the kitchen behind Rachel to the coffee pot. "Sure, sounds great. Black is good. How do you know Anna?"

Rachel handed him a cup and motioned for him to sit down at the kitchen table. "Ah, well, we met through mutual friends in Tennessee." Not a lie really. She reached inside her navy blue blazer, and her fingers caressed the pistol she'd just bought. Rachel joined Jack at the table, placed her hands around her coffee cup, and peered through the sliding glass doors across the pool to the main house where Jerry and Anna had just walked inside.

MARIA, CARY'S HOUSEKEEPER, OPENED THE door with a huge grin. "Ms. Anna. You're back. How are you?" Maria glanced over at Jerry and smiled, and he offered Maria his dimple-revealing grin.

"Maria, this is my fiancé, Jerry. Maria is the best cook in the panhandle." Maria beamed with pride at Anna's compliment. Anna said, "Is Cary home? I need to speak with him."

Maria waved them inside. "Yes, yes, Mr. Cary is home. He's in the shower. Come into the kitchen. I'm making some chilaquiles with fried eggs."

Anna and Jerry followed Maria through the foyer to the wide-open living space with incredible views of the ocean from floor-to-ceiling windows. The interior walls were painted a golden beige with white trim. A brown leather sectional couch sat on the white shag carpet in front of a marble fireplace large enough to roast a pig. Large brown wicker ceiling fans rotated slowly over their heads.

Jerry whistled. "Geez Louise, this is how the other half lives."

Anna said, "I told you, *Better Homes and Gardens*."

Anna and Jerry sat at the kitchen bar, and Maria pushed two plates of food in front of them. Anna was starving.

Maria poured two glasses of orange juice and placed them on the bar. "Ms. Anna doesn't cook very well. She likes my cooking." She smiled at Anna.

Anna reached over the bar counter and kissed Maria on the cheek. "Your dad-blamed right, Ms. Anna doesn't cook, period. Why would I want to cook when I can eat Cary's leftovers?" She chuckled. *And I have a guardian angel who cooks like a chef.*

Maria waved her hands. "Eat. Eat. It's not good cold."

Jerry took a bite and moaned in delight. "Maria, it's fantastic. Maybe you could give Anna some lessons." Anna elbowed him in the ribs, and he grunted. Jerry rustled the hair on top of Anna's head, and Maria laughed out loud. She went back to weave her magic at the stove.

Anna and Jerry had been together less than twenty-four hours, and it felt like it used to between them. It was as if the past six years had never happened. Happiness bubbled out of Anna like the water fountain on Cary's front lawn.

Cary stepped inside the kitchen and looked surprised. "Anna, you're back. Who's your friend?"

Anna began to tell Cary the condensed version of her and Jerry's love life from college to the flight out of Nashville last night.

Maria held her hands over her heart and patted it several times. "Aye yai yai. A true love story. 'Tis wonderful, no?"

Anna reached over again and squeezed Maria's hand. "Yes, it's a wonderful love story and my happily ever after." Anna turned to Cary and asked, "Cary, I was wondering if you would allow us to marry on your front lawn. I'm going to make a few calls to some wedding planners and see how fast we can pull this thing off."

Cary gave her a big smile and leaned his forehead against hers. "I'll take care of everything. My wedding gift to you and Jerry. I'll call my golf buddy, Judge McGuire, who can officiate. He owes me a favor and some money." He winked at Jerry and turned to Maria. "Maria, do you think you could handle a cake?"

With arms folded across her chest, Maria said, "Humph, I can do better than that. I'll make dinner and cake. My brother plays in a band, too. Do you want me to call him to play music for your wedding, Ms. Anna? My gift to you."

Anna leaped out of her chair and threw her arms around Maria's shoulders. "Oh, you're the best. Thank you. Thank you." She turned to Cary and said, "Would you give me away?"

Tears filled Cary's eyes, and he said, "I would love to."

Anna caught Jerry's hand and said, "Isn't it wonderful?"

Jerry put his arm around her waist and pulled her up to him, kissing her. "It is. Cary, Maria, thanks so much for helping us out on such short notice."

Cary smiled. "No thanks needed. I've never seen Anna this happy. Be good to her. She is a very sweet girl with a big heart."

Jerry playfully slapped Cary on the back. "No worries there, Cary. I intend to spend the rest of my life making her happy."

Cary pointed to the ocean and said, "You two are welcome to stay here as long as you like, but you might want to look out the window. There's a bad storm rolling in fast. It's getting dark out there."

Anna looked out at the ocean. A tropical storm was churning up the water. "Hey, Maria, flip on the TV and let's see if a hurricane is coming." Maria flipped to the local weather station. The storm brewing outside wasn't in the forecast. Anna said, "Jerry, we'd better fly, or we're going to get drenched." Anna quickly kissed Cary and Maria and then they ran out of the house and down the steps.

Anna and Jerry raced across the lawn, and the ground beneath their feet shook. Anna lost her balance and fell. "God, I think that was an earthquake or somebody just dropped a bomb."

Jerry helped Anna to her feet. The wind blew over the palm trees nearly to the breaking point, and the patio furniture tumbled into the lawn. He chuckled and shouted over the wind, "I take it back. This isn't paradise. Hurry, those clouds look like a tornado might spin out. Jesus, I had an encrypted message about this storm the night before last. This isn't a good sign."

Anna held onto Jerry's shoulder and shouted, "What? Tell me about your message when we get inside."

Anna stepped into the kitchen through the sliding glass doors, and Jerry grabbed her ass, making her squeal with delight. Anna's mouth dropped open. She stopped in her tracks, completely paralyzed with shock because Rachel stood inside her kitchen drinking coffee. Jerry tried to shove Anna behind him, but Anna wouldn't move. Anna yelled at Rachel, "What the hell are you doing in my house?" Anna noticed Jack sitting at the table. *What is he doing here?*

Jack stood and stammered, "I—I was just checking to see if you made it home all right. I have great news. The hospital has made you a good offer to stay." Jack leaned over to kiss Anna, and Jerry shoved Jack in the middle of his chest. Jack stumbled backward against the kitchen cabinets.

Jerry shouted, "Keep your damn hands off her."

Jack flushed with anger and balled his hands into fists, preparing to fight Jerry. "Who the hell are you?"

Rachel started laughing hysterically and clapped her hands. "Oh, this is just too good. I mean, this is too much." She walked over to stand between the men. "Please allow *me* to make the introductions." Rachel pointed to Jerry and said, "This is my fiancé, or ex-fiancé, as of, oh, what, sixteen hours ago. See, Jerry ran off with Anna last night, and I am just guessing here, that she's your piece of ass." Rachel threw her head back and laughed again.

Jerry's face flushed red with anger. "Get the hell out of here, Rachel, or I'm calling the cops."

Anna looked to each of them as if stuck in some bad B movie that kept rolling in slow motion. Ralph materialized beside her, and the hair on her arms rose. He said, "Rachel has a gun. Demons consume her, and they're eating her soul from the inside out."

Rachel reached into her blazer pocket, pulled out a pistol, and aimed it directly between Anna's eyes. Anna stared straight into Rachel's eyes without moving. Rachel said, "Jerry, you know how I love to pull a trigger. Step away from her and I won't kill you. But if you don't, it's no sweat off my ass to put a bullet in both of your brains."

Jack gasped, stepped back, and threw his hands up. "Rachel, put that gun down."

Rachel never took her eyes off Anna. "Jack, I told this son of a bitch last night that if I can't have him, then she can't, either. I won't be going to prison because as soon as I put a bullet in her head, I intend to put one in mine."

Jerry dropped to his knees and tears rolled down his cheeks. "Rachel, please, don't do this or kill me instead."

Rachel laughed like a madwoman. "Oh, for Chrissakes, Jerry, get off your damn knees. I can kill you, too, if that's what you really want, but this whore gets it first."

Anna's eyes widened, and she looked over Rachel's shoulder. She said, "Luwenia?"

"Hi, Anna." Luwenia walked around Rachel to stand beside Jerry.

The combination of the two angels' radiance shot forth the energy of love into the room. Luwenia placed her hand on Jerry's shoulder and said, "Hello, Jerry. Don't be afraid because I am with you." Jerry looked into Luwenia's eyes, completely dumbfounded. Luwenia turned to Ralph and said, "Do something, Raphael, because my boy's not going down today."

Jerry stood up and stared at his angel. Then he looked at Ralph and Anna. He said, "Oh, boy, this is really bad if my angel is showing up."

Anna never took her eyes off of Rachel's crazed eyes, but she addressed Jerry, "It's going to be okay, honey. There's a reason for everything in life even if we don't understand it at the time."

A sense of peace fell over Anna. She wasn't afraid, and she remembered all of the things Ralph had taught her. She could see Rachel was consumed with demons and felt betrayed, hurt. Anna understood those same feelings. She had felt the same way about Rachel marrying Jerry.

Anna had to take control and the responsibility for her actions. She wouldn't change the last sixteen hours she'd had with Jerry. He had come back to her. Anna took a deep breath and concentrated on her divine powers. The energy tingled through her every pore, and she had a sharp metallic taste in her mouth.

Anna said, "Rachel, I'm a ward of The Creator. Right now, inside you, eating away at your soul are some pretty nasty demons. They're the ones pulling your strings like a master puppeteer. But you know what? Demons can't mess around with a human's free will. You still have a choice. You still have free will."

Rachel backhanded Anna with the gun and quickly pulled the hammer back. "Bitch, you can't have him, period, free will or not."

Jerry lunged forward, and Rachel's look stopped him, "Hon, I'm anxious for her to be dead, too. You make one more step, love, and it's over. I'm debating on shooting her in a few different places, just to watch her slowly bleed to death."

Blood ran down the side of Anna's face. The energy within her began to burn, and the light of love surrounded her. Ralph stepped on one side of Anna and Luwenia stepped on the other. Lastly, Baldric, the Warrior, materialized behind Rachel.

Baldric said, "I couldn't miss the opportunity of sending those demons straight to the Eternal Blackness." Ralph and Luwenia nodded in agreement.

Angels couldn't interfere with free will, either. This was Rachel's decision, her free will. Anna believed that when bad things happened to good people it's the result of someone's free will. She was a prime example. Her life was held in the balance by Rachel's free will.

Anna remembered Ralph's letter about love having the most power in the universe. Anna forgave Rachel, she forgave Jerry, but more importantly, she forgave herself. Anna's body hummed with the energy of love like a thousand bees singing in the air around her.

"Rachel, I don't want to die today. But I will die for Jerry. I've been in love with him for over half of my life." A bolt of light shot out of Anna toward Rachel, rocking Rachel back on her heels.

A demon shot out of Rachel seeking Anna's light of love. Baldric lifted his sword, and with a flick of his wrist, a ray of light pointed toward the demon. Baldric said, "Come to Daddy." The demon shrieked with recognition, and Baldric's sword sliced the demon from belly to nose. The demon disintegrated into black ashes before disappearing into the Eternal Blackness. Baldric looked over to Anna and said, "One down, two more to go."

Anna said softly, barely a whisper, "Rachel, to see one's self as we truly are takes strength and courage and sometimes sacrifice. Do not allow these demons to take your soul."

Rachel's face suddenly softened and then contorted with a look of intense pain.

Anna reached for Rachel and Jerry shouted, "For the love of God, Anna, stop."

Anna held Rachel's gaze and in a low, even tone she said, "Do you know right this minute, in this room, stand three powerful angels, plus your guardian? They can't interfere with human free will, either. But all you have to do is ask them for help, and those angels will silence the demons within you." Ralph and Luwenia placed their hands on Anna's shoulders. Another burst of light energy shot forward from Anna, and Rachel screamed in agony.

Ralph turned his head toward Anna. "That's the other two demons screaming, not Rachel. Talk to her about her parents."

Anna took another deep breath and said, "Do you want to get rid of the demons?"

Tears fell from Rachel's eyes, and she nodded yes but didn't speak. Suddenly Rachel looked like a frightened little child.

The love of light filled the room with radiance, and Anna smiled and nodded to Rachel. "All right, do you love your father and mother?"

Rachel nodded again.

Anna didn't move, and she never broke eye contact with Rachel. "Good, that's really good. Now concentrate on your love for them. Love is the real power. Love is the real magic in the universe. Love is more powerful than all the demons who walk this earth or in hell below. Focus on the love you feel for your mom and dad. Put their faces into your heart and remember, Rachel. Remember your favorite memory with them. Can you tell me about it?"

Rachel began to cry quietly, and her fingers trembled, but the gun was still cocked and ready to fire. "My daddy bought me a pony when I was a little girl. I'm laughing as he picks me up and throws me into the air. My mommy comes over, and I go into her arms. Mommy is kissing me and telling me she loves me. Oh, I love my mama and daddy so much. I love them so much." Rachel dropped the gun to the floor, and she fell back against the wall. She covered her face with her hands and began to cry so hard her shoulders shook.

Another demon escaped from Rachel, jumped into the air, and drove fast toward Anna's soul. Baldric did an 180-degree turn at the speed of light and sliced the demon in half. The demon disintegrated into ash before disappearing into the Eternal Blackness. Baldric hopped back on the balls of his feet and readied himself for the last demon.

Ralph's hand held Anna's shoulder. He leaned in and said, "Anna, the Demon of Jealousy has possessed Rachel for a long time, long before she moved to Tennessee. This demon is strong within her and will not want to let Rachel go without a fight. Be careful. Tread lightly."

Anna started walking toward Rachel, but Jerry grabbed her arm. "Anna, please let me. Let me talk to her."

Anna shook her head slowly and placed her hand on the curve of his face. With sadness, she said, "Jerry, it has to be me. I'm the chosen." Jerry paled, and she gave him a brief kiss then she stepped over to Rachel. Anna paused and turned to Jack. "If things go badly, take Rachel to the psych ward. The phone is right behind you."

Jack said, "Anna, I'm calling them now. They'll be here in ten minutes."

"Good. But I have to help Rachel be free of this demon or her soul will be lost forever." She turned back to Rachel and took one step closer.

Rachel sprang from the floor like a gazelle and grabbed Anna by the throat, choking her. Anna couldn't breathe, and she tried to pry Rachel's fingers away, digging her fingernails into Rachel's skin.

Jerry screamed, "Let Anna go, Rachel. Stop it! You're killing her." He tried to pull Rachel away from Anna. But the demon had taken control of Rachel and was choking the life out of Anna.

Anna kicked Rachel in the shin several times as she locked eyes with Rachel, but the Demon of Jealousy looked back, and he wanted Anna dead. Anna could see the demon. He had soulless black eyes and inky black hair. Darkness oozed from within the demon and venom dripped from his sharp teeth.

Anna had always heard that your life flashed before your eyes right before you died. It was true. At once, all of her memories from loving her family, Ruby, Sandy, and Jerry flooded her mind. Anna burned bright with their love. The power of love shot forth against the demon, and this time, it was Rachel who screamed back with agony. The demon wouldn't let either of them go. The demon knew Anna was dying.

Ralph's translucent wings spanned across the room as he threw orbs of light into Anna's soul to fight the demon. He shouted, "Baelezael, let my ward go."

In a roar, Baelezael spoke in a demonic language stemming back six millennia from his descent to Earth. "I will not let her go until she breathes her last breath. I know Baldric wants to send me to the Eternal Blackness, and I'm taking this one with me."

Anna understood the demon's words. And so did Jerry.

Jerry quit yelling and brushed the back of his hand gently down Rachel's cheek. The demon flinched. Anna knew she didn't have a minute left to live as the tears flowed like a river down Jerry's cheek. He said, "Rachel, I will marry you if that is what you want. We'll get married as God as my witness and before the angels inside this room, but please let Anna go now. Please, you and I will leave here. I will never contact Anna again. I will give you my life, and I will pledge you my loyalty."

Rachel abruptly let Anna go, and Anna fell to the floor. Anna's soul separated from her body. Her spirit looked at Ralph and Jerry. Ralph began reciting a prayer, and he placed his hands on her physical body that lay on the floor.

Anna glanced at the sliding glass doors. Luc hovered outside in the dark storm. Anna could read his thoughts. Luc waited for the moment he could take Anna's power and Rachel's soul, which would be as soon as his demon, Baelezael, won the battle.

Anna gave Luc the smile this time because Jerry's love for her, his sacrifice for her, had doomed Luc's demon. Jerry's love allowed Rachel to use her free will to find love and forgiveness in her heart, which rendered Baelezael powerless. Luc turned away from Anna and dematerialized.

Rachel whipped around to look into Jerry's eyes. "You'll marry me? You would marry me to save her?"

Jerry held Rachel's gaze while he caressed Rachel's cheek with his hand. "Yes, Rachel."

Jack kneeled beside Anna, hoping to help, but it was too late. Tears welled in the corners of his eyes as he looked at her lifeless body on the floor.

Baldric pulled Jack away and said, "Pray for Anna's soul, Jack."

Anna's spirit reached up to touch Jack's shoulder and then she floated through the air to Jerry.

Jerry dropped to his knees on the floor, picked Anna up, and cradled her in his arms. "I would do anything to save Anna." Rachel cried tears of compassion for Jerry, and Anna smiled as the last demon left Rachel's soul.

Instantaneously, Anna's soul melted back into her physical body.

Baldric flew into the air, his sword held with both hands over his head, and stabbed the Demon of Jealousy in its chest as soon as it departed Rachel's soul. Baldric shouted, "The Demon of Jealousy has left the building, thank you very much." Luwenia rolled her eyes and disappeared, and then Baldric vanished.

Anna opened her eyes, and Jerry let out a half cry, half scream. "You're alive. Thank you, Jesus, you're alive." Anna smiled at him. Ralph had given her a second chance at life, and she intended to make the most out of it. Jerry said, "Do you think you can stand?"

Anna nodded and said, "I think so." Jerry helped her to her feet. Ralph had completely healed her.

Rachel's hand went over her mouth and tears fell from her eyes. "Oh, Anna, I'm sorry. I was mad and hurt, and I wanted to hurt you, too. I'm sorry. I lost it." She looked into Jerry's eyes and said, "I can see now the love you two share. I was blind and selfish. Anna tried to contact you over the years, and I intercepted the calls on your answering machine and deleted her messages. I threw away her letters, well, all except one. I still have Anna's last letter. I promise I'll give it back to you. Jerry, please call my daddy and ask him to come and get me. Tell him I'm at the Marriot on the beach."

Jerry had his arm around Anna's waist, and Anna held onto him. He looked at Rachel and said, "I'm sorry, too. I should've let you go way before this got so out of hand."

Rachel sighed heavily and turned to walk out the door when Jack reached out his hand and placed it on her shoulder. Jack said, "I'm sorry, Rachel, but I think you need to go to the hospital. It's for your safety as well as others. The ambulance is outside. I'll help you get checked in. I'll take care of you there."

Rachel looked up into Jack's eyes and nodded. "Yes, Jack. You're right, of course. I'm not thinking straight."

Jack escorted Rachel to the ambulance waiting outside.

Anna tried to wrap her head around the fact she'd died, or, at least she thought she'd died.

Jerry pulled Anna into his arms and smothered her with kisses. They both trembled with emotion. "Oh, God, Anna. I was freaking scared. I knew something bad was going to happen when we had the earthquake. My divine message said there would be an earthquake, and the chosen would save her soul. But everything happened so fast. It was like a nightmare I couldn't wake up from." He turned to Ralph. "Ralph, I'm forever in your debt. Thank you for giving her back to me."

Anna knew Ralph had healed her, but she had a feeling it was Jerry's totally unselfish love that had brought her back to life.

Ralph placed Anna's hand in Jerry's. The room filled with the light of love. Ralph said, "Jerry, love Anna and cherish her. She is a gift from The Creator, and you're blessed to have her in your life." Her cherished guardian angel leaned down and kissed her cheek. "I'll be back for the wedding." He smiled and vanished.

Anna leaned her head on Jerry's shoulder. "Let's go and sit on the patio for a few minutes. I'm still a little shaken. I was terrified when Rachel pointed the gun at my head, but a kind of peace fell over me. Life doesn't end, Jerry. My spirit watched everything, and I heard everything. It's as if my mind was still the same. I just didn't have a physical body. Love lives and lasts forever."

JACK WALKED AROUND THE SIDE of the house to the patio where Anna and Jerry were sitting at a table next to the pool. Jack had called the psychiatric ward at the hospital and pulled a few strings to keep the details of the Rachel incident quiet. Jerry contacted Rachel's parents, and they secured a private plane to fly into the Destin airport. They would be at the hospital within the next hour or so. Jack would be there when they arrived. He wanted to help Rachel.

Jack shook his head back and forth as he sat down next to Anna. He ran his fingers along his jawline. "Angels and demons—real, honest to God angels and demons?"

Anna held Jerry's hand while she looked at Jack. "Yes, Jack. They're real. The lady who hit me in the hospital was possessed by demons, too. But demons can be defeated with love."

Jack drummed his fingers on the table nervously. "You've made me a believer. A real believer. I witnessed a freaking unbelievable miracle."

Anna leaned over and her free hand squeezed his. "There's hope for you yet, Jack."

Jerry ran this thumb back and forth over the back of Anna's other hand. "Hey, Jack, I know by the way you look at her that you're kinda sweet on my Anna, but I need a best man on short notice. We're getting married, and since you live here, I was wondering if you'd stand up with us? So what do you say?"

Jack chuckled and said, "Oh, why the hell not? Or maybe I should say heck?"

Chapter 18

Against All Odds

LATER THAT EVENING, RACHEL SAT in her private hospital room pondering the life-changing events of the day. Just a few days ago, she had been leading a seemingly normal life. In fact, Rachel's life had been pretty great. She had wonderful parents, good friends, and was engaged to a sexy, fun-loving man. Rachel had been on top of the world until Joseph Campbell's death. Then her life changed overnight. Everything changed.

After pulling a gun on Anna, Rachel had watched three demons depart from her soul. She'd had no clue what had been living inside her. Rachel had lived with frequent nightmares over the years. Horrible creatures and darkness often plagued her sleep. And she sometimes found herself doing mean and selfish things to certain people for reasons she didn't always understand. She could only assume the demons had been the cause of her bad dreams and had clouded her judgment in her day-to-day life.

She was glad Jack had called for an ambulance after the debacle with Anna. He discreetly arranged for Rachel's hospitalization in the psych ward at Hall of Saints. She was left exhausted and overcome by a range of feelings—but for the first time in years, Rachel felt free.

Before the ambulance arrived, Rachel had watched Jerry with Anna. Jerry had always loved Anna. Hell, he'd told her as much, and she had listened to his stories about them as a couple, which only stirred up the jealous anger already lurking inside her. Rachel had convinced herself she could heal his broken heart and make him love her instead. She'd even resorted to sabotaging any attempt Anna made at communicating with him. But Jerry never looked at her the way he looked at Anna. If Rachel ever decided to marry, she wanted her betrothed to look at her with the same kind of intensity and the same kind of love as when Jerry looked at Anna.

Jack walked into her hospital room, and she sucked in a deep breath. Jack was beautiful, and his gaze of concern—and something more—made her want to get well fast. He said, "How do you feel, Rachel? You can tell me the truth, and it will stay between us."

Rachel sat up in bed and pulled the blanket over her. "I'm exhausted, but better. I don't feel deranged or want to slash my wrists or anything like that." She probably looked like hell and wished she had her purse, but the nurses took everything from her, including a vial of coke. God, she'd been addicted to cocaine. Rachel shook her head. She had screwed up too many times to count them all.

Jack stepped to the edge of her bed and placed his hands on the rail. "Good, I'm glad. I trust the counseling session with Dr. Adams went well?"

Rachel straightened her spine and smoothed out the covers on her bed. "Dr. Adams is good, and I like her. She's arranging for me to see someone in Tennessee."

Jack looked into her eyes with such compassion and kindness, and her heart squeezed tight. He wasn't just drop-dead gorgeous; Jack was a really good guy. He said, "Hey, your parents are here. They're right outside. Ready to see them?"

Rachel's eyes brightened, and her face lit up with a smile. "Please, I'd love to see my parents."

Jack smiled, and faint lines creased around his eyes. "Okay, I'll send them in. Oh, I have to leave the hospital, but I'll check on you later tonight. The staff can get in touch with me at any time. I've given them instructions to alert me if you need anything. Rachel, you're going to be all right."

Rachel began to cry. "Jack, thank you so much for your kindness. You've been very good to me."

Jack touched her shoulder for a brief moment. His eyes held hers, and for the first time, she had a real honest connection with someone. He said, "You're welcome and ah, well, maybe when I'm no longer your doctor we could go to dinner or something."

Rachel's eyes widened, and she grinned. "Dr. Forrester, I would love to go to dinner with you."

Jack pulled on the lapels of his white coat. "Well, then, that's the best news I've had lately. I'll get your parents." He walked over and opened the door. Nelson and Betty Doune stepped into the room and rushed to their daughter's bedside. Jack looked over his shoulder for a second, smiled, and shut the door behind him.

Three days later

JERRY LOOKED OUT AT THE white sand beach as the crystal clear waves crashed onto shore. A warm ocean breeze caressed his skin like a lover's kiss, and he smiled, thinking of Anna. The sun sat low on the horizon against a backdrop of deep blue skies, and there wasn't a cloud in the sky. A couple of seagulls squawked in the distance. Jerry glanced down at his watch and was getting a little anxious. He stood with Jack at his side. The judge had his back to the ocean, and Maria stood on the other side of the judge. They were waiting for his beautiful bride-to-be.

Jerry looked around Cary's estate. The place could be a set of a romantic movie. Maria's brother's band played a soft Spanish melody. He wore a pair of crisp white linen trousers and a long-sleeved white silk shirt. And Jack, the damn S.O.B., looked like he could star in a romance flick. Jerry decided to forget about the fact that Jack crushed on his girl.

The music switched melodies, and the band began to play the "Wedding Song (There is love)." Jerry glanced up, and Anna stood at the top of the steps with her hand in the crook of Cary's arm. Anna was his, all right, and she only had eyes for him. Jerry looked into her shining, bright eyes, and they reflected back to him the same kind of love he felt for her.

The ocean breeze caught the soft strands of her hair, and one blew across her face. Anna tucked it behind her ear and laughed. She wore a creamy white halter top evening gown with the pearl necklace he bought her their last Christmas together before she left for medical school. Jerry glanced down and chuckled. Anna was also barefoot. God, he loved her. He wanted to memorize every detail of the moment.

The soft strings of the acoustic guitars played in the background. The ceiling fans on the veranda rotated slowly, and he inhaled the salty smell of the ocean mixed with the sweet smell of old garden roses. The stress of the last few days became a distant memory as he took in another lungful of fresh air. He was looking into paradise, and her name was Anna Kelly.

ANNA SMILED DOWN AT JERRY and had the sudden urge to run down the steps to him, but Cary placed her hand in the crook of his arm. He leaned in and said, "You ready, Anna?"

Anna was giddy as a schoolgirl and nodded. "Cary, I'm ready. Let's go." Cary chuckled as they descended the steps. She kept her eyes on Jerry and his beautiful dimples. She was ready to kiss those dimples.

Ralph materialized on her other side. "You're exceptionally beautiful, daughter of my heart. I know you can't say anything, but I'm happy for you and very proud."

Anna stopped once her feet landed on the grass. She turned to face Ralph and squeezed his hand. Anna said aloud, "I love you, Ralph." He smiled.

Cary looked at Anna and said, "Honey, who are you talking to?"

Anna turned back to Cary and gave him a grin. "Why, my guardian angel, of course." Cary chuckled and shook his head.

Anna looked back at Jerry, and standing behind him was the beautiful Luwenia. Anna chuckled and noticed Luwenia only had eyes for Ralph. Anna whispered to Ralph, "You might get lucky today. I see an angel over there who has your number."

Ralph tensed and said, "Jehoshaphat, she's the most beautiful creature in the universe." Luwenia nodded and gave him a smile. She had heard every word, and Ralph straightened his shoulders and walked with renewed purpose.

Anna thought about everything that had brought her to this

moment in her life and knew she had received many blessings. She closed the gap between her and Jerry by speeding up her steps. He tossed his head back and laughed.

Anna reached over and kissed Cary on the cheek. Jerry held out his hand to her, and she slipped her hand into his. Anna didn't pay attention to what the judge was saying because her mind was on kissing Jerry, among other things that she wanted to do to him. The energy of love rose and fell around her. A faint glow of light surrounded the couple as Anna repeated her vows. A tear of joy trickled down her cheek, and Jerry stopped it with his kiss.

Jerry repeated his vows, and before he slipped the ring on her finger, he said, "I give this ring to you as my wedding gift. Think of me when you wear it and always remember that I love you with all of my heart."

Anna slipped the wedding ring on his finger as she stared into his dreamy blues. "I give you this ring as a symbol of my love for you. I will never stop loving you. My love for you will never end because it will last through eternity."

Before the judge could get the words out, Jerry scooped Anna up and kissed her as she circled her arms around his neck. The judge coughed and said, "May I present Mr. and Mrs. Jerry McDaniel." Everyone clapped and laughter scattered among the guests.

Maria's brother's band began to play their guitars and sing "Novia Mia." Jack kissed her on the cheek and shook Jerry's hand, but Jerry grabbed Jack and hugged him. Then Jerry kissed Maria, who blushed several shades of red. Cary gave Jerry a hug and Anna a kiss on the forehead before hugging her tightly.

The wedding party began to stroll toward the veranda where the food and cocktails were waiting for them. Jerry caught Anna's hand and pulled her back behind one of the old moss oak trees. His hands cupped her face, and he kissed her again, slow and passionate. Time seemed to stand still, and in the distance, the roll-and-crash rhythm of the ocean waves sang in the air.

True love was a gift. Some people never recognized true love, while others allow true love to slip through their fingers. Then there are the fortunate few who do realize true love, lose it, and by the grace of The Creator are given a second chance. Anna and Jerry were the fortunate few who received a second chance at love. She would never take Jerry's love for granted again, ever. Anna would always cherish his love unto her dying breath. And when the time came, true love would take them—together—when they crossed over to the other side.

Epilogue

Heaven

December 1985

JERRY SURPRISED ANNA A MONTH after she moved back to Tennessee by buying the old white plantation house next to Ditch Lane. Anna and Jerry spent the next six months renovating and restoring the property. The old place had been in such disarray, but with Jerry's enthusiasm over the place, Anna saw all kinds of possibilities. The house had a wide wraparound porch with an old-fashioned charm. They replaced the old windows and added a screened-in back porch with a breezeway giving them a back entrance from the barn.

The old house needed a complete renovation. Jerry hired local subcontractors to repair the old foundation, replace old wiring and plumbing, and even knock out a couple of walls to give them a more open-space atmosphere. Anna picked out wide-planked hickory floors throughout the house and worked with a local contractor to create a huge kitchen. Jerry had also added a fireplace she could see from their great room on one side and kitchen on the other. The end of the project had resulted in a home of their dreams.

Tonight, Anna and Jerry, along with Sandy, were throwing Ruby and Reed a baby party with all of their old friends and family. It was going to be the first time she and Jerry entertained as a married couple.

Anna pulled a tray of homemade sugar cookies out of her double oven and placed them on the cooling rack, then slipped a tray of fried chicken wings back inside the oven and set the thermostat to warm. Anna's mother, Christine, had helped her cook for the party all day. Her father, David was spending the day with Jerry.

The sweet smell of sugar and vanilla made her stomach growl, so she grabbed a cookie and took a bite. God, she loved homemade Christmas cookies. Her mom had just left to get ready for the party.

After placing the cookies in a container, Anna took off her apron and headed toward the back stairs when the phone rang. Anna glanced down at her watch. She only had an hour before guests would start arriving and needed to get dressed. "Hello."

Sandy said, "Hey, jellybean. I'm leaving the station and just need to run to my apartment and change clothes. Do you need me to pick up anything from the store before I head out?"

Anna thought for a minute and said, "Grab a couple of bags of ice. I have two, but you never know if people are going to drink beer or cocktails. I'd rather be safe than sorry. Hey, be careful driving. It's spitting snow out here."

Sandy laughed and said, "Uh... I work at a news station. We're supposed to get several inches of snow by morning, so I'm spending the night, okay?"

Anna started up the stairs with the phone when Jerry walked in the back door and smiled. She said, "We would love for you to stay. Jerry just picked up the rocking chair, and he's holding a huge teddy bear. It's adorable."

Sandy sighed. "Aw, I can't wait to babysit."

Anna giggled when Jerry started kissing her ear. "We'll have to draw straws. See you soon. Gotta go."

Sandy replied, "Gotta plow."

The rocking chair had a huge red bow around it. Jerry placed the rocker next to the Christmas tree in the great room and sat the teddy bear in the seat. Anna came up behind him and circled her arms around his waist, and he grabbed her hands. She leaned her face against his back. "That's the cutest teddy bear, and I love the rocking chair. Come on, let's hurry upstairs and get ready."

Jerry turned around to face her and dropped his hands to her waist. "Woman, you just want to take advantage of me before the party gets started." He grinned and kissed her.

"You're damn straight. The last one in the shower is a rotten egg." Anna ran toward the stairs before he could catch her.

Jerry yelled as he ran behind her, "First one has to eat it."

SANDY PARKED IN FRONT OF her apartment building in a tow-away zone and placed her press pass in the window so her car wouldn't get towed. She grabbed her purse, threw it over her shoulder, and sprinted through the double doors of her apartment building to the elevators. When the doors opened, she pressed the button to the third floor. Right as the doors were about to shut, a man wearing black trousers and a black turtleneck slid inside. He looked at Sandy and nodded, but she didn't make eye contact.

As the elevator cables jerked and pulled in ascent, the man leaned over and pressed the stop button. Sandy said, "What the hell are you doing?"

The man swung around, slammed Sandy against the elevator wall, and pressed his forearm to her throat, cutting off her air. Sandy jabbed the heel of her pump into his foot, and he yelled but kept pressing harder until she was on the verge of passing out. A thunderbolt of panic shot through her when a sudden flash of white light filled the confined space. The man who had her pinned against the wall of the elevator was pulled away. Sandy held her throat, coughed several times, and tried to catch her breath.

Sandy's hand went to her mouth in complete shock at the beautiful being who was beating the ever-loving shit out of her attacker. In horror, Sandy watched a demon depart from her attacker's soul.

The demon hissed and yelled, "You're breaking the rules, Baldric."

Baldric yelled back, "Tough shit." And he ran the demon through with his blinding blade of light. The demon turned to ash and disappeared.

Baldric spun around and reached out to touch Sandy's face but stopped himself before he made contact. He said, "Are you okay?"

Sandy catapulted herself into his massive arms and cried, "Thank you, oh, thank you."

Sandy leaned her face against his golden-armored chest in relief, and Baldric stroked her hair and then her cheek. "It's okay, little girl. Everything is going to be all right, but we need to get you to your room before this asshole wakes up."

Sandy glanced down at her attacker. "He's not dead?"

Baldric chuckled. "Nah, but he may wish he was when he wakes up with not only a massive headache but no memory of the last ten years." He leaned over and pressed the third-floor button, and Sandy clung onto Baldric's bicep.

Inside her apartment, Sandy couldn't take her eyes off Baldric. He stood, at least six foot six and had to weigh two hundred and fifty pounds of pure muscle, or what she thought was muscle. He was solid regardless. Baldric had long wavy blond hair that fell over his shoulders, and she stared into the depths of his sea-green eyes. Sandy smiled because she remembered him. The last time Sandy had seen Baldric, she'd been nine years old. "Why did you wait so long to come to me? Why? I needed you."

Baldric's expression softened, and when he locked eyes with hers, she completely forgot to breathe. He said, "I should've, but I've always been with you since you were born. It was just safer to watch over you."

Sandy narrowed her eyes, and she shouted, "Bullshit. You're afraid of me, and you desire me—you desire me right now. I see it in your eyes, and you smell like chocolate pie. You want me, Baldric?" She went over to him and ran her hands across the top of his shoulders and down his bulging biceps. Sandy reached down, brought his hand to her mouth and pressed a kiss.

Baldric was breathing hard. His nostrils flared, and his fingers twitched as he pushed her away. "Stop it, Sandy. I'm not just a piece of ass. I've loved you your entire life. I know all of your weaknesses and your strengths, and I know why you sleep with all of those men. I've always known. I read your thoughts just like you read others."

Sandy stumbled backward and dropped down on her loveseat. "You don't know me. You don't know what I feel."

Baldric walked over and leaned against the brick wall next to the eight-foot window that overlooked Broadway and Second Avenue in downtown Nashville. "That's where you would be wrong. You have walled off everyone except your best friends from Everglade. You can't fulfill the loneliness in your heart with casual sex." Baldric crossed his arms over his chest and revealed the most arousing set of forearms and biceps Sandy had ever seen.

Sandy stood up, walked straight up to him, and cupped his chin with her hand. "Wanna find out?"

Baldric grabbed her wrists. "Saints preserve us, woman. You haven't listened to a thing I've said. You need to get dressed. You have a party to go to, remember?"

Sandy smiled at him wickedly and reached up behind her neck and unhooked the clasp to her dress. She slowly unzipped it and followed his eyes as her dress hit the floor. He may be her warrior angel, but he liked her the way a man likes a woman.

She said, "You know, I run around in here naked all the time." Baldric's eyes went atomic bomb, and she could smell cocoa and vanilla. Yep, he desired her. Baldric always gave off this completely decadent scent when he was aroused. Sandy chuckled. "Ah, but you already knew that, didn't you?" She turned and sashayed her hips back and forth. Right before she went into her bedroom, she turned back to him and blew him a kiss, then slammed the door.

BALDRIC WONDERED IF HIS SUPERIORS were merely testing his resolve or punishing him for his previous lapses in judgment over the last two millennia. Sandy was one incredible human female, and he wanted her. He was shaking so badly that the wall he leaned against shook, too. Dust fell from the rafters.

Baldric materialized into the hall corridor so he couldn't smell her sweet scent like ripe peaches ready for the plucking. Then he slapped himself on the forehead. That demon in the elevator had meant business this afternoon, and Baldric couldn't allow his sexual weakness to interfere with the safety and protection of his ward, the lovely Sandra Daireann Cothran.

Sandy's apartment door opened, and she stepped out in the hallway wearing a little black dress. Baldric went stiff as a freaking board. *Ah, Michael must be laughing his ass off right about now.*

Sandy glanced over and said, "You might as well show yourself because you smell like hot chocolate, and I could smell you even if I were standing on Capitol Hill. Come on, you can ride up front with me on the way to Everglade." Sandy walked to the elevator, and Baldric appeared behind her. Without looking at him, she said, "You have to tell me everything you know about the man's brain you just peeled. I know Cole Steele sent him. I could see him when the attacker choked me." That was when she turned, and the air backed up in his lungs. Sandy pinned him with a stare from her beautiful eyes—hazel with tiny specks of golds and browns that surrounded her pupils.

She said, "You have to prepare me for battle, Baldric. I can't continue being a pantser." He chuckled as he read her thoughts. She was tired of flying by the seat of her pants. Baldric followed her into the elevator and readied his sword to strike at a moment's notice.

Once inside her Corvette, Sandy said, "You look a little squashed. Let me show you where the lever is so you can push the seat back, and you'll have a little more leg room." She leaned across him and reached down for the lever. "Touch my fingers, see? This lever pulls up and then just scoot back."

Baldric tensed when she intentionally pressed her breasts against his arm. The smell of her shampoo and the caress of her hand made him light-headed. He lifted the lever and pushed back. "Thanks."

Sandy quirked a smile. "No problem, big guy. I want us to be friends, Baldric. You meant so much to me when I was a little girl. I'm glad you're back."

Baldric grinned and remembered the little, fun-loving girl. *Yeah, he could do the friend thing. Sure, why not?*

Sandy laughed and teased, "Hey, Rudolph, can you turn down that glow?"

Baldric bellowed with laughter. "Sure, Santa."

RUBY AND REED PULLED INTO Jerry and Anna's driveway. Ruby was thirty-seven weeks pregnant and ready to have this baby, sooner rather than later. Ruby said, "After leaving my OB today, I meant to tell you Susan Hopkins was induced last week. You used to play softball with her husband back in college."

Reed glanced at her and said, "Yeah, how did that go?"

Ruby shifted uncomfortably in the seat. "Her doctor induced her at thirty-eight weeks. I wonder if my doctor will induce? I keep having Braxton Hicks. I know she said the baby is fine. It just makes me nervous our baby's movement has nearly stopped."

Reed had been wonderful to her. He rubbed her feet every night after work and her lower back while she tried to sleep. He loved holding and rubbing her belly while they lay in bed at night and in the morning before they got out of bed. Reed never once mentioned anything about how fat she had gotten. Ruby knew she was pregnant, but she'd gained nearly fifty pounds. He said, "Honey, your doctor is the best OB in the 'Boro. I trust her. You have to trust her, too."

"Of course, you're right." Ruby was excited about seeing everyone at the party. She just hoped she could last until it was over. She stayed so dad-blamed tired all the time. "Reed, do I look really fat?"

Reed chuckled and said, "That's a loaded question. Princess, you're more beautiful to me right now than you were the first day I saw you."

Ruby rested her head on his shoulder. "Thank you, honey. You make me happy, even though I know I look like a walrus."

Reed rubbed her thigh and said, "You do not look like a walrus. I like my woman with a little meat on her bones. Hey, look. Jerry has lights strung all the way down the fencerow. It's surreal they bought the old place right beside Ditch Lane. You know, my friend from the county road commission said they're opening Ditch Lane up—all the way to Highway 99."

Ruby's eyes widened with surprise. "Aw, naw, an end to an era. Well, at least we have our memories. Man, it's packed. I love what they did to the place. It's like something you'd see in a Norman Rockwell painting." Ruby twisted in the seat and arched her back.

Reed stopped the car and turned to face her. "Don't overdo it tonight. If you get tired, come and get me. I'll take you home. Everyone will understand."

"I promise, Daddy."

ANNA WAS THRILLED. NEARLY EVERYONE invited to the party had shown up. All of their families and friends were mingling with each other in the festive spirit of the deck-the-halls kind of merriment. Ruby looked like a picture-perfect healthy mom-to-be in a long red velvet empire dress. Ruby's cheeks were rosy from all of the attention everyone lavished on her. Anna did make a mental note to check Ruby's blood pressure before the night was over.

Christine and Sandy made sure everyone had drinks and kept the dining room table stocked with hors d'oeuvres and holiday treats. Anna's dad, David, helped Lee and Harry stack the gifts for the baby, piling them next to the Christmas tree. The wall of windows in the great room gave everyone an incredible view of the big fat snowflakes falling in the backyard.

Jerry, Reed, Brent, and George had stepped outside in the breezeway to smoke cigars in celebration of the coming birth. Anna giggled when she stuck her ear to the door to listen to the advice they were giving Reed, more myth than fact.

Anna glanced around the room and caught sight of the guardians, who seemed to be laughing at Baldric about something. Ralph and Luwenia seemed to be cozying up to each other nicely. She had noticed how Baldric kept staring at Sandy all night. If she didn't know any better, she'd say Baldric was in love. *Hmmm, another question for Ralph.* Anna wondered what the good folk of Everglade would think if they knew an elite force of warrior angels was among the partygoers tonight.

The conversations filtering around the room were light and fun. Lizzie sat down at Anna's upright piano and began to play "Have Yourself a Merry Little Christmas." Anna went over to the stereo and turned down the volume and joined George at the piano. They began to sing. Sandy and Ruby walked over to the piano. Jerry, Reed, and Brent walked inside. The old gang gathered in a circle. They sang, and Anna's heart filled with such joy. The entire room glowed with love. Suddenly, the rest of the partygoers joined in their impromptu Christmas caroling. It was a memory Anna would not soon forget.

At the end of the song, Ruby leaned over to Anna and said, "Do you mind if I go to your room and rest for a minute?"

Anna placed Ruby's hand in the crook of her arm. "Of course not.

I'll go with you. I just want to take your blood pressure. You look flushed."

Ruby sighed and walked slowly up the stairs with Anna. "I'm having fun. I just probably ate or drank something with too much sodium. I'm so happy for you and Jerry. I love your home. It's perfect. I wish Sandy could fall in love. Not because she needs a man, mind you, but to know what it feels like to be in love. Good times and bad times and happy and sad times, I wouldn't trade my life with Reed for all the tea in the freaking world."

"Me either, Well, with Jerry, not Reed." Anna and Ruby both laughed.

Ruby and Anna walked down the hall to the master bedroom. Ruby stopped before walking in the master bathroom. "Let me pee first and then you can take my blood pressure."

Anna grabbed her medical bag from her closet. Ruby screamed, and Anna ran into the bathroom. Ruby's face turned white as a sheet of paper. Anna looked down and smiled. "Honey, your water broke. You've been having contractions?"

Ruby nodded. "Yeah, but they're not close, and I didn't want to spoil the party."

Anna hugged her. "Spoil the party? Silly goose, everyone's going to talk about this party for years."

Anna helped Ruby get cleaned up and then they went downstairs to the great room. She grabbed Sandy and asked her to whistle. Sandy had a whistle that would make dogs bark. Anna said, "May I have everyone's attention, please? Please, everyone, I need your undivided attention." Anna asked Sandy, "Do we happen to know where the guys are?"

Lee walked over and smiled at Ruby and looked over to Anna. She said, "They're doing shots in the breezeway. You want me to get them?" But the guys walked back inside, laughing and smacking each other on the back. Reed looked over at Ruby and paled.

Anna waved her hand over her head and excitedly said, "I have great news, everyone. Ruby is in labor." The room erupted in an uproar of shouts and whistles, and Reed fell backward, but Jerry caught him.

Reed ran to Ruby. "Do we, do you, do we need to go? I mean to the hospital?"

Anna placed her hand on Reed's shoulder and smiled. "It's okay, Reed. Ruby's contractions are about fifteen to twenty minutes apart." Anna turned to Lee and said, "Lee, could you and Harry go to her house and get her suitcase? I've not been drinking, so I can drive her to the hospital in my suburban. It holds six people comfortably." Anna turned to her guests. "The rest of you, please stay, eat, drink, and be merry. And if you need to spend the night, make yourselves at home. I'll call Mom when I have some news."

Sandy brought her forefinger and thumb to her lips and whistled again. "Hot damn, Ruby Jane. You've always known how to get attention at a party."

LEE GLENN WAS ECSTATICALLY HAPPY. December 8, 1985, at 2:05 a.m, her baby girl delivered a beautiful baby boy named Joseph Lee Jackson. In Ruby's birthing room, Lee held the baby boy in her arms while Anna, Sandy, and Ruby stared at the little red-haired miracle. Jerry had taken Reed and his parents, along with Harry, to the Waffle House for breakfast, and George and Lizzie had gone home after the baby was born.

In the quiet stillness of the room, Lee sang softly to little Joe while she rocked the baby boy back and forth in her arms. "Hush, be still like a mouse, there's a baby in our house. Not a dolly, not a toy, just our precious baby boy." Ruby and the girls had happy grins on their faces when Lee looked down at Ruby and said, "So, I wonder what power Joe will have?"

The three girls said in chorus, "What?"

Lee looked over at the girls and smiled, then looked back at Ruby. "Yes, my darlings, I've always known. See, I'm a ward, too."

Ruby squealed with delight. "*Mom*. Why haven't you ever said anything?"

Lee bounced Joe and patted his bottom. "There's been a ward in every family that's ever lived on Campbell Ridge. Your granddaddy told me pretty much the same way I'm telling you now. He knew about all four of you, too. He was the only ward in his generation, and I'm the only one in mine. But you all are the first ward grouping from Campbell Ridge." She looked at Anna. "You know, I almost interfered when Jerry was going to marry that loud-mouth woman." Lee laid the baby boy down in his bassinet. "Aw, he's asleep. He is precious, darling girl."

A nurse came into the room and walked over to the bassinet to check Joe, and Lee tensed. Lee said, "Ruby, dear, I need to run down the hall to the vending machine and get a drink. Does anyone need anything?" The girls replied no. Lee made eye contact with the nurse and frowned. The nurse walked out, and Lee followed and shut the door.

Ruby's room was located at the end of a corridor. In the hall, the nurse who had been in Ruby's room instantly changed with a brilliant flash of light into Luc. He wore a black leather trench coat with a black turtleneck, blue jeans, and black boots. He said, "Lee Campbell, you've grown into a lovely woman, and you're still too perceptive for your own good."

Lee's guardian angel, Erinelle, materialized by Lee. The female angel had weapons strapped on her back and a sword aimed at Luc, poised for battle. Lee said, "Luc, in the name of the Father, the Son, and the Holy Ghost, leave my family now. I will not hesitate to command every angel available from here to the in-between to bind you from my family!"

Luc threw hands up in mock surrender. "Take a chill pill, Lee. I was merely checking out the new ward. He's going to look like his mother. Don't you agree, Erinelle?"

Erinelle never faltered from her battle stance; her wings spanned the width of the hall corridor. "Dragon, you aren't welcome here. Begone or I'll beckon the Prince."

Luc chuckled and stuck his hand in his pocket. "Dragon—so that's what they've been calling me. Cool, I love it." Luc gave them a deep bow. "Ladies, until we meet again." He vanished in a blink.

Lee looked at Erinelle and sighed. "Thank you for always having my back." Erinelle nodded and dematerialized. Lee walked back inside Ruby's room.

"Oh, shucks, the machine needs exact change. Oh, well, is our baby boy still sleeping?" Lee asked.

Ruby yawned and said, "Yes, he is still sleeping, and I'm not far behind. Mom, why didn't you tell me about being a ward?"

Lee had told Ruby and Anna when they were little girls, but

Erinelle made her wipe the memory of the story. Lee held Ruby's hand and kissed it. "My darling, I wasn't allowed. It wasn't my time to tell you until a new generation was born. Now, Joe is here."

Ruby's eyes widened in fear. "Joe will go to the cave? He'll find a stone and receive power?"

Lee smiled at Ruby and rubbed her hand. "Yes, my love. Never fear. We're the chosen, and we're making a difference." Lee looked at Anna and Sandy. "Anna and Sandy will have children, too. Wards work for the good of mankind, and now the legacy continues."

Sandy placed a hand on her right hip. "Well, Jerry and Anna may have children, but for me, it's gonna be a little harder unless I have a test tube baby." Anna held Sandy's hand, and Sandy held Ruby's.

Unbeknownst to the humans, five guardians appeared in the hospital room. Seneca placed an invisible veil over the women and nodded. A warrior angel stepped forward to the bassinet and placed the baby boy in his arms. He said, "I'm Thane, son of Ahgard, Guardian of Campbell Ridge. I pledge my life to guard and protect you, Joseph Lee Jackson. And while you walk this world, I will walk with you until you cross over to the next one."

The Guardians of Campbell Ridge clasped their hands around each other's wrists to join in a circle, forming a protective shield over their newest ward, Joe. The guardians' shimmering wings spanned out and upward and they sang in chorus, "May love light the way."

Books by D.F. JONES

RUBY'S CHOICE
Ditch Lane Diaries, vol. 1

ANNA'S WAY
Ditch Lane Diaries, vol. 2

SANDY'S STORY
Ditch Lane Diaries, vol. 3
coming soon

ANTIQUE MIRROR
a short story

For all buy links, please go to
http://dfjonesauthor.com/buy-the-book/

Follow me on social media
https://Facebook.com/DFJones.author

https://twitter.com/Author_DFJones

https://Instagram.com/D.F.Jones_author

https://www.goodreads.com/GoodreadscomdfjonesAuthor

Excerpt from

RUBY'S CHOICE

DITCH LANE DIARIES 1

D. F. JONES

Prologue

Campbell Ridge Cave, 1972

RUBY, ANNA, AND SANDY HAD their backpacks filled with water, extra flashlights, and batteries for spelunking the cave on Campbell Ridge. Ruby had discovered the entrance to the cave with her brother, George, five years ago when they were looking for Indian arrowheads. George had told her never under any circumstances to go inside the cave. But today, Ruby and her best friends, Anna and Sandy, were looking for new adventures.

The girls were deep inside the cave, surrounded by complete darkness with only their flashlights to illuminate the interior walls. The limestone cave had beautiful rock formations, crystals, and stalactites. The cave underground seemed alien, almost unworldly. The air smelled of the dank earth, and the only sound was running water from the stream that ran through the cave.

Ruby was forced to climb over a boulder on her belly to squeeze through a narrow pass. The boulder opened up into a hidden room. Ruby was still hanging onto the rock when she yelled back at the girls, "Hey, guys, you have to see this." And then she slid down the rock into the room.

Anna and Sandy scrambled up and over the boulder, shining their lights into the hidden room. Anna slid down the boulder and entered with Sandy right behind her. The hidden room was roughly the size of a bedroom. "Holy cow, there are ancient drawing's on the wall."

Thousands of years of groundwater had caused the rocks on one side of the cave to drop down, forming large stalactites the size of a pickup truck. The large drawings revealed intricate details of each person etched in the stone wall. Sandy inspected the drawings closer as she walked down the length of the wall. "It's a story. I read about ancient drawings like these in one of my *National Geographic* magazines. This is far out."

Ruby tripped over a small rock, dropping her flashlight. The light on the ground lit the far left corner, revealing a massive figure carved in the stone. "Geez Louise. This dude looks like a freaking astronaut. Look at his helmet."

Anna bumped into Ruby, nearly making them both fall. She held onto Ruby's shoulder and said, "That's some spooky shit."

Anna walked past Sandy to the next group of drawings. "Here's the same dude again. He's holding a totem, and there are three people kneeling before him. This looks like a ritual or rite of passage."

Sandy sat down on a rock, mesmerized by what they had discovered. She flashed her light toward Ruby and Anna as they traced their fingers over the different drawings. Sandy asked, "Do you think we should tell our parents or teachers?"

Anna and Ruby walked over sit to on the ground next to Sandy. Ruby's light fused with Sandy's as Anna's light circled to the other parts of the room. There was only one wall dedicated to the drawings. Anna replied, "I don't think so. A tribe sealed this room for some reason. We should leave. I've got a weird feeling like we're being watched."

Sandy stood, tipping over the rock she had been sitting on, causing her flashlight to point downward. "Hey, look, somethings under this rock. Bring your lights over here." Anna and Sandy shined their lights over the place where the rock had been as Ruby knelt down, reached in, and pulled out the object.

The girls plopped back down on the hard ground, staring wide-eyed at the totem. Ruby's voice trembled. "It's the totem in the drawing, the same one the deity is handing over to the people kneeling on the ground. I know this sounds weird, but this thing is pulsing in my hands."

Sandy reached over to pluck the totem out of Ruby's hand. The totem was around six inches tall, made out of crystal and quartz with piercing sapphire eyes. The detailed carvings made the image of the face appear real, smooth as glass to the touch, as though sculpted by a master artisan. No matter which way they turned the totem, it seemed to be watching them. "It's a smaller version of the big guy in the corner. He is looking at me."

Sandy handed the totem to Anna, who turned it over in her hands. "I see what you mean. This little dude is shooting energy to my fingertips. We need to place this thing back where we found it and get the hell out of Dodge. I have the creeps in here."

Ruby took the totem and put it back in the hole. In another part of the cave, she could hear rocks falling. "We need to get out of here because the cave is shifting." The girls rolled the boulder back in place and made a hasty exit.

Outside in the daylight, they sat on a rock ledge, out of breath and speechless. Ruby opened her backpack and pulled out an amber-encased spiderweb. "Well, shut the front door, what the heck? Look, y'all, it's a spiderweb inside a piece of amber?"

Anna found an amethyst stone in her pocket, and Sandy opened her thermos, finding a hiddenite stone. Anna shook her head in bewilderment. "Well, I'm pretty sure these stones weren't with us before we went inside the cave. If I wasn't so dad-blamed scared, I'd take this back inside the cave, right now."

Sandy stared at her stone and then spoke quietly. "I don't want to spook you any further, but holding this stone gave me a vision of the deity who gave us the stones. In the vision, he is relaying that we're to keep the stones on our person at all times. He will reveal to us in time what it means, and we aren't supposed to talk about this again until he reveals it to Ruby in a dream."

The girls looked at each other wide-eyed, holding their stones in eerie silence. They never uttered a single word about the totem or the stones again—until years later.

About the Author

After years of developing creative advertising for my clients through my media company, I had the compelling desire to write something for myself. If you love to read and get immersed in the characters of a book, then you will catch a small drift of how incredible it is to write your characters and breathe them into life. I fell in love with writing and trust you will enjoy my books.

I'm happily married to the love of my life and my best friend, KJ. We have two gorgeous sons whom I love and adore more than life itself. I love to laugh, and my husband keeps me in stitches.

D.F. Jones